WITHDRAWN

For more than forty years,
Yearling has been the leading name
in classic and award-winning literature
for young readers.

Yearling books feature children's
favorite authors and characters,
providing dynamic stories of adventure,
humor, history, mystery, and fantasy.

Trust Yearling paperbacks to entertain,
inspire, and promote the love of reading
in all children.

THE TOUCHSTONE TRILOGY

THE VARIOUS
CELANDINE
WINTER WOOD

Celandine

Book Two in the Touchstone Trilogy

STEVE AUGARDE

A YEARLING BOOK

Copyright © 2006 by Steve Augarde

All rights reserved. Published in the United States by Yearling, an imprint of Random House Children's Books, a division of Random House, Inc., New York. Originally published in hardcover in Great Britain by David Fickling Books, an imprint of Random House Children's Books, a division of the Random House Group Ltd., in 2005, and subsequently published in hardcover in the United States by David Fickling Books, an imprint of Random House Children's Books, a division of Random House, Inc., in 2006.

Yearling and the jumping horse design are registered trademarks of Random House, Inc.

Visit us on the Web! www.randomhouse.com/kids

Educators and librarians, for a variety of teaching tools, visit us at www.randomhouse.com/teachers

The Library of Congress has cataloged the hardcover edition of this work as follows:
Augarde, Steve.
Celandine / Steve Augarde.
p. cm.
Prequel to: The Various.
Summary: In Somerset, England, during World War I, Celandine becomes involved in the lives of the little people living on a hill near her family's farm, while also coming to terms with her own healing abilities and psychic gifts.
ISBN: 978-0-385-75048-6 (trade)—ISBN: 978-0-385-75049-3 (lib. bdg.)
[1. Fairies—Fiction. 2. Self-acceptance—Fiction. 3. Extrasensory perception—Fiction. 4. Farm life—England—Somerset—Fiction. 5. Somerset (England)—Fiction. 6. Great Britain—History—George V, 1910–1936—Fiction.] I. Title.
PZ7.A9125Cel 2006
[Fic]—dc22   2005033836

ISBN: 978-0-440-42216-7 (pbk.)

Printed in the United States of America
10 9 8 7 6 5 4 3 2
First Yearling Edition

For Grace and Eric

Chapter One

She was running away for the third time. How terrible it would be if she were caught yet again. The thought of it was unbearable. Even now they might be discovering the damage that she had left behind her, the awful revenge that she had taken.

There would be no more chances after today. She *must* succeed.

'Celandine, Celandine,
Caught the seven thirty-nine.
Seven thirty-nine was late,
Now she's back inside the gate!'

The mocking chant of the Lower School tinies rang through her head. Poor stuff it was, though not so very far from the truth.

She had indeed tried to escape by train, and twice she had failed. How stupid she had been to go to Town station whilst still in her uniform. No wonder the stationmaster had been suspicious of her and telephoned the school. At the second attempt, dressed in mufti, she had almost got away with it but had then been recognized by the very same man – who had no

1

other business to attend to, apparently, than the business of others. The result had been a further interview with Miss Craven, another long letter to her father, and another beating from the Bulldog. If she was caught now, then it would surely be the end of her.

Celandine splashed down the dreary little lane, avoiding the worst of the mud by walking along the blurred channels made by the cartwheels, occasionally stepping up onto the rain-sodden grass verges when the puddles in the road became too wide to jump.

Her walking shoes were tight and uncomfortable. The stout leather soles made the arches of her feet feel as though they were being stabbed at every step, and the stiff backs nipped at her heels. She was sure that she had blisters, but she dared not stop to look – nor would she examine her leg where the buckle of her heavy canvas bag continually rubbed and snagged at her woollen stocking. These things would have to wait. And besides, the walk was a necessary part of her plan. This time she would catch a train that would make it seem as though she was travelling *towards* the school rather than away from it. She glanced up at the black rain clouds, and pulled the collar of her mackintosh a little closer about her neck.

'*Raining, raining, raining. Always bloomin' well raining.*' That's what they sang in Flanders, according to Freddie – only they used another word instead of 'bloomin''. When he first put on his uniform he was just Freddie, her brother, dressed up in a uniform. But when he came home on leave he looked like a soldier.

Even when he was out of his uniform he still looked like a soldier.

Raining, raining, raining. They shot you in Flanders for running away. It was letting down the side, Freddie said, and an example had to be made of cowards.

Celandine walked up to the ticket office at Little Cricket station and put down her bag. 'Second-class single to Town, please,' she said, 'half', and wondered whether she would ever have a nose as red and drippy as that of the ticket man. She hoped not. The sad-eyed clerk looked at her over the top of his spectacles, glancing at the badge on her straw hat before taking a ticket from his board. 'Going back to school?' he said. 'Bit late, aren't you, miss? Term started weeks ago.'

'I've had scarlet fever.' Celandine tried not to stare at the drop of moisture at the end of the old man's nose. 'I've been in quarantine.'

'Ah, yes,' said the clerk. 'Quarantine. Over the bridge, then. Platform Two. Next one due in . . .' He glanced at his pocket watch '. . . thirteen minutes.'

She wandered towards the single lonely bench, painted in cream and brown, that stood next to a tub of flowers halfway down the platform. The cast-iron bench-end was made up of a pattern of interwoven letters – GWR. God's Wonderful Railway, somebody had once said. What was so wonderful about it? The bench was too wet to sit on and the geraniums in their concrete tub looked shabby and weather-blown.

Celandine thought that perhaps the ticket man might be watching her, and so she pretended to be interested in the damp wrinkled poster and the two enamelled advertisements mounted on the wooden fencing behind her. The advertisements told her to take Dr Collis-Brown's Mixture, and to smoke Craven 'A' cigarettes, and the poster informed her that the Women of Britain said 'Go!' – meaning that they told their menfolk to go and enlist as soldiers and fight in the war. The women who represented the Women of Britain didn't look like any women that *she'd* ever seen. Stupid poster. Telling people to go. They hadn't needed to tell Freddie to go – he had gone of his own accord. Freddie was brave and would never run away, but they had killed him all the same. Killed in action, fighting for King and Country. Just as dead as if he'd been a coward.

It didn't seem real, though. Celandine could not make it so, and she could not cry for him. Not properly.

She heard the whispering of the rails, and knew that the train was approaching at last. A heavy plume of smoke rose through the dripping trees that obscured the distant bend. Celandine watched as the smoke trail drew nearer – and then a wonderful thing happened. As the engine appeared from behind the trees, the clouds parted and a shaft of brilliant early evening sunshine fell upon the angular boiler, sparkling on the fresh water droplets that had fallen from the trees, making rainbows in the steam, so that the whole train – the little square engine with its grubby coal tender and four cream-and-brown coaches – was transformed into something shining, something beautiful. God's Wonderful Railway.

A sunshine train, towing its own sunshine with it. Through all the bright countries of the world this train might have travelled, scooping up sunlight against days like these, to arrive before her wrapped in splendour, as cheerful as a maypole.

Celandine reached up to turn the brass door handle of the second-class carriage, and felt that this time she *would* succeed, that the sunshine train would take her away from all that was hateful and bring her safely home, at last, to her friends.

It was cramped in the little washroom, and the carriage lurched annoyingly as she tried to balance on one leg in order to unlace her shoe. Celandine leaned against the rounded edge of the tiny sink and managed to remove her uniform, which she then replaced with her gardening clothes – the anonymous muslin blouse and plain brown skirt she wore for duties in the school allotments. Both were a bit grubby and stained, but so much the better, she felt, for now she might pass as a kitchenmaid or a laundry worker, at least until she spoke. Then her accent might give her away, but there was no point in worrying about that for the time being. She delved further into her canvas bag and found the pieces of bread and greengage jam, wrapped in greaseproof paper, that she'd stolen from the staffroom. She had taken some cake as well, but she was saving that. The walk from her school to the station at Little Cricket had made her hungry. She rested against the sink and took a mouthful of the slightly squashed and sticky sandwich – but immediately had to steady herself, accidentally biting her tongue as the train began to brake, jerkily. It was pulling into Town station already. This was where her ticket said she should get off.

The washroom windows were frosted glass and Celandine could see nothing but vague shapes and colours, flashes of sunlight turning to deep shadow as the carriage slowed down and finally came to a squeaky halt beneath the overhanging station roof. There was a noise of carriage doors repeatedly slamming, the rumbling grind of the porters' trolleys, echoing voices, and footsteps shuffling up and down the corridor outside the washroom. Somebody tried the door, rattled the handle a couple of times and then passed on. Celandine looked at her piece of bread and jam, took another cautious bite and chewed slowly, willing the train to start moving again. Come *on*. What were they waiting for? More slamming of doors. A long *peep* from the guard's whistle, and the carriage jerked forward. Celandine gripped the edge of the sink. They were away at last.

And from here onwards she was travelling illegally. There was no turnstile at Withney Halt where she intended to get off, and once there she would be safe from ticket collectors, but could she last that far without being caught? She simply had to trust to luck that the inspector didn't make his rounds before then.

When she had finished her sandwich, she washed her hands and looked at her reflection in the mottled oblong mirror above the sink. Her hair always came as a surprise to her. The frizzy mane didn't match her dark solemn eyes somehow – didn't even match her eyebrows. It was like some frightful wig that had been put on her head for a joke. She hated it. She hated brushing it and brushing it, because it never did the slightest good. It wouldn't plait properly, wouldn't go up into a bun, wouldn't do *anything* but remain as it was, all springy and horrid. Well, she thought darkly, she had plans – though they would have to wait a little longer.

The door handle was rattled again and a loud female voice outside said, 'Come along! Come along!'

Celandine flushed the lavatory, briefly turned the tap on and off, and unlocked the door. A large woman in a nurse's uniform was waiting in the corridor, and it was a struggle to get past the bulky figure. Celandine caught the odour of hospitals and antiseptic on the woman's rustling blue cape as she squeezed by. There was something comforting about the smell of antiseptic. It reminded her of the time she had spent in the school sanatorium, finding there a haven of tranquillity, a delicious respite from the misery of school life.

Celandine struggled along the corridor towards the rear of the train, glancing into each compartment as she passed, praying that she wouldn't meet the ticket inspector. Her stomach felt tight now and she wished she had not eaten the bread and jam.

She slid back the door of the last compartment, and nearly turned and walked straight back out again. A man in khaki uniform was huddled, alone, in the far corner, next to the window. He had an army blanket slung loosely round his shoulders, and a stick resting across his knees. But the stick was a white stick and, most terribly, the entire top of the man's head was bandaged – covering his eyes so that he couldn't see. He could still hear, that was apparent, for the swaddled head turned in her direction as she stood at the doorway.

It seemed rude, somehow, to leave. But it also seemed rude to stay. Celandine felt as though she were intruding. The man turned away. Celandine sat down on the opposite carriage seat, as near as possible to the door, and tried not to stare. The soldier's bandaged head was leaning against the window. He casually drew a packet of cigarettes from his tunic pocket and tapped one out.

Celandine hated the smell of cigarette smoke, but would not say so, of course. The soldier calmly searched his pockets, for matches presumably, and once again Celandine had to force herself not to stare. It was ill-mannered, surely, to stare at someone who couldn't stare back. Strange, though, how the man turned his bandaged eyes in the direction of his hands as they moved from pocket to pocket, as if he was still able to see what he was doing. Eventually he found what he was searching for – a box of lucifers, as she had guessed – and settled back, apparently relaxed, as he tried to strike a light on the side of the box.

'Would you like me to do that for you?' she said. The soldier was struggling with his box of matches, having succeeded so far only in burning his fingertips and singeing the cigarette halfway along its length. Celandine moved along the seat a little, wondering if he would think it impertinent of her to offer help. To address a strange man, alone in a railway compartment, and to offer to light his cigarette! What would Miss Craven say if she ever got to hear of it? Well, it didn't matter what Miss Craven would say, any more – or what anyone else would say, or think. It just didn't matter. The man was injured, horribly wounded by the look of it, and in need of help. She moved still closer, reaching out towards him, but then stopped herself. The soldier's hands were shaking. He had lowered the matchbox into his lap and his hands were shaking like anything. His poor bandaged head dropped forward and he sat, desolate, the ruined cigarette hanging from his lips. The coarse army blanket rose and fell as the man's shoulders began to quake. He was crying. Underneath the bandages he was crying, though no tears were visible – either because the bandages would soak them all up, or because there were no eyes beneath those bandages for tears to flow from.

'Jesus!' His voice was a cracked whisper, bubbling with spit. He flung the little box of lucifers across the compartment and brought his shaking hands up to his face, dashing the blackened cigarette away in order to wipe his mouth and nose on his fingertips. His white stick fell to the floor. Celandine could see, suddenly, that he was just a boy. He was a wounded soldier, foreign to her, unshaven, blasphemous and frightening, but just a boy. Not much older than Freddie.

She quietly collected up the lucifers that had spilled over the opposite seat and put them back into their cheap matchwood box, saying nothing, whilst the soldier gradually gulped back his emotion to become calmer once more. Then she leaned over and took a cigarette from the pack beside him. She had never touched a cigarette before, and it felt strange – a smooth and delicate thing. How ever did they make them? Celandine looked at it for a moment, curious, then put it in her mouth – an act that made her hands shake almost as badly as the soldier's had. She struck a lucifer on the rough side of the box, as she had seen the man do, and clumsily lit the end of the cigarette. It tasted foul, absolutely foul, and she gagged slightly as she blew out the match. But she managed to say 'Here you are', without coughing, and gently put the cigarette between the soldier's fingers. He flinched at her touch, not realizing at first what she was doing. His shoulders heaved and it seemed that he would cry again, but then he relaxed, gave a long sigh and brought the cigarette up to his lips. He took a deep draw on it and let out a thin stream of smoke. Celandine wrinkled her nose and turned her head away. .

'What's your name?' The soldier's words were so faint that she could hardly hear them.

'Celandine.' She paused for a moment. 'What's yours?'

'Tommy.' Again the word was barely a whisper, as though the effort of speaking was almost too much for him. Then the door slid open and the big woman in the nurse's uniform came in. She looked at Celandine in surprise and said loudly, 'How are you feeling now?'

'Very well, thank—' Celandine began to say, and then realized that of course the nurse was talking to the soldier.

Tommy said nothing, but merely blew out another stream of smoke and nodded his head. The nurse seemed to accept this as a reply. 'Good man!' she shouted, still looking at Celandine, and she sat down heavily next to the soldier, causing the upholstery springs to squeak in alarm. 'Soon be there now! Shouldn't be smoking though – you know that, don't you? I've told you about that, haven't I?' The nurse leaned forward, bringing the faint smell of antiseptic with her, and her large shiny face seemed to loom across the carriage like a huge piece of waxed fruit. She reached over, took the white stick from Celandine's grasp and sank back comfortably in her seat without another word. Celandine felt awkward and tried to avoid the nurse's gaze. She sat in silence, regarding her sore feet and thinking about Tommy, and Freddie. She wondered why any Women of Britain would ever say 'Go' if this was what their sons were going to.

The compartment door rumbled back with a bang, and there was the ticket inspector. Celandine felt her stomach jump, and she momentarily clutched at the material of her skirt, just for something to hold on to.

The grey-haired inspector, horribly official-looking in his blue serge uniform and peaked cap, glanced at her briefly, but then noticed the soldier huddled in the far corner. 'Dear, oh dear,' he said. 'Copped a packet then, lad? You look as though you've been in the wars *good* and proper. Talk about the walking wounded.' The soldier huddled deeper into his blanket and didn't answer. Celandine offered her useless ticket. Her hand shook as though she were holding it out for a beating.

'He's in my charge, Inspector,' bellowed the big nurse. 'I'm escorting him to Staplegrove Hospital. I have his ticket here, with mine.' She reached into the large leather bag on her lap and drew out her tickets. The inspector took them, and punched them with his machine, but it was clear that he was more interested in the soldier than in tickets. 'Where'd you get that little lot then, son?' he persisted.

'He's not well enough to talk, I'm afraid,' said the nurse.

'Blimey,' said the inspector, taking Celandine's

ticket, but barely glancing at it before punching it. 'Got your tongue as well, did they? Well, good luck to you.' He nodded to the nurse and stepped back into the corridor, closing the sliding door behind him with a smart click. The train gave a sideways lurch and Celandine swallowed. She thought for a dreadful moment that she might be sick.

But the crisis had passed. The nurse sat staring at Celandine and absently tapped her fingernails on the white stick . . . *tap-tap* . . . *tap-tap* . . . an irritating echo to the rhythm of the wheels.

The Somerset countryside, cheerful now on this sunny spring evening, passed by the grimy window until the train eventually began to slow down on its approach to Withney Halt. Celandine got up. She opened the compartment door and turned to pick up her bag. The soldier raised his head at the sound of the sliding door, listening to the movement in the compartment.

'You going?' he whispered.

'Yes,' said Celandine. 'I get off here. Goodbye, Tommy. And good luck.' As she pulled the door closed behind her, she heard the nurse say, 'Well! You're a dark horse, I must say. Do you *know* that extraordinary-looking girl?'

The steam-engine smell of oil and cinders hung upon the still country air long after the train had gone. Celandine stood on the little greystone platform of Withney Halt and looked out over the Somerset Levels – the lush patchwork of flat fields and withy beds that

13

stretched to the far wooded hills. The marshy land was criss-crossed with rhynes and irrigation ditches, and the familiar figures of pollarded willow trees stood, dipping their heads towards the still waters.

Celandine squinted into the last rays of the sun, and plotted an imaginary course across the darkening wetlands. She could just see part of the roofline of Mill Farm, her home, nestling beneath the shadow of Howard's Hill.

The rapidly darkening countryside felt lonely and deserted, and so quiet that, when a heron suddenly rose from a nearby ditch with a horrible *kraaark* and a loud splashing of wings, Celandine thought her heart would stop. But she doggedly followed the muddy paths trodden by the labourers and withy-cutters, dragging her monstrously heavy bag, and told herself that this was Somerset and not France, and that at least she wasn't being shot at. Better, too, than going by the road, where she was sure to meet someone who knew her, or her father.

The air had grown cold by the time she finally reached the scrubby paddock that stood behind the farm stables, and yet her journey had been such hard going that her muslin blouse was sticking to her back and shoulders. She cautiously leaned against the corner post of the paddock fence and looked at the dark huddle of buildings that made up Mill Farm. Faint chinks of light escaped from beneath the eaves of the stables. There would be harnesses yet to clean, and tack to mend, water to be drawn, feed and bedding to be provided for the teams, and a host of other things to be done before the stable hands could safely leave their charges for the night and go to their own rest.

The lower windows of the farmhouse itself were by now ablaze with light, and one upper window also – her mother's room. Downstairs her father would be sitting at the kitchen table, discussing the day's business over a knuckle of ham with her elder brother, Thos, and coughing his dry persistent cough – explaining why this must be done and why that must not. And Thos would be listening, impatient, scratching the back of his neck, trying to keep his temper and then, when he got the chance, explaining why this must *not* be done and why that must. The two lurchers, Cribb and Jude, would be lying at the foot of the stairs, sullenly waiting upon the hour when they would be put out for the night to shelter beneath the open barn and do their duty with regard to rats and foxes and other intruders. Cook would be in her room, with her half glass of milk stout, getting ready to turn in. How familiar it all was.

And there would be a bed for her there, thought Celandine, and food on the table if she chose to enter, but there would be no welcome. There would be only angry words from her father, bitter tears from her mother, and no gesture of comfort from Thos. A bed for the night, a meal, and then back they would send her – back to school, where they were paying good money for all her nonsense to be knocked out of her.

Celandine felt chilly now, conscious too of the open ground she had yet to cross and how her light-coloured blouse might easily be visible to anyone who happened to step outside and look about them. She undid the buckle of her canvas bag and hauled out her dark mackintosh. She also took out the envelope that she had been carrying.

It didn't take long to find a suitable stone. Celandine placed the envelope on the top of the paddock corner post and weighed it down with the stone. Now the wind wouldn't blow it away. It wouldn't be long before someone found the letter and delivered it to the farmhouse. Turning her collar against the cool night air, and her back against the lights of Mill Farm, Celandine picked up her bag once more and began the long slow climb that took her up Howard's Hill.

There had been a lot of rain recently, and so the stream that trickled down the gully on the hillside was quite lively. The stillness of the night air made the bubbling sound of the water seem unnaturally loud, and Celandine became worried that her signal might not be heard – or even recognized. Months it had been, since she was last here. Would they even remember her? She crept along the rising bank of the gully until she was as close as she could get to the thick mass of brambles that bounded the edge of the high woodland. Resting her bag on the grass she cupped her hands, put her thumbs together, and blew into the gap between her bent knuckles. She was breathless from the climb, and also out of practice, so it took two or three attempts to get it right – but eventually she managed to produce a sound that was supposed to be

16

that of a hooting owl. Was it loud enough? Could anyone hear her? She tried again a few times and looked towards the dark jumble of briars expectantly, but nothing happened. Celandine began to panic. What would she do? To go back was quite impossible.

Celandine sat down upon her bag and concentrated – no longer on imitation, but on volume. She began to experiment with finding a note, and then gradually opened her cupped hands to make the pitch and volume of the note rise as she blew harder.

Whatever it was, then, that landed with a thump upon her shoulders took her so by surprise that she was flung sideways from her perch – squealing with shock as she tumbled and rolled down into the gully, clutching at the flailing wiry limbs that clung about her neck, and then hearing the throaty little sound '*ah-ah-ah*' that made it all clear. She reached the bottom of the gully and managed to struggle to her feet – one of which was in the water by this time – laughing and trying to disentangle herself from the frantic little creature that continued to cling to her. It was no use. He *wouldn't* let go. She dropped to one knee again and hauled the wriggling being from her shoulders, managing to get one arm about the skinny waist to grasp the rough material of his tunic, pulling him around to the front of her where she could then grab him by the upper arms and force him away from her. At last she was able to hold him – just – at arms length, as he continued to writhe like a puppy, clutching hanks of her hair in his tiny fists, his whole face alive with the delight of seeing her again. His wide innocent eyes flashed white in the darkness and the huge gap-toothed smile was wider still. 'Cake!' he said, triumphantly. 'Cake-cake-cake!'

'Hallo, Fin,' she said. 'It's so *lovely* to see you.' And it was too. She gave him a hug – and it was good to feel the childish arms tight about her neck, the affection so freely given.

'Come on,' she said, and, releasing Fin with a sigh, she stood up and pushed back her hair. Fin tucked his own straight black hair behind his ears and looked up at her hopefully. 'Yes,' she couldn't help laughing, 'I've brought you some cake. But you must lead me through the tunnel first.'

The dark little figure hopped barefoot over the wet stones that were strewn along the bed of the gully, and carefully began to part the overhanging brambles. Celandine followed, clutching her canvas bag to her chest and stooping low, one foot squelching uncomfortably in her soaking wet shoe.

Chapter Two

Celandine had first met Fin over three years ago, on the 22nd June 1911, shortly after her tenth birthday. She was hardly likely to forget either the date or the occasion, for it was the Coronation of King George and Queen Mary. There would be parties up and down the land in honour of this event, and the Howards of Mill Farm would be celebrating along with everyone else.

Celandine's father, Erstcourt Howard, had been persuaded to put his hand in his pocket for once, and it had been decided that a grand picnic should take place on Howard's Hill.

The hill rose from the surrounding fields like a wooded island. Too steep and stony to plough, it had been allowed to run wild for generations. Occasionally a few sheep or cattle might be turned out to graze the rough slopes, but only if the pastures below were too flooded to use. The ancient woods that covered the hilltop had become so surrounded by brambles that only a fool or a rabbit would attempt to enter – and the Howards were solidly conscious of being neither. They left well enough alone.

For the Coronation picnic a stone platform was being specially built, about halfway up the hillside, and this was to be large enough to hold all the big trestle tables that were normally used for Harvest supper.

The Howard children – Thos, Freddie and Celandine – each viewed the coming party in their own various ways. Thos, almost fifteen at the time, pretended not to care and outwardly took his father's grumbling view that the whole affair was an unnecessary expense. He was sure that he had better things to do. He may well go and shoot some rabbits instead, come the day. Inwardly, however, he was in a breathless agony of excitement and anguish – for here was a golden opportunity to talk once again with the enchanting Emily Swann, or at least it *would* be a golden opportunity, if only the Swann family had been invited. But they had not. He knew this because he had overheard his mother and father in discussion. His mother, whose Austrian upbringing still caused her to struggle with her English, had said, 'What about the Svanns – Swaaans?' And Erstcourt had replied, 'Don't see the need of it. Blasted man still hasn't settled up for the team I hired him last autumn. Always looks the other way whenever I see him. No, Lizzie, I think not.' So Mrs Howard had timidly returned to her guest list, pegging away at it with her perpetually worried expression – so *difficult* it was for her to *organize* such an event, Erstcourt, when it was with no *back-around* she had in which things.

Freddie, thirteen years old but still glad of any

excuse to dress up, decided that he might spend the day in costume – something British perhaps, to suit the occasion. He already had a large Union Jack that would serve as a cape, and a small red gardening fork lashed to a rake handle for a trident. Now all he needed was a helmet and a shield, and he could go as Britannia. It didn't help matters that his mother had only the vaguest idea of who Britannia might be. Freddie showed her the brown penny with a likeness of Britannia on it which he was using as his model, but his mother, after raising her spectacles and peering closely at it, had said, 'And this is a *man*, Freddie?' Well of course it was a *man*, he said. Did she think he wanted to spend the day dressed as a woman? Britannia was like Neptune, only . . . British. A small seed of doubt had been sown, however, and he wondered if he should go as John Bull instead. Did John Bull ever carry a trident? It would be a shame to waste the trident.

Celandine had grasped the fact that the party was to be a very special occasion, and so she was not much looking forward to it. Very special occasions usually meant pain and discomfort. Her hair would have to be more tightly scraped back than ever and Miss Bell, her governess, would be continually fussing over her manners and appearance. Best boots and best behaviour would doubtless be required, and each were too tight a fit for Celandine's liking. She wondered if she would be able to escape from the awful Miss Bell and play with the kittens in the cider barn instead.

By seven o'clock on the morning of the picnic, the

great trestle tables were standing on the newly-built stone platform on the side of Howard's Hill, and by eight o'clock Freddie was dressed as a Christian.

He had solved the problem of his costume, having remembered a picture he had once seen of a man fighting a lion. All the man had to defend himself with was a trident and a net. It was something to do with Roman times. But Freddie was sure that the brave man with the trident was a Christian – and what could be more British than that?

Freddie already had the trident, and now he had managed to borrow one of the nets used for ferreting. He was looking forward to the day.

Thos was also remarkably cheerful. Mr Swann had suddenly paid off his debt to Farmer Howard, thus securing a last-minute invitation to the party for himself and his family. Emily Swann would be coming after all.

Celandine was not so happy. Miss Bell had caught her before she had even finished her breakfast egg, and had rigged her out in calico so starched, and ribbons so numerous, that she felt like a Christmas parcel.

'Miss Bell, I don't think I'm very well,' she said.

'Then you shall have a dose of castor oil,' said Miss Bell, promptly. 'Very good for the tongue is castor oil. It helps to keep it truthful, at the least.'

Celandine scowled at herself in the mirror, and tried to think of a good act of revenge.

At midday the whole company of guests were assembled. Besides the immediate family there were friends and relatives, the farmworkers, local tradespeople, the vicar and various other dignitaries. And there was one baby – the youngest of the Swanns – in a wicker bassinet. Over eighty people in all made up the cheerful procession that eventually began to drift through the paddock at the rear of the stables and wind its leisurely way up the sunny slopes of Howard's Hill towards the heavily laden picnic tables.

Mrs Howard set about positioning her guests.

'Erstcourt, you are here *of* course, at table head, and then I. Here. Brigadier . . . no, Mrs Brown is *you* there, then Brigadier. Reverend Brown, is you next to me, Miss Tvigg, and then the *ozer* Miss Tvigg. Josef and Sarah, you are here . . .'

When each had found a place, Erstcourt Howard rose to his feet. 'Now then,' he said, and paused for silence. 'If all have a drink to hand, I shall ask the Reverend here to lead us in a prayer and a toast to Their Majesties. Reverend?'

The atmosphere at the head of the first table soon became awkward. Mrs Howard's younger brother, Josef Wesser, had got into an argument with Brigadier Locke. Josef Wesser was a doctor, specializing in what he called 'the science of the mind', and had made the mistake of challenging the Brigadier on that retired soldier's home territory – the battlefield.

'You'll forgive me for saying so, *Doctor* Wesser, but you're talking tripe. Absolute tripe. Cowardice is cowardice, plain and simple. If a fellow hasn't the stomach to fight, then he has no business being in the army. There's only one way to deal with that type of shilly-shallying, in my opinion.'

'Oh?' said Josef. 'And that would be . . . ?'

'Court martial, sir. Certainly in the case of desertion.'

'I see. And the penalty for that would be – what – execution? I think there is a difference . . . yes? . . . between cowardice and nervous collapse. The mind works in strange ways. A man cannot always be held responsible for his actions . . .'

'Talk like a dam' fool, sir! What are you – one of the white feather brigade?'

Mrs Howard was embarrassed that her guests should be arguing, and did her best to change the subject.

At the far end of the second table sat Thos, Freddie and Celandine, in various states of disgruntlement as the afternoon wore on. Thos was only inches away from the delightful Emily Swann, but as this young lady was seated with her back to him at the next table there was little opportunity to talk.

Freddie had eaten all that he wanted to eat, which wasn't very much, and so he was bored. And Celandine, to her disgust, was seated right next to her governess, Miss Bell, who was showing off to Tom Allen the blacksmith by finding fault with everything she did. She must sit up *straight*, or she would end up round-shouldered. She must not speak with her mouth full, or she would choke. She must not kick the bench, or she would spoil her shoes. And no, she may *not* leave the table. And no, Freddie may not leave the table either. They must sit still and wait for their food to digest properly.

On and on she went. Celandine noticed that one of the Swann girls – a heavy-set child with short dark hair – was smirking at her discomfort from the next table. Celandine poked her tongue out at her. Unfortunately Miss Bell saw her do it and said, 'Celandine, stop that! Really! Your behaviour today is quite disgraceful! Do you see what I have to contend with, Mr Allen?'

A wicked thought came into Celandine's head. 'Miss Bell, do you remember that time when you were sick in a bucket?'

'I *beg* your pardon, Celandine?'

'That time when Father said you must have been at the sherry—'

'*Celandine!* That's *quite* enough, thank you! And if *you've* had quite enough, then I think you'd better get down after all – yes, yes, and Freddie also. I shall certainly speak to you later, you *sinful* child. Mr Allen, I must assure you that there is *no* truth to this whatsoever . . .'

Miss Bell was quite scarlet. There *had* been an occasion when she had been rather ill, in the school-room unfortunately, and the girl had witnessed it – but she had *not* been sick in a bucket, and neither had sherry anything to do with it. Wretched little liar!

'Come on, Freddie,' said Celandine.

The two of them made their gleeful escape, and scuttled around the side of Howard's Hill until they were out of sight of the party. In an ecstasy of freedom they threw themselves onto the warm grass – Freddie's idea – and rolled down the steep hill, over and over, until they came to a halt. Then, reeling with dizziness, they clambered back up the hill, higher this time, to begin again, gasping and shrieking as they rolled once more, recklessly allowing gravity to do what it would with them, spinning them like bobbins along the bumpy turf. At some point, then, Celandine lost all control over what was happening and knew only that she was tumbling head over heels, arms and legs hopelessly flailing, quite unable to help herself.

Freddie, having reached the end of his travels, was dizzily aware of his sister landing with a sudden thump close by, and of the dull sickening smack of bone upon rock. A tiny whimper was all that followed, then silence.

'Dinah? *Dinah!*' Freddie scrabbled over to where Celandine lay – saw the loose slab of grey stone half-buried in the grass beside her motionless head. He shook her shoulder, but there was no reaction, no sound. Her eyes were closed and she was very white.

Still dazed from his own descent, Freddie scrambled back up Howard's Hill, gasping and shouting for help. Nobody seemed to be taking any notice. Even when the party came back into view, nobody took any notice. They just kept *talking*, right up until the moment where he grabbed his mother's arm.

'Mama! I kept shouting for you! It's *Dinah*! I think she's dead!'

* * *

'No, do not move her. This is not a good idea. Lizzie please . . . let me see.' Josef Wesser knelt by Lizzie Howard, his sister, and tried to prevent her from lifting the child. Poor Mrs Howard was frantic, and Josef glanced up at Erstcourt in appeal. Erstcourt said, 'Come, Lizzie, let Josef do his work,' and at the same time placed his hands about his wife's shoulders and drew her towards him.

Josef held the child's wrist and felt for her pulse, leaning forward so that his ear was next to Celandine's mouth. He listened closely. 'Don't worry,' he said, almost instantly. 'She is breathing.'

As if to confirm this, Celandine began to move, rolling her head from side to side and setting up a continuous high-pitched moan. Her eyes were still closed and Josef said, 'She remains unconscious. But I think there are no bones broken.'

Mrs Howard knelt once more beside her daughter, still distraught. 'Oh, Josef – what can we do? What can we *do*?'

'Should we take her down to the house?' said Erstcourt.

'Perhaps.' Josef looked doubtful. It was quite a long way, and he was worried that the child might suffer more from being carried than from staying where she was. It would be good to get her out of the sun, though. He glanced up at the crowd of people who were now standing on the slope above them, looking down upon the scene, and then spoke to Lizzie.

'There was a baby in a carriage. Somebody had a . . . a bassinet. Might we borrow it, do you think?'

'Oh yes – I'm sure we could. Mrs Svann would never mind, I am sure. Mrs Svann!' Lizzie called up to Mrs Swann, who was among the crowd up on the hillside. 'Could we borrow the baby's carriage? The bassinet!'

Mrs Swann turned and spoke to somebody behind her, and in a few moments Mr Swann and Thos were bringing the big wicker carriage rather clumsily down the side of the hill.

By the time they had gently lifted Celandine into the baby carriage and made her as comfortable as they could, she had begun to regain consciousness. She had not yet spoken, but her eyes were open and she seemed aware of what was happening.

'I think perhaps we could take her back up to the platform,' said Josef. 'You would want to be with her, Lizzie, and it would be a pity to spoil the party if it is not necessary. I also shall be there. We will watch her for a while and see how she is.'

And so Josef, Thos, Erstcourt and Mr Swann carried the baby carriage back up to the platform and let it stand by the top table. Josef mixed a headache powder with a little lemonade – and the fact that Celandine was able to sit up and drink this encouraged her family to believe that she had probably not taken too much harm from her fall. Freddie in particular was hugely relieved, although worried at the same time. Now that the crisis appeared to be over, he feared that there would be trouble – and that the blame for the whole thing was likely to fall upon him. When nobody was looking, he put a piece of cake in the bassinet as a peace offering.

It soon became clear that Celandine could not remain where she was for long. Though small, she was certainly too big to fit comfortably into a baby carriage, and Josef had propped her up with her head resting on a pillow placed over the folded-down hood. She was unprotected from the sun, and exposed also to the surrounding hubbub of the party.

'We could carry her a little further up the hill and place her under the shade of the trees,' said Josef. 'Then she would be able to rest properly. And of course we should be able to see her from here. Celandine – how are you feeling? Shall we put you under the trees? Would you like that?'

Celandine was feeling too hot and headachy and sick to answer.

She floated into consciousness once more, from a dream where a thousand Union Jacks were flying and she was heading a great procession of noisy people. They were carrying her in a litter toward a distant abbey, and her Coronation.

Her head hurt and she did not want to open her eyes. She could still hear the sound of many cheerful voices, but knew that she was not in a procession. She was lying, not very comfortably, in a baby carriage and the voices she heard were the voices drifting up from the party below. Birds she could also hear, high above her – wood pigeons – calling to each other softly.

Beneath the trees on Howard's Hill, that was

where she was. She opened her eyes just a little, and allowed blotchy shades of green to filter through her lashes. Overhanging foliage dipped down towards her, quite close, sheltering her in a leafy world, cool and comforting, despite the pain in her head. So peaceful it was, to stare up through the patterns of graceful boughs, to watch the gentle shifting colours, to breathe in the woodland scents of leaf and bark and briar rose.

But how fierce and wild those briars looked. A great bank of them climbed to her left, enveloping the trunks of the trees in thorny tangles. How terrible it would be to fall amongst them. Better to look up instead, through the friendly branches of the spreading oak, to let the shapes mingle and blur, shiny as sequins . . . coloured sequins that pulsated slightly, in time with the dull throbbing in her temples.

And now she was dreaming once again, for here were eyes that gazed down towards her – big brown eyes, set wide apart, beautiful eyes that were fixed, not upon her own, but upon something else close by.

The eyes blinked, so huge in such a tiny face, and a small brown hand was nervously wiped over the half open mouth. Celandine squeezed her own eyes shut for a few moments, and then opened them again. Still there – well-hidden among the leaves, but still there.

Calm and dreamy, she felt uncertain now as to whether she was asleep or awake.

Marmoset – the word came into her head . . . marmoset. From a travelling zoo they had taken her to. Marmoset. Like Somerset, she had thought at the time, but a creature rather than a county. A creature

30

with big brown eyes, a pretty thing . . . but not clothed. No, not clothed.

So it was not a marmoset. What, then? And what was it looking at? Celandine raised her head very slightly and glanced down at the baby's coverlet that they had lightly draped over her. A piece of cake lay on a roughly folded napkin, tucked between herself and the inner side of the wicker carriage. Cherry cake. She painfully lowered her head once more, and now the eyes were looking directly at her, peeping from behind the leaves, retreating, then peeping again. Full of curiosity they were, of innocence, and of longing. The eyes moved from her to the piece of cake and back to her again. She might have laughed if it wasn't for the pain. The wanting was so undisguised, so obvious.

And there was something else in the look of those eyes that she had seen before. Something extra – or something missing. Like Charity Hobbs. Yes, that was it. Poor Charity had just such a look about her. Imbecile, they called her, the carter's youngest child. Imbecile – though it was said in pity rather than contempt. But Charity did not hang from the branches of trees, brown and skinny, like a marmoset, and dress in bits of feathers and rags and . . . what? Rabbit skins? She couldn't see properly.

So it was not a marmoset and it was certainly not Charity Hobbs. Celandine did not want to lift her head again – it hurt too much – but she allowed her fingers to search for the cherry cake, breaking a piece off, feeling the soft crumbly texture, sticky from the heat.

31

'Cake,' she whispered, and raised her arm, holding the morsel aloft, reaching up towards the dipping branches. Her tongue was dry and her throat hurt, but she said it once more. 'Cake.'

Again the flash of a tiny brown hand, the hurried wiping of the mouth, and the deep longing in the wide-set eyes that darted back and forth from her to the cherry cake. After a while it became an effort for Celandine to keep her arm upright and she began to lower it once more. The creature seemed to panic at the sight of the cake apparently being withdrawn, and it moved forward slightly, parting the foliage, revealing more of itself. Feathers, and raggedy bits of cloth . . . fur. A tiny thing – a manikin. A boy.

It crawled towards her, upside down like a squirrel on the hanging branch, the big eyes fearful but eager, a hand outstretched, brown and grubby and as small as a doll's, yet so near. So near, the trembling skinny fingers. Marching drums beat at her temples and the foliage waved to and fro, bringing the sound of distant laughing voices in and out of focus. There, and not there. And then another voice, closer – hissing – an urgent whisper. 'Fin! *Fin!* Drat the young fool – what bist doing now? *Fin!*'

Celandine raised her arm again, automatically, and felt the piece of cake being snatched away from her, heard the quick rustle of leaves, a scrabble of movement. Her vision was all wavy, but she briefly caught sight of another face – older, bearded – and a flash of panic in deep-set eyes. A glance in her direction, angry and troubled, as though gauging the damage done. Then the leaves were still, and there was nothing more to be seen. But she heard the voice again, just one word, fading into the greenery as the light began to slip away. '*Fin!*'

The sound of it bounced around her head, a retreating echo in the closing darkness.

'Who are those little people that live in the woods?' she said.

Three figures stood at her bedside: her mother, her Uncle Josef and – most surprisingly – her father. She couldn't remember that her father had ever visited her room before, not even when she had had the mumps. They had all changed their clothes since she had fallen asleep. The party was obviously over.

Now they stared down at her and her father, his mouth unsmiling beneath his greying moustache, said, 'She's awake, at last. Well, I'd better be off. Need a word with Hughes about the grain hoist. I'll leave her to you then, Lizzie – the child has taken no great harm, it would seem. Josef, shall you stay to supper? No? I'll say good day, then.'

Her mother sat down on the edge of the bed, her skirts rustling, and leaned forward, reaching a hand out towards her. Celandine felt the cool fingers resting on her forehead and she closed her eyes again for a few moments. She heard her mother whisper something to Uncle Josef, but the words were in German and difficult to make out.

Uncle Josef's reply was clearer, easier to understand. '*Keine sorge*, Lizzie. *Sie ist stark.*'

Don't worry, Lizzie. She is strong.

Strong. Was she strong? She didn't feel it. She opened her eyes again.

'Who *are* those little people living in our woods?'

She saw her mother look sideways at Josef – a worried glance – and noticed that Josef shook his head slightly. What was the matter? It was a simple enough question.

Josef lifted up the wicker chair that stood in the corner and brought it over to the bedside. He sat on it the wrong way round, straddling it as though it were a horse, leaning his forearms across the hooped back. His bearded chin rested on his arms, so that when he spoke his head moved up and down slightly.

'You saw some people?' he said. 'Where?'

'In the wood. They were up in the trees. They were very *small* people.'

'Ah.' Josef thought about this for a while. 'How small were they, these people?'

'Ever so small. Tiny.'

'So. Like . . . ah . . . *die Fee*? What is the English word . . . fairies? Like fairies?'

'Oh no. Much bigger than fairies.'

'I see.' Josef leaned sideways slightly and lowered one of his hands, palm downwards, until it hovered about a foot above the bedside rug. 'Then . . . like so, perhaps?'

'A bit bigger, I think. I couldn't see very well.'

Josef raised the level of his hand slightly and his eyebrows lifted in comical query at the same time. Celandine laughed and Josef continued to raise his hand in jerky movements, higher and higher, until he was out of his chair, stretching as tall as he could, with his fingers almost touching the ceiling. '*This* small?'

He sat down again and lowered his chin onto his hands once more. He was smiling. 'Tell me, then.'

'They were just . . . little. Little people. There was a boy, and I gave him some cake. His father – well, I *think* it must have been his father – was angry with him. He said "drat". He had a beard.'

'Ah. Like my beard?'

'Yes. Just like yours.'

'And you were . . . where . . . in the cart? In the baby carriage?'

'Yes. They were in the trees, looking down at me. The boy was. He didn't have many clothes on – just some bits of rags and feathers. And some fur. The father was only there later on . . . he shouted something . . . *Fin!* . . .'

Celandine stopped talking, realizing that there was going to be no answer to her question. On Josef's face was an expression of concerned curiosity, and on her mother's a look of open horror. They plainly didn't know who the little people were.

Josef put his hands together, almost as though he was praying, and touched his nose with his fingertips.

'Celandine, you must not let this frighten you. And you also, Lizzie – do not be alarmed. This is not at all unusual.'

'I wasn't frightened,' began Celandine, 'only my head hurt, you see, and it was all a bit blurry . . .'

'Of course. Your head hurt, and your vision was . . . ah . . . not perfect. You have taken a bad knock, and so it is expected that . . .' Josef parted his hands and gave a slight shrug. Her mother took her cue from Uncle Josef and turned towards her with a nervous little shrug of her own. 'Yes. Of course. Is expected. My poor *liebling*. But no more strange peoples, eh? All soon will be well.'

'But I did see them. They *were* there.'

'Ah,' said Joseph. 'Sometimes our eyes like to play funny games with us. You remember the little trick I showed you, Celandine, at Christmas, with the handkerchief and the playing cards? The Knave of Hearts, yes? First he was there, and then he was not there, and then he was there again. Yes?'

'Yes,' said Celandine. She remembered. But that was different.

They didn't believe her, and she wasn't sure why. The appearance of the tree-people had been surprising, shocking even, but no more so than some of the things she had seen at the travelling zoo – where the sight of a kiwi had so impressed her that she had held on tight to her mother's hand and said, 'But there aren't *really* such things, are there?' And the baboons she had seen with their brightly painted faces, and the gorgeous macaw that had offered to take her coat – these creatures seemed no less unlikely than a very small person with a taste for cherry cake.

But the more she insisted upon what she had seen, the more agitated her mother became, and the more grave the look in her Uncle Josef's eyes. In the end she gave it up and tried another subject.

'Have they all gone home now?'

But this didn't seem to have been quite the right thing to say either, for now their expressions changed from concern to puzzlement. Then Josef understood.

'Oh, the party. Yes, they have all gone home, Celandine. You have been sleeping for some while. The picnic party was yesterday – we have been quite worried, you know.'

Freddie, at least, believed her story.

'Golly,' he said, and jumped off the corner of her bed to go and peer out of the window. 'How many, do you think? Just the two that you saw? Or are there lots of them? I wonder . . . I wonder what they *eat*.'

Celandine laughed. 'Cake,' she said.

'No, but seriously . . .' Freddie turned his head to look at her, his blue eyes wide and questioning. 'And what do they do when it rains? And what about in the winter? Come on, Dinah – we have to go and see. Are you well enough? I wonder if they'd like some eggs. Or carrots. We could get some from the garden.'

'Yes, all right.'

'Hop up, then. I'll go and see if I can find a basket.'

And that was the wonderful thing about Freddie – he had no patience. Everything had to happen *now*. He never said 'We'll have to wait and see', or 'Perhaps we'd better think about it'. He wasn't sensible, like Thos.

'What a *mixture* of children you have, Mrs Howard.' People often said this – visitors who came to call. And Celandine could see that it was true, as she sat at her dressing table and tried to organize her ridiculous hair. Thos was dark, like their father – dark hair, and dark serious eyes. He also had Erstcourt's dark and sudden temper. Freddie was fair and blue-eyed, like their mother, and his hair had to be kept very short because it was so curly. Freddie was impatient and it could be difficult to get his attention, but he was seldom grumpy. When Celandine looked into the mirror she could see Thos's grave brown eyes staring back at her. And when she tried to get a brush through her frizzy blonde curls she could see how Freddie's hair would be if it was allowed to grow. Yes, they were a mixture all right, and she was the strangest mixture of them all. No wonder people gave her odd looks.

'Are you ready?' Freddie was straight back, and he'd managed to get hold of an egg basket. 'Let's go and see if we can find them, then.'

They stood beneath the spreading oak on Howard's Hill, where Celandine had lain in the baby carriage, and shouted up at the silent trees.

'Hallooo! Is there anybody in there?'

Freddie lifted the basket so that it could more clearly be seen should anyone be watching. They had eggs and carrots, a bottle of liquorice water and most of a Bath bun, but so far no customers.

'I don't suppose they stay in the same tree all the time,' said Freddie. 'I expect they move about a bit. Wish we could get in there.'

They looked doubtfully at the heavy tangle of briars and Freddie went as far as trying to part a few of them, but they could both see that it was hopeless. 'Even if we had a billhook, it wouldn't be any good,' said Freddie. He brightened up. 'Still. There might be a better place somewhere else. We'll go and see, shall we?'

Celandine stumbled along beside her brother, happy to let him be in charge as he swished through the long summer grass. Freddie was still hopeful that they would find a way through the continuous barrier of brambles. 'And even if we don't,' he said, 'they're sure to spot us sooner or later. Once they see that we mean them no harm, they'll probably come closer. Hallooo! Are you there? We've brought you some food!'

They came to a halt at the top of a steep gully and looked down the bank at the little trickle of water that dampened the rocks below. The stream obviously started somewhere in the wood, and here was where it came out.

'Aha! This could be a good place,' said Freddie, and they scrambled down the side of the gully to take a closer look.

But the brambles that overhung the stream were as thick here as anywhere and there was no possibility of even touching them without getting their feet wet and muddy.

Freddie said that they could always come back later. 'It might be the best place after all, but we'd better make sure that there isn't an easier way in. Come on.' They clambered up the opposite bank of the gully and carried on with their search.

Right around the entire perimeter of the wood they walked, and it took hours. They kept stopping and looking up at the trees, wishing that they could find a hanging branch that was low enough to reach. They shouted and whistled and promised that they only wanted to be friendly. Occasionally they had another go at picking their way through the wall of briars. None of it did any good, yet Freddie remained cheerful. 'There might be *anything* in there,' he said. 'Bears, even. Or wolves.' Another thought occurred to him. 'If we can't get *in*,' he said, 'then how can anything get out? They might be trapped, Dinah, whoever it is that you saw. They could be just waiting for us to come and rescue them.'

Celandine, so glad at first that Freddie had believed her story, began to wish that she'd kept quiet about the whole thing. Her legs ached, her head ached, and she was scratched and stung in a hundred places. She trailed miserably after her brother, wearily wading through the patches of nettles and dock leaves, following in his footsteps like King Wenceslas's page.

'Freddie, let's go back,' she said, at last. 'I'm so tired.'

'Well, but it must be just as far to go back as it is to carry on,' said Freddie. 'We'd do better to keep going. Tell you what, though, we might as well eat the food. Here, you have the bun.'

By the time they reached the big oak tree that they'd started from, Celandine was absolutely ready to drop.

'Want me to give you a pick-a-back?' said Freddie. Celandine shook her head. She suddenly wanted to cry. Freddie had believed her story when nobody else had, and he'd never once got cross with her, although it was clear that the whole day had been a waste of time. She felt terrible about it, yet he had never complained or hinted that she must have been mistaken. He would even give her a pick-a-back home if she wanted. But what really upset her was that he'd given her the Bath bun and she'd eaten it all and not even offered to share it with him. Freddie had eaten a carrot instead. Why was she such a bad person?

'I'm sorry,' she said, and began to walk down the hill – trying to stay ahead of him so that he shouldn't see her watery eyes. And even then she realized that he was still being kind, that he was carefully keeping a pace or two behind her because he knew that she was crying and he didn't want to embarrass her.

'Don't worry, Dinah,' said Freddie. 'We'll find them, you'll see. Shall we try again tomorrow?'

'Yes. If you like.'

She knew that they never would. Tomorrow was tomorrow, and something else would have claimed Freddie's attention by then – and his company. By tomorrow he would probably have forgotten all about today.

And as the tomorrows came and went, Celandine also began to forget – there being more immediate troubles to occupy her thoughts.

After the Coronation picnic, Miss Bell's attitude towards her turned to open dislike and she seemed deliberately to make life difficult. No piece of work that Celandine produced was ever quite good enough for Miss Bell. Celandine could not write satisfactorily, nor paint, nor draw, nor make fingerprint pictures without smudging them, nor embroider nor sew, nor play music – she did nothing well enough to suit her governess. Everything she attempted resulted in criticism and punishment.

'What a pity, Celandine, that you had to spoil your map of Norway by decorating it with drawings of mermaids,' said Miss Bell one morning. 'I'm afraid it just won't do.' She studied the map for a few moments longer before screwing it up and dropping it into the wastepaper basket. Then she said, 'And do you really think that blue and green are suitable colours for your embroidered lettering? You had better unpick it and start all over again.'

Celandine came to dread the very smell of the schoolroom, but worst of all were the piano lessons, held in the parlour.

Every afternoon at four o'clock, Celandine sat at the piano to play her scales, and every afternoon she got something wrong. Miss Bell stood beside her with a wooden ruler poised above Celandine's hands as they made their uncertain progress up and down the keys. And whenever those hands stumbled upon a wrong note, down came the ruler with a smart rap on the offending knuckle.

There was more torture as they moved on to 'The Bluebells of Scotland'. Celandine had played this wretched little tune so many times that it still jangled in her head when she closed her eyes at night.

'Please, Miss Bell, *can't* we have another piece of music?'

'Yes, of course, Celandine. As I've told you before, we shall select another piece directly you are able to play this one without these silly mistakes. Again, please.'

And the wooden ruler continued to hover above her outraged fingers, waiting to strike.

Celandine had appealed to her mother on several occasions, and one Sunday evening, with the prospect of another painful week before her, she tried yet again.

'I *hate* Miss Bell,' she said. 'And Miss Bell hates me. I wish you'd get rid of her, Mama, and find me a better governess.'

Her mother looked up from her sewing. 'Miss Bell

is a very *good* governess,' she said. She lowered her spectacles and peered around the spirit lamp that was set upon the little table beside her. 'And of course she does not hate you. You must not keep saying such a thing. There was no trobles with Freddie, or with Thos. If there is trobles now, then perhaps is with you, Celandine. You did not hate Miss Bell, did you Freddie?'

Freddie mumbled something. He was sitting at the parlour table, surrounded by bits of angling tackle, concentrating upon trying to tie a fishing fly.

'Well, Freddie doesn't have to be with her any more,' said Celandine. 'Now that he's going away to school. And anyway, Miss Bell was never as awful to Freddie as she is to me. I wish somebody would hurry up and marry her, then she'd *have* to go away.'

'Tom Allen might marry her,' said Freddie, 'if he could only forget about her being sick in a bucket.' He gave Celandine a sly grin.

'Sick in a *bucket*? What is this?' Mrs Howard looked from one to the other.

'It's your own fault, you know, Dinah.' Freddie held up the brightly coloured fly and brought it towards his mouth, gulping at it as though he were a fish. 'If you didn't tease her she'd be much nicer to you.'

'Freddie, that's so unfair! She's just horrible to me – it's not *my* fault. She hits me with a ruler. I keep trying to tell everybody, but nobody believes me.'

'No, no. I'm sure that this is not so and that Freddie is right.' Mrs Howard picked up her sewing

44

again. 'And I shall hear no more, Celandine. But I shall speak with Miss Bell tomorrow, and see what *again* she has to say of this.'

'Hmph.' Celandine glowered at Freddie and then went back to practising her scales. She struck the piano keys as hard as she could and wished that the hated instrument would collapse into a heap of firewood. It was plain that she would have to fight her own battles and take her revenge wherever she could find it. Celandine frowned at her right hand as it stumbled up and down the keys – like a clumsy spider. Yes. *That* was something to think about: the big spider that she had hidden upstairs in the Bovril jar . . .

Miss Bell's spectacular fear of spiders was a great discovery, and it gave Celandine some real ammunition. Nothing could be easier than to catch one or two of the really leggy ones that inhabited the stables, pop them into an empty jar and transport them to the classroom, where they could be re-housed in Miss Bell's desk. It was a delight to watch her governess trying to control her choking horror upon the discovery of yet another of the appalling creatures, to see her attempting to stand her ground when all her instinct was to cry out and flee the room. But Miss Bell had quickly grown wise to this trick and now opened her desk with extreme caution – and a ruler held at arm's length. The element of surprise had gone.

It was a shame, because Celandine had managed to catch a real monster earlier that evening, just before supper – a spider so big that she had felt it pinching furiously at her finger as she hastily clapped the pierced lid of the Bovril jar into place. She had poked a couple of dead flies through the holes in the lid and hoped that these would keep the beast going until the morning.

Plink-plink-plink . . .

Her spider-fingers crept along the piano keys more stealthily now, taking their time, quietly stalking their prey.

The next morning Miss Bell left the schoolroom at two minutes to eleven, as she always did, to fetch her cup of coffee.

Celandine waited for the footsteps to die away, her heart beating faster at the opportunity that now lay before her: Miss Bell's summer gloves were lying neatly folded on the little table that held the classroom globe.

When all was silent, Celandine jumped up and quickly crossed the room. She picked up one of the long cotton gloves and half-fitted it over the lid of the Bovril jar. Then she unscrewed the lid and shook the massive spider down into the glove, instantly folding the end of the material over a couple of times so that there could be no escape. She gently placed the glove on the table once more, tried to make everything look as it had been, and scuttled back to her seat.

It was agony having to wait until lunchtime. Every once in a while Celandine saw the glove give a little twitch, and her stifled sniggers continually threatened to give her away. Miss Bell watched her suspiciously. But at last the hands of the clock reached twelve-thirty and Miss Bell said, 'Very well. You may put down your pen.'

Celandine was in no hurry, for once, to leave the classroom. She took her time organizing her exercise books, and was rewarded by seeing Miss Bell walk over to the globe and reach for her gloves.

Miss Bell picked up the top glove and thrust her hand into it. She jumped backwards with a loud shriek, vigorously shaking her arm. It was clear that she dared not touch her gloved hand with the other one, and so was unable to rid herself of the horror of whatever was wriggling about next to her skin.

Celandine could not have hoped for more, but when she saw the spider appear and run straight up Miss Bell's arm, she thought she would collapse from laughing so much. Miss Bell scrunched her head down to her shoulder and spun round, banging against the desk as she tried to knock the spider off her. She grabbed wildly for her ruler but missed her grip, and the thing clattered across the room. Even when she had managed to shake the creature from her – a dark scurry across the lid of the desk and down to the floor – Miss Bell continued to screech in panic and disgust. She leaned against the chalky blackboard for support, her gloved hand clutching at her unpinned hair, until gradually she was able to calm herself.

An entire morning's worth of bottled-up anticipation exploded from Celandine and she hugged her ribs, exhausted with laughter but unable to stop.

Miss Bell, her terror suddenly converted to fury,

strode across the schoolroom with her arm raised to strike. Celandine lifted her own arm in defence, and for a moment the two of them remained motionless, glaring at one another.

Miss Bell finally lowered her shaking arm. She turned and walked over to her desk once more. Celandine stared at the smudge of pink chalk dust that stained the back of the retreating white blouse. Miss Bell stood at her desk and slowly removed her glove. Her breathing was still heavy and her neck still very red, but she was back in control. There was a look of triumph almost about the pursed lips, the upright bearing.

'Right, Miss *Howard*, that is the final straw.' The words hissed out of her. 'Now let me tell you something in private, whilst there is no one else to hear it. I don't like you, and I never have. I believe you to be an entirely wicked, spoilt, and sinful child – an ugly little farm urchin who will never come to the slightest good. You have no ability whatsoever. Your only talent is for mischief, lies, and tittle-tattle. Oh yes, I know all about your complaints to your mother. Fortunately, Mrs Howard is more inclined to believe my story than she is yours – and this is hardly surprising when you are known to be such a liar. Do you see, Celandine? This is why you will never win. I have your parents' full support. It doesn't matter how many times you dip the chalk in the glue-pot, or put spiders in my desk. Your silly crimes will always bring you more pain than pleasure – I can promise you that – and it will do you no good to complain.'

Miss Bell drew the long cotton glove across her palm, smoothing it out between her finger and thumb.

'No doubt you are hoping to get rid of me, Celandine, but I have every intention of remaining here for several more years yet – certainly until something better comes along. My salary is generous enough, and I shall not be driven away by *your* antics – in fact I enjoy a challenge. I shall report this morning's little episode to your mother, of course. I'm sure she'll understand why I've kept you from your lunch, and why I'm now going to give you an extra music lesson. You may pick up my ruler and then follow me.'

Miss Bell threw her glove down onto the desk and strode out of the room. Open war was finally declared.

Chapter Three

A bitter highland wind rattled through the pines, scattering the rooks and jackdaws and flinging them to the skies like bits of rag. Summer was barely gone, yet here in these northern woods the days already grew bleak.

The two Ickri guards turned their backs to the weather, their wings tight-folded against the buffeting squalls. They huffed into cupped hands and drew their hoods close about their stubbled faces.

Peck glanced behind him, at the covered entrance to Avlon's shelter. The oilskin flap had worked loose, so he laid his spear aside and stooped to peg the material down once more, pushing the forked stick into the damp earth with fingers too numb to properly grip.

'Talk talk talk,' he muttered. 'How much more o' this?'

Rafe said nothing, but slapped his arms and jigged from one foot to the other.

Occasionally the murmur of voices inside the brushwood shelter rose above the gusting wind as

Avlon and the Elders talked on. Warm it would be in there, huddled around the charcoal embers, and there would be a stoup of hot tansy to pass from hand to hand.

Rafe looked up at the darkening sky. Their watch was nearly over. Soon Ibru and Acer would come to relieve them.

Beneath the dome of woven saplings, Avlon poked at the charcoal fire with his stick, gently tapping one of the surrounding pebbles back into place. The Elders sat cross-legged in a circle and stared into the amber glow. All were silent now, their shadowed faces solemn and thoughtful as they considered what Avlon was proposing.

Haima, the eldest of the Elders, shook his head at last.

' 'Tis safer to bide here,' he said. 'The lands to the south be thick with giants. How shall we be guided through such dangers?'

'I cannot tell,' said Avlon. 'Yet I know that we shall.'

'Thee knowst more than we, then.' Haima sounded unconvinced.

'Aye,' said Avlon. 'Perhaps I do.' He continued to prod at the lumps of glowing charcoal, and the silence grew.

The legend of the Touchstone had long been on Avlon's mind, and in the vivid dreams that came to him each night. As ruler of the Ickri, their king, and Keeper of the Stone, he had long been aware of the old tale – how the two tribes, Ickri and Naiad, had travelled across the span of time from Elysse to Lys-Gorji, the land of the giants, with the Touchstone as their guide. The tribes had eventually quarrelled, so the story went, and the Touchstone had been split. The wingless Naiad tribe had kept the Orbis – the metal device wherein the Stone revolved – and the Ickri had kept the jasper globe itself. Then the Ickri had journeyed into the deep forests of the north, where they now dwelt, whilst the Naiad remained upon the wetlands far away to the south, and were perhaps no more.

'Again.' Avlon spoke to the Elders. 'Let us gather all that we have, and lay it out before us, the better to decide. Come, Haima, tell us what were told to thee, and to those that came before thee.'

Haima sighed, and raised his palms towards the warmth of the fire. 'When the travelling tribes, Ickri and Naiad, were first come to Lys-Gorji, the giants were few. By the waters these ogres lived, in dwellings raised upon poles. Slow they were, and easy tricked. There was little danger from them, then. The Naiad were a water tribe, and so were content to remain. But we, the Ickri, were true travellers. We wished for deeper forests, and richer game. We wouldst not bide upon the wetlands, nor wouldst the Naiad leave. The tribes did quarrel then, and there was blood. Each tribe laid hold to the Touchstone and could not agree, so 'twere split – the Stone to the Ickri, the Orbis to the Naiad.'

'The Naiad robbed us.' Corben, the King's younger brother, spoke. 'As should never have been.'

'Aye,' said Haima. 'The Naiad were many, and the Ickri were few. They robbed us of the Orbis and drove us out. Away to the north our fathers travelled, carrying the Stone with them, but it could guide them no longer. Without the Orbis the Stone has no power. Our fathers marked their journey upon the mapskins that we yet hold, perhaps to show a path if the Ickri should someday return, but none can divine these markings now. Then the Gorji giants became many, and the danger greater, and so the Ickri were driven yet higher into these cold lands, season upon season as the Gorji grew. So here we be.'

'And we can travel no further from the Gorji without we freeze or starve,' said Avlon. 'Yet if we could hold the Orbis once more . . .' He was talking more to himself than to the gathering of Elders that squatted in the draughty shelter about him.

'If we could hold the Orbis once more,' said Haima, 'then we might return to Elysse itself. But these be *old* tales, Avlon, and the Naiad be long gone – slain by the Gorji as we must reckon. And if they live still, where should us seek for them in a land so great? We should never find them, and 'tis folly to talk of it.'

Avlon felt differently. He did not accept that the Ickri were destined to dwindle and die in these frozen forests. He knew that his tribe had not always been so earthbound. Stories he remembered of how the Ickri had once been able to appear and disappear at will, to become other creatures, to cross over into their very dreamings, and these stories were always connected to the Touchstone and the Orbis.

He believed in such things. In his own slumbers Avlon saw that he had walked this earth before, and would do so again. He dreamed that he could truly fly – not the short hunting swoop of his kind, but with beating wings that might carry him beyond the stars. His visions grew stronger, like plants that unfurled and blossomed in the night. He saw the Orbis held aloft, the revolving jasper globe within, and he awoke each morning in the certainty that he had truly been there. This he would truly see. A restored Touchstone would transport his people from a hostile world, and so it was his duty, and his destiny, to make it so.

Avlon had already spoken to the tribe of his visions, and he believed that they would follow him southwards if he commanded it, but the Elders were wavering, still unwilling to leave the safety of these highland woods. The land to the south was overrun with giants, they said, and there was no way of telling where these Naiad might be, or whether they still held the Orbis – or if indeed they still existed.

'The mapskins,' said Avlon. 'Let us look at them once more.'

Haima was beginning to lose patience. 'They be but markings on ancient squirrel pelts,' he said. 'If they would lead us anywhere, they would lead us into the arms of the Gorji. And none can find any meaning to them.'

'I would see Una try.'

'Una?' The Elders glanced at one another, and Corben snorted with contempt.

'We be brothers, Avlon,' he said. 'And I would follow thee in this, but what can your daughter see that we may not?'

'The child is witchi.'

Corben grunted, but said no more.

'Haima?' Avlon appealed to the white bearded Elder.

Haima thought about it for a few moments. Una was known among the Ickri to be a wise-child – or 'witchi'. Una could find water without the need of an amulet or a forked stick, could foretell the weather, could smell the very moment when the seasons turned. With thin hands laid upon the swollen wrists of her elders, Una drew away the pains that plagued them, and so was treated with regard. She was the king's daughter, the child of Avlon, and would have been given due respect for this fact alone, but she also was said to have been 'born afore'. She had the Touch.

' 'Tis true that the maid be witchi,' said Haima, 'but 'twill do us no good in this matter.' He shrugged. 'Ach. Let her try, then, if she will.'

Avlon turned and called out to the Guard.

'Rafe, be you still out there? Go and seek for the child – Una. Bring her to me.'

Una ducked into the entrance of the brushwood shelter where her father sat with the grey-haired Elders. The circle of serious faces turned to look at her – although Corben's head remained lowered in a scowl of irritation.

'Come, child,' Haima beckoned her in, 'and sit with us.'

Her father, at least, was smiling. He lifted a dried-out squirrel skin from the pile in front of him, and offered it to her.

'Una,' he said, 'let us see if ye can be of help to us.'

Haima grunted and Corben's frown deepened.

'These mapskins would tell us of a journey our fathers made, long ago,' said Avlon. 'But we have forgotten how to listen to such things. Now we hope to make this journey again. We would know if ye can find some meaning here that we cannot.'

Una knelt beside her father and took the squirrel pelt from him. She knew of the mapskins, had seen them before, but had never studied them this closely. How strange, the markings upon the dried-out skin – like the designs that decorated the wings of the Ickri archers. She was conscious of the eyes that were upon her.

By the light of the fire Una could make out a faint blue line that wandered from top to bottom of the cracked and yellowed parchment. There were many clumsy depictions of animals and giants, rivers and trees, Gorji dwellings and Gorji contraptions – but whether these were intended as directions or as a simple record of the Ickri's journey north was impossible to tell.

Una spread all the mapskins out end to end on a bindle-wrap, one of the lengths of oilcloth that were used by the tribespeople for both shelter and protection of their goods. Then she removed the small red stone that she kept threaded about her neck and suspended it above the line of charts, allowing it to lead her hand where it would.

Avlon and the Ickri Elders watched in silence as the little amulet twisted this way and that in the gentle glow. Its movements seemed erratic and confused. Sometimes the stone appeared to follow a definite path, crossing smoothly from chart to chart, but then it would suddenly gyrate and shoot away from its previous course altogether. Una experimented with the order of the mapskins, patiently shuffling them around until eventually the stone travelled in an unbroken line from one end to the other. She felt that this was a beginning, and noticed her father's nod towards his brother. But Corben turned away, apparently unimpressed.

What else could be learned? Una dangled the stone above the markings on the first chart once more, and closed her eyes. She tried to picture those early travellers, searching for them amid the dark landscape of the past, hoping that they would be able to tell her something.

She could see nothing at first, but she began to feel a sense of trouble and loss. The Touchstone? Was this to do with the Touchstone? Deeper into the darkness she ventured. Snatches of sound came to her – the clatter of a magpie, the humming of flies, the sudden *gloop* of a fish on quiet waters.

Then she caught a glimpse of something, shadowy figures, half-hidden by foliage. Her eyes were closed, and yet she could see them. They were laughing. Among the bright leaves they sat, flexing their tattooed wings, the sunlight dappling their faces, and they were laughing the soundless laugh of the Ickri. For a moment they were there, and she was there with them, a fellow traveller on a hopeful journey, but in that same moment the stone shifted its path and the figures faded. She was alone again in the darkness.

In vain she sought them out once more, allowing the amulet to take her where it would, but the travellers had gone. Other things she saw: Gorji constructions, the vague shapes of great dwellings, winged figures, carved, and set among grim tablets of polished stone. She heard the rumble and growl of the Gorji world, caught the burning odours of all their works, but saw no more of her own kind. The amulet guided her hand onwards until at last all had dwindled away.

A long, long period of nothingness, then once again she caught the distant humming of flies. Closer they drifted and closer, and with their humming came a terrible stench. Her insides began to turn over in nausea and terror. There was some great danger here.

Louder and louder, the humming of the flies. *'Miiiiidge! Miiiidge! You're sinking!'*

Una opened her eyes with a jump. The amulet had travelled far beyond the line of charts, and her father and the Elders were all staring at her.

Una told all that she had seen, tried to describe the confusing images that had appeared before her, and then waited in silence.

Haima said, 'So. 'Tis plain that the child do find some meaning here – but no meaning that be plain. What be there to *guide* us in this?'

'The Ickri are my own,' said Avlon, 'and Una my own also. Would I lead my own into the grasp of giants if I did not see that it must be so? We *shall* be guided, Haima, and the way to the Orbis shall become clear. Believe me in this.'

Then Corben spoke up.

'I stand with my brother in this – as should all here,' he said. 'For where be our choice? We may move yet further north, away from the Gorji, and starve. Or we may follow Avlon to the south, and hope to find the Orbis once more. The path of little chance, or the path of none. I know which I would take.'

Haima threw up his hands in surrender at last. 'Have your way, then,' he said. 'And perhaps 'tis better that we choose than have choice made for us. I shall argue against it no more. Maris, what from thee? Are we agreed? Ruven, shall us go?'

'Aye.'

'Aye.'

The decision had finally been made. Una looked

at the hard-lined face of Corben. He had spoken in support of her father – no more than might have been expected. Why then did this make her feel so uneasy?

Avlon wasted no time. On the following morning he called together the entire Ickri tribe, that they might hear what he had to say. Elders, archers, children and wives sat waiting, cloaked and hooded against the wind, huddled upon their bindle-wraps beneath the creaking pines. Most of them had an idea of why they were met, for the rumours of a coming journey had quickly spread.

Avlon stood before the gathered tribespeople, his own hood thrown back so that his greying hair swirled about in the early breeze. He raised the Touchstone aloft for all to see.

'I and the Elders have spoken yesternight,' he said, 'and are decided. Some here may already know what is to come. We shall no longer content ourselves with hiding in these forests like mice, with scuttling like insects, with crawling like worms – for we are none of these things. We are the Ickri. We are heir to powers that shall carry us across the span of ages and return us to the great kingdom of Elysse where we belong. From Elysse we came, and to Elysse we shall return, aye, when once this Stone has been restored. Then we shall live as our fathers lived, free to journey the paths of the heavens, true travellers once again. And this shall be so, mark ye. Truly so. I have seen the Touchstone united with its brother Orbis in my dreamings, and know that I was there. The Stone did turn within the Orbis once again, and our fortunes did turn with it. I have seen this as clearly as I see your faces now.'

Avlon lowered the Touchstone and looked about at the gathering before him – the worried and wondering expressions of the old, the excited smiles of the young, the hard-set mouths of the archers, unsurprised and unperturbed.

'Aye, it shall be so,' he said, his voice softer now. 'Though not on this day, nor for many to come. The Orbis has yet to be found. It lies far from here, waiting upon our return. We must travel to the south, through the lands of the Gorji to seek it out, and I do not know the path or how long it may take to get there. Nor can I see what dangers might beset us upon the way. I only see that we must find the faith for such a journey, or stay here and dwindle to naught.' He held the Touchstone high again. 'Follow me then, those who will, and let us become as once we were. Our true selves. A travelling tribe. The Ickri.'

Avlon turned and walked towards his shelter, disappearing alone amidst the whispering trees as the murmurs of his people began to grow.

Some who heard Avlon speak were inspired by the fire that seemed to burn within him, and some were dubious. All very well to talk of high times to come – but what of the distance between now and then? Who would protect them as they attempted to make such a journey? There was no knowing how they should ever find this 'Orbis', or whether it even existed.

And yet Avlon's views had long been known, and

most had been prepared for something like this. They would go. The air was warmer, so 'twas said, in the south. The winds were not apt to bite so hard, nor the snow to lie so deep. There would be more giants to contend with, no doubt, and less room to breathe, but they understood that with each passing season the opportunities for making such a journey would become fewer. Better to risk it now, than to wait till every scrap of land was occupied by the Gorji.

Avlon's archers, the King's Guard, would do as they were bidden, but the archers under the command of Corben, the king's brother, were not so easily pushed. They sat on a log beside the entrance to Corben's shelter in order to talk things through.

'I casn't see why us don't tarry till spring,' grumbled Dunch, the eldest of Corben's company. 'I be minded to put winter at the back o' me, before I goes on this old gallivant.'

'Much chance of finding us, then, if thee did,' replied Corben.

'Much chance o' finding aught *worth* finding, either way. 'Tis all foolishness, I reckons.' Berin threw in his lot with Dunch.

'Bide here, then,' said Corben. 'We'll be well rid of thee.'

'I s'll go.' Tuz, the youngest spoke up. 'I ain't afeared o' no giants. They'll not catch I.' He raised his bow at an imaginary target. 'But I might catch they. What say thee, Faro?'

' 'Tain't the giants that's the worry,' said Faro. ''Tis

their hounds. I don't want one o' they gurt things clamped to me nethers, and nor do thee if thee've any sense. And what *be* this Orbis we'm all to go a-chasing arter? Avlon do talk some blether. He'm fey as a thistle-seed o' late.'

Corben's voice grew harsh. 'Whilst Avlon be king, and whilst I be his brother, thee'll look to thee tongue, Faro. I have spoken with him many times of this. If he be right, and this thing be found, then the hand that bears the Touchstone shall bear a power as none here can know.' Corben looked meaningfully into the faces of his archers. 'Whose ever hand that shall be. 'Twill be worth the finding of, Berin, and worth the losing of *thee* to a hound's belly, Faro. Comprend? Hold thee gripes, then. We shall *all* go.'

And so the Ickri made ready to become a travelling tribe once more, to face the long journey south – and whatever might betide.

They rolled their few possessions into bindle-wraps, and these they carried slung low behind them so that they still had some use of their wings. Infants that were too young to either walk or fly were carried in bindle-wraps worn to the front. Those that were the more fit and able shared among them the loads of those who were less so – they also distributed the bindles belonging to the King's Guard, for these archers were privileged to carry nothing but their weapons.

Avlon spoke to his brother, and his General, Corben. 'We shall travel by group. I to the lead, along with the Guard – scouts to the foremost. Then shall come the main tribe. These to be flanked and protected from the hindmost by your company, Corben, and so thee must keep them sharp. We shall travel each day by first light and by last – moon-wane to sun-wax, sun-wane to moon-wax. Comprend?'

'Aye. Comprend.'

'The archers shall have a double task – Faro, Berin, do thee hearken? – for they must look out for all, and likewise hunt for all. But the main tribe must also forage as they go, whatever be found in season, and stand as a shoulder each to his companion. Are all gathered? So. We meet again at moon-wax. Lead on then, Peck, and let Rafe go with thee. Whistle us forward where 'tis safe, whistle us hold where there be danger.'

Peck and Rafe, the chosen scouts, moved off among the dark trees, heading southward. After a while a brief whistle was heard – and Avlon began to lead the Ickri towards a distant and unknown future.

Chapter Four

Celandine had seen no more of the tree-people. Three years older, she had more or less dismissed from her mind the hazy events of Coronation Day.

The world had moved on. Freddie was away at his school, and Thos was now a man about the place, eighteen years old, and working towards the day when the farm would be his. A new tractor had been bought, together with a combine harvester and a baling machine – great smoking dragons that prowled the land from dawn till dusk and never tired. Thos, like his father, was a firm believer in advancing with the times.

But if those about her had progressed, Celandine had not. She was stuck in limbo, still locked into the same dreary classroom routines, still at war with the dreadful Miss Bell – who could *not* be got rid of, no matter what the provocation. Celandine had come to understand why this should be. Miss Bell had long been in love with the local blacksmith, Tom Allen, a frequent visitor to the farm stables. Unfortunately Miss Bell had a rival for Mr Allen's affections – big Ivy Tucker, the woman who came each morning to collect the eggs. The popular Mr Allen had so far made no commitment to either of his admirers, but Miss Bell was certainly not about to depart Mill Farm and leave a clear field for the likes of Ivy Tucker. Celandine had learned this piece of gossip from Lettie, the kitchen-cum-dairymaid. It explained a lot, but it didn't make life any easier, and Celandine felt sure that Miss Bell blamed her for the blacksmith's lack of interest.

Mrs Howard had to listen to the constant complaints from either side, and was at her wits end as to how to deal with it. The more authority she gave Miss Bell, the more resentful her daughter became towards her. She tried the opposite tack and suggested to Miss Bell that Celandine's behaviour might improve if the rules were a little less strict, but this was equally wrong, apparently.

'I'm sorry, Mrs Howard, but that would be a mistake,' said Miss Bell. 'It would certainly make my life very much simpler to let the child have her own way – but then I would be failing in my duty both to her and to you. Children need discipline, and Celandine needs more than most if she is not to run completely wild. It would be a great pity to see her education suffer for the lack of it.'

One could hardly dismiss a governess who so clearly had Celandine's best interests at heart. Mrs Howard refused to interfere any further, and the cycle of punishment and revenge continued.

On her thirteenth birthday Celandine was given a pony.

'He's been used to the leading rein, but he's not

been ridden as yet,' said her father as they entered the stables. 'Robert? Are you there?' He called for the head stableman.

Celandine had begged and begged for a pony of her own, and she couldn't believe that she was about to get her wish at last. She stood between her father and mother as together they looked into the loose box.

'His name's Tobyjug,' said her father. 'Unless you want to change it, of course. Pretty little fellow, and a pretty penny he cost me, too.'

Celandine stared at the beautiful creature. His coat was creamy white – a long white mane and tail – and when he turned his head towards them she saw that he had wonderfully dark eyes that glistened in the dim light of the stable. She was overwhelmed.

'Oh . . . he's lovely! Mama, he's gorgeous, don't you think? Papa, *thank* you! I love him!'

'Well, I hope you will.' Her father's voice was serious. 'Because he comes with strict conditions attached, I'm afraid. Now then. I want to hear no more of these continuous bad reports of your behaviour, Celandine, either in the schoolroom or out of it. Miss Bell is an excellent governess, and she would be difficult to replace. Thos and Freddie both did very well with her, and so I'm sure that any trouble is entirely of your own making. It's a wonder that the woman is still with us. Am I right, Lizzie?'

'Yes, this is true, Celandine. I am worried that Miss Bell will not stay, if you do not better how you act. And so . . .'

'And so this birthday present goes straight back to

the dealer, unless you buck your ideas up, young lady. And I mean that. Any more of this nonsense and I'll sell him on. Now do you understand?'

'But I keep trying to tell you . . .' Celandine decided not to argue. 'Yes, Papa. I'll try.'

'Well, see that you do. Robert? You'd better come and show the girl how to look after a pony.'

Robert, who had been standing in the background, stepped forward. 'Right you are, Mr Howard.'

'Robert will be teaching you to ride, eventually, but that won't be for a little while yet. Now don't forget, he's your pony, Celandine, and I expect you to take responsibility for him. That means feeding him, cleaning him and looking after his tack. Understood? Good. Lecture over, then. Happy birthday, my dear. Come along, Lizzie.'

Celandine was ecstatic, and stayed behind in the stables, long after her parents had departed. She had endless questions for Robert, but at the same time wanted to be alone with her wonderful new friend, Tobyjug. Robert chopped up a few pieces of carrot, made sure that Celandine knew how to offer the pony food from her palm rather than from between her fingers, and said, 'I'll leave 'ee to it, then, miss. Just get to know 'un, for today. You'll do better by theeself.'

The little animal was as shy of her as Celandine was of him, and for a while he kept to the far corner of the loose box, ears pricked, alert but facing away from her. Celandine's arm began to ache from trying to coax him with bits of carrot, and she was reminded of the time when she had lain in the baby carriage, holding out a piece of cherry cake to an equally nervous creature.

'*Cake*,' she had whispered then, '*cake . . . cake . . .*', and the little tree boy had come to her.

She did the same now, and whispered Tobyjug's name. '*Tobyjug . . . toby-toby-toby. Come on, boy . . . gooood boy . . .*'

The pony tossed his pretty white head and snorted, but then turned to look at her. Celandine continued to whisper to him, smiling all the while into those dark intelligent eyes. Eventually, with another little snort, the pony moved away from the far wall of the loose box and took a couple of wary paces towards her.

'*Toby-toby-toby. Come on, boy . . . there's a good boy . . .*'

At last he stretched out his neck and brought his head closer to her waiting hand. Celandine felt the whiffle of his warm breath on her palm as he gently began to take the carrot, the tickle of his nose against her flattened fingers. He was hers.

He was her pony, Tobyjug. He belonged to her and to nobody else, and she needed nothing more than this – a beautiful friend to love and to care for.

Later, as Celandine closed the stable door behind her, the words 'I'm really happy', came into her head. And so she was – yet it was as though somebody else had spoken those words for her, or had called them out to her. She turned and looked across the sunlit yard, gazing up at the farmhouse until her eyes fell upon her own bedroom window. The window was open and – the strangest thing – there was a girl standing there, framed by the stone mullion, her face turned towards the paddocks. The girl's hands rested upon the window sill. She was smiling at something, or someone. Celandine stood and looked on in astonishment. Who could this intruder be? And what on earth was she doing in her room? Those clothes, that hair . . . how very peculiar the girl looked.

Celandine moved forward, out of the shade of the stable buildings and into the sunshine – but then the brightness hurt her eyes and she could no longer see properly. She stepped back into the shade again. The girl at the window had gone. There was no longer anything there to see, yet the memory of her remained. The girl's clothing had been very unusual, outlandish even. And her hair had also looked quite extraordinary – it was untidy, but somehow deliberately so. How little trouble it would be to care for hair such as that . . .

Celandine crossed the yard, took one last look up at her window, and then went into the farmhouse. She climbed the stairs, turned right at the top landing and walked towards her bedroom door, her footsteps clacking loudly on the bare wooden flooring. She turned the handle and gave the door a gentle push, allowing it to swing open by itself. The room was empty.

All the familiar sounds of field and farmyard drifted in through the open casement, comforting, normal. Celandine stood at her bedroom doorway for a few moments longer, then quietly went over to the window. She rested her hands on the sill, as she had seen the girl do, feeling the edge of the metal frame sharp against her soft palms as she gripped it tighter.

What had she seen at this window? A ghost? Something not real?

Celandine remained for a while, looking out over the peaceful landscape, not thinking exactly, just remembering. The image of the strange girl at her window was still clear in her mind. She had always supposed that it would be very frightening to see a ghost, or a spirit, or something that wasn't really there, yet she found herself not to be frightened. Curious and confused, but not frightened.

And besides – she shifted her gaze back to the stables once more – now that she had Tobyjug, there were far more important things to think about.

Celandine could hardly wait for the days to begin, or bear them to come to a close. Every day for the next week, she was up before dawn – surprising even the kitchenmaid, Lettie, who was used to stumbling around, peep-eyed, with the world to herself at that hour – and she spent every spare moment that she could with Tobyjug. The animal was a delight to her, a creature deserving of all her love. Here at last was a reason to be joyful. She insisted upon caring for the pony entirely by herself, learning from Robert how to mix his feed, how to brush out his coat, how to adjust his bridle and leading rein.

She was impatient during her school lessons, more eager than ever for the leaden hours to pass, but now there was no question of risking the loss of her free time by misbehaving. She did everything to the very best of her ability, and gave Miss Bell as little reason as possible to criticize. Miss Bell seemed almost disappointed. She looked even more sour than usual at her pupil's apparent cheerfulness.

'Pride is a sin, Celandine. We should not forget that.'

But Celandine refused to allow her spirits to be dampened. She was happy.

And then all the joy that had unexpectedly come into her life was just as unexpectedly snatched away from her. In one cruel instant it all came to an end. Tobyjug died.

Celandine discovered the stiff little body stretched out upon the cold straw as she entered the stable one morning with the feed bucket. It was horrible. The pony's eyes were open, dull and glazed in the breaking light, eyes that had been so alive and warm the night before. The tongue, black and stiff and dry, protruded from the open jaw. Celandine stood there stupidly, scarcely noticing the clang of the bucket that dropped from her helpless fingers.

'Robert?' It started out as a whisper, barely a sound at all, but then she heard herself shouting, her voice cracked and panicky. 'Robert . . .? Robert! . . . *Robert!*'

The stable hands leaned over the wall of the loose box and murmured to each other as Robert knelt beside the body of Tobyjug. Robert took off his cap and crouched lower, sniffing cautiously at the pony's mouth. He straightened up and sat back on his heels for a few moments, thinking about it. The stable hands were silent now. Robert leaned forward once more, this time to brush the backs of his fingers across the stiff protruding tongue. He brought his hand towards his nose and sniffed again. 'Hmf.' Robert pulled on his cap and looked up at Celandine. 'I reckons he've been pois—' The awful word was cut short as one of the yard boys burst into the stable, very red-faced and out of breath. 'Beamer ain't right, Robert! There be zummat the matter wi' 'un! I can't get 'un to stand up!'

Robert turned, his face twisted in astonishment. '*Beamer*? What the bl—' Robert rose to his feet and hurried after the others.

Celandine was left alone, still staring at the body of Tobyjug. She couldn't seem to move, or even blink. She was aware of the growing commotion in the yard outside, the shouted instructions of Hughes the foreman, the clatter of boots as a boy was sent running for the veterinary surgeon. She was aware of the men that were gathering further down the stable block, heard how their voices dwindled to respectful silence, and knew that her father must have arrived to see what the matter was. All their concern was for Beamer. The huge black shire was the farm's leading team horse, and of far greater importance to them than a child's pony. Tobyjug had been forgotten, and so had she. Beamer's life mattered more.

Not to her, though. Nothing could ever matter more than this. Tobyjug was dead. Every creature on the farm, large or small, might now die and she wouldn't care.

Eleven days. She had written it in her journal only last night. Tobyjug had been part of her life for just eleven days. And now he was . . . poisoned? *Poisoned.* The word floated around her head, a droning buzz, a sound with no meaning. Normally it was warm in here, warm with the living heat of her pony and the scent of fresh hay. Now a cold stillness settled upon her, and the air smelled sour. The buzzing noise in her head became an actual fly that sped across her vision, disappeared for a second, and then reappeared as a sudden dark speck on Tobyjug's white cheek. Celandine watched as the fly meandered across the dull surface of the pony's eye. Her own eyes blinked in horrified reaction and she juddered back into consciousness again. She could stay in here no longer.

Celandine left the stable and wandered out into the piercing sunlight. She shaded her eyes as a dark-coated figure dodged past her. The veterinary surgeon, just this minute arrived, though too late to be of any help to her. Celandine crossed the yard and entered the farmhouse, unnoticed, and speaking to no one. She climbed the stairs to her bedroom. It was Sunday. She automatically began to get herself ready for church.

By the next morning there had been word from the veterinary surgeon that rat poison was almost certainly the cause of Tobyjug's death. Part of a mangled brown paper bag had been found in a hay bale. It was thought that the bag, which had contained poison pellets, might somehow have become caught up in the new baling machine. The veterinary surgeon was doubtful that this could have been a deliberate act. None could have known that this particular bale of hay would have been fed to Tobyjug and Beamer. It was unfortunate, but it was an accident. The better news was that Beamer had survived the critical hours of darkness. It looked as though he might recover after all.

Celandine rose late, after a miserable night, to face the jolting emptiness of her loss all over again. She couldn't cry. Since Tobyjug's death she had hardly made a sound, had barely managed to murmur in response to her mother's few inadequate words of sympathy. She felt sick and shaky – but the shakiness was as of something trapped inside her, something that wanted to come out. The sickness made her stomach hurt as though it were she who had eaten poison.

She sat at the parlour window and watched the activity in the farmyard – all the useless, pointless routines that she had witnessed a thousand times before; the egg woman arriving on her bicycle, Young Wilfrid driving the dung cart around to the back of the stables, Mr Hughes counting the milk churns out-side the dairy before hurrying on. Why did they? How could they, after what had happened?

'Celandine – *here* you were. Always I am hunting you. To your lessons now – Miss Bell is waiting.' Her mother stood beside her, hands clasped together, the way she always stood. Celandine didn't answer at first. It took a real effort to turn away from the window.

'Must I?' she said.

'Yes.' Her mother spoke more gently than before. 'You must. This is best, I think.'

Celandine's heart sank lower still as she walked into the schoolroom and saw that the embroidery basket was ready and waiting for her, along with her sampler. How she hated the thing. *Hated* it. She had been working on the same ridiculous sampler for well over a year – so long that the once-white material had turned noticeably grey where the letters had been unpicked and re-worked so many times. *The Lord Is My Shepherd, I Shall Not Want.* But she *did* want, that was the trouble. She wanted so badly. She wanted Tobyjug to be alive and well. She wanted to be free of the terrible burning pain inside her. She wanted everything to be different.

Miss Bell's greeting was sarcastic, and predictable. 'Ah, Miss Howard. So good of you to come.' Celandine swallowed, but said nothing. She took a deep breath and made her way to her desk as though she were walking through a mist. She sat down clumsily and opened her workbasket.

'Yes,' said Miss Bell. 'You *may* open your workbasket. You *may* take out your scissors and thread. You *may* pick up your sampler and – and you *may* begin.'

Why were her hands shaking so much? She could barely hold the dressmaking scissors, clumping great things that they were, and the skeins of coloured thread quivered in her grasp so that she could not find the ends. Her sampler began to slide from her lap as she fumbled with the threads. She grabbed at it, but missed – and as she bent down to retrieve the crumpled material, she banged her forehead on the corner of the desk. Then the scissors and most of the threads fell to the floor also.

Miss Bell walked slowly and deliberately down the room, heels clicking on the age-blackened floor-boards. She stood beside the desk. Dark grey shoes and stockings, dark grey dress – all of her was dark grey. Celandine eventually managed to gather up the sampler, the scissors, and the threads, all in one arm-ful. She sat up, red-faced, and dumped the whole grubby tangled mess onto the desk. Then she slouched back in her chair, head down, arms out-stretched in front of her. Her forehead felt as though it would burst open.

There was a long, pounding silence. Finally Miss Bell sniffed, and said, 'Celandine, I can well under-stand that you might be upset about your *horse*, but—'

The scissors flashed sideways in a quick and savage motion. Through the grey dress, through the grey stockings and deep, deep into the dark hatefulness of everything . . .

Miss Bell's shriek was so loud that it could be clearly heard in the kitchen, and it caused Cook to drop the kettle. She stared at Lettie. 'Oh my sausages – what in the world was that?' The noise was coming from the direction of the schoolroom.

They found Miss Bell propped against a table for support, pushing herself backwards in feeble panic, as though trying to retreat or escape from something, and still crying out with pain. There was nobody else in the room. Cook rushed forward, holding out her arms in readiness – and only then realized that she was still carrying the lid of the kettle. Her attention was distracted and it was Lettie who first saw the scissors. She put her hands to her mouth and gasped. 'Look!'

The scissors were deeply embedded into the dark-stained folds of Miss Bell's dress, the crossed blades protruding from the soggy material, just above the knee. Miss Bell's face was sickly grey with shock and her cries had subsided into fast panicky breathing.

'Lie back on the table, miss!' Cook took charge of the situation. 'No – don't try and stand. Lean back – that's it, just lean back on me. Lettie, you run for Mrs Howard – tell her to fetch Doctor, directly. Goo on, girl – don't gawp!'

Cross-legged in the tall summer grass, Celandine sat and looked down upon the world. The gentle sound of the breeze in the treetops became a rhythmic swishing in her ears as she rocked backwards and forwards. It was peaceful beneath the trees on Howard's Hill – peaceful and safe. No samplers here. No samplers here, no samplers here, no samplers *here*. I shall not want, I shall not want, I *shall* not want, I *shall* not want . . .

She chanted softly to herself and plucked at the grass stems in front of her, trying to keep the thought of what she had done at bay. But the scissors kept flashing into her mind, and she could still feel the weight of them, the curve of them against her palm, the pinch of the open blade as she stabbed at the dark pain . . . hate you, hate you, hate you, hate you . . .

'Hate . . . hate . . . hate . . . hate . . .' Celandine muttered aloud as she rocked to and fro.

'*Cake* . . . *cake* . . . *cake* . . . *cake* . . .'

Celandine looked up, startled by the echo.

A blurred little figure dropped from the overhanging boughs and landed in the flattened grass before her. Celandine scrabbled backwards, unable to focus properly. It was a surprise to find that she was crying, and yet even through her tears she knew instantly what this was – who this was. She even remembered his name.

Fin . . .

Chapter Five

Celandine wriggled away on her hands and heels, but she didn't get up and run. She saw Fin's worried little face, his agitated hands, and realized that he was filled with anxiety at her own distress.

He rocked from side to side, stroking the back of his wrist and pressing it against his grubby cheek – making desperate little cooing noises, as though he were comforting a baby. 'Ooo . . . ooo . . . better . . . all better . . . ooo . . . ooo.' It was clear that he was confused and upset, so that Celandine's first instinct was to reassure him, despite the shock of his being there at all.

'No . . . I'm all right. Don't be . . . I'm all right.' She brought her hand up to her face and made a brief show of wiping away her tears. 'See?' Her neck was tingling, and her cheeks felt flushed and icy cold at the same time.

Yet now he seemed to have momentarily forgotten her, to be caught up in some inner turmoil of his own, moving away from her as he continued to pet the curve of his wrist, 'Ooo . . . ooo . . .' The long rough grass caused him to stumble, and he threw his arms forward in alarm. He just managed to save himself from falling, and stood with his fingers splayed, open-mouthed, as though he was balanced at the edge of a precipice. 'No . . . I all right. I all right. See?' He looked at her in delight, very pleased with his balancing.

Celandine was sure that if she blinked he would be gone. If she closed her eyes for just one moment, he would disappear – and so she kept absolutely still and simply stared at him. His long black hair was dusty with pollen, great hanks of it tumbling wildly about his small brown face so that his eyes were as startlingly perfect as birds' eggs in a ramshackle nest. The ill-fitting corduroy tunic, slung over his skinny frame like an oversized waistcoat, was so worn away that great bald patches of the weave were visible across the shoulders and his knee-length leggings hung down in baggy ruins, supported by what looked to be a strip of rabbit-skin tied about his middle. His wiry little limbs were scuffed and grazed, streaked here and there with the green of tree-bark, and on one of his bare shoulders there was a single bead of blood, as shiny-bright as a ladybird in the sun, and presumably just acquired. The poorest village urchin would have laughed to see him, and yet how miraculous he was. How beautiful, and extraordinary, and perfect.

Fin turned his head sideways, looked away for a few moments, and then glanced shyly back, pretending to see her for the first time once more. 'Cake?' he said, in his throaty little croak of a voice, and Celandine wanted to pinch herself.

So many times they had told her – her mother, her father, her Uncle Josef – that her account of what had happened on the day of the Coronation party was all her imagination. She had had a nasty bang on the head, and that was the cause of it. And yet here was the truth, the amazing truth, standing before her – fidgeting with the ragged hem of his open tunic, looking up at the sky, seeing her, not seeing her, his attention everywhere and nowhere. 'I all right. *I* all right.'

His actions seemed entirely unpredictable and Celandine felt a moment of apprehension, the same wariness with which she would regard a stoat or an owl, or any wild creature that was suddenly sprung upon her and beyond all reason and control. He might bite, she thought. He was tiny, perhaps a little more than knee-high to her, but he wasn't a child. There was something monkey-like about the length of the arms and stooping body. He could hurt her.

No, she thought, he wouldn't hurt her. He could have been newborn, for all the harm in him.

She was holding her breath, she realized, as she watched him – not daring to move lest she should frighten him away. He gazed out over the distant landscape, his small weathered hands clasped unselfconsciously together, his mouth open in a little 'o' of fascination. But then his eyes widened, as if he had perhaps recognized or understood something, and his expression became agitated. Something was troubling him.

'Fin?' She had remembered his name, and it was funny to hear herself whisper it.

He turned to her, and now there was growing panic in his expression.

'No. Ooooh! No! Bad! Not go there. *Gorji* there. *Gorji* is get you!' He ran at her and gripped her sleeve. 'Ah – ah – ah.'

'What? What is it? What's the matter with you?' Celandine drew her arm back, alarmed by the sudden change in his manner.

Fin let go of her sleeve and scuttled off a few paces – crouching low in the long grass – then ran back to grab at her again, and all the time he kept looking out over Howard's Hill as though he were expecting an attack.

'Ah – ah. Gorji! No! Come I – come I. Gorji is! Come I – me.'

His panic transferred to her, and she too looked about wildly, scrambling to her feet and wondering where the danger was. The sunny wetlands below seemed as tranquil as ever, but Fin was insistent that they should move – 'Is *Gorji* come! Is *get* you!' He looked quickly upwards at the branches he had lately tumbled out of, half raising his arms towards them. But there was obviously no possibility of getting back into the wood by that route, and with a last tug at her clothing he was off. Celandine followed as best she could, picking her way through the clumps of dock leaves and tufts of long grass, keeping close to the high barrier of brambles that surrounded the wood.

Doubled over as he was, scurrying low through the undergrowth, he could easily have been mistaken for a hare or a pheasant – but every so often his head

83

bobbed up from the grass, making sure that she was still there, his eyes wide with panic. He moved quickly and it was difficult to keep up with him, but Celandine was not going to lose him if she could help it.

Around the crest of Howard's Hill she stumbled in his wake, until they were approaching the place where the gully was – a steep cut in the hillside that Celandine remembered as having explored before, with Freddie. By this time she was convinced that she must be dreaming, that this could not be happening to her, and when the little figure ahead of her disappeared over the edge of the gully she was certain that she would never see him again.

She reached the top of the gully a few seconds later and looked down the stony bank at the damp trickle of the stream below. Nothing but brambles and bare rocks and silence. Her side hurt and she pressed a hand to her ribs as she tried to get her breath back. Whatever it was that she had been chasing had gone.

The pounding in her ears gradually subsided and the sounds of the world returned – the cry of the lapwings drifting up from the wetlands below, the doleful clank of a distant mowing machine, the chirrup of grasshoppers on the warm hillside. Mill Farm was down there, along with all her troubles, and soon she would have to go back and face up to what she had done. Celandine shook her head, trying to keep the terrible thing at bay, but she could find no escape. The very trees were whispering behind her back, as though they were telling each other how wicked she was, and the insistent warble of some nearby water-bird sounded like a mocking little laugh. She looked down into the gully, half-heartedly searching for the source of the sound, and then saw Fin once more, crouching among the brambles at the head of the stream. He had his hands cupped to his mouth. When he was sure that she had spotted him, he parted the brambles a little and gave her a hurried wave.

There was a tunnel – a dank and forbidding place – cleverly hidden behind the brambles. It looked like the inside of a long wicker basket, a loose weave of willow sticks, black with age and damp, spanning the little stream. Astonishing though this was, Celandine really didn't like the look of it. The tunnel was only a few yards long, and if she stooped low enough she would just be able to squeeze through it, but she wasn't at all sure that she wanted to try. The overhanging brambles that concealed the entrance were already snagging at her clothing, and if she went any further she would almost certainly get her feet wet. She turned and looked behind her to where the bright sparkles of sunlight danced upon the rocky shallows of the stream, then peered once more along the extraordinary basketwork construction. She caught a glimpse of Fin, briefly silhouetted against the circle of light at the far end. Then one of her feet slipped on a stone and she fell forward with a gulp, pushing her hands against the creaking wicker walls as she tried to save herself, feeling the instant shock of cold water through her shoes and stockings. She staggered on a couple of paces further, still trying to regain her balance, and it seemed as though her choice had been made for her. Yet she stopped and hesitated once more. It was chilly in here – creepy-cold – and there was a musty smell, like the smell of the black earth beneath the laurel bushes at home.

Celandine called out, her voice sounding panicky and strange in the dim confined space.

'Fin?'

But Fin had disappeared again, and there was no reply.

The end of the tunnel was only three or four yards away, and it would now be easier to continue than to try and turn around. Celandine could see a grassy bank in the sunlight, clumps of brambles, part of a mossy tree limb, but little else. Another few crouching steps forward, her feet now hopelessly soaked, and she paused again, listening. She thought she had heard Fin's voice – 'Ah – ah – ah . . .' – a brief, muffled cry. She peered ahead and waited, shouted again, but Fin did not return. There was nothing but the sound of her own fast breathing, and the soft trickle of the water over the slippery stones.

At last she made up her mind and picked her way along to the end of the tunnel, her hair coming undone and falling over her face so that she could hardly see. She kept one hand resting on the top of her head to prevent the sharp ends of the willow sticks from making matters worse, but then her bracelet became caught up instead and this delayed her further. The colour of the wickerwork had changed, she noticed. It was lighter at this end of the tunnel, newer, as though it had recently been added to, or replaced.

Celandine emerged into the dazzling sunlight and it was a relief to be able to straighten up. She stumbled blindly forward, found her footing on a large flat stone in the middle of the trickling shallows and began to push back her mass of tangled hair – retrieving the loose ribbon in the process, along with one or two stray hair-pins that dangled across her limited vision. But then, out of nowhere, some larger object swept past her face, frighteningly close, and she very nearly overbalanced as she tried to avoid it.

The thing jabbed at her threateningly – it was like a big fork – and Celandine squealed with shock, raising her arms to try and fend it off. More sharp objects . . . spears . . . javelins . . . they were suddenly all around her, all stabbing and prodding in her direction . . .

She caught terrifying glimpses of small bearded faces between her flailing hands and flying hair, as she shielded herself from the stickle of weapons that kept lunging towards her. They were going to kill her. There were lots of them, hordes of them, hissing and snarling at her, and they were going to kill her. She buried her head in her arms – dizzy with terror – quite unable to defend herself against so many assailants and certain that she was about to die. Her legs gave way and she banged her knees on the damp stone as she fell.

The material of her pinafore muffled her cry of pain and fear, and it was as though she were screaming to herself beneath the bedclothes . . . *go away . . . go away . . .*

Celandine felt hands tugging at her sleeve, gripping her wrist, yanking her arms away from her face.

'Ah – ah- ah . . .'

Fin's voice. It was Fin – clinging to her, hanging on tight to her arm. Celandine struggled to free herself, still squealing with panic, but her hair was in her eyes again – she couldn't see what was happening.

'Fin! Get out o' there!' Another voice. Then more voices, all of them shouting, '*Fin! Fin!*'

'Pato – grab a hold of 'un quick, afore she strangles 'un!'

Celandine managed to get one arm around the wriggling creature at last and lifted him off his feet in order to gain some sort of control over him. With her other hand she roughly swept back her maddening hair, shouting with anger now, not caring any more, feeling nothing but outrage towards this impossible thing that was happening to her.

'Get . . . *OFF* me, you . . . you . . . *lunatic*!'

'Ah – ah – ah . . .' Fin was still hanging onto her like a monkey, but at last she had a clearer view of the rest of the group and she realized, through the mist of her rage, that they had backed away from her. There weren't as many of them as she had imagined – half a dozen perhaps – and although they still brandished their weapons at her, they did so from a safer distance. The wild-eyed expressions on their unshaven faces spoke more of panic and confusion than of murder. Celandine struggled to keep her grip on Fin as she glared, panting and furious, at the semi-circle of agitated little figures – and waited for them to do their worst. They hopped and splashed about in the stony shallows, making short determined rushes towards her, then retreating just as quickly. So close, they came, but no closer. They were frightened, she realized – frightened of her. *They* were frightened of *her.*

Her fingers were beginning to slip. She tried to renew her grasp on the material of Fin's tunic, but could not find the strength. Her legs and arms suddenly felt useless and her head wouldn't stay upright. She let her chin fall onto her chest for a few moments, her burst of anger exhausted, weak with shock.

Fin, released from her hold, kept his hand on her shoulder as he bent down to peer into her face.

'Ah – ah – ah . . . ooooo . . . all better . . . all better . . .' He wouldn't stop jabbering. Celandine raised her head once more, in helpless exasperation now, and put a finger to her lips.

'Shhhhh!'

She didn't know what had made her do such a thing, but it worked. Fin was instantly quiet and calm, staring at her finger in fascination, following it with his eyes as she allowed her hand to fall back into her lap, continuing to watch it as though it had just performed some astonishing trick and might well come up with another.

'*Fin!*' An urgent hiss from one of the group – the one with the long fork. 'Get *out* o' there! Come away with 'ee!' Celandine tried to focus. Was this the one she had seen before – the anxious bearded face that she had glimpsed that first time when she lay in the baby-carriage beneath the trees? She couldn't tell. Her head was spinning, as it had done then. Yet there was something about him . . . something familiar . . .

Fin turned uncertainly towards the frantically beckoning figure, but remained where he was.

'Come *away* now! Fin . . . come *away*, ye dratted young zawney – if thee don't . . .'

But Fin lifted a finger to his lips; '*Hschhhhhhhhhhh!*'

The sound was as loud as a steam engine, and once again the effect was instant. All were immediately quiet and still. Fin studied his finger, apparently delighted that it held such power. Celandine was aware of him, his free hand still resting un-selfconsciously upon her shoulder, but she reserved her blurry concentration for the others as she tried to get her breathing back to normal, pressing a clenched fist to the thudding pain in her chest.

There were five of them – six including Fin – and they all looked as though they were as frightened and confused as she was. They had lowered their weapons, and she saw that these were not actually weapons at all in any real sense – or at least they weren't spears. Three of them simply carried sticks, and one of them had part of what appeared to be a window-hook, the kind of pole with a metal attachment that Miss Bell employed to open the high classroom window on hot days. Then there was the one with the strange trident – a rake handle, by the look of it, with an old gardening fork lashed to the end of it. There were traces of the original red varnish on the handle of the fork . . .

They were not quite as raggedly dressed as poor Fin, but it was plain that much of their clothing had started life elsewhere. Part of a shepherd's smock on one – the elaborate pattern of stitching across the chest contrasted with the crude tacking around the shoulders and hem, where it had been hacked off to fit. On another a labourer's shirt, collarless and similarly butchered. A bridle strap, used as a belt. A thick piece of sacking with the printed emblem of the manufacturer clearly visible, cut and stitched to form a rough tabard. Lengths of binder-twine, used as drawstrings about the waist . . . all these things were familiar to her, and yet so out of place in such an unbelievable situation. And there were bits of fur; scraps of moleskin, rabbit, squirrel, adorning their wrists and ankles. One of them wore a necklace of tiny bright blue feathers: a kingfisher?

Their hair and complexions were all the same – a dark gypsy look to them, all of a kind, a race or a tribe, like the leather-skinned travellers that camped on Burnham Common in the fruit-picking season. They were people, Celandine thought. Just little people . . .

But no. They were not just little people. They were breathtaking. As ordinary as sparrows, yet un-imaginably strange. Their locks of black hair rose gently in the breeze, and it was as though they were floating, drifting through space. The narrowed eyes, fixed upon her, glittered from the dappled shadows that fell across their brows. Fear and suspicion she saw there, a deep wariness, but also curiosity. Was she as extraordinary to them as they were to her?

'Don't 'ee hurt 'un, mind.' The bearded one with the trident. His voice was full of concern and agitation, almost apologetic. 'Only he be weak in the nog.' He wiped a nervous forearm across his face.

Celandine didn't reply – could find no voice – but instead put her hand on Fin's back, and gave him a gentle push, feeling the brief impression of his bony little spine through the material of his shabby tunic. He stumbled away from her, hesitated for a moment, and then continued to splash through the shallows, happy enough to return to his own. Several hands reached out to grab him, but their eagerness caused him to panic. He dodged past the group – 'Ah – ah – ah . . .' – escaped their clutches and ran off a little way, weaving through the clumps of brambles that grew by the stream and clambering up onto higher ground beyond. Once he saw that he wasn't being immediately pursued, he sat down on a rock and put his finger to his lips, evidently intent on playing his new game. *Hschh!*

The dark heads of the group were momentarily turned towards Fin, and Celandine was at last able to glance quickly about her, still trying to calm her shaky breathing. Everything was so tangled and overgrown. It was like another country in here, a wild foreign land that had remained untouched for centuries. The fallen carcasses of ancient trees lay all around, propped against their living companions, their shattered limbs forming strange new structures, angular sculptures, festooned with flowering creepers, ivy, mistletoe, and the all-enveloping wall of brambles. The hillside beyond the stream was rough and rocky, quarry-like, the steep outcrops of stone covered with coarse moss and orange-grey lichen. Great clumps of wild buddleia clung to the ridges, and Celandine thought she could see a dark opening behind one of the bushes, like the mouth of a cave. Higher still the land rose to another tree-line, the great battalion of ash and elm and beech and sycamore that she saw every day from her bedroom window. How different they looked from this angle, towering above her, huddling together, as though guarding some further secret. And there was movement, some little shuffle in the tall grass at the base of the trees that may or may not have been the wind . . .

'I warned 'ee, Pato – us all did – that that young vool o' yourn'd bring us to this. *Now* what be us to do?'

The stubble-faced one with the window-hook had spoken to the bearded one with the fork. They were all looking at her once more. Her knees were hurting and she wanted to stand up. Something occurred to her.

'That's my brother's trident.' Her throat was so dry that the words came out in a loud croak, the effort of speaking making the pain in her chest worse than ever. 'Where did you get it?'

The one with the trident – Pato – shrank back a little at the sound of her voice, but looked at her blankly, as though she were speaking in a foreign tongue.

He shook his head and muttered, 'Hemmed if I knows.' It was a response to his companion's question, not to hers.

'We casn't let her go.' Another spoke – the one with the feather necklace.

'Casn't let her bide, neither.'

'So what be us to do?'

Pato shook his head again and mumbled something inaudible, at a loss it seemed.

They were discussing her as though she were a stray beast, too difficult to capture, but too dangerous to ignore. Their voices were low and reedy, but the thick accents were similar to the ones she heard all around her at Mill Farm, and they spoke slowly. Celandine could understand them well enough.

She wanted to reassure them, but it was such an effort to speak. She had to try.

'There's . . . there's no need to worry about me, you know. I don't mean any harm. Only it was Fin, you see. He was frightened. He wanted me to follow him.' The words babbled out, hurried, loud, nervous.

Again they shrank away a little, and muttered among themselves.

'What did 'er say?'

'Dunno. Zummat about Fin, I reckon.'

'*Be* 'er Gorji? 'Er don't sound like no Gorji I ever heared.'

There was that word again: 'Gorji'. Fin had used it – and it had scared him.

They were obviously struggling to understand her, Celandine thought. So much for Miss Bell's elocution lessons.

Her knees were really hurting her, and she was desperate to stand up, but thought it safer to remain where she was for a little longer. She made another attempt to communicate, this time speaking slowly, quietly, trying to calm her voice, trying to match their own volume and speed.

'What does "Gorji" mean? What is Gorji?'

She could tell that this time they had understood. They looked at her in surprise, and then turned expectantly towards Pato, the one with the trident. He was obviously their spokesman.

His head was tilted to one side as he regarded her, in puzzled silence. ' 'Tis thee,' he said, at last. '*Thee* be Gorji. A ogre. One o' they gurt giants.'

'A *giant*? I'm not a giant – look!' Celandine struggled painfully to her feet and immediately regretted her actions – for they began waving their sticks at her once more, hopping from rock to rock and shouting in panic. The whole terrible scene seemed likely to repeat itself, but this time she remained quiet and still, arms folded, until they gradually calmed down.

She waited, assuring them by her manner that she was not going to make any more sudden moves. Once again they had surrounded her, but their attitude was less threatening than before.

'You see?' she said. 'I'm not a giant . . .' Then she felt ridiculous, because of course they were right. She *was* a giant.

She was a giant, a great loud and lumbering thing. No wonder they were frightened. No wonder they didn't know what to do. She looked over to where Fin was sitting, still halfway up the rocky hillside, still 'shushing' his finger.

Her eyes were drawn higher, towards the dense line of trees that topped the hill. A slight movement along the ridge made her look – and then she had to look again. Faces . . . there were faces . . . lots of them . . .

. . . a host of small dark heads raised above the long summer grass, eyes all staring down at her. Dozens of them. *Dozens.* Babes in arms . . . children raised upon the shoulders of adults, and all of them huddled together, standing on the ridge beneath the belt of trees. Watchful, wary, motionless. A whole tribe of them.

Celandine felt dizzy all over again, as she gazed up at the silent gathering. A thousand questions battered away at the inside of her aching head, confusion upon confusion. How could all this be happening to her? How could this be? But at last she was beginning to understand the meaning of what it was that she had stumbled upon. This was another world. This was the secret thing that was spoken of in countless stories. This was the world that existed behind that first glimpse she had caught of Fin, so long ago – a world that had been hidden away, maybe for centuries, whispered about and rumoured for all time. And these were its people – the little people. She was looking at the little people.

So it was all true. The muttered tales of tiny shadows that crept through the ditches at first light, the implements and items of clothing that the field-workers mysteriously lost when their backs were turned ... such things always pointed to 'the little people'. And the night lines that the local game-keeper found on his stretch of the river that were later passed around at the inn for all to see – these too were said to be the work of the little people. 'For who'd carve a fish hook out of a bit o' bone, when they could be had three-a-penny from Moffat's?'

Here they were then, uncovered at last, living in the deserted woods on Howard's Hill. It was too much to bear, too much to know. The crowd of little figures gazed down upon her, and Celandine realized that they were viewing her as they would view a disaster. She had ruined everything.

She desperately wanted to show that she would not harm them, that they could trust her, that she would bring no danger. She looked down at Pato, still stand-ing defensively before her, still holding his trident – Freddie's trident – in readiness. His small brown face looked battered, weather-worn by summer sun and winter wind. Celandine caught a glimpse of the nature of this miraculous world she had tumbled into, though it seemed more a world of hardship than of miracles.

It was overwhelming – too much to take in – and

she must go away and think about it all, if they would only let her. She had to find the right words.

'Do you know what a promise is?' Celandine looked down into Pato's eyes and spoke slowly and quietly. 'A promise? A . . . a vow?'

She thought she saw a flicker of recognition there, and although there was silence for a long moment, he eventually replied.

'I knows what a vow be.'

'Then if I made a vow to you, would you believe me? If I vowed that I should never tell . . . if I vowed that I should never say *anything* . . . not to anybody . . . about this . . . about you being here . . . would you believe me? Because that's what I *do* vow. I shall never tell. Not if I live to be a hundred – I shall never, ever, tell.'

She saw Pato shift his barefoot stance a little, saw him look sideways at his companions. One or two of them shook their heads. He returned her gaze once more, searching, it seemed to her, for a way out of this.

Celandine tried again. 'I know . . . well, I *think* I know . . . what you must be thinking. You must be thinking that if you let me go, I might bring others here. But I never would. I promise . . .'

'You brought another 'un here afore. I saw 'ee. I saw 'ee the fust time, and I saw 'ee agin – wi' another. Long-seasons since.'

'I'm sorry – what did you say?'

'I saw 'ee afore. Yere wi' another – arter a way in yere.'

'After a way in here? Looking for a way in, you

mean?' Of course. With Freddie. She'd forgotten all about that. 'But that was a long time ago,' she said. 'I was only a child then. We were just playing . . .'

'A child? A chi'? What bist now, if not a chi'? And why were t'other 'un yere, if thee hadn't already told 'un what thee saw? Now what good's this *vow* o' yourn, if 'tis already broke?'

He was right. What earthly good was it to promise not to tell, when she had already done so?

'Yes,' she said, and hung her head for a few moments. 'It's true. I thought everybody knew you were here. I was only young. I asked them who you were. They didn't know what I meant, so I told what I saw. I told . . . my brother . . . and my mother . . . and . . . well, it doesn't matter. They didn't believe me, anyway.' Celandine wanted so badly to explain, and it was an effort to remember to speak slowly. 'They thought it was just a story . . .' This was no good at all and she felt miserably at a loss as to how to continue.

'A story? Wass that – a tale?' Pato looked about at his companions and, most surprisingly, they all grinned.

'There've been many a tale about we, I reckons,' said Pato. 'And few enough believed, thanks be. No. Thee won't be the fust as've see'd us, nor the last neither.' His face grew serious once more. 'But thee'm the fust as've come in yere, and thass the worry, see. Thass the worry. 'Tis one thing to tell as how 'ee see'd us, but 'tis another to tell where we be.'

'Oh, but I wouldn't! I promise I wouldn't.'

'Thass another vow, is it? Well, thee med take thee vows, maidy, and put 'em somewhere safe – and we s'll take our chance as we always must. Away with 'ee, I say. 'Tis more sense to let 'ee go than to make 'ee stay.'

'She wouldn't be yere at all, if 'twasn't for that young zawney o' yourn, Pato.' The one with the window-hook spoke, and his voice was bitter.

Pato snapped back at him. 'What would 'ee have I do, then, Emmet? Keep 'un tethered? 'Tis more work to look out for Fin than one pair of eyes can hold a sight of.'

'Well, it still ain't your say-so to let 'er go.' Emmet sounded more subdued.

'Oh? Be it thine? Go on, maidy, get away from yere.' Pato looked meaningfully at Emmet. 'There's none as'll stop 'ee.'

'Pato, this needs more chewing on. We casn't just let 'er go.' This time it was the one with the feather necklace.

'Do 'ee not *see*, Rufus – and *all* of 'ee – 'tis done.

'Tis over and *done*. We allus knew that this day'd come, and now 'tis yere. Perhaps 'twere my blame. But 'tis done, and casn't be undone. How can us not let 'er go? What should us do? Hobble the maid to Fin and have an end to it? Put her in the ground and wait for her own to come looking for her?' Pato sounded tired. He turned towards Celandine and studied her, looking up into her eyes, making sure that his meaning was plain. 'This maid must do as she will. If she do tell and they giants believe her, then 'tis all up wi' us. They'll come wi' hounds and dig us out like moles. They'll come wi' fire and snares and never let us bide till every last one o' us be skinned and skewered. For thass the Gorji way. Go on, chi', away with 'ee – what's done is done. And we s'll see how long this vow o' yourn do hold.' He jabbed the trident towards her.

Celandine felt her eyes prickle with tears. There was nothing she could say. She put her hand in the pocket of her pinafore and felt her bracelet catching on the calico hem as she did so. The bright colours of the beads sparkled through her tears as she drew out her handkerchief. She blew her nose and saw the company jump back in alarm at the sound. It might almost have been funny, but she didn't laugh. She put her handkerchief back in her pocket and then, on an impulse, undid the clasp of her bracelet. The glass beads shimmered and glittered in the sun. She extended her arm, very slowly and deliberately, and gently hung the bracelet over one of the prongs of the trident. It felt like a gesture of friendship and, as she saw the lines on Pato's determined face soften into puzzlement, she thought that perhaps it might be accepted as such.

Nothing more was said. Celandine looked up once more at the crowd of little people that lined the ridge, then pushed her hair back over her shoulders and turned towards the tunnel, stooping in readiness for her uncomfortable return to the world she knew.

Her shoes and stockings were soaked through and stained with mud – something else to add to the list of crimes that she would be held to account for when she got home. Perhaps her muddy things would look better when they had dried out a little. Celandine shifted her position slightly, altering the way she sat, so that her legs were in direct sunlight on the grassy bank of the gully. The breeze would help.

She would go soon – she must – but not just yet. There was so much to think about, and she didn't feel at all well. Her head was pounding, aching with the confusion of everything, and everything, and *every-thing* . . . and the inside of her mouth was dry and sore. She tried to work up some saliva, but there was nothing there.

The mowing machine still clanked away in the distance and the lapwings still called to each other across the moor – *peeeeewit . . . peeeeewit.* So far away they all were, yet so clear on the soft breeze. She could almost pretend that nothing had changed.

And nothing *had* changed, really. The mowing machine clanked, and the lapwings cried, and the grasshoppers sang – and the little people lived in the woods, just as they always had done. Nothing had changed.

Except that she knew about them. That was what had changed. She knew something that nobody else knew, and if she were to ever tell . . . well, then everything *would* change. Men would come with traps and guns and shovels and terriers . . . just as Pato said they would.

Another thought came to her – a shocking, horrible thought – and she raised her head, dizzy with the awful prospect of it. She pictured the travelling zoo that she had seen when she was small, and saw Fin . . . in a cage . . . like a marmoset . . . hanging onto the bars . . .

It could happen. It *would* happen, if she didn't keep what she had seen to herself. It was in her hands. How could she bear such a burden as that? How could she keep such a secret for the whole of her lifetime and never, ever, tell? And to think that she had *already* told – had insisted over and over, that there were little people living in the wood. What if they had believed her? The thought of it made her shudder.

Well, then. She must make sure that nothing of the sort ever *did* happen. She must guard this secret with her life, because other lives depended so entirely upon her doing so. And she must guard those other lives against the murderous outside world.

Celandine stood up. Her head still felt very swimmy, but at least her thoughts were clearer. She had stumbled upon an astounding thing, a secret so deep that it made her heart jump up into the back of her throat to think of it. In fact it was impossible to think of it and be able to breathe properly at the same time. But it was for her. This had happened to her, and to nobody else. She would never be able to share it, but at the same time she knew that she would never want to. This was hers. She had been chosen.

It was time to go. Celandine made her way slowly down Howard's Hill, dazed, but determined to do good somehow. And yet the further she left the woods behind, the more her amazing discovery was pushed to the back of her thoughts, and the closer she drew to Mill Farm the more her other problems enveloped her.

The thought of her terrible attack on Miss Bell rose up like a dragon to greet her. What frightened her most of all was that she had been capable of such a dreadful thing – that she could suffer such a fit of rage and misery that her actions had been so out of control. Could she have stopped herself? She remembered picking up the scissors, the feeling of them in her hand, and wanting to stab at ... the world. Yes, she remembered that. She hadn't wanted to attack Miss Bell in particular. She had just wanted to make everything go away, to make it all ... stop. The pain – yes – she had been stabbing at the pain of losing Tobyjug. But Miss Bell had been where the pain was. So did that make her any the less guilty? No, she thought not. Was she sorry for what she had done? Yes, she was sorry. She was very sorry, and she was very frightened, for what would happen to her now? Would they put her in prison? They might. People went to prison for far less.

They would be waiting for her. They would hear the clang of the sheep-gate that she now closed behind her. They would be watching her as she came down through the paddock, the thistly paddock, forlorn and empty now, where she had spent her few happy days with Tobyjug. They would see her reach this metal gate at the corner of the stables. They would see her cross this cobbled yard.

And yes, they saw her – for there was Mr Hughes, the foreman, pausing to look at her as he stood speaking to Robert by the door of the cider barn. And there was Lettie's face, pale and shocked at the scullery window, her mouth moving – saying something to somebody – and then Cook appearing, to look over Lettie's shoulder. They all saw her, but none could see how her stomach churned, how hot she felt, and then how icy cold, the effort it took to stay upright. None could see how her knees ached as she climbed the two steps to the front path, how all her joints were so stiff and painful that her finger knuckles would hardly bend around the hooped iron door handle, how her frame was barely capable of pushing the heavy oak door on its hinges.

Celandine clung to the iron hoop. The dark hallway smelled of boiled vegetables and she felt a huge wave of red nausea rising up inside her. Her dry mouth was suddenly full of water, and though she swallowed and swallowed, it wouldn't go away. Her entire body was pouring with perspiration. The door of the study opened and her father stepped into the hallway. He was holding a newspaper. Celandine caught the flash of his spectacles in the dim light and his look of blank surprise. She saw the word 'WAR!' on the front of the newspaper, and then up it came at last, and more, and more again – the sour tide of everything she had been through – all over the coconut matting.

Later, she felt better. They had not shouted at her, as she had supposed they would, nor had they told her she would go to prison. Her mother had come in to see her, and her Uncle Josef. Even her father had looked in for a few moments, grave and serious, but with none of the cold anger that some of her lesser exploits had induced. She had cried and cried, and told them how sorry she was. She had wept, at last, for poor Tobyjug, and they had promised that he should be buried here on the farm and should not be sent to Jotcham's abattoir. She had wept, too, for Miss Bell, and begged to be allowed to see her – and they had said perhaps tomorrow. And in the end she could weep no more.

Now she lay in her clean cool bed, a jug of Cook's lemonade on the nightstand beside her, and stared out of her window at the early evening sky. She could hear the teams being led into the yard, the heavy crunch of iron-shod hooves on the cobbles, the soft whiffle of their breath, and the clink of harnesses. She heard the roll-call of the rooks, as they settled in the high branches of the nearby copse, the squeak and clank of the yard pump as the stable boys drew fresh water for the horses, the low woof of one of the lurchers, released for the night. That would be Cribb. Jude never barked.

She had heard these sounds a thousand times, but tonight was different from any other. Tonight she held a secret within her that changed the whole world, and everything she thought she knew about it. Celandine closed her eyes and let it all wash over her.

She dreamed that she was flying. She was flying across the silent universe, through deepest space, and the void was heavy and oppressive, humid, so that it was difficult for her to breathe. It made her feel queasy. Bits of white stuff floated about her – ashes, she thought at first, but then she saw that they were moths and that she was flying amongst them. A great red planet loomed silently out of the darkness, a hot globe, with a soft radiant sheen to its surface, like polished stone. There were giant fingermarks upon the globe, inky stains that shifted and swirled like weather patterns.

From the dark side of the planet a small white horse appeared, beating across the heavens on silvery wings, a thing so beautiful that her heart ached to see it. The trail of moths flew in its wake and she followed too – trying to catch it, trying to shout its name, but no sound would come out of her mouth. The horse flew too fast for her and she was left alone in the darkness, watching the last of the moths disappear like fading sparks.

'Tobyjug!' She finally managed to shout the word, but it was too late, and it was the wrong word.

Celandine opened her eyes. 'Yes?' It was still dark – but then she realized that her head was beneath the blankets. Little wonder that she was so hot. 'Yes?' She pulled back the covers, and said it again. Someone was knocking at the door.

It was the doctor, her Uncle Josef, come to see how she was feeling.

He told her that he just wanted to make sure that she was well enough to get up. He didn't have his doctor's bag with him, he said, and he hadn't brought her any nasty medicine – he just wanted to talk to her. Celandine yawned and sat herself up, whilst he took the wicker chair from the other side of the room and brought it across to her bedside.

'I had a dream, Uncle Josef. There was a flying horse.' Celandine yawned again. 'And a big red planet.'

Uncle Josef chuckled and held up a hand in mock protest. 'Then I beg you, please do *not* tell me about it. I have many theories concerning the meaning of dreams, but I am a busy man, and if I once begin upon that subject then I shall be here all day.'

Celandine rubbed her eyes and waited. What time was it? It felt quite late – the sun was streaming into her room.

'Tell me, then, Celandine. Immediately after yesterday's unfortunate . . . incident . . . with Miss Bell – what did you do? Where did you go?'

'Where did I go?' Celandine was immediately awake and on her guard. From now on she had to be so very careful of what she said. 'Oh. I went for a walk.'

'Ah yes? And where did you walk?' Uncle Josef's face was kind – it was always kind – but his Austrian accent gave his voice an authority somehow. And he was clever. Celandine felt that he would very quickly know if she were to try and mislead him.

'I walked up Howard's Hill. Well . . . I didn't exactly walk. I ran. I was running away, you see, from . . . what I did.'

'Of course. I understand.' He smiled. 'To Howard's Hill. And how are the little people?'

The question took her so by surprise that she could hardly answer.

'Wh— what? Who?' Her voice was all squeaky.

'The little people. You remember them, yes? When you hurt your head – at the party – you were seeing some little people. They lived up in the trees.'

'Oh. Yes.' Celandine desperately tried to think what line she should take. If she denied her earlier story then it might seem suspicious, but if she continued to claim that she *had* seen them . . .

'So . . . are they still there?'

'No. They're not.' Celandine tried to make her answer as definite and final as possible – hoping that Uncle Josef would now drop the subject.

He put his hands together and thought for a moment.

'But . . . you were looking for them? You were hoping that they might be there?'

What was he getting at? What did he mean?

'No. I wasn't looking for them. I was just thinking

about what . . . what I'd done. I wasn't thinking about anything else.'

Uncle Josef lowered his hands, clasped them over one of his knees, and rocked backwards on the chair. His bearded face looked relaxed and he was still smiling.

'Do you think they have gone, then? That they are no longer there?'

So that was what he was after. Of course. He didn't really think that there *were* little people living in the wood – he never had done. He thought it was all her imagination, and he was just trying to find out if she were still imagining such things. Wasn't he?

'Yes,' she said, and she felt relieved. 'They've gone.'

'I see. So – first they *were* there, and now they have gone? Is that what you mean? Or is it that you no longer believe they were there in the first place?'

Celandine was spared the difficulty of answering this question, because Uncle Josef said, almost immediately, 'Don't worry. It doesn't matter.' He turned away from her slightly, to lay an arm along the windowsill, and then said, 'There are some things we can only imagine, Celandine. But this does not mean that they are not truly there. The centre of the earth, for an example. We have never seen it, and perhaps we never will, so we can only imagine it – but we are certain that it exists. And there are some things that we *do* see, that may not really be there at all. Many of the stars, they say, have long ceased to be, and yet we see them plainly enough.' He was silent for a while, then said, 'The truth may never be as obvious as it seems, my dear, and the unlikely is not always the impossible. You know, I had to call upon a colleague's patient the other day. A . . . oh . . . what is this word? A withy-cutter. Yes, a withy-cutter.' He looked out of the window, talking quietly, as though to himself. 'A good man, I think. And a sober one. He sees little people. Yes, quite often, by his account. They steal his - withies . . .'

Celandine watched him scratch his beard – thinking – as he gazed out over the landscape towards Howard's Hill. Finally he turned to look at her.

'You would not be the first, you see. No, most certainly. *But . . .*' He rose from his chair with a sigh, and lifted his pocket watch from his dark waistcoat. 'I must go. I think that if you feel strong enough, my dear, then you might get up for a while.' He gave her a twinkling smile. 'And if you are feeling *very* strong, then you might pay a visit to Miss Bell. I have just been to see her also. She will survive, I believe.'

Celandine got out of bed as soon as her Uncle Josef had gone and poured some water into the wash basin. As she dried her face and hands, she looked out of her window. Howard's Hill rose up from the landscape, a green island in a greener sea, wild and unexplored. It was miraculous that it had remained undisturbed for so long. And yet, she thought, perhaps it wasn't so very surprising after all, for who would ever need to go there? Uncle Josef had stared up at the tangled forest, momentarily interested, but she was sure that he would never bother to take a closer look. He was a busy man, he said, and all men were busy as far she could see. This made her feel better – the realization that everything would continue as it was. There was simply no reason for anyone to go there, and that meant that it was unlikely that anyone would notice her if *she* did so . . .

Because she did intend to go there again. She had a plan. In the meantime, though, she supposed that she must go and see Miss Bell and try to apologize.

Chapter Six

Miss Bell was leaving. Celandine stood on the little attic staircase for a few moments after she had closed Miss Bell's door, and wondered how she should be feeling. She had longed for this day, it was true, but could never have imagined that it would happen as suddenly or as unexpectedly as this. Miss Bell had cut short her tearful apology and then surprised her by saying, with a note of triumph in her voice, that she had already accepted another post, '*quite* a step up from this . . .' She had been planning to leave for some while, and this unprovoked attack upon her person only served to confirm how right she was to do so. Her time at Mill Farm had been wasted in more ways than one, and the sooner she was away from here, the better.

Celandine descended the short flight of steps to the main landing. What would happen to her now, she thought? She supposed that there would be a new governess, someone strange and different to adapt to, a faceless person, unimaginable. There had never been much love lost between herself and Miss Bell, but at least they were used to one another. So how *should* she be feeling about it all? Quite glad, she decided, and made her way along the upstairs corridor to Freddie's room.

She had been in Freddie's room before, but she knew that he would be cross with her if he found out that she'd entered in his absence. She told herself that he wouldn't find out, and that it was in a good cause.

Nevertheless, she felt as though she were a burglar, that the slightest creak in the corridor outside would make her jump, that there was someone continually looking over her shoulder, that one of the dogs would start barking any minute. How silly. She looked about her – where did he keep the stuff?

The room was very spartan, and neat: Freddie's collection of birds' eggs carefully displayed in a tray lined with cotton wool by his bed; a single glass case of butterflies mounted on the wall; a bookshelf with all his books arranged according to size. She looked at the titles. *Campfire Songs* . . . *The Home Workshop* . . . *Pears' Cyclopaedia* . . . and suddenly she missed him very much. Oh, but she missed him. She sat on the corner of his bed and wished he was here to cheer her up, to do something mad and make her laugh. It was hard to imagine him in his school, learning whatever you needed to learn in order to become a lawyer or a priest, or whatever it was they wanted him to be. Freddie in a wig and gown . . . Freddie in a cassock and surplice . . . that wasn't Freddie at all. Freddie in a circus, she could see that, or on a music hall stage – that she could see.

The heel of her shoe kicked against something and she looked down. It was the end of a long thin canvas case. Of course – he kept it under the bed. She retrieved the case and undid the tapes that secured the flap, then very carefully drew the butt of the rod partway out. He had often promised to take her fishing, but he never had. Was this the right bit, though? It was a beautiful thing. There was some lettering, a name, just above the long varnished handle. 'Hardy'. No, this wasn't what she wanted.

She got down on her hands and knees and looked under the bed. There was another canvas bag, a squareish one with leather straps.

The inside of the bag smelled faintly of riverbanks – of mud and duckweed and earthworms and eels. There were several compartments stitched into the bag – interior pockets that contained curious-looking objects, for the most part unfathomable to her. Here were shiny metal things with beads and swivels, brightly coloured egg-shaped objects, painted quills and lumps of lead. How different it was to be a boy, she thought, and how interesting it must be to deal in such matters. Her own casket of trinkets – of ribbons and brooches and pins and bracelets – seemed dull by comparison. Celandine lifted out a spoon-shaped thing and held it up to examine it, gently touching the three hooks that spoke so eloquently of its deadly purpose. It dangled from its piece of weed-green line, slowly revolving, glinting against the light like a cruel piece of jewellery. A devil's earring, perhaps. Celandine wondered why any fish would be so stupid as to even go near it, let alone try to swallow it.

It was tempting, but she didn't think that this was quite the right thing. She found what she was after in the end – simple fish hooks – neatly wrapped in a piece of wax paper. Celandine carefully tipped the hooks into the palm of her hand and counted them. Twelve. How tiny they were, like parts of an insect. She took six, and tore the piece of wax paper along one of its folds to wrap them in.

On her way out she noticed a cricket ball sitting at the back of the bookshelf, next to *Pears' Cyclopaedia*. It was the bruised sheen of its polished surface that had caught her eye – so like the colour of the planet in her dream. How funny. She reached out to press the tips of her fingers against the smooth red leather for a few moments, feeling the warmth of it, and then took her hand away. There were no fingerprints that she could see.

Celandine made a promise, although only to herself, that the flat rock that she now sat upon was as far as she would go. To venture further would be an intrusion. She hoped that the little people would see that she understood this, and that she had no intention of moving beyond this point without their invitation. The trouble was, they were nowhere to be seen.

At least two hours must have passed, probably more, and there had been no sign of them. But it was peaceful sitting upon the rock, the waters of the shallow stream trickling around her, and she was happy enough to wait. With her legs tucked beneath her and one hand resting on the warm stone, she reminded herself of a picture she had once seen: the statue of the Little Mermaid in Copenhagen. Perhaps little mermaids really existed, as well as little people? It was possible. Anything seemed possible, now.

She had the fish hooks ready, still wrapped in their piece of wax paper, and she played with the packet for a while, tapping it with her finger, chasing it back and forth across the surface of the stone as a cat might play with a mouse. They would be glad of some proper fish hooks, she thought. What else might they need? A needle and thread? Yes, that would be useful. Scissors? Scissors reminded her, inevitably, of Miss Bell. She didn't want to think about that.

They weren't coming. She could sit here until nightfall, and they still wouldn't show themselves. Well, it didn't matter – she knew they were here, and that they were watching her. Somewhere up among the high line of trees, or perhaps closer, hiding among the brambles, crouching in the tall grass, their dark eyes were looking at her, waiting to see what she would do, wondering whether she brought danger to them. But she had been most careful. For a long time she had sat at the top of the gully, scanning the landscape, making sure that there was nobody in sight before slipping off her shoes and stockings and entering the wicker tunnel.

Nobody had seen her come here, and nobody would see her leave. Celandine reached forward and picked up a piece of shale from the bed of the stream, shook the droplets of water from it and carefully placed it on top of the packet of hooks. Then she folded her navy blue stockings, tucked them into her shoes and stood up. She hoped that Pato, or perhaps Fin, would see the little offering, sitting there in the middle of the flat rock. A corner of the wax paper was just visible.

Celandine bundled her shoes beneath her arm and gingerly made her way back to the tunnel.

When she returned the following day, she brought three embroidery needles, several coloured skeins of thread and most of a tea-cake. The packet of hooks had gone.

The day after that, she brought a book to read. If she was going to sit upon the rock for several hours at a time, then she might as well keep herself amused. There was another reason for the book. Her mother had told her that she must keep up her studies until a replacement for Miss Bell had been found, or until some other decision had been made with regard to her education. Celandine had agreed, but argued that it was much better to work in the fresh air than in a stuffy classroom – although she had been careful not to say whereabouts in the fresh air she intended to be. So now she sat, more or less with her mother's approval, beyond the wall of brambles on Howard's Hill, waiting for another glimpse of the little people. Once again there was no sign of them, but once again the gifts she had left for them the previous day had gone.

Celandine opened the copy of *Aesop's Fables* she had brought with her and began to read a story about a fox and a crow. The crow had a piece of cheese which the fox wanted to try and steal. The fables were quite simple, but her lesson was not so much to read as to try and work out the moral of the story – which was always printed in italics at the end. She was supposed to go through the story, and then find the meaning of it for herself. Before she read any further, therefore, she made her eyes go out of focus and quickly placed her hand over the line of italics on the opposite page. She didn't like the morals and she wished they weren't there.

The crow was sitting in a tree with the piece of cheese in its beak, and the fox was beneath the tree, looking upwards. The fox told the crow how beautiful he thought she was – how gorgeous her plumage, how bright her eyes, how pretty her dainty little feet. He was sure that she must have the most wonderful voice to match. Would she not sing for him and make his happiness complete? The ugly old crow was very flattered. She opened her mouth to sing, and so of course she dropped the piece of cheese – which the fox very quickly gobbled up. Then the fox offered up a few rude remarks and ran away laughing.

It was quite a good story, but Celandine wasn't sure what the moral of it might be. Don't sing with your mouth full? Never believe anything a fox tells you? She began to move her hand very slowly, uncovering the words one at a time, to give herself a clue.

Moral; Pride and vanity . . .

'Why do 'ee sit theer?'

Celandine jumped and the book slid off her lap. Her hands automatically scrabbled after it, just managing to save it from falling into the water as she turned to look over her shoulder.

He was different, this one – paler-skinned, a figure in grey on the bank of the stream. He wasn't waving a stick at her and he seemed less outlandish, less wild, than the ones she had seen before. Nevertheless his sudden appearance was shocking enough and Celandine glanced towards the half-obscured opening of the wicker tunnel, judging the distance lest she should need to make a run for it.

'What do 'ee want with us?' He spoke again, and again the impression was of one who was calm, un-flustered. His head was bald in the middle, like a friar's, with white hair that grew thickly over his ears, and his shabby grey gown, tied about the waist with a cord, would have made him look even more monk-like if it weren't for the short sleeves.

'Come, maid, answer. Why do 'ee come to this place?' It was not quite as easy for her to understand this one. His accent was strange.

'I – I'm sorry.' Her voice wasn't working very well. She swallowed, and made another attempt, trying to remember to speak slowly and quietly. 'I just wanted to . . . well, I just wanted to help. I thought I could help.'

'Thee thowt to help? By bringing the Gorji upon us? Thee might help us the mooer by staying away, child. Thee've no business here.' Yes, his accent was

120

unlike that of the others she had heard, as though he came from another part of the country.

'Nobody saw me come here. And I haven't brought any . . . Gorji . . . with me.'

'*Thee* be a Gorji, child. What do thee bring, if not theeself?'

Celandine took his question literally and said, 'I've brought some lucifers.' She pushed her hand into the pocket of her pinafore and fumbled for the box of matches that she had stolen from the drawing room at home. 'See?' She held up the little wooden box and shook it.

He frowned, but looked unimpressed. His bare forearms were folded and she saw that he wore a thick metal bracelet on each wrist. They were arms that looked as though they were used to hard work, and his face, though pale, was strong about the jaw, the neck muscles clear and visible. That first impression of him as being somehow monk-like began to fade.

'For a wean?'

She didn't know what he meant. A wean? A baby perhaps? Did he think that she had brought a baby's rattle? She slid open the box, and took out a match – holding it up for him to see. Then she struck the match upon the side of the box.

He flinched at the sudden eruption of flame and thick white smoke, turning his head sideways, and half raising an arm as a shield. His grey eyes darted from the burning match to her, and then back to the match – back and forth again – finally remaining fixed upon the flame as it grew and dwindled and died.

Celandine threw the spent lucifer into the stream and closed the box.

'I've siddit afore, Micas – 'tis all their nonsense. Take no heed o' it.'

Celandine recognized the voice. It was Pato, who now emerged casually from the surrounding under-growth and stepped down towards the bank. The figure in grey turned in surprise to look at him, and the two nodded to one another.

'Pato.'

'Micas.'

There was something cautious in their greeting, Celandine thought, as though they were not particularly well acquainted.

Pato was minus the trident this time. He stood with his hands on his hips and stared directly at her.

'You'm back yere again, then, maidy. I was hoping we'd seen the last of 'ee – and p'raps we would, too, if we'd only make sure thee'd seen the last of we.' He looked meaningfully at Micas. ''Tis better not to show theeself, Micas. I'd 'a thought your kind might've knowed that.'

Micas nodded, but said, 'I know it well enow – but *she* knows we'm here, Pato. She knows. And so hiding mayn't be our best play. Wha'ist she want, I wonder? If 'n we knew that, we might barter it for her going.'

How unalike they were, Celandine thought – the one so pale, the other so dark. How could that be? And why would their speech be different? And why did they seem as though they were strangers to each other?

'I don't want anything,' she said. 'I only wanted . . . to be friendly. And to bring you things that might be useful to you.'

'A box o' fire. Hmph.' Pato snorted and looked up at the sky.

'Well, what about the fish hooks? Did you find the fish hooks? And the needles?'

Pato said nothing.

'What be in the other box?' said Micas.

Celandine was puzzled. What other box? Did he mean the book? She held it up.

'In here, do you mean? Um . . . stories. Tales.'

'A box o' fire and a box o' tales.' Pato was not to be impressed. He turned to Micas. 'I means to stay out o' this. An' thee should do the same, Micas. Leave this maid be. She'll soon tire, if we pays her no mind. Come.' He began to walk away, then stopped to look over his shoulder. Micas remained where he was. Pato shook his head, and disappeared among the ferns.

Micas stepped further down the bank, so that he was right at the edge of the stream – just a couple of feet from where she still sat upon the flat rock. He nodded cautiously at the closed book. 'Show'st me,' he said.

'Read to you? Is that what you mean?'

'Show'st me how'n a tale be put in a box.'

'All right.' She was close enough to him to be aware of his slow intake of breath as she gently opened the cover of the book, as though he were tensing himself against the possibility of more fireworks.

' "*The Fox and the Crow*" ' she read. ' "*There was once a clever fox . . .*" '

The next morning Micas did not come alone. Others appeared from among the ferns, half a dozen or more shabby little figures in grey, all of them quite elderly, to stand in a silent huddle upon the bank of the stream.

Celandine looked at their bearded faces, so pale their skin and white their hair that they might almost have been albino were it not for the dark cautious eyes. She wondered once again whether this could possibly be happening.

Micas spoke on the group's behalf. 'These be Elders, maid. Some Tinklers, some Troggles. They'm come to judge 'ee for themselves. And to hear 'ee tell a tale.'

'Oh,' said Celandine. She opened her book, self-conscious now, and began to read. The bubbling waters around her were like a musical accompaniment to a voice that sounded as though it belonged to someone else.

Within another couple of days Celandine had attracted quite a respectable audience. The number of listeners was now perhaps thirty – a shy and solemn congregation – fathers, mothers, children. They stood beside the stream in silence, rarely smiling or speaking, but their huge dark eyes were wide with curiosity and wonder as she read the ancient fables of the boy who cried 'wolf', the dog in the manger, the fox that lost its tail. And she in turn was so overcome by the strangeness of it all that she sometimes had to stop mid-sentence and look up from her book, to convince herself that she wasn't dreaming, before finding her place once more.

At the end of each story the dark heads moved a little closer together, to nod their approval at one another and perhaps exchange a whisper or two – but if she spoke to any directly, or asked them questions, they shrank away from her, protectively drawing their young ones closer, shielding the tiny heads that peered wide-eyed from the folds of coarse grey material.

'How long have you been here?' Celandine wanted to know. 'And where do you live? In the trees?'

The group looked to Micas, and from him she learned a little more. They called themselves Tinklers and Troggles, and they lived in the caves. Celandine could just see the mouth of one of the caves from where she sat upon her rock. She wanted to look at the jewellery that they wore – the heavy anklets and bracelets, the medallions that dangled from the cords tied about their gowns.

'Can I see?' She spoke to one that Micas had called Mab, and the pretty Tinkler girl silently held out her wrists to show the metal bangles that she wore. The designs looked intricate, but the metal was dull, like blackened pewter.

'Where do you get these things?'

'We worken the tinsy.'

Celandine took this to mean that they must some-how make these things for themselves, and indeed there was nothing about this group that seemed borrowed from the outside world. There were no bits of binder twine, no scraps of tweed or twill, no pigskin waistcoats that had seen better days. And when it was time for her to go, and Celandine offered them whatever treasures she had brought – a hatpin, a ball of wool, the metal puzzle from her Christmas box – they shook their heads in refusal. Always she left these things upon the rock, and always they had disappeared when she next returned, but she was certain that it was not the cave-dwellers who had taken them.

Celandine soon learned that there were four distinct groups, or tribes, that inhabited this secret and forgotten world. They sometimes referred to themselves as the Various.

'Aye, Various we be,' said Micas. 'The Naiad do work the Great Clearing, and the Wisp do fish the Gorji waters. Us Tinklers and Troggles don't see much o' they, for we biden in the caves and keeps to our own.'

Pato and Fin, and the others of the first group that Celandine had seen were Naiad, so Micas told her. She had yet to meet any of the Wisp. She got the impression that those who lived below ground were inclined to avoid those who lived above it.

By the fourth day of listening to her stories, the cave-dwellers became more relaxed. They sat upon the bank now, rather than stood, and some of the younger ones dabbled their toes in the water as Celandine read to them, from another book now, of frogs and wolves, of wicked witches, and of children who got lost in the woods.

The old fairy tales could be quite frightening, and when, on the fifth day, she told the story of Little Red Riding Hood, she caught something of the nervousness of her listeners – feeling a chill across her own shoulders as she reached the part where the wolf was about to pounce. Celandine was aware of the silence around her – the eyes that stared, the open mouths that dared not breathe – and so when Fin came suddenly bounding out of the brambles behind her shouting 'Ah – ah – ah!', she scrabbled to her feet along with the rest of them, and leaped from the stone to the bank, shrieking with fright.

In an instant she was laughing, of course, clutching her chest and gasping for breath. Fin danced around her, grabbing at her sleeve and saying '*cake-cake-cake*' in his throaty little voice. He was so plainly delighted to see her that she could hardly be cross with him, but the scattered group of Tinklers regarded him from a safer distance, scowling at him as though they were cats that had just been doused with a garden hose.

He had escaped at last, for surely they must have somehow kept him away from her these last few days, and now he was making the most of his freedom.

'*I* all right. *I* all right.' He splashed back to the rock and picked up the book – which Celandine had dropped, face-down, in her panic. The pages fascinated him and he riffled his fingers through them, dangling the book above his head so that he could see from beneath how the leaves fluttered back and forth.

But his joy was cut short, for now here was Pato, bursting through the undergrowth on the opposite bank of the stream with Rufus and a few others of the Naiad in red-faced pursuit.

'*Fin!* Come away from there! Fin – I *told* 'ee . . . I warned 'ee . . . I'll give 'ee such a latherin'! *Fin!*' Pato was furious. He made a dash towards the rock, but Fin was too quick for him. He jumped across to the near bank, scampered up it, and ran to hide behind Celandine. 'Ah – ah – ah!' He was hanging onto her skirts, so that when she spun round he spun with her. For a few moments she felt as if she were a dog that was trying to catch its own tail.

Then Pato came running up, very hot and angry looking, and managed to get a firm grip on the collar of Fin's tunic. He swung back his free hand and shouted, 'I told 'ee! I told 'ee!'

'Don't!' Celandine half reached towards Pato's raised hand. 'Don't hit him! Please don't!'

Pato lifted his hand higher still – but then he paused, and his shoulders seemed to sag. He lowered his arm.

'Hit 'un?' He sighed, and wiped the back of his brown wrist across his streaming forehead. 'No, I casn't hit 'un. Casn't do it somehow – though by the Stone, I comes close to it, and thass the truth. Maybe 'tis my blame, but there 'tis.'

'He doesn't mean any harm, I'm sure he doesn't.' Celandine looked down at poor Fin who, though secured by the scruff of the neck, seemed content enough, his attention now on the nearby group of Tinklers.

'No,' said Pato. 'He don't mean no harm . . .'

'But he've brung it upon us all the same.' Rufus and the other half dozen of Pato's companions had drawn closer. It was Rufus who spoke, but he didn't pursue the point. Like Fin, his attention seemed to be drawn towards the cave-dwellers.

There was silence for a few moments, and Celandine was aware of the uneasy way in which the two separate groups regarded one another. There was a mutual curiosity there, but also a wariness that seemed strange to her.

She said, 'Fin hasn't really brought you any harm, at least . . . not if you mean me. Nobody else knows that I've been coming here, and nobody ever will – I've already promised you that. I'm very careful, you know, not to let anyone see me. And I've tried to bring you things that might be useful.' She looked slyly at the bright red stitching around the shoulders of Rufus's waistcoat. 'Did you like the wool?'

Rufus looked the other way.

'And I don't think the others mind me coming here – Micas, and Loren, and Elina . . . and the rest. I've been reading to them. They like it, I think.'

Pato looked at the book, which Fin was now clutching to his chest, and muttered, 'What *be* that thing?' He called across to the other group. 'Micas! What is it 'ee *do* . . . what do 'ee . . . ?' His voice trailed off, waiting, as Micas walked over. 'When 'ee do all sit there by the gwylie, Micas, and this yere maid do break open that . . . that *thing* . . . and she do talk to 'ee . . . well, I don't understand it, thass all. What bist she a-doin' of ? '

Micas rubbed the palm of his hand across the top of his shiny head.

' 'Tis named a boox. She do bring tales from't. Though we don't see how. It speaken to her in voices we m'nt hear, though we hearken right close. By piece and by piece it speaken to her, and she speaken to us.'

'We med all tell a tale, Micas – thee or I as well as the next – and have no need o' such things. Bide *still*, Fin, will 'ee?'

'This'm but a maid, Pato. Nor maid nor giant, nor thee nor I, would hold so much – aye, tales upon tales – in but one pate. No. We'n a-held much parley on this. It speaken. 'Tis witchi.'

'Witchi?' Pato raised his eyebrows and yanked Fin towards him, as he bent forward to take a closer look at the book.

Celandine had to stifle a giggle.

'It's just a *book*,' she said. 'There's nothing . . . *witchy* . . . about it. Look, I'll show you.' She gently took the book from Fin and let it fall open, lowering it so that Pato and Micas could see the pages. The two of them moved in a little closer – Pato, reluctant and suspicious, Micas more curious and interested.

'See? Here's a picture – of a crow. And over here, there's a fox. And these are the words that tell the tale. Can you see?'

The two faces, one so dark, the other so pale, studied the open pages.

'I sees a corben, and a renard,' said Pato. He bent his ear towards the book. 'But I casn't hear no tale.'

'Well, you don't *hear* anything. You have to *read* it – these words . . . all these marks on the page, they're words . . .' Celandine was beginning to realize how difficult it would be to try and explain. 'You see, each word . . .' – she pointed with her finger – 'each word makes a sound. Or rather, each letter . . .' She gave up.

'Tomorrow I'll bring some paper and a pencil. Then I can show you.'

Pato turned away, disinterested. ''Tis all nonsense to I. Micas, thee and I shall have this out, now we'm gathered. Be you for letting this maid to keep coming here or no?'

Micas was still examining the pages of the open book. He looked up. 'She'm a-coming here in any wise, Pato, without let from you or I. Might we not gain from her?'

'I casn't see us'd gain aught but a handful o' trouble. But you'm right – she'll do as she will.' Pato sighed and scratched his nose. 'Well, let her, then. You'll hear no more about it from I, for 'tis no more nor less than I said would happen from the fust.' He turned to Rufus – who simply shrugged his shoulders – and then to Emmet and the others. There were one or two muttered comments, but no definite objections.

'You med keep this yere *book*,' said Pato to Micas, 'if that's what pleases thee. I'll take the fish hooks.' He looked up at Celandine. 'As many as ever I zhould find.'

The matter seemed settled. The forest-dwellers would agree to trust her, and to allow her come and go as she pleased. Celandine stood among the Naiad, next to Pato and Fin. Together they watched as Micas gathered his own tribespeople together and led them back up the stony path towards the caves. Celandine was struck once again by the difference between the two groups, and the caution with which they regarded one another. On the way back to the tunnel she said, 'Aren't they your friends – the Tinklers? Don't you like them very much?'

Pato grunted. 'They bain't like we. There be some lopsided notions in they mazy heads o' their'n, I can tell 'ee. Proper crack-nogs, the lot of 'em.'

More than that he didn't say. As she splashed her way along the tunnel, Celandine could hear Fin's voice fading into the distance. 'Ah – ah – ah. *I* all right!'

When she returned the following morning she found Pato and Fin waiting for her.

'We've all thought on,' said Pato. 'And 'tis best we be warned, if 'ee be a-coming in. Then we can see if thee've kept to thee vow and have come alone. Can 'ee bird-whistle?'

Celandine shook her head.

'Then I'll show 'ee how.'

Celandine sat on the bank beside Pato and watched as he cupped his brown wrinkled hands together. 'Do 'ee see?' he said. 'Like this.' He blew into the gap between the bent knuckles of his thumbs, and produced the most startling array of bird calls: wood pigeon, curlew, heron, owl. All were immediately recognizable, perfect imitations of the sounds that Celandine had so often heard among the trees and fields about her. Fin automatically copied his father, raising his own small hands to his mouth and trilling away to himself like a blackbird as he crouched beside the shallows of the stream, off in some world of his own.

Celandine was astonished. 'I can't do *that*,' she said.

'Then 'tis time 'ee could,' said Pato. He showed her how to position her hands, one clasped over the other, how to make a little gap between her thumbs, where to blow. It took her a while, but eventually Celandine managed to make a breathy little hooting sound.

'Owl,' said Pato. And he was right – it *did* sound a bit like an owl. Celandine was encouraged, and kept on trying. After about half an hour she found that she could more or less reliably produce two different sounds: an owl and a wood pigeon. Pato decided that these were to be her warning signals before entering the tunnel. The pigeon call would be for daytime, the owl for night.

'What if nobody hears me?' Celandine said. 'Who'll be listening?'

'All o' us,' said Pato. 'We hears more than 'ee do reckon. We has to. And I s'll set Fin to watch for 'ee. He'm down here by the gwylie more times than not, anywise, if I let 'un.'

Celandine looked doubtfully at Fin. She was happy enough to give a signal before entering the forest, if that was what Pato wanted, but couldn't see that Fin would make much of a watchdog.

'But how will he know that it's not a real bird?' said Celandine. 'A proper owl?'

Pato laughed. 'A proper owl?' he said. 'You ain't like to be mistook for one o' they, maidy. Not even Fin be such a zawney as all that.'

She inhabited two different worlds, connected by a wicker tunnel, and as she daily crossed from one to the other Celandine felt as though she was two different people. When she was on the farm she was a child, a being of no great importance and of whom nobody took a great deal of notice, beyond the fact that she was a nuisance. But when she was among the Various she was a giant, and all were hushed at her coming.

It was no easier to be a giant, though, than it was to be a child.

Celandine took an exercise book and a wax crayon into the forest in order to explain to Micas and the other cave-dwellers what the alphabet was and how it worked – a prospect so daunting that she felt like giving up before she had started.

But the gathering of cave-dwellers seemed genuinely curious, and so she drew out the whole alphabet in thick black letters, one to a page, A, B, C. Then she tore the pages from the book and laid them out on the grassy bank of the stream.

'These shapes are called "letters",' she said. 'And every letter has its own sound. Do you see? This one says "Ah". This one says "Buh". This one says "Cuh". If you put the letters together, and put the sounds together, then you get a word.' The cave-dwellers looked blank at this, and Celandine sought around for inspiration. This was so difficult to get across. She felt a pang of sympathy for the departed Miss Bell.

'Look.' Celandine separated the A and the B from the line of letters, and placed them by themselves.

Then she picked up the M and laid it on the grass in front of the other two. The group of Tinklers and Troggles shuffled closer, trying to get a better view.

'See? This letter says "Muh". So now we have "Muh", "Ah", and "Buh". So if you put those sounds together, you get "Mmm . . . Aaaa . . ." '

'Mab.'

Celandine looked round in surprise. 'Who said that?'

It was Loren. The little Tinkler lad half-raised his hand and smiled shyly.

' 'Tis Mab,' he said. He pointed to Micas and Elina's daughter. 'She.'

Celandine was amazed. 'That's *right*,' she said. 'It's Mab!'

Perhaps this was going to be possible after all.

They proved to be astonishingly fast learners, although not all words were as easy to demonstrate as 'Mab'. It made Celandine's head spin to try to explain why 'T. H. E.' said 'the', or why some letters could be pronounced in several different ways. Then, of course, the pieces of paper were inclined to blow about in the breeze. On more than one occasion a carefully assembled word had ended up in the stream, to be whisked off towards the tunnel.

But they continued to persevere, and Celandine's poor teaching was more than made up for by the cave-dwellers' enthusiasm and delight at seeing their names spelt out upon the grass.

The days fell into a natural routine as summer passed. Every morning, apart from Sundays,

Celandine came to the tunnel, and Fin was always there to meet her, answering her whistled signal with a far more convincing bird-call of his own. Sometimes he stayed with her for a while as she sat and read to the cave-dwellers, but the stories could not hold his interest for long, and the bits of paper that they spent so much time pondering over meant nothing to him. Usually he wandered off to play by himself in the stream.

At around mid-morning Pato would arrive – supposedly to collect Fin, but also to accept whatever little gift Celandine might have brought with her; a length of string, a dibber from the greenhouse, or a tomato, perhaps. Celandine had come to think of Pato as a kind of toll-keeper. He always took whatever she gave him with barely a glance at it, as though this were her entrance fee to the forest.

Towards lunchtime, Celandine went home. She didn't want to arouse suspicion by being continually away from the farm, although lately she had begun to wonder whether her absence would actually be noticed, now that all anyone ever seemed to think about was the war.

The war. She didn't really understand it. Britain was apparently at war with Germany and Austro-Hungary, that much she knew, but there was no one to explain it to her. Freddie was away at boarding school, and Thos only grunted that it was all nonsense anyway. Her mother became tearful, as she so often seemed to of late, whenever the subject was mentioned. Her mother was Austrian and spoke with a German accent.

Celandine supposed that meant she must be half-Austrian herself. She had never given it much thought before, but now she was beginning to see that it might make a difference.

She entered the kitchen one morning to beg for scraps as usual, pretending that she wanted to feed the ducks. Sometimes she managed to get hold of cake for Fin in this manner. She found Cook talking to Ivy Tucker, the woman who came to collect the eggs. They were discussing the war. Both women turned to look at her, arms identically folded, and Cook said, 'Sorry, *fraulein*, I got nothing for 'ee today.' Ivy Tucker smirked.

Celandine thought about it later, and wondered why Cook had called her *fraulein* in that way. Something told her that there would be no more cake forthcoming.

The daily routine held as July burnt through to August, and then the fine weather broke. As the first summer storm crashed through the woods, it seemed natural to Celandine that she should run for cover along with her pupils, following the drenched little figures as they scurried up the steep rocky pathway that led to the caves. It was only as she crouched beneath the overhanging outcrop of the main entrance, gazing out upon the sheets of driving rain and feeling the coolness of the worn stone floor beneath her hands and knees that she began to realize what she had done. They had not invited her here. She had broken her promise.

And yet it didn't appear to bother them. The cave-dwellers stood beside her, unconcerned, as they listened to the hiss of the rain, watching it tumble in rivulets from the great overhanging rock that formed the roof of the cave. It was like being behind a water-fall, Celandine thought.

There was a pungent smell about the place, vaguely scented, as of burning oil or candle-wax. Celandine could see that further back into the cave there were other dark entrances, to tunnels perhaps, or underground chambers. Was this really their home? What did they do back there? She so wanted to ask questions, but thought that it might be rude to pry on this first visit. She looked about her at the stone walls of the cave entrance. There were cracks here and there, crevices from which tufts of grass and moss sprouted, but for the most part the stone was smooth. Big empty expanses of smooth stone. It gave her an idea . . .

Celandine brought chalk from the schoolroom and was at last able to write out a permanent display of the entire alphabet. The flat grey walls of the cave entrance were covered in rainbow-coloured letters.

'*Theer* . . . *wazz* . . . *onkee* . . . *a* . . . *clee-veer* . . . *fox* . . .' She was amazed at how quickly her reading group had progressed, but little Loren, in particular, was quite wonderful. Already he had learned nearly all of his letters. Celandine knelt beside the Tinkler boy and showed him how to move his finger along the line of words, one hesitant step at a time. She gave him a pencil and paper, and the first time that he managed to write his own name with no help from her, she felt as though she were a magician.

Her extraordinary pupils flourished, and Celandine began to have real hopes that she might truly be able to teach them to read. But then, suddenly, it was all over. Everything was about to change.

Her mother and father gave her the news one evening at supper.

'I've a letter here, Celandine, from the head-mistress at Mount Pleasant School in North Perrott.' Her father was waving a sheet of blue notepaper at her from the far end of the table. Celandine put down her soup-spoon. What was this? North Perrott was miles away. Miles and miles.

'She's prepared to take you as a pupil into the third form, I'm happy to say.' Her father folded the letter and tucked it back into its envelope as he spoke. 'Now, your mother and I decided that you've grown too old to have another governess, and so I wrote to Miss Craven a couple of weeks ago. We're very lucky to have got a place at such a good school, con-sidering recent events. Comes highly recommended – not cheap. One of Swann's girls goes there, isn't that right, Lizzie?'

'Yes, I believe is a very good school.' Her mother had been searching the sleeve of her dress for a hand-kerchief. She blew her nose, and quickly dabbed at one of her eyes.

'But Mama . . .' Celandine was horrified. 'I *can't*. Not now. You don't understand . . .'

140

'You *can't*?' Her father was already beginning to lose his temper. 'You'll do as you're told, young lady, just for once. And it's high time you did. Now then. I've had to give the school a very full account of the circumstances, and you should be grateful for this opportunity to start afresh. Miss Craven was under no obligation to take you on, and so I give her credit for doing so. I gather she stands for no nonsense. Good thing, in my opinion . . .'

Celandine was only half listening. What would happen now to the little people? All her work would be wasted. All her plans . . .

She tried to focus once more on what was being said, and could see that there was no point in arguing. Her father was adamant that she should go and her mother, though tearful, was in agreement with him. She would attend the Mount Pleasant School for Girls, for the start of the Michaelmas term in a fortnight's time, and there was a lot to be done before then. It was a boarding school, like Freddie's, and so there would be uniforms to buy, games kit, and a trunk to put it all in. She might even enjoy it. At any rate she must accept it. The matter had already been decided.

How quickly a fortnight could fly by when you wanted time to stand still, how short the days when you wished they would never end.

Celandine sat in the long grass on top of Howard's Hill, clutching a little red bridle that Pato had given her, and wondering when she would ever be back here again. She had given her last reading lesson, perhaps for a very long time, and tomorrow she was to become a pupil herself once more.

She laid the bridle on the grass beside her. It was a lovely thing, beautifully made, with three small bells that twinkled brightly against the soft red leather. Celandine shook her head at the wonder of it and what it meant. That Pato, who always seemed to accept her gifts without much thanks, should give her a going-away present – and such a present – was a surprise. But to discover that the higher woods must contain other creatures that she had yet to see, creatures that could wear such a bridle as this, was an even greater surprise. There was so much that she didn't know about them, the Various, so much that she had still to learn.

Well, it would have to wait. It would all have to wait. Celandine stood up, flapped some of the chalk dust from her pinafore and began to make her way down the hill. The bells on the little bridle made a soft jingling sound as she brushed through the clumps of wild poppies.

She arrived back on the farm to find that her mother was cross with her – again.

'*Here* you are, Celandine! Once more I am hunting you. Always you are lost to me. The photograph man! Did you forgotten this?'

'What? Oh – yes. Sorry.'

'And always you are so dirty! What is this white dust – flour? Go and put on your clean dress – is on your bed – and then let me make your hair.'

'Yes, Mama. I'm sorry.'

It had been her father's idea that the photographer should call in order to take formal portraits of the family, along with suitable views of the farm – to include the horses and the men. All of this had been done, and now it was only Celandine who was keeping the photographer waiting.

They sat her upon a square wicker basket in the parlour. She was wearing her blue shiny dress with the high lace collar and the pearl buttons. It was too tight, and she hated it. The material always felt cold and stiff and the collar bit into her neck. Her best boots were also too tight, the laces now barely long enough to reach the top pair of hooks. She must have grown recently.

Her mother had scraped her hair back and tied it so firmly that she felt as though her eyebrows were at least a couple of inches higher up her forehead than usual.

Celandine was facing the window, and so Mr Tilzey the photographer was a shadowy figure against the light – quietly moving back and forth with pieces of unfamiliar equipment; a tray with some powder on it, a black cloth, some wooden-framed objects, like drawers from a small cabinet. The camera itself was a large box – mahogany, with brass attachments – mounted on a wooden tripod. Celandine looked at the lens, a dark and mysterious thing. It reminded her of tunnels, and of caves, and she tried to peer through it into the smoky blue world beyond. What might be in there?

The photographer was taking a long time and

Celandine began to feel quite chilly. She gazed out of the window, at the distant slope of Howard's Hill. What would they be doing now, the Various, with their secret lives? Would any of them be thinking of her? Tomorrow she would be gone. Would they forget all about her?

'Now then, ah . . . Celandine, is it? I think we are ready.' He was a gingery man was Mr Tilzey, and the mid-morning light shone fiery red around the edges of his beard.

'I am going to put my head beneath this cloth, and when I say "watch the birdie" I'd like you to look into the camera and smile. Yes? And then you must sit quite still, until I tell you otherwise. Yes?'

'Yes.' (What birdie?)

'Celandine – please. You must not be so *shlumping*. Sit *tall* with your back.' Her mother was still cross with her.

Celandine straightened her back and wondered whether the pearl buttons might suddenly start pinging around the room, whether her boots might fly off, whether her hair would wildly spring from its cage of pins and ribbons . . .

'And what is this *thing* you are holding – a piece from a *horse*?' Her mother, again.

'Oh, I think I rather like that.' The photographer's voice was now muffled, from beneath his black cloth. 'Very pretty, my dear. Quite still then, please. Quite, quite still . . .'

Celandine looked at the camera and tried to smile through the discomfort. Why didn't he begin? She pinched the bridle in frustration, feeling the texture of the leather strap between her fingers and the ball of her thumb. It was smoother on one side than it was on the other. Something caught her eye – something flying past the window – a flicker of black and white beyond the humped silhouette of the photographer's cloaked shoulder. A magpie.

'Watch the birdie . . . quite, quite still . . .'

The magpie settled on the roof of the stables and stood there motionless – quite, quite still. How extraordinary. She watched the birdie . . .

The searing flare of white light seemed to burst inside her head, blinding her completely, and the smell of burning magnesium filled her nostrils. She couldn't see a thing – but in that helpless moment knew only that she felt no more pain. Her hair tumbled freely about her shoulders and her soft clothing was warm and comfortable, open at the neck, loosely creased around her knees. The fast ticking of a clock came drifting through the scented silence – a cheerful sound, and a friendly one, familiar to her. In her hands she cradled the present that she had been given, a little metal bowl, and she traced the polished rim of it, so cool and smooth to her fingertips. She felt very peaceful.

'Thank you, my dear. That will do, I think.' The photographer's voice made her jump, and the bells on the red bridle gave a little jingle.

Gradually her vision returned, creeping in around the edges of the dancing white light, and with it came a sense of sadness and bewilderment. Wherever it was she had momentarily been – or *whoever* it was she had momentarily been – she was back, and she was herself. Once again her boots pinched and her collar itched. Once again her scalp felt as though her hair was slowly being pulled from it, strand by strand.

Celandine could hear the grave wooden tick of the grandmother clock on the wall behind her, the faint creak and whirr of the mechanism. She turned to look at it. Five-and-twenty past ten.

'Come then, Celandine – we have also some more work to be done.'

'Yes, Mama.'

'You will excuse us, please, Mr Tilzey. My daughter is beginning tomorrow at her new school. We have some *boxing* yet to finish.'

Mr Tilzey looked mildly surprised at this, but said that he quite understood.

Chapter Seven

Mount Pleasant School for Girls. Founded 1851. Headmistress: Miss A. Craven. The maroon and grey lettering of the large painted sign more or less matched the colours of her uniform – maroon blazer over a grey tunic. And the pale yellow background of the sign was a similar colour to that of the ludicrous straw hat that lay upon the buckboard seat between her and Robert. The words MISS A. CRAVEN appeared to have been painted more recently than the rest, the raised outline of a previous name just visible in the Saturday morning sunshine.

Celandine had plenty of time to study these things because there was an obstruction up ahead – a motor coach and a carriage had between them blocked the steep curving driveway that led to the school. There was no point in Robert's trying to go any further until the way was clear.

It began to look as though they might be stuck there for quite a while, and Robert finally said, 'P'raps you should walk on up, miss. 'Tain't very far. I can drop your boxes at porter's lodge when I gets there.'

'Yes, all right.' She waited to be helped down from the pony trap, and then stood awkwardly holding her hat whilst Robert retrieved her large canvas bag from among the other things that were stacked at the back. She patted the horse's neck and was inevitably reminded of Tobyjug. Her hand still held the memory of him – of how he too had once felt like this: alive and warm against her palm. And then so cold.

'I'll say cheerio, miss. And I hope . . . well, I hope 'ee'll settle in all right . . .' Poor Robert looked very uncomfortable.

'Yes. Goodbye, Robert. Thank you.' She wanted to cry. Robert was a kind man.

But she put on her hat and walked along the grass verge of the drive, threading her way past the unhappy entanglement of carriage and motor coach that still blocked all progress in either direction. The problem seemed to be that neither vehicle could reverse – the motor coach because of the steepness of the hill, and the carriage because one of its wheels had caught against the coach.

There was a lot of shouting. Both drivers were offering very lively advice as to what they believed the other should do, and from the queue at either end came further loud suggestions. The carriage was a smart landau, open-topped, and in the back sat a fair-haired girl in school uniform who was also shouting – though not very helpfully, 'Oh for goodness *sake*, Stokes! Just go *on*, why don't you? I shall be *late*!'

Silly idiot, thought Celandine. Why doesn't she walk?

The scene at the top of the drive was no less riotous – there were girls and bags and boxes everywhere – so that Celandine only took in a brief impression of the school building. It was tall and complicated. There was a central clock tower, with several gables to either side, built from the local hamstone, like Mill Farm, but made ugly by the dark grey mortar between the blocks. Celandine noticed that there were metal bars fixed to the upstairs windows. These had presumably been put there for the girls' safety, but the effect was to make the place look vaguely prison-like.

She had a letter tucked into the inside pocket of her stiff new blazer, and instructions to report to Matron – whoever that might be. Celandine climbed the broad flight of well-worn steps that led up to the high archway of the main entrance and pushed her way into the echoing hall. Here there were more girls than ever and the cavernous space rang with the confusion of voices and clattering feet. A stone staircase rose in a great square spiral right up through the centre of the building, and from high above came the sounds of banging doors and footsteps hurrying along distant corridors. It was all very bewildering.

Near the foot of the staircase a group of girls surrounded a woman in a white uniform. The woman was seated at a small table and the girls peered over her shoulder, trying to catch a glimpse of the sheets of paper that lay in front of her.

'Matron, what about me? Am I in Wyndham too?'
'Where am I, Matron?'

'Matron, I'm supposed to be in Dampier, but you've got me down as Hardy. That can't be right, you know.'

Celandine moved closer. At least she had discovered who Matron was.

The woman in white threw up her hands in despair, and shouted, 'Girls! Will you please be *quiet*! I can't hear myself think! *Thank* you. That's better. Molly Fletcher – you're in Hardy. Alexandra Long – Dampier. Kathleen O'Hanlon – Hardy.'

'But Matron, you've got me on the list as an "H". I should be an "O".'

Celandine put her bag down on the chequered tile floor, and waited. She hadn't the least idea of what they could be all be arguing about. More girls came and went – big girls, small girls, pretty girls and plain girls, tearful girls who clung to their mothers and cheerful girls who galloped up the stairs two at a time. Celandine watched them all and wondered how she would ever fit in, wondered whether all this would ever become familiar to her. It was so very different from the world she was used to.

At last the group that had been gathered around Matron dispersed, and Celandine was able to approach the desk. She took the letter from her blazer pocket.

'Excuse me. I have a letter . . . I don't know what I'm supposed to do.'

'Ah. A new girl? Let's have a look then, shall we?'

Matron took the letter and opened it, holding the single sheet of paper a little distance away from her as she read it. She had a remarkably shiny face, Celandine thought – very clean and neat beneath her wiry silver hair and starched white cap.

'Celandine Howard,' said Matron, and transferred her attention to the list on her desk. 'Celandine Howard. Yes, here we are. Celandine Howard. You're in . . . Hardy. Now then . . . who can I get to . . . ?' She glanced over Celandine's shoulder. 'Ah. Jessop. Just in time to make yourself useful. You can take this young lady up to Hardy for me, if you will. You're both in the same dorm. Now then, Howard, this is Nina Jessop. Nina will be in the same dormitory as you, and so she can show you the ropes.'

Celandine turned round, and looked at the girl standing behind her – a red-eyed child who looked as though she was either just about to cry, or had recently left off doing so.

Matron continued to address the girl. 'Did you want to see me, Jessop?'

'No, Matron. Well, but only to ask you which dorm I was in this year.' Her voice was a whisper. 'It's Hardy, is it?'

'That's right.'

'Oh.'

'Off you go, then, the pair of you – and Howard, you're to go and see Miss Craven in the headmistress's study at five-thirty. Five-thirty, mind. Supper's at six-fifteen. Bell goes at six-ten. And don't forget that there'll be a locker inspection at seven, so you'll need to have your bed made and locker packed before you go to supper – there'll be no time afterwards. Jessop will show you what to do. Run along then. Oh, and Jessop,' Matron opened her eyes very wide and gave the girl an unnaturally bright smile, '*do* try to buck up a bit, this term. You're in the third form now.'

'Yes, Matron.'

'Yes, Matron. Well, see that you do. Go.'

Celandine had been a Mount Pleasant girl for barely half an hour, but already she sensed that she was in a less lowly position than the unfortunate Nina Jessop. Every question she asked – and she had many – was met with blushing shyness and a response that was as brief as possible. What was Matron like? Oh, she was 'all right'. What about the teachers – were they very strict? Yes. What was the food like? Oh, pretty foul. Some of it was 'all right'.

As they hurried along one of the dark upper corridors, three very young girls, minus their hats and blazers, came running towards them. They barged past Nina Jessop as though she had been invisible, although they seemed to acknowledge her existence as an afterthought – 'Ninky-ninky-noooo!' they chanted.

'Who were they?' said Celandine.

'Second-formers,' muttered Nina. She pushed open a heavy wooden door that bore a gold-painted sign in capital letters – HARDY – and Celandine followed.

They were in a room full of beds. It took Celandine a few moments to realize that this was where she would be sleeping. It was not that she had imagined something different, simply that she had given the matter no thought whatsoever. The overwhelming events of the recent weeks – Tobyjug's death, her attack on Miss Bell, her meeting with Fin and entering the forest – had so filled the present of each day that there had been no time to wonder about the future. In a kind of numb helplessness she had allowed herself to be kitted out and bundled off to this place, for what else could she do in the face of her father's anger and her mother's insistence? None of it had seemed real. Her mother had clung to her in parting, and wept, yet she herself had been able to feel nothing. Her father had even given her a half-crown, saying that she should have the other half if she came home at Christmas with a good report of herself – and she had caught her brother Thos's look of outright astonishment as she had taken the coin without a word. But now she was here, in a cold white room full of beds, with a weepy-eyed girl called Nina Jessop, and this was where she would be sleeping from now on. The reality of it struck her at last. She had left home.

There was a painful lump in her throat and her eyes prickled as she looked about the room. It seemed so cheerless. The iron beds – perhaps a dozen of them, each covered with a brown army blanket – were ranged side by side around the walls. There was just enough space between them for a small wooden locker. Two more beds stood end to end in the centre of the room, with lockers separating the head rails.

'Hullo, Ninky, don't tell us you've found a chum.'

Celandine looked round. There were three girls

sitting in a far corner. They had been partially hidden from view by the open door.

'Won't you introduce us?' The one who spoke looked somehow familiar. She was a big girl, with very dark hair cut into an unflatteringly short bob.

Nina Jessop, who was already kneeling beside a locker, raised her head and peered over the top of her bed. Her face was very flushed.

'Oh,' she said. 'This is, um . . . It's um . . .'

'Oh, it's *Um*, is it?' The big girl spoke again, and her two friends giggled. 'This is your friend *Um*, is it, Ninky? Well then, *Um*, how do you do? Chloe, Daphne, say hallo to Ninky's chum – Um.' The two girls giggled again. 'Hallo, Um.'

Celandine was already feeling as though she wanted to slap the lot of them, but she forced a smile and began to say, 'Actually, my name's—'

'Oh, I already know,' the big girl interrupted her. 'It's Celandine Howard. My dears . . .' she leaned forward and spread her arms in a mock curtsey, 'please allow me to present Miss Celandine Howard!'

'Hallo, Miss Celandine Howard!'

Celandine frowned and looked at the big girl, trying to remember where she might have seen her before.

'How did you know my name?' she said. 'Have we met, then?'

'Well, I don't believe we've exactly *met*, you know. But your people were gracious enough to invite us to a party a few summers ago – on Coronation Day. It was all rather grand, and dear Mama was *so* grateful.

154

You've a brother who's rather sweet on my sister Emily, so I gather.'

Emily? Emily . . . Swann? Of course.

'Oh. So you must be . . . um . . .'

'No, I'm not Um. That's you, according to Ninky. I'm Mary Swann.'

'Yes, of course. Mary.'

'But you may call me Swann.'

'I beg your pardon?'

'We call each other by our surnames here, unless we're *particularly* good friends. Don't we, Jessop?'

Nina Jessop said nothing, but returned to her unpacking.

Celandine had apparently been left to fend for herself. She looked about the room once more, and said, 'But where am I supposed to go?'

'I say, Ninky, you're not much help to your chum, are you?' said Mary Swann. 'Over there.' She pointed to an unmade bed just beyond Nina. 'That'll be yours.'

The mattress, a stiff and lumpy object covered in black-and-white striped ticking, was rolled tightly against the bedstead. A bare pillow, also striped, lay perched on top of the rolled-up mattress. On the slatted metal base was a neatly folded pile of bedding, although it seemed a rather meagre pile at that.

Celandine had never made a bed in her life and hardly knew where to start. But she reasoned that the mattress would have to be at the bottom. That much, at least, was obvious. So she put the pile of sheets and blankets on top of her locker and struggled to unroll the mattress – a heavy and awkward object that never-theless managed to look inadequate as a means of support. Finally she got the thing so that it was lying flat upon the base. The base had no springs and the lattice of metal slats didn't hold out the promise of much comfort. What next? A sheet?

She was conscious of being watched, and of the whispering that was going on in the far corner of the room. By the time she had managed to spread a sheet over the mattress and had tucked it in as best she could, it was no great surprise to find that her observers had moved in closer.

'Oh dear, I'm afraid that this will never do,' said Mary Swann, who now stood at the foot of the bed, hands on hips. 'If the Bulldog saw this, she'd have fits. Absolute fits, my dear.' Daphne and Chloe giggled – their unvarying response to all of Mary's remarks, it would seem. How stupid they looked, with their long pigtails and their identical protruding teeth. Like dim rabbits they were, a pair of silly rabbits . . . then Celandine realized that the girls were twins. It was so obvious. Why hadn't she seen it before?

'Would you like us to help?' said Mary Swann. 'Only, the Bulldog's fearfully hot on bed drill.'

Celandine was inclined to be wary of this offer, but didn't see how she could refuse. 'Yes, all right then. Thanks.'

'It's the corners, you see,' said Mary, beginning to undo Celandine's handiwork. 'They have to be done the Mount *Pleasant* way. Everything has to be done the Mount *Pleasant* way. See – we hold this bit out like this.

Then we fold that bit under, and tuck it in like this, and so we end up with . . . this. Got it? I'll show you again. Watch.'

Mary Swann moved on to the next corner and demonstrated the Mount Pleasant bed-making method once again. Celandine glanced away at one point and caught Nina Jessop staring at the proceedings – the expression on her face telling her that such acts of kindness at the hands of Mary Swann might not be the norm.

'Now you try,' said Mary. And so Celandine pulled out one of the remaining corners and made a fair attempt at copying what she had seen, expecting all the while that some blow was about to fall on her or that some trick would be played. But when she had finished, Mary said, 'There. That was very good, Howard. We'll make a proper Mount Pleasant girl of you yet, dear. Now, have you unpacked your bag? No? Well, Chloe can show you where everything goes, can't you, Chlo? Not a bit of good relying on Ninky – you'll get no sense out of her. Come on, Daph, we might as well finish off this bed, now that we've started.'

Celandine was more suspicious than ever, but she allowed the sniggering Chloe to show her how the locker was to be arranged – stockings and under-garments in the bottom drawer along with her sponge-bag, clean blouses and spare tunic in the top, toothbrush in this drawer, hairbrush in that. It didn't seem to be a very logical system. She tried at the same time to keep an eye on Mary and Daphne, sure that they would put something horrible in her bed – a dead bird, or a thistle, or some such idiotic thing. But she noticed nothing unusual, and by the time she had finished her unpacking, the bed looked neat and crisply made up.

'Have you brought any food with you, or money?' said Mary. 'Only you have to keep all that in your locker as well.'

Celandine had an orange, some barley twist, and half a bar of chocolate in her bag – exotic treats supplied by her mother at the last minute – and she put these in the top drawer of her locker on Mary's advice, along with the half-crown that her father had given her.

Once everything was done, the three drifted back towards their own corner of the room and said no more to her. Celandine was left wondering why they had paid her so much attention, but then there was a scuffling sound in the corridor and a kick at the door, and in came another girl, very red in the face and weighed down with bags and boxes under each arm. It was the fair-haired girl who had been sitting in the carriage that had blocked the driveway. Her temper seemed to have improved very little since then.

'Ye *gods*,' she cried, 'Is there anything more *pointless* than a coachman who can't drive a stupid coach?' She dropped her luggage in a heap and staggered theatrically over to the corner where Mary Swann and the pigtailed twins were sitting. She flopped face-down across a bed, where she lay drooping over the side and complaining loudly to the linoleum. 'Do you know, I've had to *walk*? I've had to *walk*! All up that hill, with all of my luggage – *and* up all those stairs. Not a porter to be *seen*. Not one. Well, they shan't blame me if I'm laid up for a week over this. Oh! I've such a *headache*, I could *scream*!' She rolled over and sat up. 'Mary, darling, come and soothe me, do. I need unctions, balms . . .'

'Oh, poor Alicia.'

'Yes, poor Alicia,' cooed the twins.

Celandine wasn't quite sure what to make of this drama. She watched for a while as 'poor Alicia' was patted and comforted by her friends, and then became aware that Nina Jessop was trying to catch her eye. Nina was still kneeling beside her locker, sorting out her belongings, but she kept glancing over the top of her bed towards where Celandine was sitting.

'They've apple-pied your bed,' she whispered.

'What?' said Celandine.

There was no time for any further explanation however, because the fair-haired girl, Alicia, was suddenly on her feet, miraculously recovered, and walking back down the room towards her jumbled heap of luggage. She stopped and looked at Celandine.

'Hallo – who's this wond'rous creature?' she said.

'Oh, that's the common-or-garden *Um*,' said Mary Swann. 'Otherwise known as Miss Celandine Howard. She's Ninky's new chum.'

'How extraordinary,' murmured Alicia. 'And does it speak, I wonder? Can it dance the quadrille? Cut a little caper for us, my dear. Distract us, do. No? Oh well . . .' She turned away and began to gather up her scattered pieces of luggage.

Celandine sat on her bed with her hands in her lap. She didn't know what else to do. Occasionally she glanced at the large clock that was mounted on the wall at the far end of the dormitory. Nina made no further attempt to speak to her.

A patch of late afternoon sun streamed in through a corner of one of the high windows, throwing long slanting shadows over the unfamiliar room. Celandine saw her own shadow for a few moments, a mocking distortion of herself stretched out upon the floor, motionless; then an invisible cloud stole softly across the sun and the light was slowly extinguished, the room descending into a final depressing gloom.

Other girls arrived in ones and twos, some laughing, some complaining, and all looked at her curiously as they deposited their bags and boxes, before joining the group at the end of the dim room. None of them made any move to be friendly towards her – possibly on the instruction of Mary Swann. Eventually there was quite a crowd down there, and their chattering grew louder, their antics more boisterous. Only Nina Jessop remained apart, lying upon her bed and reading a book, acknowledging no one, ignoring the occasional taunts that drifted her way. Celandine stared through the window at the darkening landscape, her face burning with self-consciousness.

At five-twenty, Celandine cleared her throat and said, 'Nina – I mean, Jessop – would you show me where the headmistress's study is? Only I've to be there at half-past five.'

'Yes, all right.' Nina Jessop closed her book and put it under her pillow. She stood up and smoothed out her tunic. Celandine noticed that her hands shook slightly. 'It's downstairs.'

The hubbub at the end of the room subsided to a low murmur as Celandine followed Nina to the door.

Walking down the corridor towards the main stairway Celandine felt a little burst of pity for the timid girl beside her. Despite her own worries and troubles, she nevertheless considered herself the more fortunate of the two. Nina looked as though a puff of wind might blow her away. Her legs were so thin that it was a wonder they carried her at all, though there was precious little of her to *be* carried, at that.

Celandine had intended to ask Nina about the 'apple-pie', and what that meant, but instead she said, 'They're not very nice to you, are they, those others?'

'Oh. Well . . . it doesn't matter.' Nina sounded surprised that another person should consider her feelings. She glanced up at Celandine, the paleness of her face making her eyes seem redder than ever, but then she looked downwards again and said no more. They reached the top of the stairway, and began to descend towards the entrance hall, their footsteps echoing on the smooth stone.

Celandine tried again. 'Why do they call you Ninky?'

'Don't know,' said Nina. But then she hesitated and said, 'Well, it's short for "nincompoop", you see.'

'Oh.' It wasn't a word that Celandine had ever heard before. Nincompoop. It was plainly not a compliment. 'Do you mind if I call you Nina, then? Only I don't think I shall get used to calling people by their surnames.'

'If you like. But they'll scrag you for it, you know, if you do. They scrag anyone who speaks to me.'

'I shan't care,' said Celandine, jumping the last two steps.

Nina seemed doubtful. 'You don't know what they're like,' she muttered. They walked on a little further and then stopped outside a dark varnished door, just off the main hallway. 'This is Miss Craven's office. You have to knock, and wait.' Nina Jessop's voice had lowered to a whisper and she backed away slightly, as though nervous of the very shadows beneath the portal.

Celandine knocked at the door. There was no reply. She looked at Nina, and raised her hand to knock again, but Nina opened her eyes wide and shook her head.

'Enter.' The distant voice sounded deep enough to be that of a man. Celandine struggled a little with the heavy brass doorknob, too big for her hands, but eventually managed to turn the thing. She pushed against the door, needing to use her shoulder slightly in order to move it. A final parting glance at Nina and she entered the room.

'Close the door behind you.' Again, the deep voice sounded almost masculine, and the appearance of the figure seated at her desk only added to that impression. Miss Craven's grey hair was cut severely short, and the heavy pleated black gown that she wore had the effect of making her shoulders appear square and broad. Her face was long and thin, deeply lined about the mouth. 'Come and stand over here.'

Celandine crossed the worn green carpet and stood before Miss Craven's heavy oak desk. The room smelled faintly of tobacco and it reminded Celandine of her father's study at home.

'Hands by your sides, please.' Miss Craven sat very upright in her chair, her own hands neatly folded upon the green leather desktop in front of her. A pair of gold-rimmed glasses lay on the desktop, beside an envelope. Celandine recognized the handwriting.

'Now then, Howard. I shall make it clear from the outset, that if it were not for your father's local standing in the county, there would be no place for you here.' Miss Craven raised her dark eyebrows slightly and waited for a few moments. It occurred to Celandine that perhaps she was expected to respond to this, but she could find nothing to say.

'Furthermore, I can tell you that the kind of behaviour that you have apparently displayed up until now will under no circumstances be tolerated at Mount Pleasant. Mr Howard has been very frank in his account of you, and I have to say that I am appalled. Absolutely appalled. To wilfully attack a person of authority in such a vicious manner is quite inexcusable – and I do *not* excuse it. Yours was a criminal act, and I should judge that a child from a less privileged home might have found themselves suffering the most serious of consequences, had charges been brought. As it is, you may feel that you've got away with it – but I give you fair warning now that any such occurrence in this establishment would be treated with the utmost severity. There would be no question of any lenience. What *have* you to say for yourself?'

Celandine still made no reply. There was a long set of bookshelves behind Miss Craven, and on top of the shelves was a glass case that contained several stuffed animals: an otter, a pine-marten, a stoat and a weasel. The otter had a fish in its mouth – and there was something not quite right about it.

'Nothing. Very well. Let us move on to another issue, then; these delusions of yours. Games of make-believe are one thing – persistent lies are entirely another matter. It is quite simply a *lie* to claim that you have seen things that do not exist. Yes, Howard, I know all about your past encounters with "little people" and so forth. As I said, your father has been commendably frank. Quite rightly, he and your mother believe that these stories of yours border on the ungodly –

although they do say that it has been some time since you made these wild claims. I am perfectly clear in this; no good can ever come of meddling with such things. There has been an unfortunate rise in what might be called the cult of the psychic, of late. These so-called mediums – with their talk of seances and "spirits of the deceased" and "ectoplasm" and who knows what other nonsense – it flies in the face of all Christian belief, and there will be none of it here. Do I make myself understood?'

It was a direct question. 'Yes, Miss Craven.'

'I hope I do. Because there will be no second chances. I have my eye on you, Howard, and I have assured your parents that the atmosphere here at Mount Pleasant will bring about a change in your attitude and behaviour. I intend to see that it does.'

Miss Craven leaned back slightly in her chair, and pulled open a drawer. She took out a small white booklet, and placed it at the front of the desk. *Mount Pleasant School for Girls. Rules and Regulations.*

'Take it. Read it. I shall expect you to have it off by heart before lessons begin on Monday. Either Miss Belvedere or I will be testing you on it at that time. For tonight you should read the section on locker drill – Miss Belvedere is very specific in these matters, and no exceptions will be made. That will be all. Your hair, by the way, is unacceptable. It must be tied back properly, or cut short. Go and see Matron about it.'

Celandine said 'Yes, Miss Craven,' and picked up the booklet. She glanced once again at the glass case, and at the otter with the fish in its jaws. Then she realized that it was the stuffed fish that had seemed out of place. It was a mackerel. A mackerel was a sea fish, wasn't it? Surely that couldn't be right.

'Was there something you wanted to say?' The dark eyebrows were once again raised in query.

'No, Miss Craven.'

'Then you may go. Dismissed.'

There had been no reason to assume that Nina would still be waiting outside the headmistress's office, but it was nevertheless a slight disappointment to find her no longer there. Celandine walked back into the main entrance hall and hesitated for a few moments. She supposed that she ought to return to the dormitory, but then decided that she was in no great hurry after all. Perhaps she would explore instead.

She wandered the now deserted corridors of the ground floor, pausing to look at the green baize noticeboards that still carried redundant games fixtures from the previous term – lists of unfamiliar names, and activities. '*The Dipper Club will NOT be meeting this Thursday. Please note.*' What on earth could the Dipper Club be?

Celandine peeped into those rooms where the doors were ajar, classrooms for the most part, and looked apprehensively at the rows of iron-framed desks, each with its bench seat neatly raised. She smelled the smells that the long months of summer vacation could never erase – paper-glue and chalk dust, pencil sharpenings and musty textbooks, ink-stained floorboards, and the toil of generations. One of these desks would be hers perhaps, her allotted cell, and here she would sit . . . or there . . . or there . . . in the weeks that spanned the unimaginable distance between now and Christmas.

The last classroom that Celandine wandered into turned out to be occupied by a couple of older girls – who quickly brought her out of her reverie.

'Where do you think you're going, you little squit? This is the fifth-form room! Get out!'

One of the two, a very spotty girl, shied a tennis ball at her, which missed and bounced out into the corridor. At the same moment a bell began to ring, a harsh and urgent clamour, and Celandine fled the room, dodging the grey tennis ball as it rebounded back through the doorway. The terrible clanging seemed like an alarm, warning everyone of her trespass onto forbidden territory, but as Celandine ran along the corridor she realized that of course it was only the supper bell. How silly of her. She slowed her pace to a walk and tried to appear as if she knew where she was going. But then the bell stopped ringing and, as the chaotic echoes still jangled in her head, a strange sensation came over her – a tingling to the very roots of her hair. Celandine came to a dead halt, right in the middle of the corridor. She had seen something. She had glanced through the open doorway of one of the classrooms in passing, and she had seen something – a figure standing by a far window. A girl. The girl had been on the other side of the room, half turning from the window and looking expectantly towards the door. Waiting for someone to arrive. It was the girl with the strange hair, the one that she had seen looking out of her bedroom at Mill Farm. She had been holding something in her hands – a cup? – and her mode of dress was quite extraordinary: brightly coloured trousers and a striped shirt that had no sleeves.

Celandine remained in the middle of the corridor, quite unable to move, although she was now aware of quick footsteps approaching her from behind. She felt a dull thud on the back of her head, which made her jump out of her skin, and the two big fifth-form girls overtook her, one on either side. The spotty girl had given her a passing clip with the tennis ball.

'Hurry along, squit. You'll be late for supper.'

Celandine automatically put her hand to her head in annoyance, but ignored the two fifth-formers and turned instead to look towards the open doorway. What *was* it that she had seen? A curious shivery feeling stole about her shoulders, but she finally found the courage to step backwards a couple of paces and peep in to the room. Nothing. Just rows of empty desks. Twice, now, she had seen that ghostly figure, and twice it had disappeared. Well, three times, if she were to count that business when she had sat for the photograph . . .

What was happening to her? What could it possibly mean? Chattering voices in the main entrance hall drew her attention back to the present and she began to make her way along the corridor once more. She must go in to supper.

There was no need to ask for directions – all she had to do was join the gathering crowd and allow herself to be swept along by the confusion of it all.

The dining hall turned out to be a large single-storey wooden building, separate from the main school. Bright gas lights shone down upon rows of long tables and benches that ran down the centre of the hall, and these were already filling up with schoolgirls as Celandine arrived. At the far end of the room was a single long table, not yet occupied. Celandine didn't know what she was supposed to do, and so she spoke to a girl who appeared to be about the same age as herself.

'Can you tell me where I should sit? Only it's my first day, you see . . .'

'Well, what form are you in?'

'Third form. I think.'

'Same as me. Come on. It's just over here.'

Celandine followed the girl past two or three of the long rows and was shown to where the third form sat. She recognized some of the girls that had been in the dormitory, Mary Swann among them, but they were at the far end of the table and they took no notice of her. She looked around for Nina Jessop, but couldn't see her anywhere.

'You might as well sit next to me,' said the girl. 'What's your name?'

'Howard.' How strange that sounded.

'I'm Jane Reiss. What dorm are you in?'

'Hardy.'

'Oh. I'm in Wyndham. We're all Wyndham down at this end. The Hardys are all at the other end. You'd be better sitting with them in future. It's not a rule, though.'

'I've a brother called Wyndham. Only we call him Freddie.'

'How funny.'

But then somebody shouted out 'Rise!' and there was a general scraping and shuffling as everyone clambered over the bench seats and stood up. All talking had ceased and there was an expectant silence. After a few moments a side door opened and a procession of teachers entered the room, with Miss Craven at the head. The teachers walked in single file to the top table, where they stood in a line, half a dozen of them, their long black gowns making them look like a row of jackdaws, Celandine thought.

Miss Craven surveyed the motionless ranks of assembled schoolgirls . . . and waited. For what, Celandine wondered? The cold gaze of the headmistress fell upon her and the dark brows lifted slightly in query. Celandine suddenly realized that all those about her had their heads bowed and their eyes closed. She quickly dropped her head and squeezed her eyelids tight shut.

A few more moments, and then the deep voice spoke.

'For what we are about to receive, may the Lord make us truly thankful.'

'Amen.'

There was shuffling once again as all took their places, and then a low murmur of conversation, more subdued now that there were teachers present.

The Wyndham girls were a little friendlier towards her than those in her own dormitory had been. They asked her what her name was and where she was from, and what on earth had possessed her parents to consign her to a dump like Mount Pleasant. They laughed at her book of rules and regulations – The Epistles, they called it – and told her she'd be a month learning it all. Bloodcurdling warnings, they gave her, as to the kind of punishments meted out to those who strayed, and they pointed out those teachers who were the most zealous in wielding the strap, which information Celandine took with a pinch of salt. But, inevitably, the Wyndham girls had more to say to each other than they did to her, and Celandine was eventually left to eat her meal in silence.

Platefuls of watery-looking fish pie were passed along the line from the end of the table, where a prefect sat dividing the contents of a large metal tray into more or less equal portions. Tureens of cauliflower and carrots were delivered to the tables by members of the kitchen staff, and serving spoons were provided so that the girls could help themselves. The vegetables were very overcooked and there were hardly enough to go round, so that by the time the tureen reached Celandine there were just two bits of carrot and a few damp scraps of cauliflower left. She fared a little better with the pudding, tapioca, but this was because several of the girls turned their noses up at it altogether. 'Frogspawn', they called it.

When the meal was over, all rose once more and Miss Craven said Grace, followed by the Lord's Prayer.

She, and most of the teachers, then left the room – but the girls remained where they were. One of the teachers was still standing at the top table, and apparently had a few words of her own to add. She was a great buttress of a woman, very heavily jowled, with shiny black hair that was scraped mercilessly back into a tight bun. Her upper lip was noticeably dark, even from the distance where Celandine stood, and her hips looked as broad and as powerful as those of a rhino.

'Who's that?' whispered Celandine.

The girl Jane Reiss leaned slightly towards her, and muttered from the corner of her mouth. 'Miss Belvedere – 'ware The Bulldog.'

Celandine nodded – she could have guessed as much – but there immediately came a great bellow from the end of the room.

'*Reiss!* Were you *talking*?'

'Please, miss, no, miss. I mean . . . well, I was just telling this new girl your name, miss.'

'My name? She'll learn my name soon enough, girl! And *you'll* learn not to speak without permission. Outside the staffroom, immediately after this.'

'Yes, miss.'

'Yes, miss. And what *is* my name, Reiss? As you seem intent upon helping others, perhaps you'd like to tell *all* the new girls who I am.'

'Miss Belvedere, miss.'

'That's right. Miss Belvedere! I am the Lower School house-mistress, which means – for the benefit of all you first-formers, and any others who are new to the school – that you are in my care. It is I who have the responsibility of making sure that you are all tucked into your beds at night. It is I who have the responsibility of making sure that you are properly dressed, that your kit is all in order, and that you are generally fit to be seen. And it is I to whom you should come if you have any questions, although I might warn you that I don't encourage a lot of foolish questions. All new girls will have been given a book of rules. Learn these by heart, do as you're told, and there should be no need for questions.' Here Miss Belvedere picked up a piece of paper from the table in front of her and consulted it for a few moments.

'I have a few points to make before you get ready for locker inspection. Item one. You will have noticed that during the holidays some improvements have been made. We now have the electrical lighting installed in the main school building. On no account shall any girl, other than Head Girl, be allowed to touch any part of this.

'Item two. We have begun the building of the new swimming pool. This will be ready for use by the spring term, although it cannot be guaranteed that the war with Germany and Austro-Hungary will not affect these plans. Miss Craven will be addressing the school on the subject of the war during Monday's morning assembly. For the time being, the workmen are here – and I need hardly remind you that there will be no communication between any girl and any of these men.

'Now you will go to your dormitories and wait for inspection – apart from you, Reiss, who will attend a short interview with me. Dismiss!'

After a final glare about the room, Miss Belvedere

grasped the lapels of her gown and strode towards the door.

'Oh, bad luck, Jane!' The girls who had been standing in the immediate vicinity of Jane Reiss offered their sympathies as soon as the terrifying Miss Belvedere had left the dining hall.

'First night back, too.'

'The wretched old Bulldog's worse than ever.'

Jane Reiss said nothing, but took a deep and shaky breath. She looked very pale.

'I'm so sorry,' said Celandine. It hadn't really been her fault, but she felt guilty nevertheless.

Still Jane didn't reply, but began to make her way towards the exit, her head up and her eyes unnaturally bright.

'What will happen to her?' Celandine asked one of the girls who had been close by.

'The swish, of course. Should have been you, you little dummy.'

The swish? What was the swish – the strap? So, had the earlier stories of beatings on the palm of the hand really been true? Celandine miserably followed the crowd, feeling that any friendliness that the Wyndham girls might have offered was now very definitely withdrawn.

When Celandine entered the dormitory, she felt that the atmosphere there was even more hostile towards her than it had been previously.

Mary Swann spoke up straight away. 'Well, I wouldn't be in your shoes, Howard, not if you paid me to wear them.'

'Why not?' said Celandine. 'I've done nothing wrong.'

'Haven't you? Getting Jane Reiss into trouble wasn't a very clever idea. Prickly lot, some of those Wyndham kids. Likely to give you a scragging, I should say.'

There were murmurs of agreement at this, and one or two dark mutterings.

'Yes. Better watch your step.'

'Especially in the heads.'

'What are the heads?' said Celandine.

'Washrooms.'

'Oh. Well, it wasn't *my* fault – and anyway, it's none of your business.' Celandine walked over to her bed, feeling now that she hated this place and everyone in it. What was the matter with them all? She glowered at Nina Jessop, who was perched on the iron footrail of her own bed, staring at the floor as though distancing herself from all that was going on. The ninny. The nincompoop.

Mary Swann and the fair-haired girl, Alicia Tremlett, seemed disinclined to let the matter drop. They moved in closer towards Celandine, and Alicia said, 'You'll soon learn, Howard, to be careful how you speak to us . . .' But then the girl whose bed was nearest the door, and whose job it obviously was to act as lookout, hissed ''Ware Bulldog!' and everyone immediately scuttled back to their places.

The dormitory had gone completely quiet, but there was no sound to be heard from the corridor, no warning footsteps to herald the arrival of the house-mistress. Miss Belvedere's sudden appearance in the doorway was accompanied by the merest rustle of her long black gown. This she swept back so that she stood with her hands on her broad hips, rocking to and fro on the heels of her stout brogues.

She scanned the silent room, then gave the girl by the door a long and suspicious look. 'I wonder you don't join the Nature Scouts, Fletcher. You seem to have the necessary observation skills.'

'Miss?'

'No matter. Stand by your beds, please.'

Miss Belvedere walked to the centre of the room, and brandished a copy of the Rules and Regulations. 'You should all know the drill by now – but I believe it's as well to re-acquaint ourselves at the start of each term. That way there will be no misunderstandings.'

Her eye fell upon Celandine.

'New girl,' she said. 'What is your name?'

'Howard, miss.'

'Howard. And have you been instructed in locker drill, Howard?'

'Yes, miss.'

'And do you have the rules and regulations off by heart?'

'No, miss. Not yet, miss.'

'But you will by Monday morning – yes?'

'Yes, miss.'

'Yes indeed. In the meantime you shall read them aloud. This will instruct you, and it will serve to remind others. Take this copy, turn to page twelve and begin, please.'

Celandine took the offered booklet and fumbled her way through it, searching for page twelve.

'*Rule number one,*' Celandine read, '*No food or drink shall be kept in any locker at any time. This is strictly forbidden. Personal possessions of value, such as money or . . .*' She hesitated. But the orange . . . and the sweets! They had told her to put those things there! She looked up at Miss Belvedere, decided against saying anything, and struggled to continue.

'*. . . such as money or jewellery are also forbidden.*' The half-crown they had also persuaded her to put in the locker. There was nothing she could do about it.

'*Two. Top drawer. The top drawer is for toiletries alone. Sponge-bag, hairbrush, toothbrush, tooth powder, soap-dish, facecloth and hand towel are required items. Plain hairclips are permitted.*' But she had put all those things away in no particular order. It was obvious now, that Mary Swann's intention had been to try to get her into as much trouble as possible.

'*Three. The middle drawer. The middle drawer is for clean undergarments, stockings and nightclothes. House tie and sash must also be kept here.*' Should she say something? No. Carry on.

'*Four. Bottom drawer. The bottom drawer is for clean tunics, blouses, and school cardigan. Woollen gloves (navy blue) may also be kept here (Winter Term only).*

'*N.B. Locker Drill will take place each Saturday evening at 7 p.m. but also at the House-mistress's discretion.*'

Miss Belvedere held out her hand and Celandine stopped reading. She closed the booklet and passed it back.

'We'll start with you then, Fletcher.' Miss Belvedere walked over to the girl who slept next to the door. 'Let us see whether your locker drill is as smart as your lookout drill, shall we?'

The distance between the beds was narrow and Miss Belvedere had to turn sideways slightly in order to accommodate herself in the gap. From where Celandine was standing she could see little of what was going on – the bulky rear-view of the house-mistress obscured her line of vision – but she could hear the locker drawers being opened and closed. For a brief and wild moment she wondered if she could remove the forbidden articles from her own locker whilst Miss Belvedere's back was turned, but quickly saw that it was hopeless. And anyway, her things were in such a jumble that there was no possibility of putting them right. She looked at Molly Fletcher, who stood very upright at the end of her bed, staring straight ahead of her. There was an expression of such apprehension on the girl's face that Celandine felt her own heart sink even further. *Why* had she let herself be fooled in this way? She glanced furiously across at Mary Swann and the stupid Pigtail Twins, but they also stood rigidly staring ahead – though it was very obvious that they were smirking to themselves.

Miss Belvedere straightened up and shuffled back along the space between the first two beds. She glanced at the girl, Fletcher, and said, 'Pass.' Celandine saw Fletcher's shoulders sag with relief as the house-mistress moved on to the next victim.

The following two lockers also passed muster, and

so did the third, but then, as an afterthought, Miss Belvedere stepped back into the space that she had just occupied – not to re-examine the locker, but to inspect the bed. She lifted the pillow, paused for a moment, and then reached forward, a look of grim triumph on her large downy face.

'And what might *this* be?' She held aloft a small glass object that had some sort of bulbous attachment.

'It's a . . . a scent spray, miss.' The girl whose pillow it had been did not look round. She continued to stare at the opposite wall, her face growing redder as Miss Belvedere slowly backed out from between the beds and positioned herself in front of the girl.

'A scent spray?' Miss Belvedere put the delicate object to her nose. She gently squeezed the bulb and sniffed. '*Very* pretty, dear. And is the top real *silver?*' Her voice was horribly oily and calm.

'Yes, miss.' The girl was shaking, obviously terrified.

'Very pretty.' Miss Belvedere drew back slightly, and then struck. '*Con-fis-ca-ted!*' Her face shot forward so quickly and her voice was such a sudden bellow that the whole room jumped, though they had all known it was coming. The girl's head snapped back and she staggered against the footrail of her bed.

'*Outside* the staffroom – *now!* Wait for me there! I'll deal with *you* once I've inspected the Senior girls! *Now!* Scent spray indeed!' The girl regained her balance and stumbled from the room, her face distorted with anguish.

Celandine felt herself beginning to quake. One

more inspection – Nina Jessop was next in line – and then it would be her turn. Miss Belvedere savagely attacked Nina's locker, yanking open the drawers and rummaging through the contents. Celandine could hear the bang and rattle of the process, but dared not turn to look. Her tongue was dry and her heart was thumping so much that it hurt.

'Pass.' The verdict was finally delivered and the terrible woman sounded almost disappointed. Nina had obviously done a good job on her own locker, Celandine thought bitterly, but had never offered *her* any help, even though Matron had asked her to.

She took a deep breath as Miss Belvedere bristled past her and made her way between the beds. Even now Celandine wanted to blurt out the truth – it wasn't me, it wasn't me, it was *them*. But she held her tongue instead, and waited for the sky to fall in.

Bang – the first drawer was open and Celandine drew her shoulders up, tensing herself against the inevitable storm. More bangs and rattles from behind her, and the rustling and bustling of impatient hands, delving through her possessions. Then a pause. No movement, just a long and aching silence. The opposite wall began to shimmer alarmingly and the heavy door seemed to ripple as though it were a curtain.

A final squeak of a drawer, and then; 'Pass.'

Celandine felt her knees buckle and she had to steady herself against the bedrail. Pass? She pressed her calves and her fingertips to the cool metal, desperately trying to stay upright. *Pass?*

'Stand up *straight*, girl! What on earth's the matter with you?' Miss Belvedere drew level with her and barked in her face before turning her attention to the next bed.

Celandine continued to struggle through the fog of confusion that filled her head. How could this be? She risked a dazed backward glance at her locker, as though that stolid little object might be able to explain itself to her. The drawers were closed, of course, and whatever secrets it held were invisible to her. Well, *somebody* must have . . . what? . . . removed the forbidden objects? Rearranged the contents properly? Who?

Miss Belvedere had moved on several times before Celandine eventually turned to look wonderingly at Nina. Of course. It could only have been Nina. And yet Nina stared determinedly ahead and gave no flicker of acknowledgement to her questioning glances. It *must* have been her, though. When they were all at supper, perhaps? Had she stayed behind then? But why? And where would she have hidden the . . .

'So!'

Here was more trouble. Miss Belvedere was standing by the locker of one of the twins, Chloe, or perhaps it was Daphne, and once again there was a note of triumph in her voice. She held up a crumpled little paper bag. To most of the girls the contents of that bag would have been a mystery, but Celandine quickly realized what was in there – barley twist. The expression on the face of the girl, Daphne, or perhaps it was Chloe, was one of absolute shock. She couldn't have looked more surprised and horrified if Miss Belvedere had hauled a dead cat from her locker.

'But please, miss, I—'

'*Si-lence!* How long have you been at this school, Willis?'

'Please, miss, two years, miss, but I—'

'*Si-leeeeence!* Two *years?* Two years, and you *still* haven't grasped the rules? *Outside* the staffroom *now!*'

The girl had certainly been at the school long enough to realize that it was both useless and dangerous to argue with Miss Belvedere, and with a final pitiful wail of 'But miii-iisss . . .' she ran from the room.

As Miss Belvedere approached the next locker, Celandine felt a sense of inevitability as to what would happen next. She watched in fear and awe as the Bulldog sniffed out the half-eaten chocolate bar that had lately been in her own drawer, and displayed it for all to see. The second twin's thinking processes were no quicker than the first, and she in turn looked aghast at the discovery – and made the same mistake of protesting her absolute innocence. Like her sister before her, she had been taken completely by surprise.

But Mary Swann, at least, had begun to understand what was happening.

As Chloe, or perhaps it was Daphne, was also despatched in tears to wait outside the staffroom, Mary Swann fixed Celandine with a look of hatred. Mary showed no surprise as her own locker was inspected and discovery was made of the last piece of contraband, the orange. Whilst Miss Belvedere held the orange aloft, a bright bauble in her pudgy hand, Mary Swann continued to stare at Celandine.

Celandine met her gaze and saw it shift slightly – saw a shadow of puzzlement in the dark scowl, and then a flicker of realization. Before Miss Belvedere had even come to the end of her final tirade, Mary Swann was already moving towards the exit. She was resigned to her fate, but she knew who had brought this about. Yes, she knew. In passing, her vengeful glare was directed not at Celandine, but at Nina Jessop.

Miss Belvedere waited until Mary Swann had left the room. 'A poor start,' she said, and there was a long moment of grim silence as she studied each girl in turn. 'A *very* poor start. I wonder how many more of you I shall need to interview before lights-out.' She glanced at the clock on the end wall and frowned. 'Wilson, is your locker properly packed?'

'Yes, miss.'

'And yours, Wyatt?'

'Yes, miss.'

'No stray bottles of lavender water? No mysterious quantities of coconut ice waiting to be discovered?'

'No, miss.'

'No, miss.'

'Very well. I must take your word for it – there have been far too many delays already. You will change into your nightclothes, all of you, in *silence*. You will go to the washroom in *silence*. And you will return here and wait for lights-out in *silence*. I shall be back once I have dealt with the unhappy band of smugglers downstairs, and have inspected the Senior girls – and if I hear a *peep* out of any of you in the meantime, then there will be trouble. And I *mean* trouble. Is that clear?'

'Yes, miss.' A faint and dismal chorus.

'Oh, and Fletcher,' Miss Belvedere paused by the door, 'if I see your ugly little head poking out into the corridor when I return, then its next public appearance is likely to be on a spike above the school gates. Do we understand one another?'

'Yes, miss.'

The silence held whilst the girls put on their night-gowns. Celandine dumbly copied the actions of those around her; folding her tunic neatly and laying it on top of her locker, taking her sponge-bag from the top drawer, carrying her shoes out into the corridor and placing them at the end of the row, ready for cleaning. She followed the subdued procession to the huge brightly lit washroom, took her turn at one of the great square porcelain basins, studied the crazed patterns of blue cracks in the enamel as she lowered her head to brush her teeth. Still nobody spoke. She waited in line for an available lavatory cubicle, looked at the initials scratched on the outside of the mahogany panelled doors, and then at more initials scratched on the inside, as she sat alone and wondered how much more alone she could ever feel.

Perhaps she could sit here for ever and never have to come out and face the world again. Perhaps she could just stare at the scratched lavatory door for the rest of her days. '*DH is a sneak*'. Who was DH? It could stand for Dinah Howard – Freddie always called her Dinah. What was Freddie doing now, at his school? Was he as miserable as she was?

Something had happened outside the cubicle. The silence had changed. It wasn't simply the lack of talking – all movement had now ceased as well. There was no brushing of teeth, no swill of water in the basins, nothing but the rhythmic drip of a cistern in one of the other cubicles ... *pip* ... *pip* ... *ta-pip* ... *pip*. What was happening? Celandine stood up, listening intensely, fully expecting that the door would burst open and that she would be attacked.

Another sound, very faint and distant, and Celandine felt herself flinch instinctively. Again. And again. The sounds drifted up from far below, whispered through the corridors, vibrated along the water pipes of the hushed washroom; *shwack* ... *shwack* ...

Celandine gently opened the cubicle door. Pale and motionless they stood, the Hardy dormitory girls, frozen into random poses around the central block of washbasins. Pink tooth powder foamed at their lips and trickled down their chins unheeded, giving them the grisly appearance of hungry animals, poised for the kill. And their eyes – dark eyes, pale eyes, blue and brown – all of them were wide open, and all of them were looking at her.

Still nothing was said. The whole room was listening and waiting.

And now here was another sound: uneven

footsteps, hurrying, half-running along the empty corridors. The spell was broken and the girls seemed to come back to life. Heads turned towards the doorway as the twins appeared – one behind the other, their tear-strewn faces screwed up into identical expressions of pain, shoulders hunched forward and forearms crossed, fists pressed into their armpits.

'Here, Chloe!'

'Daph – over here! Over here!'

The twins stumbled across the washroom and plunged their hands into the basins of cool water that the other girls had prepared for them. With heads hanging down, they jiggled from one foot to the other, gasping and choking as the group gathered round them.

'Nan – over here! Quick!'

The 'scent spray' girl had entered the room in a similar state, and Celandine watched as she too was helped towards a waiting basin, her long auburn hair obscuring her face as she leaned forward to thrust her hands into the water.

Celandine saw that Nina Jessop stood apart from the rest, clutching her sponge-bag. How frail and vulnerable she looked. Her eyes were cast downwards, staring at the green linoleum that was now wet with splashes from the overflowing basins. She seemed to have cut herself off from what was happening around her – or perhaps she was contemplating the enormity of what she had done. For Celandine was now more certain than ever that it had been Nina who had tidied up her locker and distributed the contents among those who had tried to get her into trouble. Why would she risk such a thing, though? They were hardly friends.

Mary Swann was in the room. Celandine hadn't seen her come in, but here she was – surrounded, as the others had been, by willing helpers.

'Here's a basin, Mary! Quickly – over here!'

But Mary would have none of it. She shrugged off the arms that reached out to comfort her, and ignored the washbasin that had been filled in readiness.

'I'm all right.'

Instead she stood with her hands raised to her mouth and gently blew onto her open palms, taking her time. The two spots of colour on her broad cheeks were the only indication of any pain that she might have been feeling.

Celandine waited, knowing that Mary would eventually look her way, and that trouble would surely follow. Mary did indeed look at her, but only momentarily – a dark flash of bitterness over the top of her hands as she continued to blow on them. Then the vengeful gaze shifted away from Celandine and beyond her, to where Nina Jessop stood.

'I know it was you, Ninky.'

Celandine looked around at Nina. The girl was plainly terrified, her face pinched and pebble-white. Her cotton nightdress was too big, and it made her seem thinner than ever, the square yoke hanging precariously on her slight shoulders. Nina made no sound, and no movement, but still kept her eyes fixed on the wet floor in front of her.

Celandine turned towards Mary Swann once more and was struck by the contrast between the two girls. It seemed hardly possible that they were of the same species, let alone the same age.

Mary, broad and sturdy, still dressed in her dark school tunic and heavy black shoes, moved forward. She was now threateningly close to Celandine, but she continued to look at Nina.

'I *know* it was you, Ninky, so you might as well confess. Not that it'll help you much. Shall I tell you what I'm going to do?'

'I don't know what you're talking about,' muttered Nina. Her head was down and her words were only just audible.

'Don't you? I think you do. See that basin of water? I'm going to push your stupid head into that basin, *Jessop*, and I'm going to hold it there. Yes, and I shall keep on holding it there until you jolly well drown. I'm going to drown you, *Jessop*, like a rat in a bucket. I shall—'

'No you shan't.'

Celandine heard herself say the words. They were out before she'd had chance to think about it, before she had even begun to consider the consequences. *No you shan't.* Then, to make matters worse, she said, 'And anyway, it wasn't Nina. It was me.'

Mary Swann gaped at her, the scowling eyebrows rising into an arch of astonishment.

'What?'

Celandine edged sideways a little, so that she was in between Nina and Mary. 'I said, it was me.'

She found that she wasn't afraid. She *ought* to be afraid, but she wasn't – and the hesitation she now saw upon Mary's ugly face made her bolder still.

'*I* put those things in your lockers – and it serves you right, too.' She stretched her luck yet further by taking a deliberate step towards the big girl. 'You tried to get me into trouble on purpose – telling me that I was to keep food in my locker, and . . . and the money . . . and making me do everything wrong. You did everything you *could* to get me into trouble – and so I did exactly the same to you. And now you can't blame *me* if Miss Belvedere gave you the switch, or the swash, or the swish, or whatever the stupid thing is.' A couple of the girls sniggered at this.

Mary had stepped back a pace, an instinctive reaction to Celandine's advance, but now began to recover herself.

'*You?* How could it have been you? I don't believe you.'

'I don't care whether you believe me or not. It was me.'

'Well *when*, then? You were at supper with everyone else. When would you have had the time?'

'It doesn't matter when. It was me.'

Mary Swann was plainly unused to any such confrontation. She was big and she was strong, and smaller weaker girls simply did not behave towards her in this manner. She looked confused. And yet, with her classmates around her, watching her, it would be

189

impossible for her to back down. She nodded her head slowly, as if coming to a decision, and some of the other girls moved in a little closer.

Celandine forged blindly ahead, relying on heaven knew what instinct.

'So perhaps you'd better try and drown me instead. Go on then, if you like. Try it.'

It was a bluff – but such tactics had been known to work. Many a time Celandine had watched one of the skinny farm cats see off Cribb, the great lurcher, just by standing its ground and hissing defiance. Yes, she had seen it succeed. But she had also seen it fail – for where Cribb might be deflected, the other dog, Jude, would not. Nothing would stop Jude.

Celandine stood with her arms straight by her side. She clenched her fists and saw Mary glance down at them, as if gauging her determination. A moment of hesitation perhaps, but only so that the coming attack could be better judged.

'Get her, Mary . . .' A whispered urge of encouragement from one of the other girls – Alicia perhaps – and once again Mary nodded. Celandine clenched her fists tighter.

She had one more gambit, one last barricade to hide behind, and there was no time to consider what might follow.

'You know why I was sent to this place, don't you, Mary?' Already she was regretting her hurried decision, but it was too late to stop. 'I was sent here as a punishment. Do you know what I did?'

Mary Swann, caught off-guard again, was obliged to answer.

'No. What?'

'I stabbed my governess.'

The words bounced off the walls of the washroom, and the echoes quickly faded into a horrified silence. She had said it. The awful phrase hung there, still audible somehow, long after its departure. *Pip . . . pip . . . ta-pip . . . pip.* The drip of the cistern crept into the empty space and danced its solemn jig. Nobody moved. Celandine pressed home her advantage – there seemed no point in backing out now.

'So if you think that I'm frightened of *you*, Mary Swann . . .' She looked about the room, hearing the shock of her own voice, booming back at her. '. . . or of any of you . . .'

The girls seemed to emerge from their trance, and the ones who had moved in closer now shrank back. Yet still they were silent. This was the unknown. They were on dark and unfamiliar ground, with a creature that apparently dealt in acts of violence far beyond their imagining. They looked at her in wary speculation, as though she might have knives or daggers concealed beneath the thin folds of her nightgown – weapons that might be drawn forth and used upon them at any moment.

One of Celandine's feet felt damp. Water from the washroom floor must have seeped through the thin leather soles of her carpet slippers. She should move, yet she found herself unwilling to do so – as though it might break the spell.

'Most commendable.' The loud voice made everybody jump. Miss Belvedere was standing in the doorway. 'I see that for once my words appear to have had some effect, and that you have finally understood that silence means silence. Perhaps my toil is not in vain, after all. You girl – Howard – is there any reason why you should be standing in a puddle? No matter. Back to your dormitory, all of you. Lights out in four minutes. Go.'

Miss Belvedere remained half in and half out of the doorway, and every girl automatically ducked as they brushed past her.

As she clambered into her unfamiliar bed, Celandine remembered Nina's curious warning about the 'apple-pie'. She cautiously wriggled her legs down between the chilly sheets, half expecting to find herself up to her ankles in sticky fruit and pastry, but all seemed normal. She caught an exchange of glances between Mary and the twins, and it was clear that some other plan of theirs had been foiled. By Nina?

Nina still would not meet her eye. Either she was protecting herself by refusing any contact, or she was as horrified as everyone else by what she had heard in the washroom.

Miss Belvedere had followed the silent troupe of girls to the dormitory and waited whilst the four she had lately 'interviewed' got changed into their nightgowns. She stood near the door with her hand on the electric light switch. Where once it had been necessary to extinguish the gas mantles one by one, it was now miraculously possible to turn all the lights out with a single movement.

'Who is on bell duty this week?' she asked.

Molly Fletcher, the girl by the door, spoke up. 'I am, miss.'

'Well, don't forget that it's Sunday lie-in. First bell at seven-thirty.'

'Yes, miss.'

'And I very much hope that I shall not have occasion to speak to any of you before then. Absolute silence, *if* you please, between now and first bell.'

Miss Belvedere took one last long look around the room, making sure that all heads were on pillows, and that all eyes appeared to be closed. 'Very well. Good night, Hardy.'

'Goodnight Miss Belvedere.' A last sorrowful chant, and in an instant the room was dark.

There was a faint creak from the door-hinge, but no sound of the latch clicking into place. Miss Belvedere might be lurking outside even now, and consequently there was no talking or whispering.

Celandine lay curled up on her side for a while with her eyes closed, yet knew that she wouldn't sleep. The bed was as lumpy and uncomfortable as she had supposed it would be, and the strangeness of her surroundings was impossible to ignore. She eventually rolled over onto her back and rested her hands behind her head, staring upwards into the shadowy darkness. The heavy wooden shutters had been drawn across the high windows, but a little light still penetrated here and there. It was only early

September, and not quite dark outside. Celandine could just make out the black lines of the roof beams, and the shape of a redundant gas fitting mounted on the wall above her bed.

What was she doing here? She listened to the sighs and rustles and muffled coughs of the other girls, and it felt as though her own quiet room at Mill Farm was a million miles away, and that she had left it months ago, rather than hours. For that was all it had been, a dozen hours, and in that time she had probably succeeded in making a dozen enemies. Could any day have seemed longer, or gone more badly? Yes, she thought – the day that Tobyjug had died. That had been worse than this. And the day that she had attacked Miss Bell had seemed longer – the day that began so horribly, and yet ended so magically.

So magically.

Yes, she would think of that. She still had her secret, her strange and wonderful secret, and nobody could take that away from her. She would hold that secret to her, and hug it in the darkness, and though every hand might be against her – Miss Craven and Miss Belvedere, Mary Swann and the stupid Pigtail Twins, and the whole jumbled up lot of them – they could never take that secret away. She had seen things that they would never see. She knew things that they would never know. She was special.

Her eyelids began to droop, and she eventually left the snuffles and creaks of the restless dormitory behind. Once more she sat beneath the trees on

Howard's Hill on the day she had attacked Miss Bell, watching in tear-blurred amazement as Fin dropped from the overhanging boughs to crouch awkwardly before her, clasping his hands in child-like anxiety, wanting to help her and not knowing how.

Chapter Eight

Perrott's Orchard and Five Springs are out of bounds to all Juniors except as part of supervised Hare and Hounds . . . The Bell Monitor Rota is posted on the noticeboard outside Tratt . . .

What on earth was Tratt? It didn't matter – just try and memorize it, along with all the other rules and regulations.

'Come in!'

Celandine pushed open the staffroom door in response to the muffled summons from within, and nearly tripped over a Sealyham terrier that was apparently keen to leave.

'Don't let him out!' Miss Belvedere's voice thundered across the room from somewhere amidst the noisy huddle of black-gowns at the far end.

Another girl was present, just inside the doorway – Molly Fletcher – but it was Celandine who automatically reached down and grabbed the dog's collar. The little animal came to a halt without much of a struggle. It looked up at her for a moment, a vague glance from eyes that seemed filmy and dull, and then stood still, head down, listless. Celandine waited awkwardly, holding onto the stiff leather collar as Miss Belvedere crossed the room. One or two of the teachers turned to stare at her.

The dog was shivering. Celandine could feel the tremor of it against her knuckles. A curious feeling came over her, a chilly moment of darkness that drifted by her and then passed on. There was a funny smell about the little animal, and a sudden image of Tobyjug came back to her, lying white and still on the stable floor.

'Carol – basket!' Miss Belvedere came to the doorway, and pointed backwards into the room. Celandine let go of the dog's collar, and straightened up. The terrier wandered off a few paces, but then stopped once more and looked around uncertainly.

'Basket!' Again Miss Belvedere barked out her command and the dog moved away a little further.

'Now then – Howard, isn't it? Let us see how productively you have spent your first Sunday at Mount Pleasant. What do we never do in corridors?'

'Loiter or run, Miss Belvedere.'

'And where must we keep our tuck boxes?'

'In the . . . in the common room, Miss Belvedere.' The dog – Carol – was now walking in circles. It didn't look at all happy.

'And when may we whistle?'

'Um . . . never. Under no . . . um . . . no . . .'

'Circumstances. Under no circumstances. On what occasion is it permitted to wear white socks . . . ?

Howard! I seem not to have your full attention! What is it that you keep *looking* at, girl?'

'Sorry, Miss Belvedere. I was . . . I was watching the dog. Your dog, I mean. I don't think it's very well.'

'My *dog*?' Miss Belvedere turned briefly. The terrier had finally decided to go to its basket and was now ambling in that direction. It seemed content enough, all of a sudden.

'Howard, if this is some ploy to distract my attention then I can assure you that I'm not so easily fooled. The dog is *perfectly* well, thank you very much – fit as a flea, in fact – and is in any case no concern of yours. School motto, *if* you please.'

'Um . . . *Venite filii, obedite mihi . . .*' The loud clatter of the Assembly bell suddenly filled the corridor outside, an urgent disorientating sound. Celandine could hardly hear herself speak. '*Timorem domini . . . um . . .*'

'Come along girl! *Timorem domini . . .*' Miss Belvedere had no difficulty in raising her own voice above the clamour of the bell.

'*Timorem domini . . . ego . . . ego vos docebo.*'

'Right. Well. We seem to have run out of time, and so that will have to do – for the moment. Off you go to Assembly. But remember, Howard, I may well decide to continue this little interview at a later date. I know something of your history, and I shall be keeping a very close eye on you. Go. Now then, Fletcher, let us see what you have learned about remaining in bed after lights out . . .'

Celandine hurried away – thankful that at least she had not been required to translate from the Latin.

Stupid language. But anyway, she had survived. She joined the jostling stream of girls who were now making their way to Assembly, and wondered at her own sad certainty about the little white terrier, Carol. The dog was dying. Why on earth did she think that?

'It should be the duty of all Mount Pleasant girls to follow the progress of Great Britain and her allies in the war against Germany and Austro-Hungary. Where there are men fighting on our behalf, our prayers shall accompany them. In mind and spirit we are at their side, and there we shall remain until the enemy is overthrown.'

Miss Craven stepped aside from the Big School lectern and grasped the lapels of her long black gown. The rest of the staff stood in a row behind her, silhouetted against the tall stained-glass window.

'Naturally I shall keep you informed as to events. Today's news is that the British army has crossed the Marne and the Germans are in retreat as a consequence. Yes – we *may* allow ourselves a brief murmur of approval and relief, but this does not mean that the war is over. There could be many more weeks of fighting to come before we are able to lay aside our arms. In the meantime you will be asking yourselves "What can *we* do, to help?" – and I shall tell you. Number one; minimize wastage . . .'

Miss Craven went on to list the ways in which materials could be saved, how she intended to set up extra sewing and knitting classes to provide the troops with socks and balaclavas, how it had been decided to exclude certain luxuries from the dinner menu. The use of hot water was now to be monitored and limited, and a correspondence was to be started, strictly regulated of course, in the form of a weekly newsletter to the local regiment – the Somersets – via the adjutant at Taunton barracks. This newsletter would bring uplifting thoughts of home to those who were battling abroad.

'And finally, we must do all that we can to boycott German goods. We shall *not* be seen to be assisting the Hun economy. All items of German origin shall be confiscated – pens, jigsaws, pocket-watches, games equipment – and no more shall be purchased or used until further notice. Now let us pray.'

Celandine closed her eyes and put her hands together. A startling image appeared before her of the stained-glass window and the figures standing in front of it. It was like a photographic negative, the window-glass darkly clouded, the lead patterns and solid mullions picked out sharply in white. The motionless figures of the teachers were also shown up in white, a ghostly tableau.

The strange picture continued to float around the corners of her vision as Assembly came to an end and she shuffled off to first lesson, lost in the murmuring crowd.

Celandine spent most of that first week expecting some sort of blow to fall upon her. Mary Swann did not seem the type to simply let bygones be bygones, and revenge for the business with the lockers was surely on its way. In the classroom Celandine felt safe enough, but on the games field, or in the changing hut, and particularly in the dim echoing corridors between the washrooms and the dormitories, she was continually prepared for the worst.

Yet nothing happened. Mary and her group of followers acted as though she were invisible. They never spoke, never acknowledged her presence. Other girls, not of Mary's set, ignored her less pointedly but kept their distance nevertheless, and treated her with extreme wariness whenever contact was unavoidable.

Nina Jessop was the only girl who would willingly talk to her, although Nina's stammered half-sentences could hardly be called talking. Really, the girl was impossible – reddening like a strawberry at every question or remark. It was rare that Nina had any observation of her own to make, or any opinion to voice that was not extracted from her as though with a corkscrew. Her words were as carefully rationed as the Thursday night bath-water. And yet she could be stubborn, in her own shy way. She continued to deny all knowledge of how Celandine's locker had come to be neatly and correctly packed, and no amount of public threatening from Mary Swann, or private cajoling from Celandine could shift her. 'I really don't know what you're talking about' was her unvarying, if blushing, response.

Mary Swann held herself back from outright physical assault, and eventually seemed to give up. Outwardly at least, she ignored both Nina and Celandine, and the others followed her example, but among her own set she began to take a slightly different tack. 'What if Ninky's telling the truth? I've heard some funny rumours, at home, about that Howard girl. They say she's not *normal.* It's very strange, isn't it, how those things just moved from locker to locker, all by themselves. Like magic. Almost like *black* magic . . .'

Nobody was quite prepared to swallow this, but it gave them something to talk about.

On the second Saturday of term, exactly a week after she had arrived, Celandine was summoned to Miss Craven's office. Miss Belvedere was also present, and together they made a formidable sight – the one seated, gaunt and pale, the other standing, buckled and belted in acres of Norfolk tweed.

'Come and stand over here, Howard.' Miss Craven looked sourly displeased. 'I have some sad news to report – sad and disturbing. Miss Belvedere has suffered a loss.'

Celandine knew instantly what was coming, and her knowledge frightened her. It was the dog, Carol. She could feel her face begin to redden.

'A most *sudden* loss, and I was very sorry to hear of it. Miss Belvedere's terrier has unexpectedly passed away.'

The headmistress stared at Celandine for a few moments, the pale grey eyes unblinking, cold as a bird's.

'The news seems to agitate you, child. I am wondering – though it barely seems credible – whether you are implicated in some way.'

Implicated? What did that mean – involved? At fault?

'N-no, Miss Craven – Miss Belvedere. How could it be my . . . anything do with me? How could it be my fault?'

'Don't question *me*, girl!' Miss Craven brought her hand down flat on the leather-bound desk. 'I'm asking *you*. Do you or do you not have any knowledge of this sad event?'

'No, Miss Craven.'

'And yet I am told that you remarked upon the dog's ill health at a time when it was apparently quite well. How do you explain this *expert* diagnosis?'

'I don't know, Miss Craven. It . . . looked ill. I just knew.'

'Nothing wrong with the animal at all, I can assure you, Miss Craven.' Miss Belvedere's booming voice filled the room. 'It was perfectly fit – *at that time.*'

'Thank you, Miss Belvedere. I shall take your word for it.' Miss Craven leaned forward in her chair. 'Well, Howard? Was this seemingly prior knowledge of yours a prediction? Or was it . . . a *threat*?'

Celandine knew that her face must be burning red. She could feel the tingle of it right through her scalp.

'No, Miss Craven, I honestly just thought that Miss

Belvedere's dog didn't seem very well. And I never saw her again after that. I haven't been near her. But I just knew. I . . . I don't know how. I'm . . . I live on a farm, you see. That's my home. I suppose I'm just used to seeing sick anim—' The thought of Tobyjug came into her head, and her eyes welled up with tears. A great wave of homesickness suddenly swept over her, choking her, drowning her, and she longed to be in her own room, in her own bed, listening to the chink of the horses' harnesses through the open window as the teams returned to the stableyard. She could say no more.

'I see. Well you can spare us your tears, Howard, whether of guilt or of remorse. I can hardly think that they are tears of mourning, for an animal you saw but the once – according to your account. However, in the light of the veterinary surgeon's report, and in the absence of any evidence to the contrary, we must accept that the animal suffered from some sort of heart ailment. Yet I still find it *extremely* suspicious that you somehow "just knew" about this illness, whereas the dog's owner, Miss Belvedere, knew of no such thing. If this incident doesn't smack of foul play, then it smacks of psychic mumbo-jumbo, neither of which will I tolerate in this school. I believe you capable of anything, Howard, and you've a long way to go before I am likely to revise that opinion. Is that understood? I hope so. Now you had better return to your lesson. And if you suffer from any further *premonitions*, you'd do well to keep them to yourself. It would be safer. Dismissed.'

'She *looks* a bit like a witch, I must say.' The lounging inhabitants of Tratt, the sixth-form study, regarded Celandine with mild interest as she stood on the mat just inside the door. Very comfortable they looked in their low cushioned chairs ranged around the cosy little fireplace. One of them was busy with a toasting fork and there was a sizeable pile of bread, sliced and ready, on a plate by the glowing hearth. A large heavy-framed mirror hung above the fireplace, and Celandine could see her own pale face reflected there as she stood in the doorway. The hair took her by surprise, as always.

'Yes, it's the hair, isn't it?' The cool eyes of the group continued to look her up and down, the neatly groomed heads tilted this way and that as they considered her.

'Tell me, child,' the girl with the toasting fork waved the thing lazily in her direction, an invitation to come closer, 'do you read tea leaves, that sort of thing?'

'Um . . . no.'

Celandine was aware of a slight rustle behind her, and in the mirror she saw the reflection of another girl entering the room, bringing with her an atmosphere of newly-ironed starch, and faintly perfumed soap. It was Aberdeen, the Head Girl.

'Hullo. What are you doing here?' Aberdeen carried an armful of large books before her, and the title of the top one stared out like a red banner – *Beethoven.*

'I . . . I don't really know,' said Celandine. 'I was told to report here.'

205

'Oh, we thought we'd better have a look at her, Gillian, that's all.' One of the girls in the armchairs stifled a yawn. 'This is the Witch – the kiddie that laid a curse on poor old Carol, you know, the Bulldog's terrier. Ha ha! That's rather good, isn't it? The Bulldog's terrier.'

'Not something we should be joking about, though.' Gillian Aberdeen walked over to a table and lowered her pile of books onto the brown velveteen cloth. 'And in any case, I don't believe it for a moment. Witches and curses, indeed. Right, that's the last of the German books from the library. Now then.' She turned to look at Celandine. 'Howard, isn't it? You've already been interviewed by Miss Craven, so I gather?'

The blue eyes of the Head Girl seemed tired, and there was a little worry-frown across her brow that looked as though it might be there permanently. Her appearance was immaculate – the pleated skirt crisply pressed, the long dark hair clipped firmly into place – but there was a distracted air about her, as though she had too many things to think about.

'Yes. I had to go and see Miss Craven this morning, during lessons.'

'Well, in that case I see no reason for you to be here. Help me with these books some of you, for goodness' sake – there's simply a ton of them to find a home for. *And* we've all these pens and things to sort through.'

'Purged of all evil German influences, are we? What a lot of nonsense this whole business is. As if we didn't have enough to do.' One or two of the fireside-loungers began to stir themselves, grumbling.

'It isn't nonsense at all.' Aberdeen sounded cross. 'We must help in whatever way we can.'

'Oh, you're such a priss, Abbers. What possible difference can it make to the war whether Tiny Lewis in form 2b uses a German nib or a British one? I'll bet the Kaiser's not scouring Bavaria for pen nibs made in *Sheffield* . . .'

'*Is* Bavaria part of Germany?'

'Here you – Witch.' The girl who knelt by the hearth spoke to Celandine, her toasting fork brandished like a demon's trident in the fireside glow. 'That's all right. You can cut along now. But if you come up with any good curses to lay upon brutal house-mistresses, then let us know – do.'

Celandine wondered why they called her Witch. She wondered also whether she would ever be eighteen, and a prefect, and allowed the privilege of making toast whenever she felt like it. It seemed doubtful, somehow.

She backed towards the doorway but then stopped, to avoid colliding with yet another girl about to enter the room – a face at her shoulder, glimpsed in the mirror opposite. It was a face she had seen before, slightly freckled, not pretty exactly . . .

Celandine quickly turned, but there was nobody there. She stood staring at the empty doorway.

'Yes, Howard? Was there something?' Aberdeen was speaking to her.

'Um . . . no, Aberdeen. Nothing.'

207

'Off you go, then.'

Celandine closed the sixth-form study door behind her and walked slowly back down the echoing stairwell.

She later assumed that the rumours of her supernatural powers had been started by Molly Fletcher. Molly had been present in the staffroom when the incident with the dog had occurred. But though she began to hear the word 'Witch' being whispered behind her back, nothing was said to her face, and most of her peers continued to ignore her.

Celandine was therefore glad of Nina's company. Whenever some activity required that girls be split into pairs – walking to church, dancing lessons, nature trips – it was a comfort not to be left standing alone. Celandine realized, with a jolt of sudden sympathy, that standing alone must so often have been Nina's lot before her own arrival at the school.

They lived a curious half-life, the two of them, thrown together by circumstance rather than choice, part of the teeming crowd of bodies that moved through the relentless routines of bed, lessons, meals and bed again – yet as separate from that crowd as the poor Siamese twins that floated in formaldehyde on the chemistry lab shelf.

Gradually they learned to understand one another and become friends. Beneath Nina's stammering shyness lay a quiet resilience that Celandine couldn't help but admire, a quality much better suited to this imprisonment than her own unpredictable temper, she felt. And Nina, so mistrustful of any offer of friendship lest it should suddenly be withdrawn, slowly allowed herself to accept that Celandine would not drop her the minute it became convenient to do so. Together they managed to survive the lonely weeks, outcasts though they were, without feeling too miserable.

As half term approached, Celandine was shocked to discover that Nina would be remaining in school for the holiday.

'My parents are in India,' said Nina. 'I've nowhere else to go. Other girls stay as well, so I'm not the only one, you see – and I've done it lots of times.'

But Celandine said that she was sure nobody would mind if Nina came back to Mill Farm with her, and so asked permission of her mother in her fort- nightly letter home. It wasn't until permission had been given that Celandine realized, with a pang of dis- appointment, what Nina's presence at Mill Farm would mean; there would be no possibility of any visits to Howard's Hill, and all her plans to do so would have to be postponed. She would not be able to go and see Fin, or any of the little people.

The little people. How far away and impossible and dreamlike that world seemed to her now.

Chapter Nine

As it happened, the weather over half term was so appalling that Celandine doubted whether she would have ventured as far as Howard's Hill in any case. The October rain swept across the wetlands and hurled itself against the rattling panes of the farmhouse, seeping in below the window frames and forming little puddles on the sills. The girls traced their names in wet fingermarks upon the painted wood and looked despondently out at the stableyard, now awash with mud and sodden straw.

They played endless games of Old Maid, and Nine Men's Morris, read to each other from *Aesop's Fables* – taking it in turns to invent the silliest of morals they could think of – and picked out the tunes from Freddie's book of *Campfire Songs* on the piano in the parlour. Freddie would not be coming home for half term, which was another blow. He was apparently going off somewhere with a school friend instead.

Once, during a fleeting break in the weather, Nina looked up at the dark hump of Howard's Hill and said, 'What's that place? It looks *very* mysterious, don't you think?' And Celandine, more to relieve the tedium than anything else, came very close to telling all. How Nina's watery eyes would widen in astonishment if only she knew just how mysterious 'that place' really was. Yet it wasn't so much the breaking of her vow that made Celandine hold her tongue, rather that she had almost ceased to believe the whole fantastic story herself. How ridiculous it seemed, that there could be a whole other world up there. At any rate, she simply said, 'Yes, I've always thought so too,' and dealt another hand of Old Maid.

'I'm sorry we can't go outside. It's a bit of a bore, when the weather's like this.'

'I'm not bored.' Nina sounded surprised at the suggestion. 'If you think this is boring, you should try staying in school for the holidays. I love being here. I wish *I* lived on a farm.'

'Really?' Again Celandine caught a glimpse of how Nina's life must have been before they had met. 'Do you miss your mother and father?'

Nina nodded, and said nothing. Celandine saw that she had touched a nerve. 'Sorry,' she said. 'Is it my go?' She laid down a card, and tried to imagine what it would be like if her own mother and father were constantly away. Would she miss them? She wasn't at all sure that she would. Was that wicked of her? She missed Freddie. And Tobyjug.

'I'm so glad you're here, Nina, honestly I am. You must come and stay every half – if you'd like to, that is. It does get a bit lonely by myself, and it's so much better if you have a . . . a friend.'

Nina nodded again, and managed to whisper, 'Yes. It is.' But now her eyes looked more watery than ever and so Celandine decided that she had probably said enough.

Ten minutes later, they looked up from their card game. The unfamiliar sound of a petrol engine came rattling into the yard, and a few moments after that two heads flashed past by the window, one of them wearing a peaked cap. Both faces were screwed up against the rain.

'Gracious,' said Nina, above the rhythmic *thumpeta-thumpeta* noise outside, 'whatever's *that?*'

Celandine looked at her blankly. 'Freddie,' she said, after a moment. 'I think one of them was Freddie. Not the one in the hat.'

They got up from their chairs and peered through the streaming window. A brief exchange of raised voices was just audible above the engine noise and the squalling wind. Then they saw a large motorcycle swing around the yard and roar towards the open gate once more – ridden by a young man in a cap and greatcoat, his passenger now no longer visible. He looked wet through. The motorcycle disappeared through the gateway in a cloud of smoke and steam.

'Come on,' said Celandine. 'Freddie's home! Don't know why, though. I thought he was supposed to be staying with someone from his school.'

They arrived in the hallway at the same time as Mrs Howard. Freddie was standing on the coconut matting, shaking the drips from his summer jacket – an entirely inadequate piece of clothing to be wearing on the back of a motorcycle in mid-October. His trousers clung to his legs, and muddy rainwater simply streamed from him onto the mat. He was carrying a small leather suitcase.

'Freddie! What is this? Are you here—? Oh, I am so glad! Give me a kiss! Come – come out of these clothes. Yes, yes, at once! I will fetch Cook for bringing a hot *bath*.'

'I've no time, Mother. No – really. I have to be gone again in three-quarters of an hour. Just popped in to get changed, you know. Hallo, Dinah! And er, hallo . . . er . . . oh, Nina is it? Hallo.'

'Changed? You are leaving again this *shortly*? Freddie – no! There are no clothes here ready, nothing is *ironed* on . . .'

'Now don't *worry*, Mother. I have a suitcase here, with clean clothes . . . won't take me a minute. Is there a towel in my room? I'll be down again directly – then I'll explain. Back in a jif. What have you done to your wrist, by the way?'

'I *boiled* it on the teapot.'

'Oh. Bad luck.'

Freddie bounded up the stairs, taking his suitcase with him. Mrs Howard and the two girls were left to stare wonderingly at one another.

'What is this place – a house for mad ones?' Lizzie Howard threw up her hands in despair. 'Accchhh! Well, he shall have some thing to eat, in whatever case. Celandine, lay a little plates in the parlour, and I shall find Cook.'

By the time they could hear Freddie coming back

downstairs, there was a tea table laid in the parlour, with a plateful of bread and butter, a dish of damson jam, half a fruit cake, and a fresh pot of tea. The parlour led directly on to the dim hallway, and something about the deliberate and measured tread of the footsteps on the stairs made them all look towards the open door. Through the banister rails they caught a shadowy glimpse of khaki and brown leather, and Mrs Howard already had her hands to her face in shock as Freddie appeared in the doorway. He was dressed in army uniform.

'No ... oh no ...' Celandine could hear her mother beside her, breathing into her cupped hands, but she could not take her eyes off Freddie. He looked ... foolish. He had scampered up the stairs an excited schoolboy, and had come back down a soldier – except that he was not a soldier. He couldn't be. He was just Freddie, dressing up again, and in a costume that didn't fit very well. It was too big.

'Jock's coming to pick me up again in half an hour.' The voice was as familiar as ever, but the booted feet sounded foreign and strange, a leathery creak as Freddie walked towards the table, and the smell of the new serge uniform was somehow ominous. Mrs Howard sat down heavily on one of the parlour chairs.

'Well, I wish somebody would jolly well *say* something.' Freddie picked up a piece of bread and butter and put a blob of jam on it. Celandine watched the knife spreading the home-made jam, saw how the tip of it carefully picked out one of the damson skins ... he never would eat the skins. She looked at the scrap of dark skin, curled up and glistening now on the side of Freddie's plate, and knew that she would remember it for ever. There was something so sad about it that she had to turn away, swallowing back the tears. She didn't want Nina to see her cry.

'Freddie . . . *no*! You are too young.' Mrs Howard had found her voice at last. 'Too *young*. You must listen to me . . .' She struggled to stand up again.

The sound of the front-door latch clicked out in the hallway and Freddie put down his plate, expectantly.

'It's too late,' he said. 'I've already enlisted.' It was apparent that he was bracing himself against his father's appearance, for when Thos put his dripping head around the door, Freddie looked relieved and picked up his plate once more.

Thos looked anything but relieved, however. He stood open-mouthed in the doorway for a few moments, then slowly began to remove his wet coat.

'What the devil's all *this*, Freddie? Did I just hear you say . . . you were enlisted? *Enlisted?* You're *sixteen*, for God's sake! How can you possibly . . . ?' He seemed to realize that he was dripping water onto the carpet. 'Wait *there*,' he said.

Freddie shot a glance at Celandine and raised his eyebrows. Thos's deep voice echoed out in the corridor. 'And anyway, it's *illegal*. You're below minimum age.'

'It's too late, I tell you,' Freddie shouted back. 'I've signed up. And what's more, I think you should do the same.'

Thos reappeared in the doorway, wiping his head and neck with a scarf, red in the face now, with fury.

'The *same*? I should do the *same*? You don't think I might have more important things to worry about, you blithering little fool? Do you imagine I have the time to go chasing around the continent with a lot of Frogs for company? There's a farm to run here, if you hadn't noticed. Perhaps *you* can afford to miss a few Latin lessons and go off on the spree, but I have to work. Now get out of that stupid uniform and go back to your school desk.'

'I tell you, I've signed up,' said Freddie. 'And there's an end to it. I'm leaving in about fifteen minutes and reporting to barracks.'

'Reporting to . . .' Thos looked as though he might explode. 'Reporting to *barracks*? You're barely out of short trousers, you dolt! And just *look* at you! You're . . . *ridiculous*. I tell you, it's illegal. They simply wouldn't sign a schoolkid. How old did you tell them you were?'

'Sixteen,' said Freddie.

'Well, there you are then. And what did they say to that?'

'Told me to walk around the corner, and see if I wasn't eighteen by the time I came back.'

'*What*? And you were stupid enough to *do* that? What do you think the school will say when they hear of it? For that matter . . .' – Thos played his trump card – 'what do you think Father will say? Do you imagine he'll just let you go waltzing off without a word?'

'Where is he?' said Freddie.

'He's gone to Radstock for a few days. And when he comes *back*—'

'I shall be gone.'

'Freddie . . .' Thos gave a long sigh. 'Freddie, listen to me . . .'

'Yes, Freddie,' said Lizzie Howard, 'listen to your brother. He has more of the good sense.'

Celandine looked at Thos. He was obviously trying to calm his temper now, trying to reason with Freddie rather than simply bully him.

'Freddie . . . it just won't work. Father will be down at those barracks the minute he hears of this, you know he will, and he won't leave until he gets you out – and then you'll *really* be for it. I'm sure that you just want to . . . I don't know, help your country and all that. But they don't need *school*kids. They're not sending *boys* out to France.'

'I shan't be going to France,' said Freddie. 'Not for a while, I don't think. There's training first. I shall be in England for ages yet. It'll probably all be over before they let me anywhere near the fighting.'

'Well, then – why go?'

'Because . . . because I'm sick of everything else, that's why. I don't want to be at school . . . don't want to be a priest, or a lawyer . . . or a *farmer*. And things like this don't happen very often. Thos, there's a *war* going on – thousands of people are enlisting. Thousands every day. We're at *war*. It might not seem like it, stuck down here, but we are. I want to be doing something . . . real. Something that matters a bit more than Latin and Greek. As *you* say – some *work*.'

'Oh, for goodness sake, Freddie. They don't need *you*. What *you* do can't possibly make the slightest difference.'

'It can to me.'

There was silence. Freddie would not change his mind, and everyone there apart from Nina had known it from the beginning. For all their differences in temperament, the Howard children were similar in one respect: their stubbornness. There wasn't one of them who would readily let go of something once they had a firm hold on it – and each recognized this in the other.

Freddie said, 'Dinah, I want to show you something – quickly – before I go. It's only a new butterfly, but you might like it. Come upstairs a minute.'

The two of them could hear Thos's voice, angrily rumbling away beneath them, as they stood in Freddie's room.

'Dinah – can you keep a secret?'

Celandine had to smile to herself, despite her sadness. Oh yes. She could keep a secret.

'I expect so,' she said, looking around her. 'Where is it?'

'Where's what? Oh, the butterfly? There isn't one. Dinah, I would have gone straight to the barracks, but I wanted someone to know where I was . . . where I *really* was . . . and you're the only one I can trust. Thos is right – Father will come to get me as soon as he hears about it, and so I've enlisted under another name.'

'What? But he'll still find you, won't he? Taunton barracks can't be that big. He's sure to know people there, and he only has to see you . . .'

'I haven't joined the Somersets. I'm with the Dorsets. Can you remember that? Dorsetshire Regiment. I enlisted at Sherborne, not at Taunton – and I'll be based at Dorchester. Will you remember that?'

'All right. But Freddie – don't do this . . . please don't go . . .'

'I must. And you mustn't worry. And you mustn't tell. Promise?'

He looked so young and anxious in his too-new army jacket, his fair hair still wet from the rain – how could anyone believe he was eighteen?

'All right. What name did you give?'

'Frederick Thomas. I just took my first name and Thos's. Wasn't really thinking about it at the time – but at least I shan't forget it.'

'No.'

The deep growl of the motorcycle made them turn towards the window, and they saw the greatcoated rider swing into the yard once more. The machine came to a halt and the rider sat astride it, casually adjusting his gauntlets. He pushed his army cap back a little and grimaced up at the rain. This time he wore goggles – like a strange disguise, they were, but a disguise that could never hide what lay beneath: another face too young for this venture.

'Come on,' said Freddie. 'Jock's here.'

* * *

Erstcourt Howard's reaction, two days later, was predictably noisy – and his voice carried as far as the stables, where the grooms bent their heads a little further to their tasks as a consequence. Why had word not been brought to him *immediately*? What on *earth* were Thos and Lizzie thinking to simply let the boy go? Could he not turn his back for two minutes at a time without some disaster should occur? Was he to attend to every little *detail*? Without stopping for sup or bite, he strode out into the yard and yelled for Mr Hughes, the foreman.

'Hughes – get that wretched gig out, and any lump of horseflesh that'll stand the whip! Yes, *now*! I don't *care* which. It's two hours to the barracks, and damned if I don't do it in one!'

Celandine and Nina peeped fearfully out of the parlour window and watched Erstcourt rattle out of the yard at a very smart pace.

'I think Freddie's awfully brave,' said Nina.

'To go and enlist, you mean? Hmph. I think Freddie's idiotic. Quite . . . preposterous,' said Celandine – although she couldn't help but feel just a little bit proud.

'No, I mean to risk getting caught by your father. I think I'd rather be caught by the Hun than by him.'

'Oh, Father's preposterous too. My whole family is quite preposterous.'

Chapter Ten

Mary Swann had simply been biding her time, of course – waiting for the right weapon with which to attack. Now she had found one. At breakfast on the first morning of the new half, the talk was of the war. One or two of the girls could now claim a personal connection in that they had neighbours or family friends who had gone away to fight, and at the Hardy end of the long refectory table Alicia Tremlett was gaining some attention for herself in this respect. She had a cousin, she said – 'dear Peter' – who had just enlisted.

'Oh Alicia! How brave of him – but how awful for *you*. Were you *very* close?'

'Yes,' said Alicia, lowering her eyes, 'we're . . . well, perhaps I shouldn't say. But if anything should happen to him . . . you know . . . I should be . . .' She looked as though a tear or two might not be out of the question.

'Oh! How terrible – and how *romantic*. What's his name, dear?'

'Peter Breugel. His family were Dutch, although now they're *completely* British of course. They were

221

descended from a famous painter called Peter Bruegel. Peter – my Peter – is named after him.' Alicia took a delicate bite of bread and marmalade.

'Oh *Alicia*! Listen, dear, you must be brave too – for *his* sake. Which regiment is he with?'

'Oh. It's the er . . . the um . . .'

'Alicia – it mightn't be wise to give away too much information . . .' Mary Swann leaned forward and looked pointedly at Celandine, who was sitting a little further along the table, opposite Nina.

'Why – what do you mean?' said Alicia.

'Only that you can't necessarily trust *everyone*, you know. Your cousin might be completely British, even though he has a Dutch name. But there are some people with *British* names who aren't completely British at all.'

Mary continued to look at Celandine, and gradually all heads turned in that direction.

'Yes,' said Mary. 'There are some people with British names who are actually half-German. It makes you wonder whose side they might be on. But . . .' Mary sighed. 'That's up to them, I suppose.'

'Who do you mean – the Witch? Is she half-German?'

'Of course, the other thing you have to be careful of is *sympathizers*,' said Mary, directing her gaze towards Nina. 'My father was talking about them. People who might *be* British, but who are actually friends with the Germans. Sympathizers are even worse, according to Daddy. They're as bad as the white feather brigade – cowards. He'd shoot the lot of 'em. Is there any more milk in that jug, Chlo?'

It didn't take long for the word to get around; Celandine Howard was not only quite possibly a witch, she was also half-German. And that meant that Nina Jessop must be both a witch's assistant and a German sympathizer – a dangerous if unlikely mixture of black cat and white feather. Mary Swann had played her hand well, so well that she could now afford to sit back and let others do the rest of her work.

Whereas Celandine and Nina had previously been ignored mainly by those in their own dormitory, it now became an unwritten law of the entire Lower School that nobody was to speak to them. This would have been more bearable if it wasn't for the low hissing that accompanied them wherever they went. If a question was asked of either of them in the classroom, the unsuspecting teacher would look up in surprise at the brief '*ssss*' that erupted at the mention of the name Howard or Jessop. In morning Assembly, as the third form filed past the first and second forms to take their places, the barely audible hissing sound followed the footsteps of the two girls like a shadowing snake – so that the prefects at the end of each row had to repeatedly call for silence, though they well understood what was going on and made no serious attempt to stamp it out. On the hockey pitch no ball was ever wittingly passed to either Celandine or Nina, which actually suited Nina very well, and if either of them should accidentally find themselves in possession, then the hissing would begin and continue until the wretched ball had been surrendered. In the washrooms no girl would ever touch a bar of soap that had come into contact with the tainted skin of the two outcasts, and at the dinner table no jug or dish would ever be accepted from their sullied hands.

Of the two, Nina suffered the worse treatment. Like pack animals, the Lower School instinctively singled out the weaker prey, and if ever Nina was alone she was in trouble. Celandine was regarded with more caution. She was understood to be violent by reputation, perhaps truly dangerous, and so was never physically jostled or slyly kicked – and certainly never cornered. Besides, there were growing whispers that she was possessed of mysterious powers, whispers made the more believable by her wild appearance: the gypsy-dark eyes, the Medusa-like hair. Hadn't she laid a curse upon poor Carol, as revenge against Miss Belvedere? Hadn't she caused oranges and sweets to levitate and float from locker to locker? These were the rumours. Who knew what she was, or what she might be capable of? No, Ninky was easier game, and far safer to deal with.

'Ninky-ninky-nooo!'

The chanted words became a kind of battle-cry, a tally-ho, and a signal that Nina was temporarily without Celandine's protection. Girls then descended upon her and cheerfully gave her a 'scragging' – pulling out her ribbons, pelting her with apple cores or twisting her ears until they went bright red. It was usually Mary Swann who was behind it all, although she never touched Nina personally. No, Mary was careful to remain at a distance, merely directing operations and offering sly encouragement to her minions.

Nina put up no resistance, but neither did she beg for mercy. She submitted passively to each assault and waited until her attackers had had enough before picking herself up, red-faced and dishevelled, from the washroom floor or the muddy playing field, or wherever they had cornered her. She was entirely vulnerable, an easy target to hit, yet not an easy one to break. Nina was no fighter, but neither was she a coward – and even though she was often reduced to tears, the bullies could never quite make her give in.

Celandine was furiously aware of what was happening to her friend, but as the attacks only ever occurred when she was elsewhere, there was never any direct evidence for her to act upon. Even so, she would instantly have reported matters to the Head Girl if Nina hadn't repeatedly begged her not to.

'I'm all right,' Nina said. 'They'll get tired of bothering in the end.'

Celandine was not so sure. She was concerned that things might easily get worse rather than better, and as she peered around the door to the washroom one late afternoon she was more apprehensive than ever.

She couldn't find Nina. She had already looked in the common room, the third-form classroom, and the library – the three most likely places.

'Nina?' One of the cubicles was occupied, but there was no reply.

Celandine hurried back down the corridor and glanced briefly into the dormitory – out of bounds at this time of day, but she was running out of alternatives. Not there. Where else could she be?

The playing fields and the gym weren't even worth considering. Nina would never be doing anything physical unless it was compulsory. Celandine wandered out into the quad. It was gone half-past four and very nearly dark, the late October mist descending all around, so that the lights from the dining-hall windows were blurred and softened. Soon it would be teatime. Celandine was so worried, and yet she really didn't know why. Something was wrong, though. She could feel it.

Footsteps – she heard them coming across the quadrangle – and the urgent whispering of voices, out of breath.

'*Nothing* – do you hear me? You must say *nothing*. You don't know anything.'

'But *Maaary*—'

'Shut up.'

Celandine moved into the shadow of one of the great stone buttresses that projected from the walls of the main building, and watched. A knot of girls hurried by on the opposite side of the quad, four or five of them perhaps. They too were deep in shadow, but not so far away as to be unrecognizable. Mary Swann, the Pigtail twins, Alicia . . .

The group disappeared through the entrance to Big School. They shouldn't be going that way – it was forbidden to third-formers. Why would they risk that?

Celandine stepped out from behind the buttress and considered what she had seen. Where had they been coming from? *Could* it have been the playing field? But what would they have been doing up there at this time of day? It was too dark to have been throwing a ball around, and they hadn't been dressed for gym. She walked uncertainly past the brightly-lit dining hall, where the rattle and clink of cutlery spoke of preparations for the evening meal, and turned the corner next to the fives court. From here the long flight of steps to the playing fields rose up and disappeared into the misty darkness above her.

Something had happened. Something terrible had happened, she was certain of it. Celandine began to climb the greasy wooden steps – old railway sleepers they were, worn and splintered by generations of hockey boots.

At the top of the steps she paused, listening in the darkness. Had she heard something, or was it just her nervousness? It was cold, and the hazy orange lights of the school buildings below seemed welcoming now, comforting, as they had never done before. Perhaps she should go back down. The quick scrunch of footsteps on the cinder path behind her made her spin round.

'Who's that?'

'Who's that?' Another uncertain voice echoed her own, and her heart jumped in fright. A pale face appeared out of the mist, disembodied for a few moments, floating like a balloon, until the dark school tunic became suddenly visible beneath it. It was Molly Fletcher.

Molly looked surprised, then frightened, her eyes

wide with panic. She tried to dodge past, but Celandine reached out and grabbed at the thin woollen sleeve of her cardigan.

'What are you doing up here?' she said. 'What's been going on?'

Molly jerked her arm back and the neck of the cardigan slipped down over her shoulder, but Celandine managed to get a grip on the girl's wrist with her free hand. There was another moment or two of struggling and then Molly gave up.

'Where is she?' said Celandine. This was all to do with Nina, she knew it – something had happened to Nina. Molly's face was white. She was shivering, and plainly terrified. Celandine tightened her grip.

'Where *is* she?'

'Pool . . .' It was more of a gasping sound than a word.

'What?'

'The swimming pool . . . we . . . I didn't want to . . . I said no . . .' Molly's nose was streaming now.

'Come on.' Celandine waited to hear no more. She hurried Molly along the cinder track, yanking at the reluctant wrist, quite prepared to drag the little wretch by the hair if need be.

The area beyond the gymnasium, where the new pool was being built, was unfamiliar to her, it being out of bounds, and it was now made the more difficult to negotiate because of the darkness. Celandine had to let go of Molly and stumble alone among the piles of earth, heavy tarpaulins, concrete blocks and builders' planks – picking her way through the obstacles until she found herself at the edge of the vast pit that had been dug.

'Nina?' It was so dark down there. She couldn't see a thing. 'Nina? Can you hear me? Are you all right?' Her voice sounded loud and strange, echoing back at her from the void.

No reply. Celandine gingerly moved around the perimeter, peering down into the gloom. There was a rectangle of solid concrete at one end of the pool, and she could see what looked like a board extending out above the pit. Yes, a long springboard, mounted on metal stanchions in the concrete.

'Nina?' There *was* something down there. She could see just it – a vaguely crumpled shape in the darkness below her.

'Nina! Is that you?'

Still no answer. Celandine tried to stay calm. What did she need? A ladder . . . a ladder and . . . some planks? No. It was too dark, and it was too dangerous – she could not do this by herself. What she needed was some help.

'Fletcher – where are you? Are you still there?' But again her voice bounced back at her, a brief mocking echo, then disappeared into the empty darkness. Molly Fletcher had gone.

Celandine burst into the crowded dining hall and ran straight to the top table – where the teachers looked up at her in astonishment as she blurted out her news.

'There's a girl in the swimming pool – Nina Jessop. I think she's hurt!'

The low murmur of conversation at the rest of the tables quickly dwindled to silence. Somebody dropped a piece of cutlery at the far end of the room.

Miss Belvedere folded her napkin and scraped back her chair. 'In the *swimming pool*? Right. *I'll* deal with this – *with* your permission, Miss Craven. Aberdeen! Run to the caretaker's flat and fetch Mr Blight – tell him to bring lanterns. Matron, perhaps you'd better accompany me. And as for you, Howard, you may go and sit at your table – where you should have been these last fifteen minutes. I'm sure that there will be plenty of questions for you to answer in due course.'

'No! I mean . . . I want to be there . . . to help . . .'

'Howard! *Do* as you're told this instant, and let us have less of your insolence! Go and sit down!'

Celandine walked slowly past the rows of refectory tables, aware that every face was staring at her, and as she passed she heard the murmurs and whispers of conversation that sprang up behind her. She approached the third-form table and looked at Mary Swann and her cronies. Of all the girls in the room, theirs were the only eyes that were not fixed upon her – Mary Swann, the Pigtail twins, Alicia Tremlett . . . and Molly Fletcher; none of them would look at her. Instead they appeared to concentrate on their food, staring at their plates, tight-lipped and white-faced, saying nothing.

No. She would not do this. She would *not* sit meekly and wait for news. She had to know what was happening to Nina.

At the last minute she bolted – fled from the dining hall and out into the chilly night air once more.

'*Howard!*' Celandine heard the house-mistress's voice bawling at her, but she ignored it. Instead she ran past the fives court and again clambered up the long flight of steps to the playing field. She might not be allowed to help, but at least she would watch – and she would worry about the consequences later.

They came with swinging lanterns and urgent voices, hurrying along the cinder track: Miss Belvedere, of course, and Aberdeen, and Matron. The caretaker, Mr Blight, she could also see, and another man – one of the porters? Yes, old William.

Celandine crouched between a pile of cement bags and a stack of wooden doors, ducking her head lower still as the lantern beams threatened to expose her.

'William – some light over here, please!' Miss Belvedere's bulky shadow moved along the side of the pit. 'Yes, just here. Hurry up, man – give me that lantern. Aha! Matron – Mr Blight! I think we've . . . yes, there she is. Just down there – do you see her? *Stupid* girl. What on earth did she think she was doing . . .'

Celandine peered around the side of the cement sacks, desperate to know what was happening.

'We'll need a ladder, Mr Blight – ah, you've already found one. Good.'

The two men were lowering a builder's ladder over the side of the pit. One of the lanterns disappeared from view as the caretaker descended into the depths. The light shone upwards, stabbing out erratically, illuminating the faces of those who remained above ground. A muffled voice; 'No movement as I can see, Miss Belvedere. Shall I pick her up?'

'No – don't do that.' Matron was leaning forward. 'We should put her on a stretcher . . .'

'Except that we don't have one . . .' Miss Belvedere again. 'Well, we can't just leave the wretched child down there.'

'What about a plank?' The caretaker's muffled voice once more. 'Could we lift her up on a plank?'

'Matron? What do you think?'

'Well, I suppose . . .'

'*I* think we have very little choice. William! See what you can find.'

The porter, William, began casting about for something suitable, and his search brought him almost immediately to Celandine's hiding place. There was a pile of white-painted doors just behind her, and it seemed that old William had quickly spotted them. Celandine watched him draw closer. When it became certain that he was about to trip right over her, she stood up. It was pointless trying to hide any longer.

'Oh my Gawd . . .' William's arms jerked up defensively. 'What the bleedin' . . .' He put his hand over his heart. 'Gawd's *sake*, miss! Are you tryin' to *kill* me?'

Miss Belvedere looked round. She raised the lantern that she was holding.

'Ah, Howard,' she said. '*There* you are. And I can't say that I'm surprised – in fact *wherever* there is trouble I should not be surprised to find you in the thick of it. Well, you are in trouble now, girl, I can assure you, and I shall be dealing with you directly. Aberdeen – keep an eye on this child, please. I should hate to lose her again. In the meantime, William, if you've quite recovered . . . could we have one of those changing-hut doors?'

They slowly carried Nina down the steps, the men taking an end of the narrow cubicle door apiece and walking sideways – carefully negotiating the railway sleepers, one at a time. Miss Belvedere and Matron led the way, and Cleandine followed, under the watchful eye of Aberdeen.

It was like a horrible kind of funeral march: step . . . pause . . . step . . . pause . . .

Nina lay on her side, motionless upon the makeshift stretcher, her clothes rumpled and filthy, one of her shoes missing. There was a smear of blood on her forehead, a bright glistening patch that appeared again and again in the swinging light of the lanterns. What had they done to her? What had they *done?*

Celandine felt a tingling fury that ran right through her. Her hands were clenched so tight that her fingernails were digging into her palms. They would pay for this. They would suffer. She thought of the scissors – the time she had attacked Miss Bell. Would she do the same again now? Would she . . . ?

They had reached the bottom of the steps.

'Better get her straight to the san, Matron,' said Miss Belvedere. 'I'll be along shortly, as soon as I've interviewed Howard and got to the bottom of this. Howard, you will come with me.'

It occurred to Celandine, for the first time, that there would be questions about all this, and that she would have to answer them. What was she to say? She was as sure as she could be that Mary Swann was involved, but she wasn't so sure that she could tell Miss Belvedere that. And what about the fact that it had been Molly Fletcher who had told her where Nina was? Should she tell Miss Belvedere *that*? Above all, she didn't want to unwittingly get Nina into any more trouble than she might already be in. Perhaps it would be better to say nothing – for the moment.

They had reached the staffroom. Celandine had been so caught up in thinking about what she would say, that the silent journey across the quad and through the main building had barely registered.

Miss Belvedere unlocked the staffroom door, and switched on the electric light. 'Wait there,' she said. She walked across the room, pushing back the sleeve of her right forearm in what seemed like a practised movement. She pulled open the drawer of a large bureau, took something from it, then walked back again. She was carrying a broad leather strap – a thing that looked as though it might once have belonged on a steamer trunk.

'Right,' she said. 'Let us begin.' Miss Belvedere folded the leather strap in two and tapped the loose ends against the meaty palm of one hand. 'What were you and Jessop doing up by the new swimming pool in the first place? I'm sure you must know that it is strictly out of bounds.'

'We weren't up there, Miss Belvedere. At least—'

'What do you mean, you "weren't up there"? You very obviously *were* up there!'

'I mean that we weren't up there together. I . . . found Nina, I mean Jessop . . .'

'You *found* her?'

'Yes. I was looking for her . . . I didn't know where she was . . .'

'And you just happened to think of looking in the swimming pool – a place that is entirely forbidden to you? It doesn't sound very likely, does it?'

Celandine could think of nothing to say.

'Well?'

The whole building had become eerily silent – no sound but the tap-tapping of the leather strap against the heavy palm.

'I do not consider this to be a reasonable explanation, Howard. I feel certain that you are attempting to conceal the facts from me – a very foolish thing to do, under such serious circumstances, and tantamount to lying. No doubt we shall learn more in due course. Be that as it may, you deliberately defied my order to return to your seat – and you once again flouted the rules by entering an area that is out of bounds. There can be *no* excuse for this, nor can any exceptions be made. Have you anything further to say?'

Celandine tried to steady her breathing. The

roaring in her ears – the sound of her own blood pounding through her – had drowned out the tapping of the leather strap.

'Very well. Hold out your left hand.' The words seemed to echo from a long way away. Celandine watched her hand as she hesitantly held it out, concentrated upon keeping it steady, tried to stop it jumping around.

'Palm flat.'

Celandine somehow managed to straighten her fingers. A blur of movement at the outside edges of her vision . . .

Shwack!

The pain cut through everything – her fear, the roaring in her ears, all her troubles – all blown away by the unbelievable explosion of pain. It was almost a relief. She snatched her hand backwards and instinctively pressed it to her ribs.

'Again.'

Again? For a moment the word seemed to have no meaning – it was just a jangle of sound. Again? Celandine dragged her hand away from her body, forced it away from her, and held it out – again – but now her fingers wouldn't straighten properly. She couldn't seem to . . .

Shwack!

This time it was worse – much worse – and she doubled forward, gasping at the shock of it, pressing her stinging palm hard against her ribs once more.

'Right hand . . .'

* * *

It was over. Celandine looked at her white-faced reflection in the mottled surface of the washroom mirror, and told herself that it was over. It was done. It was as bad as it could be, but it was done. She let her hands float gently in the basin, motionless in the aching cold of the water, and stared into the mirror at her dark resentful eyes. Soon she would go. Once she was able to stand without support, once she could bear to lift her beaten palms from the swirling comfort of the basin . . .

Another reflection appeared in the mirror – another white face to match her own: Molly Fletcher.

'Are you . . . all right?'

'Go away.' Celandine found that she could speak. Her voice was shaky, but she could speak. She continued to look at the mirror, watching as Molly cautiously drew a little closer.

'I'm sorry, truly I am. We all are.'

'Are you? You will be. And don't you *dare* come near me!'

'How's Ninky – did she . . . did she say anything?' Molly shrank back again, wringing her hands, uncertain.

Celandine turned her head, and looked at Molly directly.

'No, she didn't say anything, *Fletcher*. She's unconscious – she *couldn't* say anything. She might be dying, for all you know. She might even be dead. What did you do to her? What did you *do*?'

'Oh . . . oh God . . .' Molly began to cry. 'We didn't mean to . . . we didn't think she'd . . . oh God. She

237

jumped. We . . . we made her walk the plank – they did. I said no. They were making her walk the plank. On the diving board. It was just a joke. But she *jumped.*'

Celandine snatched her hands from the basin, sending gouts of water splattering heavily to the floor. Molly turned and ran from the echoing washroom.

The dormitory was silent as Celandine entered. She stood at the threshold for a moment and looked around. Most of the girls were in their nightgowns, just sitting on their beds. Molly Fletcher, closest to the door, was already in bed – hunched forward, face hidden against her drawn-up knees.

Mary Swann was in the far corner of the room, casually perched on the bar of her iron bedstead – one bare foot on the floor, the other resting on the cross-rail.

Nina's bed stood empty, of course. It looked so neatly made and sad somehow, the tartan dressing gown carefully folded at the foot of the bed, that the sight of it made Celandine's fury rise again. What cowards they were. What stupid, ugly . . . brainless . . . pig-faced . . .

The loud clack of her nailed heels echoed the rhythm of all the bad words she could think of as she strode down the length of linoleum between the rows of beds. Her swollen palms burned with outrage.

Mary Swann pushed herself upright from her bedstead. She folded her arms, defensively, as Celandine came storming towards her.

'Don't you touch *me*, you little savage . . .' she muttered – then louder, beginning to panic; 'I'm *warning* you, Howard! You'd better not touch *me . . .*'

Celandine marched straight up to her, holding Mary's eyes with her own, not allowing them to be diverted for a moment. She knew exactly what she was going to do. Without losing a single beat of the rhythm that pounded through her, she raised her right foot high at the final stride and *stamped* her booted heel down as hard as she could onto Mary's bare toes. A quick step back, in order to brace herself, and she hurled herself forward again, straight-armed, and shoved the big girl in the chest with all the force that raged within her. Mary Swann shot backwards, tumbled straight over the bedstead and bounced sideways – hitting her head against the distempered wall with a dull thump.

Mary howled in agony and rolled over, clutching frantically at her foot as Celandine swung herself around the bedstead and grabbed a fistful of hair. She began shaking Mary's head from side to side, as a terrier might shake a rat.

''Ware Bulldog! Bulldog!' Celandine caught a glimpse, even through her red fury, of Molly Fletcher wildly signalling from her position by the door. 'Bulldog!'

Miss Belvedere was coming. Celandine's own sore hands were a reminder to her of what that meant, and it brought her back to her senses. She did not want another interview with the house-mistress. With a last twisting wrench of Mary's hair, she finally let go. Her footsteps, as she walked back up through the room, were quite inaudible now for the shrieking behind her.

She reached her own bed just as Miss Belvedere sailed through the door.

'What is the meaning of this *appalling* noise?' The house-mistress put her hands on her hips and stared in disbelief towards the writhing figure of Mary Swann.

'You girl! You down there! Cease that infernal screeching immediately!' Miss Belvedere quickly walked down through the room and stood by Mary's bed.

'Are you *deaf*, child? Stop this thrashing about!'

Celandine tried to calm her breathing. She wiped her damp hands on her tunic. A wisp of dark hair and a few grey flakes of distemper floated to the ground. It occurred to her that she ought to get herself undressed whilst Miss Belvedere's attention was elsewhere. She quickly opened her locker drawer and took out her nightgown – all the time keeping a watchful eye on what was happening at the end of the room.

Mary was still holding her foot and rocking backwards and forwards in pain, but she was merely sobbing now, no longer screaming.

'Now then.' Miss Belvedere's voice dropped to a tone of weary patience. 'Perhaps you can tell me what the trouble is. Quietly if possible. *Reasonably*, if you are capable of reason.'

'She ... she ...' Mary was still struggling to control her sobs. Her intake of breath came in short painful gulps. She shook her head, unable to continue.

'She – she . . .?' Miss Belvedere's prompting was unsympathetic. 'But who – who? And what – what?'

Celandine straightened her nightgown, and tied the drawstring ribbon in a bow at her neck. Should she bother taking her boots off? It was apparent that Mary was going to tell all as soon as she was capable of speech, and that would mean another walk down to the staffroom. Well, she didn't care. It was worth it – and Mary would be in far more trouble than she, once the truth was out.

'Now let us try again,' said Miss Belvedere. 'What has been going on here?'

'She . . .' Mary looked towards Celandine, then hesitated. She glanced around at her friends, then looked at Celandine again. Finally, she dropped her head. 'I . . . I . . .'

'Ah,' said Miss Belvedere. 'It's "I – I" now, is it? And what did "I – I" do?'

'I . . . stubbed my toes. On the bedstead.'

Celandine sat down, and began to pull off her boots.

Miss Belvedere stood with her hand on the electric light switch. The expression on her slab-like face, never cheerful, was particularly grim this night.

'You will all be aware that a very serious incident has occurred in this school – as serious as any that I have had occasion to deal with during my time here. I have just returned from the sanatorium, where I have talked with both Matron and Doctor Nichols, and the news is not good. Nina Jessop is breathing, apparently, but has yet to regain consciousness. She appears to be most severely concussed. It is too early to say what the outcome will be.'

Miss Belvedere's gaze fell on Nina's empty bed, then shifted towards Celandine.

'I am in no way convinced that I have got to the bottom of this. Such information as I have so far received has been inadequate to say the least. If there is a culprit here . . . or cul*prits* . . . or if anybody has any knowledge of this matter at all, then they would do well to come forward now. Does anybody wish to say anything?'

Miss Belvedere looked slowly around the hushed dormitory, taking time to study every face. Eventually her eye fell upon Celandine once more, and remained there.

'Very well. But please don't imagine that you have heard the last of this. I strongly suspect that *somebody* in this dormitory is in a very great deal of trouble – and if so, I shall find them out. I'd like you to think about that. Goodnight, Hardy.'

'Goodnight, Miss Belvedere.' The faintest whisper of a reply, and the room fell dark.

Celandine lay on her back in the gloom and listened to the creaks and shuffles of those around her. She would not be the only one who would find it hard to sleep tonight, and that was some comfort. The palms of her hands burned and throbbed, and she clenched them tight as she remembered how she had dealt with Mary Swann. She wondered whether that would be the end of it, or whether there would be more trouble to come – and decided that she no longer cared.

The sound of muffled sobbing was coming from one of the beds opposite. Molly Fletcher, probably. It was Molly who had told her where Nina was. It was also Molly who had warned her of Miss Belvedere's approach. Molly had betrayed Mary Swann – and the rest of her tribe. No wonder she was crying. What would happen to her now?

But more importantly than any of this, what was happening to Nina? How could she just lie here, doing nothing, whilst Nina lay unconscious in the san? She couldn't. Visitors were only allowed into the san during the hour between afternoon lessons and tea. She couldn't wait that long for news. She had to see Nina for herself, somehow, and help in any way that she could.

Go now – after lights-out? Was that what she was intending to do? Was she? Celandine began to test the idea, to rehearse the journey in her imagination. Put on her dressing gown and slippers and creep over to the door. Make sure that the Bulldog was not still lurking in the corridor outside. Tiptoe past Wyndham dormitory and down the main staircase. Go to the front door . . . no, that was too close to Miss Craven's study. Perhaps the back door would be better. Yes, past the downstairs washrooms and up the short flight of steps to the back entrance. Unlock the door . . .

An hour later she finally sat up and forced herself to make a decision. Molly's whimpering had ceased. Others might still be awake, but then they might be awake all night. Now would be as good a time as any – if she really dared do it.

It wasn't until the cold and damp of the night air hit her that Celandine realized she had forgotten to put on her dressing gown – the very first stage of her plan. She gently pulled the heavy arched door towards her, closing it as quietly as she could, and shivered. It had been horribly creepy, tiptoeing alone through the panelled corridors and down the unlit stairwell. Every creak and tick of the settling building had startled her as though it had been a whip-crack, every draught of air through a loose casement had felt like a passing ghost.

Outside was little better. It was cold. The earlier mist had blown away and a damp drizzly breeze folded itself around Celandine's hunched shoulders. Her hands still ached and now her head was beginning to ache also. She didn't feel well. But she had come this far and she would not turn back.

The pathway to the san was bordered by high foliage on either side. Shadowy fronds of rhododendron reached lazily out towards her, like clumsy fingers, and the rustling of nameless creatures in the undergrowth made her catch her breath. This was a feeling she had not rehearsed.

Celandine was surprised to see light in one or two of the sanatorium windows, a faint glow. Did that mean someone was awake? She began to wonder how she would ever find Nina without perhaps accidentally finding Matron first.

The glass-fronted door to the porch, at least, was unlocked. Celandine hesitated for a moment, then crept quietly in. A tiny light glowed from a gas-mantle.

It was enough to illuminate the porch – the rubber boots, the walking stick, the mackintosh that hung upon the wall.

Celandine gently turned the brass handle of the front door and pushed. It was open!

The surgery was on the right of the hallway that she now found herself in. She knew that much. She also knew that Matron lived on the premises – upstairs perhaps? If that was the case, then the other downstairs rooms could be sick wards.

This was worse, much worse, than creeping through the school itself. This was like being a burglar. Celandine told herself that she was here to find Nina, not to commit a crime. And if she *was* caught then perhaps she could simply say that she felt sick – something that was not so very far from the truth.

She could see that there were two more doors – one on the left, and one at the end of the passage. Celandine reached for the handle of the first door, but then changed her mind. There was something

about the other door, the one at the end of the passageway, which made her think it the more likely one. There was no telling why – it was just an instinct, and she crept towards it.

The handle turned easily and the hinge was smooth and silent. Celandine peeped into the room. Here too there was a soft glow of light, another mantle turned down low, and she immediately saw that the room was occupied. A bed stood in the near corner, and there was a sleeping child in it. The girl lay with fists clenched and arms flung out, as though she was running a race. Her face was familiar, but it was not Nina's face. Tiny Lewis? Yes, Tiny Lewis. One of the second-formers, probably down with a cold.

Her instinct had been wrong, then. Celandine began to close the door, but then realized that there was a second bed at the far end of the room. It was partly hidden behind a folding screen. Was that her? She moved forward, so that she could see around the angle of the screen. Yes, that was Nina.

There was a canvas chair next to the bed – one of the tubular-framed ones that were sometimes used for school concerts. A tumbler of water stood on the bedside cabinet, and against the glass was propped a pale blue envelope, a letter, addressed to Nina. The water was apparently untouched, and the letter unopened. It didn't look as though Nina had yet regained consciousness. Celandine sat on the chair, put her hands between her knees, and tried to control her shivering.

They had bandaged Nina's head. It was very neatly

done, the broad strips of white gauze criss-crossing perfectly, like a diagram from a textbook. And the pillow and bedclothes were smooth and unrumpled – further indication that Nina had not moved during the hours that she had lain there. She was motionless now, lying flat on her back, as still as a waxwork. Celandine leaned closer. The very slightest rise and fall of the starched cotton sheet, tucked so tightly across the thin shoulders, reassured her that Nina was actually alive and breathing.

'Nina,' she whispered. 'Can you hear me?'

No response. Not a flicker. Celandine glanced beyond the folding screen at the sleeping figure of Tiny Lewis, whose tousled hair and sprawling pose seemed so full of life and energy by comparison.

Gingerly she put out her hand as if to touch the bandaged head of her friend, but then thought better of it. Nina looked so pale and vulnerable. She would not disturb her. Instead she held her palm uncertainly for a moment above the neat bindings, before slowly withdrawing it.

Curious, though, the brief sensation of heat that she had felt in that moment: as if her outstretched fingers had passed through a wisp of steam. Had she imagined it? Celandine considered for a while longer, before hesitantly extending her hand once more, allowing it to hover just above Nina's forehead.

A tingling sensation in her palm – it was definitely there – but then it was probably just a reaction from the beating she had taken. That must be the reason. Celandine closed her eyes and slowly moved her hand from side to side, surprised at how the feeling strengthened and faded accordingly, and yet she did not find it alarming. It was peaceful to just sit in silence, to let the turmoil of this day recede. Her thoughts began to drift, as though she were upon the edge of sleep, and she gradually let her consciousness float where it would.

She was looking down into the darkness. A pool of darkness it was – a pit, an ocean, a millpond, black with leaf-mould. It was an unhappy place. There was pain down there. The darkness itself was a concentration of pain, and she could feel herself being drawn towards it. No, it was the other way round; the pain was being drawn upwards to meet her, a ragged cloud of swirling substance, attracted to her outstretched hand . . .

Stop – this was too strange a feeling. Celandine briefly opened her eyes, became aware once more of her surroundings. The quiet room was still there and she was still sitting next to Nina, with her hand steadily resting above the bandages. Nothing had changed, except that now her heart began to beat a little faster. Had she momentarily fallen asleep? She felt woozy, uncertain.

Again she allowed her eyes to close, and this time she ventured a little further into the darkness. Nina's pain, that was what she could feel. Her hand was resting above Nina's head, and she could feel the pain in there – the inky cloud that reached out towards her and sucked at her palm. It clung to her, greedily attached itself, thick as road-tar, sticky as the cobwebs that festooned the corners of Mill Farm's dusty stables. If she withdrew her hand, then the pain would come with it. She would somehow bring the pain from its dark hiding place, draw it upwards and into the light, set it free. Could she?

The thought frightened her. Her heart was beating so fast now that it hurt, and her shoulders trembled. A trickle of perspiration ran down onto one of her eyelids and she half blinked it away, catching a sparkled glimpse of the room around her as she did so. She was still here, and all she had to do was bring her hand back, if she could only find the strength.

It seemed so heavy. The dead weight of it sapped at her fading energy. She reached out with her other hand, in order to grasp the wrist of the first, to drag it back, to gradually reel in that long tangle of confusion, waterlogged, from the silent depths.

Up it came then, in one twisted mass, a skein of pain, a monstrous catch. As she lifted her aching hands, the thing unfolded itself before her imagination; a creature of oilskin, a bat-winged sail, a tattered tarpaulin that covered her in its circling shadow before drifting away. Far and away it spun, whirling up into the heavens, around and around, until it became no more than a leaf upon the wind. One among many. It was gone.

Celandine let her hands fall back into her lap, dizzily conscious once more of her own being. She didn't feel at all well. For a long time she sat with her eyes closed, waiting for her beating heart to subside, waiting for everything to be normal again. She tried stretching her neck from side to side, but this made her dizzier than ever, and she was frightened that she was going to be sick. Slowly she opened her eyes. Tiny Lewis was staring at her, propped up on one elbow in her bed, a look of outright astonishment on her small white face.

'Hallo.' Nina's voice, faint and distant. 'How long have you been there?'

Nina was awake, then. Awake, awake . . . That was good – but it was a struggle to reply.

'I . . . I don't know.' It might have been hours. It might only have been minutes. Celandine felt hot, then cold, then horribly faint. The room was slowly turning about her. A jug and washbasin on a corner stand. If she had some water . . .

Nina had closed her eyes again. The glass at the bedside – Nina wouldn't mind. Celandine reached out towards it, but her fingers fumbled against the blue envelope and the glass tipped up. She watched it roll over the edge of the little cabinet, saw it shatter on the tiled floor. Harsh echoing sounds. Bright jewels of glass and water droplets, arcing upwards, rushing to meet her – so close – and then an unfamiliar voice, high and panicky, spinning away into the darkness. 'Matron! *Matron!*' Tiny Lewis . . .

She could hear the rooks calling to one another, and thought at first that she was in her bed at home until the explosive sound of a nearby coughing attack suggested that she must still be in the sanatorium after all. Celandine kept her eyes closed and listened.

The sound of whispering – two low voices. She thought that she recognized one of them: Tiny Lewis, talking to another girl.

'She *did*, I tell you.'

'Who? Ninky?'

'No, you dilly. Howard. The *Witch*. It was like a . . . like . . . What are those people called – the ones who talk to dead people?'

'Priests?'

'*No*, idiot. Not priests. Medi— somethings . . . medians . . . ?'

'Mediums?'

A brisk footstep, and the rustle of starched cotton. The whispering stopped.

'Lewis – I don't *think* I gave you permission to come in here and talk to Price. Are you all dressed and ready? Good. You've just two minutes before Assembly to take your sponge-bag and nightclothes back to your dorm – and you can tell Miss Belvedere that I've excused you from games for the rest of this week.'

'Yes, Matron. Thank you.'

'Off you go, then.'

The footsteps came closer. Celandine cautiously opened her eyes. Matron was standing at the bedside, looking down at her.

'Ah. You're awake then, Howard.' Matron reached into the top pocket of her crisp white uniform and drew out a thermometer. 'Pop this under your tongue and I'll come back in a minute or two. In the meantime you might like to think about giving me a good reason for your sudden arrival in the middle of the night.'

They'd moved her in with Nina, into the bed lately occupied by Tiny Lewis. Her explanation to Matron – that she had been feeling too ill to sleep and had then wandered down to the san in a kind of daze – seemed to have been accepted. It was possible that she had a chill, although her temperature seemed normal. She was to be kept here for a day or so, but away from other infected patients, just to be on the safe side.

It was so peaceful, just to lie there and do nothing but think. Celandine looked across the room at Nina. Asleep. The strange experience of the previous night came back to her, but now it seemed unreal, something that she had imagined. Yes, she must have fallen half asleep in the chair and simply imagined it all, although the shocked expression on Tiny Lewis's face had been real enough. 'Witch' – that was what they were calling her. She thought about it. It was true that some very odd things had happened to her – the ghostly figure of the girl that kept appearing, the business with Miss Belvedere's dog, and with Nina . . . and the little people, of course. The little people – that was the strangest thing of all. But did that make her a witch? She didn't think so. But perhaps she was . . . different.

Nina rolled over and opened her eyes. Her hands were outside the bedclothes now, and one of her wrists was bandaged.

'Celandine? Is that . . . what are you doing here?'

She tried to prop herself up, but then said 'Ow,' and lay back down again. 'Were you here last night? Only . . . owww . . . my head . . . only, I thought I woke up once, and saw you. Something got broken.'

'Yes. I was worried. I came down to see how you were. Then . . . then I didn't feel very well. I think I fainted. Now Matron says I might have a chill. But never mind about that – what *happened* to you? What did they do?'

'Oh.' Nina sighed. 'The swimming pool. It was horrible. They said . . . Mary and everyone . . . they said to come up on to the playing field. They said they'd found something, and they wanted me to see it, but they wouldn't say what it was. I thought it was something to do with you, so I went. Over by the swimming pool, they said – that's where it was. Then they made me walk the plank. Made me stand on one leg. Then the other. They kept throwing bits of mud at me, and laughing. So I turned around and jumped. I . . . I don't know why. I just did.' Nina managed to push herself up into a half-sitting position. She looked away, staring out of the window for a few moments. Then she turned back again. 'I don't think I was trying to kill myself,' she said. 'I think I was trying to frighten them. To make them sorry. I didn't care about me, or what happened to me, as long it would make them sorry.'

'Well, they *are* sorry,' said Celandine. 'Mary Swann is *very* sorry. I think I broke her toes, I stamped on them so hard. And she's probably got a bald patch where I pulled out most of her hair.'

'No! Did you?' Nina looked half horrified, half delighted. 'But . . . she'll kill you . . .'

'She won't. She'll not dare touch me. And she'll not touch you either. They're frightened half to death, the whole lot of them, of being found out. Miss Belvedere's on the warpath, and if *she* ever discovers the truth . . . well, they know what would happen to them. They'll leave us alone from now on, you'll see.'

'Mm.' Nina's face looked troubled. She picked up the blue envelope that lay on her bedside cabinet. 'Actually, it doesn't really matter any more. Not for me.'

The envelope had been opened, and Nina ran her fingers along the rough edge of the torn paper. 'My parents are moving back to England. Because of the war, I think. They've taken a house in Taunton, and so they say there's no need for me to be at a boarding school any more. They're taking me away from here. I'm leaving.'

'What? No! You *can't* be leaving. You just *can't*. When?'

'End of this term. Christmas.'

Christmas. Who would have thought that its advent could be so dreaded, or that it could ever arrive so quickly? It came around all too soon for Celandine, who found herself counting the days in quite the opposite of the usual spirit. How would she ever survive at Mount Pleasant once Nina was gone? She would be entirely friendless. There would be nobody at all for her to talk to. To make matters worse, she could see that she was far more upset at the prospect of remaining than Nina was at leaving. Perhaps she shouldn't blame her friend for that – for who would not gladly escape this place if they could?

Some things, at least, had changed for the better. Just as Celandine had predicted, Mary Swann and her followers kept themselves at a very safe distance during the last weeks of term, and there was no longer any threat of violence. Miss Belvedere, despite her most vigorous investigations, learned no more of the swimming pool affair than she had upon that first night – and the culprits were at pains to keep things that way. Celandine and Nina felt relatively safe.

Life had become a little easier, then, for the time being. But there was an atmosphere growing around Celandine that spread far beyond her own dormitory or classroom. Miss Craven's daily bulletins suggested that the war was now unlikely to be over by Christmas. The battles raged on, and although the Germans were perpetually being 'held in check' or 'suffering great losses', it was plain that the Allies were far from actually winning. Miss Craven called upon all girls to pray to God and do their duty with a will. The Sewing Club would be rescheduled to accommodate extra sessions, and half of all produce from the kitchen garden would be sold to aid the War Loan. Miss Craven reminded the school that any trace of the Hun – pens, geometry equipment, sheet music, anything that was suspected of being German in origin – was now strictly forbidden. All to be impounded, or destroyed.

Anti-German feeling had risen so high that it was close to becoming a second religion – or a witch-hunt.

It would not be long, Celandine thought, before they got around to her.

And Nina was leaving. She would have to face it all alone.

Chapter Eleven

The atmosphere at Mill Farm had become tense. Several of the farm hands had enlisted, and there was now a shortage of manpower – a matter of great inconvenience to Erstcourt Howard and his remaining workers.

Mrs Howard was beginning to have problems domestically. The egg woman no longer called, having declared that she could live without 'German eggs', and Cook had taken to muttering '*Jahwohl*' to each and every request. The local shopkeepers seemed suddenly to require that all bills be paid promptly, and social invitations had dwindled almost into non-existence.

'What do they think, these *schtupid* people?' Mrs Howard complained to Celandine. 'I am a submarine, with . . . with *bombs* in my skirts?'

Celandine shrugged her shoulders. She wasn't really listening. She had more than enough troubles of her own, but at that particular moment she was trying to write a letter, and was also thinking about the possibility of a visit to Howard's Hill. This wouldn't be so easy in the winter. The ground was sodden and muddy from the persistent rain, and for all she knew the little wicker tunnel could be knee high in water, perhaps worse. Would Freddie's wading boots fit her, she wondered? It looked as though she might have to put it off once again.

She and Nina had faithfully promised to see each other if they possibly could, though a visit over the Christmas holiday didn't seem very likely. She could write, at least.

'*Dear Nina . . .*'

The end of her dip-pen had been gnawed to a splintery pulp, and bits of paint were sticking to the tip of her tongue. So far she had found very little to say.

'*It's Christmas Eve, and I'm sitting at the parlour table where we played cards at half term. It's still raining, and I don't feel in the least bit Christmassy.*'

Celandine looked up in wonder. She had been remembering how she had sat here with Nina, and how Freddie had suddenly appeared on the motor-cycle. Now, amazingly, here was that very sound again – *brpp-mmm . . . brpp-mmm . . .*

It was as though she were watching a moving picture, a newsreel that she had already seen. The motorcycle flashed past the window, the two great-coated figures hunched against the rain, and then disappeared from her view. The engine slowed to a steady beat – *thumpeta-thumpeta-thump* – and she heard Freddie's voice, faint upon the gusting wind. 'Thanks, Jock! Monday . . . yes . . . Merry Christmas.'

The engine speed picked up again and faded away in the lane. Celandine turned to look at her mother, saw the apprehension on her face – and knew that they had both been thinking the same thing.

'Oh! . . . Erstcourt . . .'

Freddie looked thinner. And yet bigger somehow – taller, more angular. The roundness of his face had gone, and his cheekbones were clearly visible. His uniform no longer hung so loosely about his shoulders.

'Where's Father?' It was all that he said – just two words – but it seemed to Celandine that his voice had changed as well. The cold wind blew into the hallway as Freddie stood holding the door open, ready to either come in or to go back out again, whichever was necessary. Lizzie ran forward as if to hug him, and then held back, awkwardly. She merely touched the wet sleeve of his army greatcoat instead.

'Oh Freddie, it is so *good* you are safe . . . but your father, he is with Mr Hughes. I think perhaps the cider barn . . . Yes, I hear the machine. But, Freddie . . .'

'Better get it over with, then. Back in a minute . . .'

He closed the door, and was gone. But Mrs Howard, after waiting uncertainly for a few moments, opened the door once more. Celandine joined her mother at the threshold. Together they stood and watched, narrowing their eyes against the sleeting drizzle, as Freddie crossed the yard and disappeared into the barn.

It wasn't long before Mr Hughes came out, followed by Robert the head stableman. Whatever was

being said in there was obviously not for their ears. The two men hurried over to the stables.

'Will it be all right, do you think?' Celandine needed her mother's reassurance.

'Yes, I think so. Your father is still very angry – yet he was too a soldier, when he was young. He will become over this. But I – I shall worry always. Come. We are wet, and we can do nothing.'

Celandine sat with her mother in the parlour and listened fearfully as the boots came stamping into the hallway, Erstcourt's loud voice haranguing, questioning, criticizing.

'Now you listen to me, boy. You will tell me exactly which regiment you are with, and the name of your commanding officer – because as far as the Somersets are concerned, they've never dam' well heard of you! No record of you whatsoever!'

'Well, I'm *not* going to tell you, and so it's not a bit of good your carrying on. All you need to know is that I'm safe and well. I've got forty-eight hours leave for

Christmas, and then I'm going back to barracks on Monday.' Freddie's voice was calm and unflustered, but absolutely adamant.

'Back to barracks? You'll do no such thing, my lad! Now that you're here, you'll dam' well stay here and do as you're told!'

'I'll go right now if you don't stop shouting at me!' Freddie was beginning to get angry. 'Yes! And you shan't stop me. I'm *sorry*, do you hear? I'm *sorry*, Father. Truly I am. I don't mean to cause you worry and . . . and pain. But it's done. I've joined the army. I'm a soldier now. There's an end to it.'

The two men entered the room, both red-faced, uncomfortable. Erstcourt appealed to his wife.

'Lizzie – what are we to *do* with this . . . this . . . *foolish* little drummer boy?'

'Let him beat his drum, Erstcourt, as once you beat yours.'

Celandine felt the tears spring to her eyes. It was quite the best thing that she had ever heard her mother say – and the first time she had known her father to be defeated. She saw him shrink somehow, as his anger collapsed within him, and she knew that there would be no more argument. Freddie had won his battle.

The atmosphere at Christmas dinner the following day was a little strained, though it might have been a lot worse. Thos remained disapproving of Freddie's actions, but was no longer openly scornful, and Erstcourt went as far as to say that there was no better life for a man than the army, under the proper circumstances. He still maintained that these were *not* the proper circumstances and that Freddie had acted most unwisely, but no son of his would be disowned for attempting to do his duty, however misguidedly.

'Nevertheless, this is still unfair on your mother, Freddie, to refuse to tell us which regiment you're with. It's a great worry to her, not knowing where you are. I'll trouble you for the parsnips, Lizzie, if I may.' Erstcourt's gentler tone had more effect than his previous bluster, and Freddie gave ground.

'Well, all right, then,' he said. 'I'm with the Dorsets, not the Somersets. So now you know. I'd still rather not say where, though. But you mustn't worry, Mama. I shall write. Training is nearly over, and once I'm posted I promise I shall tell you where I am. I've already given you as my next of kin. If I was ever, you know . . . hurt . . . they would know who to write to.'

He looked tired, thought Celandine, tired and distant. And he looked like a soldier. They had cut his hair, and changed the shape of him and the sound of him, and made him theirs. Somebody else owned him now.

All he wanted to do, he had said to her privately, was sleep. The training was hard, and they kept them at it from dawn till dusk. Soon he would be sent to France or Egypt – perhaps even to Gallipoli. It all depended.

When dinner was over, Thos and Erstcourt left to attend to some farm business, a necessary thing be it Christmas or not, and Mrs Howard went upstairs for her nap. Freddie and Celandine settled down in the parlour for a game of canasta. Freddie soon lost interest, however, and they ended up simply building card houses, and talking.

'How's school?' said Freddie.

'Terrible. I wish *I* could run away and join the army.'

Freddie laughed, and once again Celandine was aware of how different he sounded, how much he had altered. 'Yes,' he said, 'I can just see you stabbing at sack-dummies with a fixed bayonet. Or a pair of scissors.' Then he looked embarrassed. 'Sorry. I didn't mean to . . . you know . . . remind you.'

'Oh . . . it doesn't matter.' She thought about it for a moment, remembering. 'I can't believe I actually did that.'

'Can't you? I wish I knew that I could "actually do that", if I had to. We talk about it quite a lot, you see . . . wondering whether we've really got it in us . . .' He carefully balanced another card on the construction in front of him, to make a roof. 'And we hear stories in the mess. About deserters. They shoot them for cowardice, as an example to the others. They have to, because it's letting down the side – can't have men just wandering off and deserting. But some of them can't help it, you see . . . they get the jim-jams . . . can't take it any more. And so they blindfold them . . . sit them in a chair . . .'

'Freddie, don't!' Celandine was horrified. 'That's dreadful! Aren't you very frightened?'

'I don't *think* so.' He stood up, restless again, and walked over to the window. The little parlour seemed too enclosed for him now, too small to hold him. 'Not that I think I'm particularly brave or anything. I just want to *be* there. Just want to get *started*. I can't bear all this waiting around.'

Some things about him hadn't really changed after all, Celandine thought. He was just as impatient as ever.

'Do you remember that time we walked all the way round Howard's Hill,' he said, 'looking for fairies?' He was still standing at the window, although little could be seen of the darkening afternoon landscape.

'They're not really fairies . . .' Celandine had been taken by surprise, and the words simply came out. 'I mean, I didn't really see any fairies.'

'Oh. Was it all a joke, then?'

'No. Not exactly. I . . . oh, I don't know *what* I saw. It was so long ago, I can't really remember.' Celandine felt miserable. She didn't want to lie, not to Freddie, but she couldn't tell him the truth. She just couldn't.

He turned towards her and she pretended to concentrate on her card house, unable to look him in the eye. If he asked her again, she thought, she would tell him.

'I'm sorry I didn't bring you a present, Dinah,' he said. 'I didn't know I was going to be able to get away until the last minute, and there's been no time for anything. Tell you what, though. I'll get Jock to let me take you for a spin on his motorbike before I leave. He won't mind, I know. Would you like that?'

She nodded, unable to say anything for the moment.

Chapter Twelve

The Ickri were making better progress. The cold forests of the north were far behind them, and now they were travelling through softer country. Season had turned upon season until it was winter yet again, but it was nothing to the winters they had previously known. Here, as they entered the south-lands, there was at least water to be drunk rather than ice to be cracked, roots that could be dug from ground less hard than rock.

In the early days of their long journey they had attempted to travel southwards by keeping strictly to the forests, picking their way along the woodland trails made by deer and fox and rabbit, but this had proved slow going. They began to risk crossing the open moorland, but although they walked in semi-darkness, after dusk and before the dawn, the bare heath felt too exposing. There was no cover if any threat should suddenly appear, and the ground was so rough and rocky that few could cope with it for any length of time.

In the end they decided that they must follow the

ways made by the Gorji – the cart-tracks and the tow-paths, the quiet lanes and the metalled roads that led so conveniently towards the south. Where there were hedges and ditches and stone walls there was always somewhere to hide, and there were few roads that had none of these things.

By and large the giants were slow and un-observant, easily avoided. They were intent upon their own business, and this did not include hunting for little people by moonlight. The real danger came from the Gorji hounds. Every other giant seemed to be accompanied by a great dribble-snouted beast whose purpose it was to go sniffing for trouble.

Mustard dust was the answer. When the wet muzzle came thrusting through the sheltering bullrushes, or into the dark hedgerow, when the hot stench of hound's breath blew into their very faces, then the Ickri travellers would return the compliment – blowing clouds of the yellow dust into the inquisitive nostrils of the hunter, whilst taking care to pinch their own noses well.

No hound could stand it. The most determined attacker would give a choking yelp, and immediately back away, snorting and pawing at its ugly face, and crying to its master for comfort.

The giants took little notice. Sometimes they would laugh, as they continued along the road. 'What did 'ee find then, old Bowser? A fuzz-peg? Serve 'ee right, then.' Their swinging lanterns would disappear into the night, and once again it would be safe to move on.

It was Una who had suggested that each of the travellers should carry a little pouch of mustard dust – the ground seed of the yellow flowering plant that grew wild at the edges of the fields. And it was Una who had suggested to her father that they should travel by the Gorji roads. She seemed to have some instinct for the direction they should take, the dangers they were likely to face, and how those dangers might be met. It was Avlon's vision that carried the tribe onwards, but it was Una who pointed the way.

Una was secretly worried, however. It was easy enough to keep to a southerly line – the stars and seasons could guide them thus – but how would they know how far to the east or the west they should be? And how would they ever find the exact spot where the water-tribes supposedly dwelt? The land was vast, and the Orbis might be anywhere, or nowhere at all.

By day the tribe usually found woodland in which to eat, sleep and plan the next stage of the journey. Sometimes they were lucky enough to find a barn or cattle byre that was far enough from Gorji habitation to risk an overnight stay, or perhaps a remote bridge that they could safely shelter beneath. As the Gorji world began to wake, so the Ickri took their rest. At sun-wane, as the Gorji fieldworkers laid down their tools and went home for the night, so the Ickri rose to go to work. There was food to prepare, and there was foraging to be done for the next day's provisions. The archers took to the trees in search of birds and squirrels, whilst others collected berries or nuts, mush-rooms, greenstuff – whatever there was to be had.

Each was expected to supply something, and to carry it safe in a pecking bag until the following morning.

Una was excused these duties. As the rest of the tribe hunted for food, she sat alone, studying the parchment charts in the failing light and trying to determine the path they should take. It was a difficult task. There was no doubt that the charts related to the original journey of the Ickri into the north, but as a guide to making the return journey they were almost useless. The faded marks drawn upon the parchment meant little to her, and the movement of her small jasper amulet as she dangled it above the continuous blue line was uncertain, and difficult to interpret.

Eventually the matter was resolved. Una was kneeling beside her father's makeshift shelter one evening, puzzling over the charts as usual and studying the movements of the amulet. There were a few scrawled markings on one of the parchments that looked as though they might represent a Gorji bridge – an arch spanning a stretch of water. The tribe had crossed such a thing a few nights previously, but now the amulet seemed drawn towards it once again. Should she tell her father that they must turn around and go back? She covered her eyes with one of her hands and tried to think.

'Why do 'ee bother with such foolishness?'

It was Maven-the-Green. Rarely glimpsed, always on the fringes of the travelling company, Maven was nevertheless still with them. How she lived was a mystery, for she never ate with the tribe and was never seen to drink or sleep or to even rest her ancient bones. The Elders had warned Una against all contact with Maven, for the mad old hag was viewed with deep suspicion. She was known to carry a hunting blowpipe, and darts tipped with fearful poisons of her own mixing. It was considered bad luck to even look upon her, lest she strike you down. Where had she come from? Nobody knew. She was certainly not one of the Ickri, wingless and humpbacked as she was, yet it was said that Maven had been with the tribe for all time, a wild and lawless creature, beyond all reason. She was dangerous, a dabbler in curses and potions. No, it would not do for the daughter of Avlon to associate with such a one.

And yet Avlon himself did not disapprove. 'I have spoken with her many times,' he once said, as he put his arm about Una's shoulder. 'And I see that she be here to a purpose. Maven will do thee no harm, Una, and much may be learned from her.' Her father was right. Una had come to regard Maven as her friend and guide, and had learned many secrets from her – some of them healing, some of them deadly.

Maven's appearance was strange and terrifying, her face and hands and hair all streaked with green dyes of her own devising. Trails of ivy creepers festooned her crooked frame, so that she rustled as she hobbled along, and yet Una had not heard her approach on this occasion.

Una looked up from her charts, unconcerned to find Maven standing there, her thick skeins of green-tinged hair writhing in the wind like a nest of adders. 'I must find the way,' she said. 'These things are all I have to help me, whether they be foolish or no.'

'Bits o' skin,' said Maven. 'They'll not help 'ee. 'Tis the stone that knows.'

Una held the amulet in the palm of her hand. 'Aye,' she said. 'I think that it does. It tries to show me, but . . .' She closed her fingers over the small fragment of jasper, and squeezed it tight.

'Not that stone,' said Maven. 'T'other 'un.'

Her father was not pleased at the idea. 'The Touchstone?' he said. 'No. The Stone is not for thee to carry, child. 'Tis for me alone, whilst I am ruler of the Ickri. Some day, when I am gone, and if thee should become Queen . . .' He glanced at his brother, Corben, who stood nearby, and who looked equally displeased at Una's suggestion, '. . . *when* thee become Queen – then 'twill be yours to hold. But for now, it belongs to me.'

Later, though, when her father was alone, Una tried again to persuade him. Was not the Touchstone once their guide, was that not its purpose? Where was the harm in seeing whether it could help them?

'It has no power, without the Orbis,' said Avlon. 'Or I would feel it.'

'Let me try,' said Una.

She knew immediately, once the Stone was cradled in her hands, that it held the answer. The pull of it was so strong. Whichever way she turned, the Stone continued to exert a force, a clear and constant magnetism towards one direction. Maven had been right – the Stone could point the way to any that had the gift of interpreting it. No longer would she have to rely on the uncertain twists and turns of the little jasper amulet, the vague markings on cracked parchments. Here was an energy that spoke directly to her at last, drawing her forward as if she were hanging on to a shooting star. She was unable to understand, as yet, why her hands left faint marks upon the Stone – fingerprints that faded away even as she watched them.

Avlon spoke to the assembled company that night. 'I have news,' he said. 'My daughter has made a great discovery.'

Una watched her father as he spoke, saw how he raised the hopes of every heart, assuring each that their purpose was true, and that no matter how long the journey, or how dangerous, they were now at one with their lodestar and would surely find their way.

'We are guided at last,' said Avlon. 'As I knew 'twould be.' He raised the jasper globe aloft, for all to see. 'We have only to follow the Stone, and to survive.'

Avlon was right – they had only to follow the Touchstone, and to survive. But if following the Stone was easy, survival was not. The Ickri were tough, well used to the ravages of northern storm and gale, but in the forests of the north they had at least had shelter and provisions prepared against such times; here they were exposed to all weathers and could only provide for themselves day by day.

The air grew a little warmer as they moved steadily onwards, but there was no let up as yet in the storms that whipped through the countryside, and the trees were still struggling to clothe their winter bones.

In dripping copses, or by trickling roadside ditches, the tribe made whatever shelter was possible, ate whatever could be found, and clung to Avlon's dream of another existence – a world that was waiting for them, perhaps not so far away from this sodden trench, this winter wood.

No, survival was not easy. Moreover, the Stone itself could present them with problems also, for if Una had become more confident of the path they should take, that path had become more dangerous as a result. Where once they had avoided going anywhere near the Gorji settlements, it now appeared that they must pass right through them if Una and the Stone would have their way. Time and again the tribe were led to the borders of some Gorji settlement, and days of travel might then be spent in skirting round the place. Would it not be quicker to hurry through under the protection of darkness, whilst the Gorji slept?

There was a lot of argument over this. To many it was utter madness to think of creeping through Gorji territory by dead of night, but others thought it worth the risk. Avlon took the opportunity to call a general parley. The tribe had found warm shelter in a remote and disused cattle byre, and for once all could be accommodated beneath one roof in relative safety, though that roof sagged and leaked a little. Bindle-wraps and clothing were spread out upon musty hay-bales to dry, and it was comforting to be able to huddle together after the long hours of travelling, and to eat and talk as the rain beat down outside.

Avlon gathered the Elders about him in a corner

of the byre, along with any others that cared to listen.

'What shall we say, then, of this business? The Stone would lead us straight if we would allow it, aye, and oft-times through Gorji settlements if we would follow. *Should* we follow, and put all our trust in the Stone? Haima?'

'I say no. For who can tell what us'd find in such places – or what'd find us?' Haima spoke, and most of the Elders were of the same opinion.

'Aye,' said Maris. ''Twould only take one wean to cry out and they'd have us on all sides.'

'And what o' the hounds?'

'Best keep away. 'Tis naught but foolishness.'

But there were others on the outside of the circle, mostly archers, who thought it worth the risk, and especially where the settlement was not too large.

'They Gorji bain't so lissome as we,' said Berin. 'They be slow.'

'Aye, and all a-snore, anywise.'

'We'd be through and gone afore they knowed it.'

'And see what we should save – a deal of hard travel.'

Avlon was inclined to agree with the Elders, and to follow the path of caution. 'For myself, I should take the chance,' he said. 'And the archers and scouts – they also can look out for themselves. But I have the whole tribe to think of, the old and the young. The risk be too great. We have come too far to lose what has been gained.'

Corben thought differently. 'What ails us?' he said. 'When did we grow so faint of heart? We be Ickri, and we may go where we will. Did thee not say, Avlon, that we should no longer hide like mice? The Gorji be

273

nothing – wingless ogres, slow in head and foot. The least among us could run a ring about the greatest of them. Listen to the Stone, I say, and to your daughter, and let us travel the straightest path.'

The argument moved back and forth, with little new to be added. Avlon was not to be quickly swayed either way. He needed more time to consider.

'Come,' he said. 'Enough for this day. I shall think on, but now we must take some ease.'

Moon followed moon, and still Avlon would not risk coming closer to the Gorji than was necessary. They continued as they had done, skirting around the Gorji settlements no matter how much extra effort it took.

Una was surprised to find that she had an ally in Corben. Her father's younger brother had never shown any great liking for her – but she was grateful to receive whatever support was being offered. She felt strong in her belief that the Touchstone was not only their guide but also their protector, and that somehow the Ickri would come to no harm whilst they carried it towards its destination.

She tried again to explain this feeling to her father as they took in their surroundings one damp and drizzly evening. 'Aye,' said Avlon. 'I also believe that we are treading the way laid down for us and that we are meant to reach our journey's end unharmed. And we draw close – I feel it. But our survival yet hangs upon the right choice at every turn. Who is to make that choice, if not I?'

They were standing at the fringe of a high copse, father and daughter, looking down upon the Gorji

274

town that now lay in their path. The evening sky was growing dark and already they could see lamplights in some of the windows of the distant stone dwellings. Soon it would be time for the tribe to move on.

A broad river ran through the middle of the settlement, and the Ickri would have to cross this somehow. In the town itself there would be bridges, but in the darkening countryside there were none visible. Much of the surrounding landscape was flooded and the thought of passing through this in the blackness of night was not a happy one.

Una drew the hood of her shoulder-wrap more tightly about her face and waited for her father to decide. In summer, she thought, with lighter clothing and nothing to carry, they might almost fly such a distance. They could perhaps launch themselves from the trees and glide over the town, to land safely on the other side. But in the last clinging embrace of winter, cold and wet, burdened with heavy cloaks and muddy bindle-wraps, they were as earthbound as the Gorji themselves. It was plain that they were never bred for such climes. They had adapted as best they could, but this was no world for the Ickri. They belonged in warm treetops, bare-skinned beneath the bright sun – not trudging among rain-soaked hedgerows and claggy fields. Spring was here, and yet the season refused to turn.

Avlon turned his draggled head, a faint look of surprise on his tired face.

'Greetings, Maven,' he said. 'Do thee come to advise us?'

The crooked figure was standing a little way off, peering out over the landscape from beneath a ragged shawl. Una had not seen her arrive.

'What would 'ee hear from I?' said Maven. 'What 'ee do already know? That 'tis a danger to come so close to the Gorji? The choice be already made, maister, as all choices be already made. And all shall be as 'twould ever be.'

Avlon wiped the droplets of water from his beard, and looked down at the Gorji settlement. The lamp-lights were becoming more numerous, now that the night was drawing in, and the surrounding country-side, flooded and treacherous, grew correspondingly darker. 'Come, then,' he said at last. 'We shall take the risk – and the shorter way.' He put his arm around Una's shoulders and together they walked back to where the tribe was waiting, huddled in groups beneath the soaking trees.

By the time the lights from the Gorji settlement were extinguished, and it was judged that the giants must be sleeping, the drizzle had stopped. A chill breeze blew along the turnpike, and the moon appeared, high and hazy, among the ragged clouds. The Ickri crouched in silence beside a low wall at the edge of the town, nervously waiting for a signal from the scouts.

Peck and Rafe eventually appeared, hanging over the wall to whisper their report to Avlon. 'All quiet.' A general shuffle, and the entire tribe had clambered into the roadway. They were on Gorji territory, closer to the giants than most of them had ever been.

The scouts moved cautiously ahead, together with three of the King's archers. Then came Avlon, and Una – who carried the Touchstone – accompanied by more of the guard. The rest of the tribe followed, with Corben and his own archers bringing up the rear.

There were too many of them. As the great stone dwellings began to loom above them, dark and solid against the watery moon, it seemed impossible that some pair of wakeful eyes would not catch sight of them, creeping in a straggly line through the rain-washed streets. Somewhere behind those threatening casements there must surely be an ogre who had chanced to observe them, and who might be rousing his comrades at this very moment . . .

Una felt sick now, sick with the thought that she had been the one to bring them to this. She wanted to turn around, to go back to the relative safety of the fields and spinneys. The smells of the Gorji, and all their world, was in her nostrils – the mingled odours of baking bread and stale fermentations that wafted up through metal gratings, the strange fruits that lay discarded and rotting beside the raised stone path-ways, piles of horse manure, damp ashes. She could smell, too, the scent of her own fear, and the fear of those around her as they hurried past the long lines of black metal railings – cruelly tipped like spears – or hugged the slimy walls of dripping archways and side-stepped the iron-bound wooden doors that were set into the pavements and which spoke of echoing cavernous spaces below. The place was far bigger than it had seemed from their distant hilltop, and Una felt foolish to have imagined that they could ever have floated over it. It was huge.

Whenever they came to a halt, or a fork in the roadway, the leading party paused and turned to look at her, their anxious eyes searching for hers in the darkness. Which path should they take? And according to the pull of the Stone she would signal the direction, this way or that. The rear body of the party could not always be seen, and so it could only be hoped that nothing had happened to them. Una glanced up at her father and he smiled encouragement at her. She saw that his brow glistened damp in the moonlight, although the rain had stopped some time ago.

They found a long set of slippery steps that led them up onto a massive bridge, triple arched over a broad river, and here they gathered for a few moments, gazing through the stanchions at the roaring waters below as they waited for the rear guard to join them.

To either end of the bridge a lantern burned, throwing curved shadows across the long stretch of glistening cobbles, and the thought of crossing such a distance frightened them. Once out in the middle the entire tribe would be completely exposed, trapped if they were seen, and with no way of escaping but to throw themselves into the black torrent that rushed beneath them.

Yet this was the reason they had risked passing through the settlement – to cross the floods – and now was no time to turn back. One last look around and

Peck and Rafe were away, scurrying low, keeping to whatever shadow they could find. There was no possibility of hearing a signal above the roar of the waters, and the main company could only wait until they judged that the scouts had safely reached the other side. Nervously they began to follow.

Halfway across the bridge Una dropped the Touchstone. A great clanging sound split the night, a single note bursting through the darkness, and in her fright she stumbled against her father. The orb slipped from her grasp, landed on the cobbles and began to roll towards the edge of the bridge. Una staggered forward, lunging for the Stone, but was knocked off balance completely as one of the archers ran into her. She fell and caught a last horrifying glimpse of the orb about to disappear between the stanchions. Her vision was blocked for a few moments, and by the time she had managed to disentangle herself from the fallen archer, the Touchstone had gone.

Gone! The clanging sound rang out once more, but now Una paid it little heed. She clambered to her feet and stared dumbly at the gap between the stanchions.

'Come *on*, chi'! 'Tis but a Gorji thing – a tang – a bell.' Her father's whispered voice. He was gripping her upper arm, urgently drawing her away . . .

A hand miraculously reached out and placed the Touchstone in hers. It was still safe! The waters roared louder as Una allowed herself to be hurried onwards through the confusion. A tang. Yes, she had heard them sometimes, tolling across the distant landscape.

A Gorji thing. She clasped the Touchstone to her chest. As they passed beneath the lantern on the far side of the bridge, Una recalled that the hand that returned the Stone to her had been streaked with green.

The road out of town now lay straight ahead, but it seemed to go on for ever. There were many distant buildings yet to pass, and the nerves of the travellers had been shaken. Could they not find some route other than the main highway? From their vantage point upon the bridge they could see a large area of moonlit parkland bordering the roadside. The parkland was bounded by ornate railings – and a long hedge. A hedge would at least give them shelter and a chance of safety. If they could enter this enclosure, they might make their way forward by keeping close to the line of foliage. There were even some trees in there, a group of tall elms that stood out in the open, some distance from the hedge. That was good – although a cluster of dark and mysterious shapes beneath the trees made them hesitate. Peck and Rafe would scout ahead.

They descended the steps at the side of the bridge, slipped between the railings by twos and threes, clambered through the hedge beyond, and were glad to find grass and earth beneath their feet once more. The ground was sodden by the heavy rain, but not flooded. This was better.

Once assembled beneath the shadow of the hedge the tribe felt safer. They began to creep forward, listening for the whistled signals of the scouts. It gradually became apparent that the dark objects beneath the trees were wagons of some sort, although not of the broad open type used by the Gorji field-workers. These were taller, for the most part, and covered. Some of them were simply draped over with cloth. Others were like the wagons that occasionally appeared in the woods – the travelling dwellings of those giants who called themselves Romni – that stayed for a few days and then disappeared, leaving only a patch of flattened earth and a pile of woodash to tell of their coming and going.

And yet there was something else here, something more dangerous than the mere presence of giants.

The entire company instinctively came to a halt, listening. There was some distance between the hedge and the group of silent wagons beneath the trees, but the long line of tribespeople were nervous of passing by. Why was there no signal from the scouts?

Una moved out into the field a little way, towards the wagons, gently breathing the damp night air through her nostrils. She heard her father's whisper – '*Una!*' – but she continued just a few steps further. The breeze was blowing away from her, and yet she caught a whiff of something. Horses? No . . . not horses. Animals, though. A little closer, and she might learn more . . .

There was a sharp crackle of breaking branches behind her, and she jumped forward in alarm, turning her head to look fearfully over her shoulder. The Ickri were disappearing like rabbits beneath the hedge, and something – *someone* – was coming over the top of it.

Gorji. Two of them. One was floundering on the ground, the other balancing on the railings. The second giant leaped forward – and crashed through the hedge. Una fled.

She scuttled over to the wagons and threw herself beneath the nearest one, crouching low behind one of the wheels. A strong animal smell surrounded her, heavy with musk, unfamiliar.

The giants were whispering to each other – 'Shhhhh!' – and softly giggling. They picked themselves up from the ground and clumsily attempted to brush the mud from their clothing. They were dressed in black and white. The moon sailed bright in a clearing sky now, and Una could see their every move. The figures began creeping towards the wagons – coming her way. She tried to stay calm. Breathe out . . . breathe in . . . breathe out . . . breathe in . . .

A soft creak from the wooden planking overhead startled her, and the wheel that she was hiding behind rocked slightly. Una risked a glance upwards. Something above her, something very heavy, had momentarily shifted position – an alarming thought, but there was more immediate danger from the approaching giants.

'Which one, do you think?' They were whispering again.

'Can't say, old man. Might have to try them all.'

'Hallo, though. What's this?' One of the shadowy figures was stooping – picking something up from the ground.

Una put her hand to her mouth, and tried not to cry out. She could scarce believe it – had not realized what had happened until that moment. It was the Touchstone. Twice – *twice* – in one night, she had dropped it. In her panic she had failed to even notice. This time it was surely lost to her.

She was frantic. This could *not* be. One of the Gorji was holding the Stone up to the moon and staring at it. He was swaying slightly.

'What is it – a co . . . a coc'nut ball?'

'Bit heavy for that, I sh'think. Jolly little thing, though. Keep it for luck, eh? I'll put it . . .' The giant pulled at his clothing and nearly overbalanced. He let out a long breath, as if to steady himself, '. . . in my . . . pocket. There.'

'Very good. Now for the bear. Lesh try this one.'

'Right you are, dear boy.'

They came staggering towards the very wagon where Una lay hidden. Now she could only see their legs and feet – close enough to touch, they were – and she shrank back behind the spokes of the wheel. Their footwear was very strange, black and shiny in the moonlight. What was she to do about the Touchstone? Breathe out . . . breathe in . . .

'Lift up the canvas, old man. Anything in there? See any fur?'

'Shhh.'

'Two hairs from a bear's backside. One for you, one for me. Bring us luck when we're soldiering, eh? One f'r you, one f'r me . . .'

'Shhh.'

'Don't keep saying "shhh". Make a feller nerv—
Good Lord! What's *that* thing?'

'What? I can't see what's in there . . .'

'Not in *there*. Over there – under the trees. See it?'

The feet moved back from the wagon a little. Una
crept further into the shadow.

'Where? Under what tr—? Oh . . .'

The feet were quite still now, and there was a long
silence. Una could hear the giants breathing –
uneven, panting slightly.

'Is it ash . . . ash . . . ash*leep*, you s'pose?'

'Dunno. I 'spec they must sleep standing up. Like
horses. Tell you what – I'll keep an eye on it. You have
another look in there, and I'll jus' . . . I'll jus' keep an
eye . . .'

'Right you are, then.'

One set of shiny black feet moved uncertainly back
to the wagon.

Una heard the voice begin to mutter. 'Aha! Steady
does it, then. One f'r *you* . . . and one . . . f'r *me* . . .' –
and then it seemed as though the world had
exploded. There was a low rumbling noise above her,
a deep gurgling snarl, that burst into a roar so terrible
her entire body was shaken by the thundering
vibration of it. Una clung to the wet turf for an instant,
cowering beneath the awful sound, but then her nerve
broke altogether and she wriggled out from beneath
the rocking wagon, squealing, with her hands covering her ears. Oblivious to whatever the Gorji might be
doing, she scrambled to her feet and ran.

She ducked under two more wagons, banging one

of her wings against a heavy wooden shaft, not caring, desperate only to escape.

The trees. If she could but find a low branch, she might be safe – anything, anywhere . . . Into the purple shadows of the elms she ran, as yet another dreadful roar made her instinctively turn her head. Then the darkness swallowed her up completely. Una stretched out her arms to save herself – too late – and blindly crashed into a tree-trunk.

No, not a tree-trunk. As she fell backwards with the impact, she heard a deep snort of alarm, a bellow of anger, and knew that she had stumbled against something warm and alive. This thing moved – and it was moving now, a massive bulk, swaying in the darkness above her, bigger than a Gorji wagon, bigger than the sky. Una scrambled to her knees, caught the sharp clink of metal upon metal and was suddenly whisked upwards – gasping as the earth shot away from her. Her wings spread automatically and she flapped them in panic, though the world was spinning head over heels. A thump that knocked the breath out of her and she was on her back in the mud again, momentarily helpless, but away from the elms at least, and away from the awful creature that was chained there in the darkness. She rolled over and over, terrified at how the very tree roots shook beneath her.

The shrill bellows of the trampling monster under the trees were even louder than the roars from the creature in the wagon – such a noise that Una could hardly keep her feet – and amid the roars and bellows came the baying of Gorji hounds, and the angry shouts of Gorji voices.

'Who's there?'

'Isaac! That you? Flares – get the flares!'

Flickers of light appeared, flaming brands that threw long sinister shadows across the encampment, so that the leaping figures of the Gorji seemed to be everywhere.

More shouts:

'Hold the dogs! Hold 'em, Reuben! A pound to a penny it'll be some o' they College boys larkin' about – and we can't afford to be killing the customers.'

'College? Well, just let I get a sight of 'em, then. I'll give 'em some larnin' they'll not forget.'

The hounds barked and yelped, demented with frustration at being held back from their quarry.

Una dodged between the wagons, anywhere to escape the mayhem, whimpering with terror. The hedge. She had to get away from this monstrous din and back to the hedge, where there was at least some chance of safety. She could see the long dark line of foliage, not so very far away, but the idea of covering that stretch of open ground was terrifying. Would they see her? There was no time to wonder – just run. A deep breath, and she broke cover, scampering across the moonlit grass and keeping as low as she could.

Almost immediately there was a horrible choking noise from somewhere behind her – a strangled yelp – and then a howl of triumph. They'd seen her! One of the hounds had seen her . . .

'Towler!' A shout, raw on the night air.

'Damn*blast* the thing – he's loose! Towler! Leave it! Leave it!'

Una dared not look. The hedge was dancing towards her, but not quickly enough. She would never be able to reach it in time, could never outrun the horror that was chasing her. The splatter of heavy paws and the eager panting breath – so near – drove her to one last effort. Just as it seemed that the thing must drag her down, she flapped her wings and rose clumsily at the hedge, heard the dreadful click of powerful jaws snapping around her legs, felt the rough brush of leaves against her toes, flapped once again, and she was over.

Over the hedge and the railing spikes she tumbled, exhausted . . . and landed straight into the lap of a giant. Too late she saw it coming – a glimpse of shiny black footwear, a huge upturned face – but there was not a thing that she could do about it. Her shoulder crumpled against the giant's stomach, and she grabbed frantically at loose material, struggling to right herself.

The giant said 'Oof!', and one of his big arms knocked against her, so that she was sent spinning away from him. Una crashed into the railings, banging her head on one of the metal bars, and for a few moments was utterly helpless. The hound was barking and whining on the other side of the hedge, and the giant was struggling to sit up, but Una was unable to move for the deep dark pain in her head.

The Gorji appeared to slowly split himself into two, to grow another torso – an awful thing to behold – but then Una realized that there really were two of them after all, one of them appearing from behind the other. It was the same pair that she had been hiding from earlier. They must have clambered back over the hedge, and now *they* were hiding – sprawled out on the flat wet paving stone behind the railings, hoping not to be seen. Why could she not move? The hound had stopped barking. Perhaps it had gone away.

The blurry sound of a voice seemed to wake her.

'Maurice, old man . . . can *you* see it as well? Or is it just me?'

'No no no. I see it too. Do ass . . . assure you, John. See it perf'ly well . . . Must have escaped from the men . . . menajry. Zoo. Monkey of some sort.'

'Don't think it *is* a monkey, though.'

'Nor do I, old chum. Perf'ly honest.'

The giants were both sitting up now, one leaning forward to peer unsteadily at her.

'Tell you what, John . . . Make a dam' fine mascot, eh? For the reg'ment. *Dam'* fine – don't you think?'

'Agree with you, abshlutely. Better than some mangy old terrier.'

'Shall we keep it?'

'Got to catch it first.'

'Tally-ho, then.'

The giants began to struggle to their feet, and the movement brought Una to her senses at last. She grasped one of the metal railings and pulled herself upright.

Along the opposite side of the road ran a wall, too high for her to scramble over, but there was a large

288

open gateway set into the stonework, and beyond the gate she thought that she could see yew trees. Trees meant safety. After the horrors she had witnessed this night, these two stumbling ogres were not so very frightening, but she was dizzy with pain and as unsteady on her feet as the Gorji themselves.

As she pushed herself away from the railings, she heard one of the giants gasp in amazement.

'My . . . my *God*, Maurice! Look at that! Do you see? It's got . . . it's got *wings . . .*'

Una staggered out into the muddy roadway, slipped and almost fell, yet still managed to reach the wall before the Gorji had even stepped from the side path. Beneath the arched gateway and into the shadows beyond she crept, looking about her for a place to hide. She found no shortage – for there were large blocks of stone set in the grassy earth, row upon row of them in the moonlight, some tall and strangely carved, cross-shaped, some plain and squat like great caskets. Amid the rows of stones a curving pathway led towards a massive dwelling, dark and alone, with a tower that rose tall against the night sky. In such a place as this she could hide from a whole tribe of giants. There would be no need for her to fly up into one of the yew trees, and thus risk being seen. Una ducked down behind one of the cross-shaped stones, pressed a hand to her aching head, and waited.

The giants appeared in the gateway, their silhouettes swaying against one another. They began to move forward along the path, looking from side to side, crouching slightly with arms outstretched, as though in readiness to catch her. What crack-nogs they were, she thought. She would wait until they had passed her by, then slip back out through the gates. It would be simple enough. The edge of the settlement could not be so very far away, and the tribe would surely be on the lookout for her there. Una gently rubbed the side of her head, feeling the swelling where she had collided with the metal bars. Once she was returned to the tribe, she would be able to remedy her pain. Perhaps Maven might help her . . .

Then she remembered the Touchstone.

Her heart jumped at the thought. How could she have forgotten about it? And how could she now leave without it? She could not.

Somehow she would have to get it back.

The giants had left the pathway and were now creeping among the stones, still bent low and whispering to one another.

Una watched them as they lurched back and forth. There was little danger of her being caught, or even seen. The greater fear was that they should tire of searching for her and so leave this place. What would she do then? Follow them?

They had stopped. They were sitting on a step at the base of a tall cross-shaped object, talking. Una dodged from stone to stone, drawing closer. Their speech was loud enough now, but she could barely understand their words.

'Gone to earth, old boy, I'm afraid.'

Una peeped from the shadows of a large stone carving. One of the giants was lying down on the step beneath the tall cross. The other was still sitting up.

Clanggg! A huge metallic sound rang out in the night, and Una shrank backwards in fright. It was the tang – the same clamorous noise that they had heard from the bridge – but closer now. She looked up. The sound came from the high tower. *Clanggg!* Again. And again. She counted the times . . . ickri . . . dickri . . . dockri . . . That was it – no more. The sound echoed into the darkness, and died away.

'John! John – get up!'

One of the giants was looking directly towards her.

'Look, old man – there it *is*!'

'Wha . . . ?'

They'd seen her – one of them had. The giant that had been sitting was now standing, leaning forward, peering towards her hiding place. The other began to push himself upright.

'What? Where?'

'*There!* See it?'

Una quickly glanced about her, trying to decide which way to run, then turned back towards the giants. They were looking her way, but their eyes were raised slightly, not focused directly upon her. She was still in deep shadow behind the stone carving – *had* they seen her? The figures swayed closer, and now Una was certain that whatever they had spotted, it was not her, for one of them came to a sudden halt and said,

'Maurice, you dam' . . . fool. That'sh a ruddy angel.'

'Eh?'

'Itsh an *angel* – can't you see? Stone thing . . .

291

marble thing. Shtatue. Def'nitley not eshcaped from the zoo.'

'D'you know . . . b'lieve you're right. Angel, yes. 'S the wings, you see. The wings . . .'

'Yes. The wings. Very pretty, all same.'

'Very. Do you know, I'm 'bout done in, old man.'

'Me too. We'll sit down again, shall we?'

The giants staggered back to their step at the foot of the cross, and lay down. One of them yawned, and said, 'Never mind, though. We got two hairs from a bear's backside, didn't we? Bring us luck, when we're soldiering.'

'Perf'ly honest, old man, don't believe it *was* a bear.'

'No? What, then?'

'Tiger.'

'Ah. Oh well. 'Night, old man.'

'Night night.'

Una stood up and rubbed her shoulders, trying to warm herself. The giants had been still for a long while. Did they sleep?

She thought of the tribe – how they would be worried about her. They might perhaps even be searching for her. That would be dangerous. She could wait no longer.

On silent footsteps across the wet grass she ran towards the great stone cross. The two figures huddled beneath it were breathing heavily, eyes closed. Their faces, resting on the cold stone step, were level with hers. How helpless and foolish those faces looked, so pale and distorted in the moonlight. They were young, she realized. Giants they might be, but only lately full-grown. Long white wraps about their necks, they wore, grass-stained now, and torn. Their curious black footwear, so shiny when she had first seen it, had since become clagged and spattered with mud.

One of them had the Touchstone, had hidden it somewhere in his clothing. But which of them? And where would he hide it? Una stretched out a hand and gingerly touched a corner of dark material that hung over the side of the step, watching the eyes of the sleeping giants as she did so, lest one of them should suddenly wake. There was no reaction, and so she grew bolder, lifting the corner of material, and gently letting it fall again. A tiny clink of sound resulted from this movement. Still the giants slept on.

I'll put it in my . . . pocket. Those were the words she had heard, as she had knelt beneath the wagon. Pocket. Did he mean pouchen – one of the pouches that the Gorji sewed into their clothing?

There was a flap on the piece of hanging material. Una lifted it, and found that she could put her hand inside the cloth. Again the faint jingle of sound. The tips of her fingers touched . . . metal? Bits of metal – loose, and separate. She drew a piece from its hiding place and studied it in the moonlight. A small metal disc, smooth-edged, faintly patterned – and of no interest to her. She threw it lightly onto the grass.

How many pouchen would two giants have between them? She might still be searching at sun-wax, and it was too cold to hope that they would sleep for so long. *I'll put it in my . . . pocket.* It had been the deeper of the two voices – that much she remembered – but which giant did that voice belong to? She must find it . . . must find it . . .

A thought came to her. Perhaps if she could not find the Touchstone, the Touchstone might find her? Aye. Perhaps. She would try.

Una placed her hands as near as she dared to the body of the second giant, allowing her outstretched fingers to hover above the torso of the sleeping form. Eyes half closed, she tried to leave this strange place behind, to let her hands be drawn where they would go. Find me. Tell me where to look . . .

Her breathing fell into the deep sighing rhythm of the giant's breathing, slowly in, slowly out . . . slowly in . . . and slowly out. Her eyes were closed now, and she drifted into the darkness. Once again she knelt beneath the Gorji wagon, breathing out . . . breathing in . . . out . . . and in, watching, listening. Frightened. And once again she heard the giant's voice. *I'll put it . . .* breathing out . . . *in my . . . pocket.* She heard him say it, saw him do it, felt him breathe it now. This was the one. Aye, this was the one.

She half opened her eyes again, watching her hands, floating like pale birds' wings above dark waves . . . searching . . . circling . . . descending. And finding. Here. It was here. She could feel the pull of it, seeking for her . . .

Her fingertips touched the creases of the material, gently explored the rumpled folds, found the opening

of the pocket. Breathe out, breathe in . . . slowly . . .
slowly . . . there. Her hand closed around the
Touchstone, and . . . *Clanggg!* She was no longer
breathing.

The tang pealed out again and again. Ickri . . .
dickri . . . dockri . . . quatern . . .

Una watched in horror, unable to move, as the last
echoes of the tang faded into silence. The giant
opened his eyes. He looked straight at her and smiled.

'An angel . . .' His voice was soft, barely a murmur.
'Angels to watch over me . . .' he raised a hand
towards her face, but lowered it again without touching her, 'when I'm . . . soldiering . . .' The eyes grew
vacant, rolled upwards slightly, and then closed once
more.

Una waited, motionless, feeling the silence steal
about her shoulders. Then carefully, carefully, she
drew the Touchstone from the depths of the giant's
garment and stepped back, watching for a little
longer. He was asleep.

The Stone was safe, and she could breathe again.
She backed away a few more paces, still cautious, still
unwilling to believe that the Gorji could really
slumber through the sound of the tang. Finally she
turned away – but then very nearly let go of the
Touchstone for the third time that terrible night.
She was standing face to face with the thing that she
had been hiding behind earlier, the stone carving
that one of the giants had mistaken for her, and
called . . . *angel*.

Pale and beautiful it stood, a winged figure on a

raised platform of stone, head bowed so that it looked down upon her. In its cupped hands it held something small and round, so that Una, with her own hands cupped about the Touchstone, felt that she was staring up in wonder at an image of herself.

And yet what a poor imitation she was of such a perfect creature. The wings of this vision were the graceful wings of a powerful bird, feathered pinions that could fly across the universe – to Elysse and back again, if need be. Her own wings could scarcely lift her over a hedge. And the descending folds of that glistening gown mocked the earth-stained shift that hung about her scratched and bruised body. She looked closer. The object that was born so lovingly in those cupped hands was a heart.

Had the Gorji made this? Were the foolish ogres, the destroyers, the wreckers of all that existed, truly able to fashion such things? This was some creature of a higher tribe – more akin to the Ickri than the Gorji – and yet she had never heard tell of them. *Angels*.

Una knelt and touched one of the delicate bare feet, letting her palm rest on the smooth white stone, half surprised not to find it warm and alive. The figure was raised upon a block of darker stone into which strange markings had been carved, small groups of shapes divided into rows. Some of the shapes were repeated. Here was one like another, and there it appeared again. Una let her finger trace the shapes, following them along the lines, feeling the clean precise edges of the cut stone. She was reminded of the faded blue markings on the parchments that had been her guide at the beginning of this journey. Some of those markings had been similar to these. Did they have some meaning that the Ickri had once understood, but had now forgotten?

The wind had changed. Una was aware of it as she stood up and backed away, still puzzling over the lines of markings. The air was warmer. A small sound made her glance over her shoulder at the giants. One of them had moved a little, but still they slept.

The Ickri tribe's journey was nearly over, Una realized. Something in the urgent beating heart of the Touchstone told her so, and she must leave this place now and carry that news to her father. The tribe would be waiting for her. She knew that they were safe. And spring was here at last, born on the changing wind, this she also knew. But the strange markings beneath the angel's feet – these had no meaning for her. Some things she could divine, and some things she could not.

In Loving Memory
Pte. Wyndham Frederick Howard
"FREDDIE"
1898 - 1915

Chapter Thirteen

Now that Nina had left Mount Pleasant there was no longer any proof of what had really happened that night at the swimming pool, and so Mary Swann and Co. were in little danger of ever being found out. Celandine felt vulnerable once more, for who would be inclined to believe her side of the story – she who was supposedly half-German, and a witch to boot? Nobody.

The whispers around her grew louder and ever more persistent. She was evil, violent. She was practised in the use of vicious weapons – possibly knives, certainly boot heels. She laid curses upon her enemies, and was rumoured to dabble in black arts. Tiny Lewis's lurid account of what she had seen in the sanatorium had been embellished many times over, so that now the entire Lower School were half-prepared to believe that the Witch had raised Jessop from the dead and caused her to float about the room like a hovering Lazarus. Such a person was too dangerous to be tolerated, would have to be dealt with, must be stopped.

And yet they were frightened of her, Celandine knew that. If ever she chanced to find herself alone with one of her enemies – walking towards her in a corridor, coming out of one of the washroom cubicles, picking up a book from the library – then that person would sidle past her nervously, eyes half averted but still watchful. None would dare confront her, yet the very thing that protected her, her reputation, was also the thing that set her apart. They were frightened of her, and so they hated her. She had seen things that they would never see, knew things that they would never know – but she also knew that eventually they would destroy her for being different. She must escape.

Escape! The thought of it was like a window opening on to the day. Why had it not occurred to her before? This was a school, not a prison. She would write to her mother and beg that she might be taken away, just as Nina had been taken away.

No. That would take too long – and her mother might refuse. She would simply leave. Straight after supper would be the best time. If she was missed at prep, it would probably be assumed that she was seeing Matron or something. She would walk down to Town station, catch a train, and go home to Mill Farm . . .

It hadn't worked. How stupid to have tried to run away whilst still in her school uniform. Once again Celandine found herself in Miss Craven's office, staring at the strange collection of stuffed animals

299

behind the glass door of their display case, wondering about the otter and why it had a mackerel in its jaws. A mackerel was definitely a sea fish. Perhaps the animal was a sea otter? But in that case it was surely the wrong sort of otter to be in the company of a stoat, a weasel, and a pine-marten . . .

'I have written to your father, naturally, and I imagine that I will hear from him in due course.' Miss Craven was still droning on. 'I have given him my assurance that this will *not* occur again. From now on you are gated – by which I mean strictly confined to school premises. You are barred from going into town, and from all excursions, including those that might take place during nature lessons. Under those circumstances you will remain in school and do extra classwork. I shall consider further action once I have received a reply from your father. In the meantime you will take five hundred lines, to be handed in to me on Monday morning – '*I must learn that the only remedy for self-pity is self-discipline.*' Yes, Howard, you have displayed nothing but self-pity and cowardice in running away. Where would this country be if our soldiers at the Front all decided to simply run away, as you have done? What would happen to *them*, do you suppose? Would *they* simply be given five hundred lines and sent to bed without any supper? No, I think not. Go away, then, and consider just how fortunate you are. Dismissed.'

The following week Celandine received two letters – one from her father, and one from Freddie. She very much wanted to open Freddie's letter first, but she made herself put it to one side. It would be better to get the one from her father out of the way. There was just a little time before first bell, and so she took the letters back up to the dormitory and sat on the end of her bed. The thought of reading her father's letter made her feel quite ill – a feeling that was made worse by the strong smell of paint that filled the upper floors. The corridors were being decorated and the distemper fumes made her head ache.

Her father was angry, of course. Celandine skimmed through the pages, wincing as the criticisms jumped out at her – throwing away her opportunities . . . great personal expense . . . enough worries already . . . your mother has become quite ill with strain . . .

It was unbearable. She read through to the end as quickly as she could and stuffed the folded pages back into their envelope. Later, perhaps, she would try again, but for now she was desperate to hear what Freddie had to say.

Dearest Dinah,

At last I have a little time to scribble some letters, and have already written home as I promised I would. I have given Mama and Father all details *so you don't have to keep it a secret any more. We are in France, but I'm not sure where, quite. My geography was never very good, and I don't suppose I'd be allowed to say in any case. I can at least say that I am safe and well, and some way back from the front line. Most of our regiment has been sent to* ———, *and just a few of us have been brought over here to help with the horses. There was a shortage of men who had experience with horses, and so I was picked to go. I wish I had kept quiet, because this isn't much different to being back at Mill Farm, apart from the noise, which is terrible and goes on day and night. I spend most of my time mucking out, and holding the horses while Corporal Blake tries to shoe them, and when I'm not doing that I'm loading up the wagons with crates of munitions. I have only held a rifle once since we arrived here.*

The worst of it is the rain and the mud, although I am not so badly off as those poor blighters in the forward trenches. At least I have somewhere dry to sleep. Last week a man was ——— for ——— . . .

Most of the last couple of paragraphs had been obliterated, inked out with a heavy black pen. The letter had been censored. Celandine held the page up to the light, trying to work out what Freddie had been trying to tell her. *Last week a man was . . .* what? Shot for desertion? For cowardice? This was her guess, because of the conversation they had had at Christmas. She imagined the picture that Freddie had perhaps tried to paint, of a poor frightened soldier sitting upon a chair, blindfolded and shaking in the early morning drizzle. Unable to take it any more . . . an attack of the jim-jams . . . a deserter. A coward.

Was she a deserter and a coward too? Perhaps she was. Perhaps her father was right, and she should simply try harder. Perhaps Miss Craven was right, and she should count herself lucky.

So she tried, for a while. Instead of simply accepting her solitude, she made an effort to be friendly, to ignore the taunts and whispered comments and just be nice to everyone. She tried especially hard to be friends with Molly Fletcher, who always appeared to be on the outside of Mary Swann's group of followers.

It didn't work – in fact it only seemed to make things worse. Her eagerness to please was seen as a sign of weakness, and any effort to join in a game or a conversation was met with open hostility. Go away, Witch. Did you say something, *fraulein?* Sorry, we don't understand *German.*

Go away. If only she could . . .

Celandine stared vacantly at the hunched shoulders of the girl in front of her. Another hour of prep to go. No sound but the scratching of pens, the occasional sigh, the shifting of uncomfortable bodies on hard wooden seats. Gillian Aberdeen sat at the head of the class, on prep duty for the week, and looked as weary as those in her charge. The hour would pass, the bell would ring, and then it would be supper and bed. And again tomorrow, and tomorrow and tomorrow. She couldn't stand it – couldn't take it any more. Anything would be better than this.

But even if she did escape, where should she go? There was no welcome awaiting her at home, that much was clear. Her father would simply send her back to Mount Pleasant. She could run away to . . . to London, for instance, but what then? She had no money to speak of, and where would she live, and how?

It was no good. There was nowhere else for her to be. If only she had her own desert island. If only she could sit for ever beneath the trees and eat blackberries and catch fish, and have no more worries, like Robinson Crusoe.

Or like Fin.

Fin! The sudden idea of him, and of Howard's Hill, and of that secret other world she knew, ran through her with such a shock that it made her gasp out loud. She could go there!

Could she, though? *Could* she?

'Something the matter, Howard?' Aberdeen was looking at her, stifling a yawn as she spoke.

'No, Aberdeen. I . . . I just thought of something, that's all. An answer.'

'An answer? I should write it down, then, if I were you.'

She had failed a second time, and she felt utterly ridiculous. To imagine that she could just try the same method of escape, albeit in her ordinary clothes, and get away with it had been brainless. The stuffed animals grinned at her horribly as Miss Craven lectured her yet again.

'I can see that I have been far too lenient with you, Howard – a failing of mine, so I am told. I try to be charitable, where I should simply chastize. I try to persuade, where I should punish. Very well. Enough. It appears that mere words have no effect upon you, and so we must resort to something more fundamental. We shall not be beaten in this. But you *will* be, I'm afraid. Miss Belvedere,' the headmistress turned to her colleague, 'I wonder if you'd be good enough to spare a little of your time and show this girl how we deal with persistent truancy? I would do it myself, but I find that I have yet another unfortunate letter to write.'

'Certainly, Miss Craven. You can leave it to me. Come along, Howard.'

Celandine followed Miss Belvedere to the staffroom, where the leather strap would be waiting for her, coiled and ready in its dark wooden drawer.

This time she felt as though she *had* been beaten – and not just on her hands. Celandine looked at her tear-stained face in the washroom mirror and saw that she was helpless, her spirit all but gone, drowning in the icy water that swirled around her aching palms. She was ready to give up. There was no escape. There was no alternative to this. Her daydream of running away and living with the Various seemed ridiculous to her now. The Various! For all she knew, they were another of her silly imaginings, like the girl at the window, or like Nina's 'cure'. She wasn't *different*. She wasn't *special*. She was just stupid, and strange. And lonely.

They sensed her defeat, the girls who had once been so wary of her. They jostled her in the corridors now, flicked wet towels at her in the changing rooms, chanted her name in derision. '*Celandine, Celandine, caught the seven thirty-nine...*' She was no witch. She had no powers. She was a limping fox, a blind snake, a creature that could be kicked with impunity by the smallest among them. There was no fight left in her.

Mary Swann, who had waited so long for her revenge, made an announcement one Saturday at lunchtime. 'I've been thinking about what I should do when I leave school. I shall have to have a career of some sort, you know – and I've decided to become a hairdresser.'

'Well, I think that's a *lovely* idea,' said Alicia Tremlett, and there were murmurs of general approval up and down the length of the dining table.

'Yes,' said Mary. 'The thing is, I want to start practising now – today. I have some *very* sharp scissors and a jolly good hairbrush. Now all I need is a volunteer to practise on. I could do with someone with *lots* of hair so that I can get plenty of practise in, you see.'

Celandine was aware that all eyes were now looking her way, but she took another spoonful of tapioca and said nothing.

'Howard has lots of hair,' said Alicia.

'Yes, that's true,' said Mary. 'And being *German*, it would probably look well on her if it was cut quite short. Like the Kaiser's. What do you think, Howard? Let's make an appointment for later on today shall we? Just after the hockey match with Queen's. At about half-past four – would that suit?'

'She doesn't look very happy about it,' said Alicia.

'Probably a bit nervous,' said Mary. 'I may need a few of you to help me hold her down.'

Just as lunchtime was coming to a close, Celandine was summoned from the dining hall. A message to go and see the headmistress. Miss Craven's office *again*? What had she done this time?

Halfway along the main corridor, she faltered. A horrible cold feeling had come over her – a creeping about her shoulders, a cloudiness of vision. This was something bad. She forced herself onwards, and knocked at Miss Craven's study door.

The headmistress was seated at her desk, an opened letter in front of her – a depressingly familiar sight.

'Come and sit down.' Miss Craven's voice was quiet and serious. A chair had been placed in front of the heavy oak desk. Why?

Celandine sat on the chair and placed her hands in her lap. The cloudiness seemed to fill the room. She could almost smell it – an atmosphere, faintly acrid, like Guy Fawkes Night. She watched Miss Craven's thin mouth, and waited.

'I am afraid that I have some bad news for you, Howard. I hope that you will be able to accept it with courage.'

Celandine knew, then, what it was. She knew what had happened and she knew what it was that she could sense: the ghost of smoke and gunpowder.

'Your father has written to me, asking that I should inform you personally, rather than you should first learn of it from his letter. Your brother has fallen in France, fighting for his country.'

Miss Craven's mouth had stopped moving, and the room was completely silent.

Ages passed, with no sound and no motion.

The creases deepened around Miss Craven's mouth as it opened once more. 'Naturally this will have come as a shock to you, and so I am giving you special permission to return to your dormitory. There you will be able to sit for a while and reflect, and read Mr Howard's letter for yourself. Sad as this news may be, I must advise you not to give way to grief or hysteria. There is no nobler cause for which to give one's life than King and Country, and we must honour that sacrifice by displaying similar courage. Once you have had time to reflect, you will go to lunch as usual, and you will then attend this afternoon's hockey match against Queen's College.'

There were just two sheets of paper. Was that all? Had her father no more to say to her than would fill two sheets of paper?

'How ... did it ... how did it ... ?' She couldn't get the sentence out.

'Mr Howard has wisely limited himself to the facts. Detail can only cause unnecessary distress. I understand that your brother's death was due to an accident whilst handling munitions, rather than to enemy bombardment. There was an explosion.'

An explosion. The word itself exploded in Celandine's head and became a spreading cloud, a rolling white fog that filled every corner of her. She could feel nothing.

'Howard ... you must understand that it is not only our soldiers who are fighting this war. We at home are fighting also, and we shall not give in. We must stand upright, and never allow the enemy the satisfaction of seeing us bowed. I therefore expect to see you up on the playing field at 3 p.m. in support of the First Eleven hockey team against Queen's. This is a very important match, and I want the entire school there to cheer our side on, without exceptions. As we play our games, so we fight our wars. Here is your letter, Howard. Please remember what I have said. Dismissed.'

Celandine wandered towards the dormitory window, where there was better light, and read through the letter once again. The words were plain enough – Freddie had been killed – but the words refused to mean anything. They were just patterns. She saw how her father's neat lines of handwriting became slightly cramped at the bottom of the second page, as though he had not wanted to begin a third. There would be a memorial service next week, he said. Robert would be sent to collect her.

Yrs. affectionately, Father.

Yrs. That abbreviation had saved a little space.

Celandine remained by the window for a while, trying to get her dazed thoughts in order. Eventually she took her fountain pen from her blazer pocket, turned her father's letter over and wrote a few words on the blank side of one of the sheets of paper. She put the letter back in its envelope and altered the name and address on the front.

Then she knelt at her bedside. There was plenty of time, but she might as well get started. She hauled forth her canvas bag from beneath the bed, and began to undo the stiff leather straps.

Celandine sat for an hour or more on the edge of her bed, packed and ready to leave, her feet gently kicking against the bag. The second luncheon bell came and went. The building grew quiet.

Later, she became aware of the distant sound of a motor coach, grinding its way up the steep curving drive. That would be Queen's College hockey team arriving.

Later still, she stood up and opened one of the dormitory windows, listening for the signal that would be her cue to leave. She could hear nothing but the birds, cheerful as always, despite the dreariness of the weather.

She had reflected, just as Miss Craven had advised, and this time she had a better plan. This time she would not be caught.

A muffled cheer drifted across from the hockey pitch – the sound that Celandine had been waiting for – and she picked up her bag. The match had started. The whole school would be safely up on the playing field, and it was time to go. The bag felt quite heavy, and she wondered whether she would be able to lug it all the way to Little Cricket. Perhaps she should leave her mackintosh behind? No, she would need that, and everything else that she had in there.

Outside in the corridor she stopped. Two galvanized buckets had been left standing near the doorway, each covered with a folded sheet of news-paper. A piece of wood had been laid across the top of each bucket, presumably to keep the newspaper in place. Celandine put down her bag and uncovered the buckets. There was pale green distemper in one, white in the other. The decorators had obviously finished work for the week and would not now be back until Monday.

Celandine picked up the pails and carried them, milkmaid fashion, back into the dormitory.

Neither bucket was much more than half full, but it was surprising to see just how far it went. She was able to tip green paint all over the beds of Mary Swann, the Pigtail twins, and Alicia Tremlett, and still have plenty left over. Give her a haircut, would they? Hold her down, would they? Around the dormitory she walked, steadily pouring the creamy distemper up and down each bed, along the linoleum, into locker drawers and slippers and the laundry bag that hung by the door, over pillows and dressing gowns, anywhere and everywhere. And when she had shaken the last few drops from the green bucket, she started on the white . . .

By the time Celandine had finished, the room looked so spectacularly ruined, so deliciously shocking, that she was half tempted to stay, just to witness the screams of outrage. It would almost be worth the consequences.

Almost, but not quite. Celandine picked up her bag once more and hurried through the silent corridors.

Outside in the deserted quad she felt more exposed. Anybody might be looking down upon her from those high windows. She scuttled across to the dining hall and hid herself around the back, where the dustbins were kept. From here she would only have to push her way through the scraggy hedge that bordered the croquet lawn, pass through the little wooden gate on the other side of the lawn, and then she would be in the lane. After that she had a good chance, by taking the back roads, of getting to the railway station at Little Cricket unseen. Then she would buy a ticket back to Town, and make it look as though she was travelling towards the school rather than running away from it. Except that she would not be getting off the train at Town station, not if she could help it . . .

She peeped around the corner of the building, waiting for the right moment. The croquet lawn was for prefects only, and she wanted to make quite sure that there were none about before crossing that open space.

It was smelly by the dustbins; the remains of yesterday's supper, if she wasn't mistaken. Yes, a loosely wrapped piece of damp newspaper had a fish's head sticking out of it. Phew. Another cheer from the playing fields reassured her that she had done well to bide her time. The entire school would be up there by now. Celandine glanced down at the dustbin again, gingerly pulling a corner of the newspaper away between finger and thumb to expose the fish. A mackerel. Complete, and raw, and very smelly.

The filmy eye of the dead fish regarded her, drawing her hypnotically in to its blue-black depths. It slowly suggested an idea to her – and what a wonderful idea it was.

How long would it take, though? Five minutes? Ten? Was it really worth the risk of being caught? She had been lucky so far. To go back into the school again would simply be foolhardy. Foolhardy, stupid . . . and irresistible.

The door of the glass case opened quite easily, although Celandine's hand shook as she fumbled with the little metal clasp. To be caught in the head-mistress's study! That would surely be the end of her. The stuffed fish was tight in the otter's jaws, but she wiggled it to and fro, and it began to crumble – the dusty surface of it breaking up around the otter's teeth. Celandine drew it slowly out and placed it on the open newspaper. It was dry and almost weightless, and it looked curiously unconvincing lying beside its damp and leaky brother.

She struggled to make the real mackerel fit into place. It was fatter, and she had to press the silvery flesh down hard onto the otter's lower teeth – until the skin was pierced – before she could squeeze the body under the top two fangs. Finally it was done, wedged into place. Celandine stepped back. It looked very good, and the stoat, the weasel, and the pine-marten all grinned their approval. What a *little* thing a weasel was, she thought. Like a bit of skipping rope.

Now that the glass door was closed, it would need an unusually sharp eye to detect any alteration to the display. Days might pass – weeks – before the source of the dreadful smell could be tracked down. Celandine picked up the piece of newspaper, folded it about the stuffed fish and tucked the package beneath her arm. That was that.

One final small act of revenge occurred to her as she tiptoed from Miss Craven's study. She would have to pass by the staffroom on her way out of the building – and if that room should just happen to be empty, well then, why not?

Celandine knocked softly at the staffroom door. If there was a reply, she would say . . . well, she would think of something.

Silence. She opened the door and peeped in. The room was empty.

A minute later she closed the door again and walked calmly down the corridor, gently tapping Miss Belvedere's leather strap against her palm as she did so. What a pity that she'd not had the foresight to bring a big bunch of nettles with her, or a dead rat, or a nest of scorpions, and put *those* in the drawer in place of the strap. But there. She couldn't think of everything.

There had been another bonus; one of the teachers had left some food on the staffroom table. It was only a sandwich and a piece of cake, but the items came ready-wrapped in greaseproof paper and just about fitted into her blazer pocket. They would come in useful for the train journey.

Celandine pushed the newspaper package and the leather strap well down into the dustbin, picked up her canvas bag, and made her way across the croquet lawn. The cheers from the playing field rang out louder than ever. They might almost have been for her, she thought. And all in all she felt that she deserved them.

Chapter Fourteen

She had succeeded at last, and this thought kept her going as she followed Fin into the pitch-darkness of the wicker tunnel, blindly feeling her way forward, and trying at the same time to keep her bag from slipping into the water. Her feet were soaked and her hair was being pulled out in strands by the sharp ends of the wickerwork, but she had escaped – third time lucky. She was free. Nevertheless the sound of her own breathing became increasingly panicky, and it was a huge relief to emerge from the tunnel and stand upright again.

Celandine staggered onto the flat rock in the middle of the stream, and awkwardly jumped across to the shadowy bank where Fin was waiting for her.

'*Cake-cake-cake . . .*' He hadn't forgotten her promise, and she had to stop and fumble through her bag for the crumpled and sticky little package that she had saved for him.

'Come on,' she said. 'I'm getting cold now.' She began to move away from the stream.

'Ah-ah-ah . . . *I* all right.' Fin took a quick bite of his cake before catching up with her.

There was a little more light than there had been in the tunnel, but it was scary out here just the same. The creaking limbs of the sycamore trees loomed above them, massive and forbidding against the night sky, and Celandine was so glad that Fin was with her. She would not care to be stumbling through these cold black woods all alone. How different the world was after dark. The well-worn pathway to the caves, friendly and familiar in daylight, seemed treacherous to her now – with dips and hummocks and exposed roots that threatened to catch her out at every gasping step. She had not stopped to think of how this part of her journey might be. She had thought only of catching that train, and escaping. Anything to escape. Beyond that, she had hardly dared venture or imagine. Now the enormity of what she was doing crept up behind her and breathed upon her neck.

She had run away from school, and from the whole world, and she was staggering through the darkness on Howard's Hill, weighed down by her heavy bag, cold and tired and homeless.

No, not homeless. She *could* go home, if she wanted to. Mill Farm was only at the bottom of the hill, and she could turn around and go there now if she chose. She could give up this foolishness and be in her own bed in half an hour. There would be a price to pay – for she would certainly be sent back to Mount Pleasant in the morning. But she did have a choice.

'Fin!' Her voice was gulping, shaky with exhaustion. 'Slow down. I can't see you.' She caught the brief flash of Fin's white teeth as he stopped to wait for her, a Cheshire cat grin in the surrounding gloom.

The air at the mouth of the cave was warmer. From the distant passageways there came a faint orange glow, and Celandine could smell the same oily perfume that she remembered from before, but stronger, now that it was night-time. It reminded her of incense, and of church.

Fin would not come any closer. He remained at the bottom of the loose pile of shale that sloped away from the cave entrance. His eyes glinted up at her.

'Ah-ah-ah! Nooo. Not go *there*. Come is me. I.'

'Halloooo!' Celandine's voice echoed around the cavern. 'Can anyone hear me?'

Fin was still hissing at her from the bottom of the slope; 'Noooo! Shhh! Is *Tinklers* there! Is *get* you . . .'

Celandine peered into the shadows of the cave, and waited. 'I'm all right, Fin. Don't worry.' Again her words bounced back at her – too loud for this place – and again there was the sense of something church-like in the quiet scented atmosphere.

Two small figures appeared, fleeting shades against the distant glow, and then vanished. Back they came, three, four – more – standing in a huddle at the far end of the cave. One of them separated from the group, and came towards her. Micas. Celandine recognized the shape of his head, the way that his hair grew at the sides but not on the top, like a monk. He carried a light before him, a dish of oil with a crude wick that flared and guttered as he walked. Celandine saw a host of chalk marks on the flickery walls of the cave, and was surprised at how many had been added since she was last here. Months and months it had been. It looked as though they had been working hard.

'Micas! It's me – Celandine.'

'As I see – I as thowt to see thee no more. What do thee want, child?' Micas drew close, and looked up at her. ' 'Tis gone moon-wax. Bist not a-bed then?' His face was puzzled, but his voice was as calm as she had remembered it.

'I've run away,' she said. 'And I've nowhere to go. I hoped that I could stay here. For a while.' She was so tired. The thought of Freddie entered her head – a white explosion, quite soundless. It made her blink.

'Stay? Bide wi' us?'

'Yes. Just for a while.'

'Dost have troubles, then?'

'Yes. I have. Lots.'

'Om. And shall they seeken for 'ee here? Wast followed to this place?'

'No, Micas. I promise. Nobody knows that I'm here.'

Micas stood beside her at the cave entrance and looked out upon the darkness. The little clay lamp sputtered unevenly in the damp night air, giving off a smoky pungency. Lavender. Celandine recognized the scent of it now. Fin seemed to have disappeared.

'The wind don't turn,' said Micas. His bald head was tilted backwards as he regarded the shifting skies. 'Nor yet the season. Come, then.' He began to retreat into the cave once more, and gestured to her that she should follow. 'Thee med stay this night, at the least. Elina! Mab! Bring a bolster and pallets – and make up a tansy. We ha'en a Gorji traveller among us, though I never thowt to hear me speken such a thing.'

In a hollowed-out side chamber close to the cave entrance, Micas and Elina laid down three wicker pallets, end to end. They looked a bit like flat picnic baskets. Elina draped a rough woollen coverlet across the pallets and said, 'Can 'ee sleep on that?'

Celandine's head was rocking with weariness. She lowered herself dizzily onto the wicker bed. 'Yes,' she said. 'Thank you, Elina. I'm sorry to put you to so much . . .' Her voice faded away. She was too exhausted, suddenly, to even be polite. All she wanted to do was disappear into endless slumber.

They gave her a sacking pillow filled with aromatic leaves, so that as she lay upon it and pulled the coverlet over her, the scents of the forest instantly swept her away on a perfumed tide.

She was too tired to search for a single thought through the fog that filled her head. And when she heard Elina's quiet murmur, 'Rest theeself then, maid,' she could find no voice to answer with.

Celandine awoke briefly that first night, and lay in the dead silence, waiting, as the strangeness of her surroundings descended upon her. A dim yellow light filtered through the chamber entrance, from a lavender oil lamp in the main tunnel beyond. She put out her hand to touch the rough stone wall beside her. It did not feel cold.

The thick woollen coverlet was wrapped about her – she had rolled herself up in it, as though she were a cocoon – and the wicker pallets creaked softly beneath her whenever she moved. She was warm, and she was dry. Beyond that there was no sensation. Blurred images of her long day drifted through her head; sitting on the chair in Miss Craven's office, the letter from her father, the distemper paint and the glass case, the railway clerk at Little Cricket with his drippy nose, and the injured soldier on the train – Tommy. Again the thought of Freddie burst before her – a puff of white smoke that slowly spread to all the corners of her vision. But she could feel nothing, no pain. She closed her eyes again. Tomorrow, perhaps, her senses might return.

Tomorrow came and went, and the day after that. To Celandine it was as though she was disconnected from all that was happening around her, seeing herself from a distance – during the few hours that she was awake. For all she really wanted to do was sleep. She couldn't remember when she had ever felt so sleepy. Her little side chamber was warm, and it was so comforting to just sleep and dream, sleep and dream. And when she was awake, it was equally comforting to lie on her back and look up at the stone roof of her sanctuary, to follow the encrusted patterns of the tiny barnacle-like things that grew there, and to float through the hours like a mermaid in a cavern beneath the sea. No lessons, no freezing cold showers, and no war. All her troubles had been left behind her, banished beyond the wall of briars that separated her from the outside world. They couldn't find her here.

Celandine was aware of the quiet comings and goings of the cave-dwellers, as they passed by the entrance to her darkened room, the muffled snatches of speech that told of their normal everyday lives.

'Bist going arter kindles, Tammas?'

'Aye, whilst rain do hold off.'

'Bide, then. I'll come with 'ee.'

What were kindles, Celandine wondered? Kindling? There must be fires, then, somewhere beyond the deep tunnels at the back of the main cave. Perhaps that was why the cave walls never seemed as cold as she would have expected.

'Bron! Do 'ee mind that crock o' spadger's eggs! Thee've feet like Gorji shovels.'

'Well what be 'em doing down theer, for all to hop round? Much wonder they ends up scraddled, if that's where 'ee lays 'em.'

The footsteps came and went.

Celandine could hear the excited whispers of the cave-children, playing at some game in the broad main entrance, but the confused echoes made it hard to tell whether there were a dozen of them out there, or only two or three.

'Goo on, Bant, gi' un a gurt flick!'

'I got 'un! Ohhh . . . 'Tis out agin.'

'The worse for thee, then, for now 'tis Goppo. In his eye then, Gop!'

'Blinder! Good on' ee, Gop!'

What could they be doing, Celandine wondered?

She was curious, but not curious enough to leave her bed. She closed her eyes and listened to the muted echoes, soft starbursts of sound, bouncing through the darkness.

Sometimes Elina or her daughter Mab brought food – a porridgey mixture of dried fruit, and grain, and seeds that Celandine did not recognize, all stewed up together and ladled onto a wooden trencher. For drink there was either water or a hot infusion which they called a 'tansy', and which was a bit like un-sweetened tea. It was plain stuff, and plain that the cave-dwellers lived upon little else at this time of year, but Celandine automatically ate and drank whatever was given to her, lost in the nothingness of her own cloudy daydreams.

'Thee be more like a mousen than a giant.' Elina had come into the side chamber to collect Celandine's wooden dish. 'I've heared a mousen make more of a noise, leastways. Will 'ee not come through the tunnels and sit wi' us?'

Elina had a kind face. The long grey hair that fell in a single plait over one shoulder, and the coloured scarf she wore about her neck, made her look like a tiny version of the old fortune-teller that came to Goosey Fair each year. Her dark wrinkled eyes were full of concern.

Celandine shook her head.

'I don't really like tunnels,' she said. 'And I just feel like being quiet. I'm just happy to be quiet. And to sleep.'

'Ah. 'Tis the same wi' us all,' said Elina. 'We'm

none of us so lively. Once the season do turn, then we med turn wi' it.' She paused at the chamber entrance. 'Little Loren have been asking after 'ee,' she said. 'Most taken wi' his letters, he be, and wanting to show 'ee.'

Celandine laughed. 'Is he? Then I'll get up, soon,' she said. 'It's time I did.'

Her legs felt weak and achy as she stood barefoot at the cave entrance, her navy mackintosh slung around her like a cloak. She looked out upon the dripping woodland and shivered. She had not arrived at a good time. Winter had yet to loosen its grip, and the endless wind and rain made venturing from the cave almost impossible.

Loren, standing beside her, gave a little cough, and Celandine saw the tiny cloud of his breath on the cold morning air. 'Come on,' she said. 'I'll go and put some warmer clothes on and then we can read a story. Would you like that?'

He looked up at her and nodded. His nose looked sore and runny, and the red rims around his eyes made his taut skin seem whiter than ever.

'Aye,' he whispered. 'I would.'

He was half-starved, Celandine realized, and immediately felt shocked and guilty. The blue veins were visible at his temples, and the skin so stretched about his cheekbones and jaw that his teeth protruded slightly. He had not been as thin as this the previous summer.

And, now that she looked about her, Celandine saw that they were all of the same appearance, the cave-dwellers, gaunt and frail and pale as milk-water, their wide eyes staring from the lamp-lit shadows. They were at the mercy of the seasons, even more so than the farming community that she knew. An over-long winter, a miserable summer, and they might actually die. It was horrible to imagine. What could she do to help them? She could stop eating so much of their food, she decided.

Later, with her mackintosh still draped about her shoulders, Celandine knelt among the cave-children to watch them play. She wrinkled up her nose at the gruesome focus of their game – a battered and ancient ram's skull with great curving horns and long yellow-stained teeth. A ghoulish sight it made as it lay in the middle of the cave floor, grinning horribly at all around, as though it had just risen from the underworld.

The ram's head was positioned between two chalked lines near the cave entrance. Behind these lines the children crouched, one group to either side of the skull, so that an empty eye-socket faced each team. With their pinched little faces frowning in concentration, the cave-children pushed up their ravelled sleeves and took turns to flick tiny coloured pebbles at the skull – the aim being to try and land the pebbles into the gaping hollows where the eyes had once been.

'Blinder!' This was the name of their game, and it was the quiet exclamation that went up whenever a score was made. Even in the excitement of the moment the players' voices were seldom raised.

When each child had taken a turn, any pebbles that had lodged in the eye-sockets were fished out again, to be counted up. 'Ickren, dickren, dockren, quatern, quin . . .' So strange, the murmured words that kept the tally. The side that had scored the most took a corresponding number of pebbles from their opponents. It was a cross between marbles and tiddleywinks, thought Celandine, if a rather sinister one.

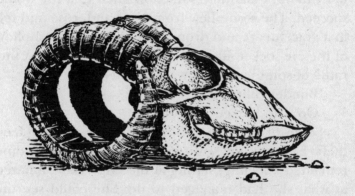

Loren leaned towards Celandine and placed a bright red pebble in her palm. She looked at the little stone. It was beautifully polished – as shiny as a blob of sealing wax, or a jumping bean.

'Goo on,' said Loren. 'Gi' us a blinder.'

'Ay, Celandine. Try thee hand.' Goppo, the champion player, grinned up at her. He spat into his grubby palms and vigorously rolled his own pebble between them – an encouragement for her to do the same.

'Shall I?' Celandine could not quite bring herself to spit on the pretty stone that Loren had given her, but she blew upon it instead, just for luck, and then balanced it between finger and thumbnail as she had seen the others do. She looked across at the skull, ignored the mocking challenge of that deathly grin, and tried to concentrate upon judging the distance.

In the very wishing-moment that she flicked up her thumb, Celandine somehow knew that she would succeed. The stone flew from her hand, rose and fell in a graceful arc and dropped straight into the hollow of the eye-socket, like a bird into a nesting box. A tiny rattle of sound and that was it. Perfect.

'Blinder! Blinder!'

'Oo! Did 'ee see 'un goo?'

Some of the cave-children jumped to their feet, their faces lit up with excitement, but Celandine remained kneeling, staring at the ram's skull, amazed at what she had managed to do. She could see the little red stone, a demon's eye that winked at her from its black socket so that the skull seemed eerily alive again in the dim light of the cave.

'Oo! She'm *witchi*, that she be.'

Witchy? A witch? Others had said the same, and now Celandine was starting to wonder. Perhaps she really did have magic powers . . . perhaps she really could perform miracles . . .

But it was nothing more than beginner's luck, of course. Celandine played the ram's-head game many more times after that, taking it in turns to join with one team or the other. Nevertheless her first miracle turned out to be her last, and although she huffed upon her stone and rolled it between her palms, and cast a hundred magic spells upon it, she never managed to score another Blinder.

There were other side chambers leading off the main cavern, Celandine discovered, rooms that were used for work or for storage. Micas and Elina showed her what little they had to show; the collection of earthenware pots, mostly empty, wherein they stored dried food against the winter months – rose-hips, crab apples, nuts and wild grain. They showed her the weaving chamber, and how they divided the precious scraps of wool and fur and horsehair that they found into separate baskets, to be eventually woven into something like cloth upon a rough wooden frame. They showed her the wash-place – an eerie echoing chamber where icy water trickled among the black rocks, to disappear through cracks and crevices far below.

They would have shown her, too, what lay further beyond, through the honeycomb of low tunnels that led away from the main chambers, but here Celandine would not venture. Where the cave-dwellers could just about stand upright to enter these places, she would have to crawl, and she was nervous of doing so. From time to time she heard metallic tapping sounds echoing along the passageways, *tink-tink-tink*, and when she asked Micas what they did back there, he simply said, 'We worken the tinsy.'

Later he emerged from one of the tunnels with a sack over his shoulder. Celandine almost laughed when he opened the sack, because it contained metal-ware – plates and bowls, and bits of jewellery – and she thought he looked like a burglar who had lately robbed a mansion. The objects were dull and tarnished, but when she looked closer she saw that they were finely engraved. Tiny figures she could see in the flickering lamplight, beautifully drawn, amid many scenes. She looked closer still, beginning to take an interest. So exquisite, these things were, in such primitive surroundings. What were the figures doing, and what did it all mean?

' 'Tis we,' said Micas. 'And all our story. We maken our tales so, as the Gorji do maken theirs i' a book, as 'twould seem. See – here be old Emra, that was slain b' the Ickren, and here be a Gorji dwelling, a-standing on wooden legs long afore the waters dried. We were but tribe and tribe, then, and lived upon the waters, the Naiad, and the Ickren alike.'

The words made little sense at first, but as the rainy days passed Celandine came to understand more, learning to unravel the pictorial account of the woodlanders' history. She was drawn in by the story of the Touchstone, the magical object that had been stolen by the wicked tribe that Micas called Ickren, although she didn't really believe that it could be entirely true. There may have once been such a stone, she thought, but never a one that could lead its followers up to the very heavens. And these Ickren, if they had ever actually existed, had also been exaggerated. She could accept the bows and arrows, but the wings were surely an added fancy. She became fascinated, though, and she continued to work her way through the picture fables, as the cave-dwellers themselves worked their way through the Gorji fables that were hidden within a different kind of code – letters.

They had made progress in her long absence, and now when they gathered in the draughty cave entrance to look at the chalk marks upon the wall, their cleverness astounded her.

MICAS

Celandine wrote the word upon the wall and said, 'What do these letters spell?'

'Micas! 'Tis Micas!' She had hardly got the question out before Loren had got the answer.

'Yes! That's *very* good. All right, then. Let's see if somebody else can answer the next.'

One by one she wrote out their names, and with very little prompting each could recognize their own – Tammas, Garlan, Esma, Poll. Whatever she wrote on the wall, they could eventually decipher. They learned faster than she could teach them, and the dreary days of confinement were illuminated by simple chalk marks upon stone.

Still the wind and rain continued, and spring seemed as far away as ever. Celandine struggled to work out exactly how long it had been since she had run away. Eight days? Ten? And what was happening now, in that other world beyond the briars? She thought of the note that she had left on the paddock corner post and, not for the first time, she felt a stab of guilt.

'*Dear Mama, I shall be staying with some friends and neighbours for a while, near Taunton. I am perfectly safe and well. Please don't worry about me. Love, Celandine.*'

How inadequate those few words had been, and how misleading. But if she had written more, and been more truthful, would that have caused less worry? Probably not. She pushed the thought away from her.

Celandine grew tired of reading from *Aesop's Fables* and fairytales, and wished that she had more books. If only she had thought to bring some with her. It occurred to her that she might write stories upon the wall, but this seemed too laborious. A song. She could write the words of a song.

The cave entrance looked as though it had been smeared with whitewash, so many times had it been written upon, and then wiped down with a wet scrap of cloth, but the fresh words were readable, and she could hear the ragged little group whispering behind her – already attempting to translate as the chalk marks appeared. 'E-arly on . . . one . . . mo . . . morn . . .'

'This isn't a story,' she said. 'It's a song that I learned when I was little. If I sing it, then . . . well, you can look at the words, and see if you can read them. Then we could all sing it together.'

The pale faces looked up at her, puzzled but attentive. She was hungry, she realized. Her tummy was making funny noises. Outside the entrance the wind had dropped, and she was aware of the silence.

'*Early one morning, just as the sun was rising,*
I heard a maiden sing in the valley below . . .'

Celandine faltered, and nearly stopped singing altogether – so shocked were the expressions that greeted her efforts.

'*Oh never leave me, Oh don't deceive me . . .*'

What on earth could be the matter with them?

'*How could you use a poor maiden so?*'

They were regarding her as though she had just thrown a fit – shrinking against one another as if for support. Was her voice so very terrible?

'What is it?' she said.

A slanting sunbeam stole into the entrance of the cave, fiery bright, so that the dusty little gathering was bathed in its glow. The huddled cave-dwellers shielded their faces from the unaccustomed glare, but still their eyes were fixed upon Celandine, in awe and wonder . . .

'Again,' they whispered. 'Show us how 'twere done . . .'

It took Celandine a while to understand what they meant.

'Don't you know how to sing?' she said. 'Has nobody ever taught you?'

Spring had finally arrived then, with that first shy beam of light, and every creature, every twig and leaf, seemed in a hurry to make up for lost time. The sun shone warm upon the damp forest, so that it steamed like a tropical garden and hummed with the activities of its inhabitants. Everything was alive, and awake and busy.

Celandine viewed it all from the mouth of the cave, and felt oddly reluctant to venture out. She had been content to hide away in the darkness, neither happy nor unhappy, floating in a mist of pictures and stories. But here was bright daylight to be faced once more, sharp and clear, and beyond the bounds of the forest lay the world that was the cause of all her pain. If she once stepped forth into the brilliant sunshine, she would be that much closer to everything she had run away from – and that much closer to being hauled back. She didn't want to be awoken from the comfort of the darkness.

Yet if she imagined that she might simply dream away her time among the sheltering shadows at the mouth of the cave, she was wrong. There was too much to be done.

Elina gave her a large square piece of cloth and showed her how to tie the four corners together in order to make a kind of bag. In this she was expected to collect food – wild mushrooms, hawthorn leaves, rapunzel, birds' eggs – whatever she could find. From Elina she learned how to dig up the tuberous roots of the cat-tails that grew beside the stream, and the most likely places to hunt for the winter stores of hazelnuts that the squirrels had forgotten. She also learned, to her surprise, that the buds, stalks, leaves and roots of her namesake – the celandine – were edible, as were the roots and leaves of dandelions. All these things were food to the woodlanders, even nettles.

Pretty Mab, the grown-up daughter of Micas and

Elina, showed her how to pick nettle leaves without stinging her hands.

'Look close,' she said. 'See they little hairs, how they do point towards 'ee? Thee've to catch 'em firm. Come at 'em from behind, then they can't hurt 'ee.'

Mab demonstrated, plucking each nettle leaf as she brought her hand towards her so that her finger and thumb flattened the stinging hairs and rendered them harmless.

But Celandine was still nervous of trying.

'Don't 'ee be afeared o' it,' said Mab. 'You show 'un who be maister, and 'twill do 'ee no harm.'

Finally Celandine plucked up the courage to do it. She grasped the nettle leaf between finger and thumb, making sure that her grip followed the direction of the wicked little hairs. To her amazement, it worked. The nettle did not sting her, and she pulled the leaf from its stem feeling as though she had worked a true miracle.

'See?' said Mab. 'Now thee knows as it *can* be done, thee can do it so again – and every time. And there s'll always be nettle broth for 'ee, though there med be naught else.'

Her clothing was unsuitable, and something would have to be done about it. The calico dress that she had brought was all very well for work in the school garden, but here it was a hopeless encumbrance – forever getting caught up on brambles and bushes. And her heavy walking shoes would not do at all. But what was the alternative?

She laid down the bunch of celandines that she

had picked and wandered up to the high ridge, looking for more. It was best not to handle the flowers too much, but rather to tie them in bundles and put them in the shade to be collected later – otherwise they became bruised and damaged.

Some of the Naiad were working in the main clearing, and Celandine watched them for a while. Their backs were bent as they tended to the neat patches of plants that were laid out across the open ground. They looked almost oriental with their wide-brimmed grass hats, their plain smocks and short leggings. The Naiad lived a different kind of life to the Tinklers and Troggles – growing their own food upon small allotments, rather than foraging for it in the wild. Perhaps it was better that way. She would very much like a potato for a change. She would also like a smock, and some leggings.

One of the figures straightened up, then slowly turned to look directly at her. It was as though he had sensed that he was being watched. He made no gesture, said nothing that Celandine could hear, but almost immediately the rest of the fieldworkers followed suit – raising their heads and looking her way, like a herd of deer, alert to every whiff of danger. They regarded her calmly for a few moments, then returned to their work – tolerating her presence, yet careful, now, not to turn their backs to her. Celandine knew that those eyes were still upon her, mistrustful beneath the dappled shadows of their grass hats. They would not feel comfortable until she had moved on.

Had she enough celandines? She began to make

her way back down through the wood, and in doing so startled a group of Naiad horses that were coming along one of the narrow pathways. They were being herded by Pato. Celandine waited for the horses to pass, turning her face from the dust that they kicked up. They were odd-looking little things, with their spiky manes and tufted tails – more like donkeys than horses. Or like miniature zebras, without the stripes. They had quite a strong smell about them, and that too reminded her of donkeys – the ones that she had once seen on a trip to Weymouth sands. Astonishing creatures they had seemed to her at first, but she had soon grown used to them, and now they appeared no more exotic or out of place than the peacocks that wandered the vicarage lawn.

The little red bridle that Pato had given her had led Celandine to assume that the horses were ridden, but she had never seen this happen.

'What do you do with them,' she said to Pato, as he drew level with her, 'the horses, I mean?'

'Do wi' em?' Pato came to a halt and looked up at her as though she might be making fun of him. He removed the chewed end of a willow stick from his mouth. 'We milks 'em, o' course.'

'You *milk* them?' Celandine thought that he must be joking in turn. 'Horses can't be milked!'

'Oh, can 'em not? Well drat 'em, then, I says. For they'm no use to we if they casn't be milked. I'd best catch up and give 'em the tidings.' Pato put his chewing-stick back in his mouth and sauntered off into the dust-cloud with a chuckle.

Celandine stared after him and shook her head. What on earth did horse's milk taste like, she wondered? She wasn't sure that she wanted to know.

She sighed. It was time to get back to the matter in hand. What *was* she going to do about her clothing? Celandine tried to brush some of the dust from her dress. Then a thought came to her. She could go back to Mill Farm, and find something more suitable there. Could she? Yes, and she could collect more books as well. And some scissors . . .

Celandine stood still, among the sunlit trees, and explored the idea.

There was a chest full of old clothes on the landing, outside Freddie's room – and there were the canvas boots that he used for fishing. Freddie wouldn't mind if she took them. Not now . . .

She had tried to think of Freddie so many times, but something wouldn't let her. The fog came down, so that her thoughts could never quite reach him. But this time her vision became a starry blur and she had to wipe her eyes. A quick flicker of colour danced through her tears, puzzling for a moment, then shocking as she realized what it was. There was someone coming – a figure walking along the woodland path. Celandine quickly dodged back among the trees, blinking, trying to focus. Still there.

It was the girl in the window – that extraordinary child – coming her way. Again the strangest clothes . . . green trouser things, with a bib, like overalls . . . a yellow shirt with no sleeves and no collar . . . pink boots, made of . . . canvas? And now she carried before her a bunch of flowers. Celandines.

Who *was* this person, and how on earth could she possibly be here? And was that *her* bunch of celandines that she was holding? The figure drew closer, about to pass by. Celandine decided find out once and for all. She wasn't frightened.

'Hallo?' The twigs crackled beneath her feet as she stepped forward, but the girl seemed to have heard nothing.

'Hallo?' Celandine called out again, but still the girl kept walking – no turn of the head, no falter in that boyish stride. The grass did not move beneath those footsteps, nor was there any sound. The blonde hair rose and fell, cool and comfortable, as if in a breeze. And yet the air was still.

Celandine watched sadly as the child continued on her way. There was no point in chasing after her, no point in saying more. She knew that she was seeing something that wasn't really there – and yet she also knew that she was seeing something that she could not have invented, or dreamed up. That hair, those clothes; her imagination could never have pictured them. If the girl wasn't real now, then she once had been, or someday would be . . .

There was a distant bend in the pathway, and Celandine waited for the figure to turn the corner. But then, just before reaching this point, the child simply faded away, dissolving like the passing of a rainbow. She was gone, whoever she was.

Gradually the busy sounds of the forest came back

into focus – the whirr of a dragonfly, the noisy cooing of the pigeons in the tall cedars. Celandine examined the bunch of flowers she was still holding, limp and spoiled now, in her hot sticky hands. She supposed that she had better go and find some more.

Chapter Fifteen

Una stood at the fringe of the high woods, and looked out over the wetlands below. To have come so far – *so far* – only to be struck down at the last was too hard to bear. The sickness that gripped the Ickri tribe was the worst they had ever known. One of the Elders, old Maris, had already died of it, and one newborn also. Many more lay ill – including Avlon himself. What would she do if he left her?

In vain she collected bunches of holly and wolfsbane, sweet violet, feverfew. Her infusions and poultices did little good. This was some Gorji plague, a sweating, aching fever that was beyond her power to heal. But where was the cause of it? For almost a moon the tribe had been laid low in these woods – for as one recovered so another fell sick. Now her father was ill. She had done what she could to help him, but had little faith that it would be enough.

The weather, at least, had been kinder than fortune. Out over the moors, the bright evening sun-shine glinted upon the waters and warmed the greening willows, still stranded, some of them, in the remains of the winter floods. It would not be a hard land to cross, compared to some that they had seen.

And they were so close, now, Una was certain of it. Indeed, she had come to believe that she could see their destination from this very ridge. A mysterious hill rose from the sunny landscape – separate from its line of brothers beyond – and even without the aid of the Touchstone her eye was drawn constantly to it. The long crest of the hill was thickly crowned with dense foliage, and it seemed to Una that there was a tense stillness about it, as of a crouching animal caught in the open whose best hope of going unseen is to remain motionless.

This evening she carried the Touchstone with her, and the pull of it was stronger than ever, the direction clear and unwavering. She was sure that she was looking at their journey's end . . .

'What does it tell thee, child . . .?'

Una flinched at the deep voice, and spun around.

'. . . That which we would hear?'

It was Corben.

Her father's brother had taken more notice of her of late. His words had become friendlier, and his eye seemed to be often upon her.

'Aye.' Una turned to look at the hill once more, and nodded. ' 'Tis not so far, no.'

Corben stood beside her and followed the direction of her gaze.

'The wooded hill? *There*, reckon ye? Then we be close indeed. And what of the Naiad – do they yet dwell here?'

'The Touchstone seeks the Orbis. It would not have brought us here if there were naught to find. Aye. The Naiad be close by.' Una was talking as if to herself, and as if seeing something that only she could see.

There was a long silence, and when Una glanced up she realized that Corben was no longer staring at the landscape but at her. What was there in that cool regard that made her mistrust him so?

'Ye have a great power, Una. We should not to have come so far but for thee – and Avlon be justly proud of thee. Our one desire be to see him well again, and all our tribe. But more shall die, I fear, before this scourge be over. Even now I have come from the King's side, and it pains me to see him ailing so – my poor brother.'

Una felt reproached then, and said, 'I should be there also. I'll go to him.'

She knelt inside the arbour of woven hazel and willow branches that they had made for her father – and wondered what more she could do. Maven had helped her in the mixing of healing potions, but no physic seemed able to quiet that rattling breath, no poultice could draw out the fire that burned within him.

The heat seemed to rise from his very being, so that when she passed her hand above his forehead she could feel a prickle of warmth against her palm. She thought of how her empty fingers had once brought the Touchstone from a giant's garb, and wondered if she could bring out this pestilence likewise. What harm could come of trying? Una placed the Touchstone at her father's side, then closed her eyes and let her hand hover above the streaming brow. The night closed in about her and she floated away on the failing rhythm of her father's breath. Breathe in . . . breathe out . . .

She saw herself kneeling beside dark waters, the star-forsaken pools of the woodlands, known only to the brocks and toads – and to one lost tribe. Spiny-fish there were, down there, and deeper creatures, warty and blind. The murky pools that she saw in her vision were connected to the troubled darkness that lay beneath her outstretched hand. Whatever evil lurked in those depths, she felt it now against her palm. Here she must fish, with charms and webs, delving and dipping into the brackish swirl until she found the gulping sickness that lay in wait for those who would foolishly drink therefrom. Aye. Those who would foolishly *drink* therefrom . . . Now she understood. *This* was the source of all their ill, the very water they daily collected. She saw it now . . . breathe out . . . breathe in . . . some Gorji poison buried there. She must draw it out, the poison, the knowledge of it, and lift it from her father's frame. Raise it high in all its ugliness, and fling it to the heavens . . .

Get out. Be gone. Leave him.

For a long time Una waited, her eyes still closed, until she had the strength to lift her head once more.

Already there was a change. She could feel it. The breathing was calmer, and the brow cooler. She wiped a hand across her own forehead, exhausted now.

'Come, child, thee've done as much as thee are able. I will sit with him through the night.'

It was Corben, again. How long had he been standing there?

'Una.' His voice was soft. 'To your rest, I say. No daughter could do more.'

'Yes,' she said. 'But he improves, I know it.'

'Perhaps.'

'He improves, and he will be well again. But Corben – if my father should waken, let him take no water to drink. The pools here be fouled – I see it now, and know 'tis so. We must collect from the lands below, not from these woods.'

'The water? Have this been the cause of our ailing? Such a wise chi' ye be. Aye then – I shall see it done. Now rest.'

Una awoke in fright as the chilly light of dawn crept through the branches of her shelter. She had entered into another life during her sleep – a dreaming – and was startled to find herself back again. The sounds and images of that other world still danced around her. Her wings still ached.

Across the universe she had been flying, a moth amongst many moths. She had led them all, beating through the velvety darkness towards a far-off light. They travelled beneath a fiery orb, a jasper moon, that both sheltered them and guided them onward. Her father's voice echoed about her: '*Briefly parted, soon united.*' She could not see him anywhere, but she heard him clearly. '*All are one, Una, all are one. And on and on we live. I am gone, but shall return, though many and many a fourseason pass. And you shall not age, Una, as others age, though aged you will seem. Briefly parted, soon united.'*

The echoes of the turning seasons fell upon her ear again and again, the sounds of summer birdsong and winter storms circling her in the darkness of her dreaming. Onward she flew among the other moths, exhausted beneath the looming orb, yet the light ahead drew no closer. A Gorji maid she saw, and then another, sleeping giants that drifted among the cloud of moths for a while. Una saw their faces – and knew that she would always remember them – but soon they were left behind. Who they were she could not tell, nor what part they might play in this endless journey. She felt that they were somehow important to her.

At last it seemed that she and all her kind must fall into the black depths for ever, their strength gone. And then a flying horse appeared – rounding the curve of the great red orb on silvery wings. *'Briefly parted, soon united.'*

It was the shock of this that brought her back – the familiar voice, and the fear that came over her as she understood its meaning. She awoke and knew that she was now alone in this world.

Dazed and fearful, she stumbled from her shelter. The early morning light filtered down through the trees, and she drew her shoulder-wrap close about her as she hurried to the spot where her father lay. She must see him.

Too late. Even as she arrived she met Corben,

stooping beneath the woven arch of hazel branches to emerge from the shelter. Una halted in her tracks and stared at him. He appeared surprised to see her – irritated – but his expression quickly changed to one of sorrow. In his hands he carried the Touchstone, cradling it to him as though it were the head of a child.

'Una. I was coming to seek for thee. Here is a black morn indeed – and I am saddened to see it. All our care has been in vain – the King . . .'

'No!' Her voice was cracked and not in her control. 'No . . .'

'Aye, though it pain us all. He is gone.'

'But he *improved* . . .'

'Yet not enough. He is gone, Una. The fever has taken him in the night. And now ye must take this.' He held out the Touchstone, offering it to her, the hand steady but not fully outstretched – as though it might be snatched back at any moment.

'Come to me, Una. Ye be Queen now, and the Stone belongs in your care. Take it, child, and then kneel with it before your poor father. We shall look upon him together.'

There was something dangerous in Corben's expression, some deadly purpose in the grim set of the mouth, the hint of a sneer about the cruelly hooked nose, and Una backed away. She looked up into Corben's narrowed eyes and felt a creeping horror of what she saw there. If she entered that shelter she knew that she would never emerge alive. Those powerful hands, reaching out towards her, meant her nothing but harm. They had killed once – she was certain of it now – and they would kill again.

Una glanced behind her, quickly judging her best path, then ducked back into the undergrowth.

At the edge of a high woodland ravine Una sat and stared down at the rocky pools far below. From here the tribe had collected their water, and from here they had brought the Gorji sickness upon themselves. Too late she had understood. But for her slowness of thought they might all be safe, and her father still strong and well. Now her father was dead, murdered by his own brother, and her own life under threat. How long had Corben waited for his opportunity? Had he planned this from the very start of their journey – that he would wait until the end was in sight before seizing his moment? Or had her father's illness given him a chance that had been unlooked for?

How little she had seen of what was happening about her. For all she knew, the whole tribe might have plotted in this – Peck and Rafe, Corben's archers, the King's Guard . . .

She could trust nobody, could go to nobody for help, until she learned more. In the meantime she must remain hidden, watching and listening to all that she could. She must stay close to the tribe, yet become invisible. And she must somehow get back the Touchstone . . .

The faintest rustle of leaves broke the eerie silence about her, as of a whispered breeze through the low foliage of the hawthorn bushes. And yet the air was still. Una slowly turned her head. Maven-the-Green was standing beside her.

Corben held his brow in deep sorrow as the Ickri elders took their turn to look upon the dead body of Avlon.

'A dark day for our tribe,' he said, 'and one I hoped never to see. I thought that he improved. The child bade me give him water – but then he fell worse in the night and was gone.'

'Where is she now – Una? She should be here, to claim the Stone.'

'She ran into the woods at the news, and has not been seen. I held the Stone out to her, but she would not take it. If any should find Una, then they must bring her to me – to gain what is rightfully hers. Until she returns, the Stone shall be safe in my charge. Tonight I shall lay beside my brother, and tomorrow we shall carry the Stone forth to seek for the child.'

But when the morning came, the Touchstone had gone.

Stolen in the night! The word quickly spread. Corben had awoken to find the jasper globe no longer at his side. Had the child crept into the shelter and taken it? Why would she do such a thing when it was rightfully hers? And why did she not show herself? The scouts and the Guard were dispatched into the surrounding woods to find Una.

Corben spoke to his own archers. 'She'll not be far away – though I doubt the Guard'll catch her. Too slippery she be, for their like. Come the night, 'twill be our turn.'

'Why've she run, though?' said Berin. 'She be Queen, now.'

'She runs from me,' said Corben. 'And if the Guard cannot find her by nightfall, then I shall tell why.'

As evening began to descend, the archers of the Guard returned. There was still no sign of Una, and the Elders' talk became more agitated. Where could the child be, and why had she run away? Without her, and the Stone, they were surely lost. The King was dead, many of the tribe were ailing, and their destination was still unknown. Who else but Una had the power to guide them from this place? They might all die before an answer could be found.

Corben had taken up a humble position, sitting among his own archers, and patiently listening to the Elders' talk. Eventually, with the reluctant air of one who must speak out even though it pain him to do so, he rose to his feet.

'My friends. I fear that I have been foolish. I thought to protect my brother's child until she were found and able to give account of herself, but now I see that truth must be told before more harm comes to us. Yesternight, when I held the Stone in my hands, it spoke to me. Aye, it spoke to me, and it told me much. I know now what ails our tribe, and brings us sickness – 'tis the water in this place. And I believe Una knew this also.'

'The *water*?'

'Aye, the pools that we take from be fouled by the Gorji. They bring this plague upon us.'

'And ye think Una *knew* of this? Why would she not have told us?'

Corben looked uncomfortable. 'My brother lies dead – poisoned by the water from the pools. And who is now become Queen because of his death?'

'You say Una would have seen her father *die* that she might become Queen? This could never be!'

The Elders were horrified, and the surrounding archers of the Guard muttered threateningly. Even Corben's own archers looked shocked.

Corben's voice was low and regretful, yet persistent.

'Believe my words. When Una went to her rest she bade me give Avlon water to drink, as she had done, and as much as he might take. 'Tis often said that the chi' has the Touch, and so I did as she asked. I saw my brother grow ever weaker, and I feared for his life, yet I kept faith in his daughter and let him drink as he would. And so at last he died, in my arms, and at my hand. Aye, at *my* hand – though another guided it. From moon-wane to sun-wax I sat with him, and wept for him. Then I lifted the Touchstone, thinking to rightfully place it at his side. 'Twas then I first felt its power, and so held it awhile in great wonder. I saw many visions, my friends, and much became clear to me. I learned that our journey's end is hard by – aye, we may see it from these very woods – 'tis but a step beyond here to where the Naiad now dwell. This the Stone told me, and Una surely knows it too, she with her witchi ways, yet she has said nothing. I learned that all our sickness be from the water we

349

drink. This also Una must know, and yet she has said nothing.'

'And the Stone told thee all this?' Haima glanced at his fellow Elders.

'Aye.' Corben's voice grew defiant. 'The Stone spoke to me, as it will speak to any who have the right to bear it, and are able to listen. 'Tis not only Una that has the gift of seeing what will be. I too have such powers, though I make less play of it. When the child returned and saw that I held the Stone, and saw that at last I understood her wiles, she feared my anger – and the anger of all here. And this be the reason she ran away. Now she has stolen the Touchstone for herself and hides from us yet.'

Corben sighed, and bowed his head amid the shocked silence. 'Una be nought but a chi'. We must mind this in our judgement of her, and be not too harsh. Her head be weak and fey, and her senses were turned by the Stone – and her wish to be Queen. Aye, the Touchstone has more power than we had thought, and Avlon should never have trusted it to her. 'Twere not for a child to hold, but for a king.'

By degrees, and with much apparent regret, Corben persuaded the gathered company that Una had betrayed the faith that had been put in her. She had been swept away by her own childish ambitions. She had come to believe that the Touchstone was hers by right – and this had led her to use her gifts to do a great wrong. Avlon had been foolish to place in the hands of a maid that which was meant for a king alone. He had paid a terrible price for his doting, and had left the Ickri weakened and leaderless.

The furious Elders demanded that Una be found at all costs, and brought to swift justice, but Corben raised a plea for calm.

'Give me the task of seeking for her. She be yet my kin, and I would see no harm done to her – nor see her driven into deeper hiding. If we lose her, we may also lose the Stone. Let us see what soft words and a gentle hand may do.'

'Do as thee will, then,' said Haima. 'But be wary. If what thee say is true, then the child is evil. She has learned too much from Mad Maven, aye, and I have always advised Avlon of this. Yet he would not listen – and now see how soft words and a gentle hand have served him.'

Corben later summoned his own archers to the king's shelter, and spoke to them privately.

'So then,' he said. 'Here my brother lies, dead, and it is now our task to seek the one who has murdered him. What should we do with a child who would slay her own father so that she might bear the Stone?'

'Cast her from the tribe,' said Dunch, and spat on the ground. 'She'm not fit to be Queen.'

'Yet she is Queen,' said Corben. 'And none may cast her out. Perhaps she should be sent to her father, for him to judge . . .' He watched the archers' faces, as they slowly caught his meaning. 'Perhaps she should be joined with him.'

'If she were gone to where her father be, then she'd be dead also,' said Dunch. 'And thee'd become King, Corben. We sees that plain enough. But to slay her? A queen?' Dunch shook his head. 'This be no small task . . .'

'She murdered her *father*,' Corben's voice was angry now. 'My brother. Your king. Does she not deserve the same?' Corben leaned across and grasped Dunch by the forearm. 'A strong hand is needed now,' he said, 'with other hands as strong about. If I were become King, then *thee*, Dunch, would be King's Guard – and thee Tuz, and thee Berin – all of 'ee here. No more would ye carry the bindle-wraps, and walk with the ruck o' the tribe. Thee'd walk with me – the chosen ones. And when the Stone was restored, then those who were my Guard would share in its power, for I would raise thee high. Together we would stand at the gates of Elysse, returned to our own. This my brother saw in all his visions, and I believe it also – the Stone and Orbis together have the power to take us back to Elysse.'

'This Orbis have yet to be found, Corben. And now the Stone be lost to us also.'

'Do thee not reckon theeselves to be hunters? Both are but a step from here, Dunch. But a step. Only bring me the Stone, and I shall lead us to the Orbis.'

'And Una?'

'Her father calls her. Send the little witchi to him and see his cruel death paid for.'

The archers were persuaded. They strung their bows and prepared to search the darkening woods.

As a parting thought Corben said, 'Seek for Maven – if she still be with us. Find Maven, and the chi' will not be far from her. Kill them both, if needs must. I care only that 'ee bring me the Stone.'

A clear still night, and an archer's moon. Well and good. No leaf would shiver upon the bough unseen, no crackling twig would go unheard. The sharpened ears and eyes of the hunters were aware of every little flicker of movement, every tiny tick of sound as they moved slowly through the moonlit woods.

Faro and Berin took to the high trees, swooping expertly from branch to branch, silent as owls. Dunch and Tuz crept among the shadows of the forest floor below, arrows notched to their bows, ready to shoot in an instant. The four of them were well spread out, able to cover a good deal of ground between them.

Back and forth they moved, and from side to side, holding their line, sweeping the acres of woodland with that grim patience that is at the heart of the hunter. They were the Ickri, and this was their game. They had played it many times, and they had seldom lost. So long as there was prey to be found, then found it would be, and no creature that remained above ground could escape them. Through the woods and up towards the ravine they slowly worked their way.

It was Tuz, the youngest and the least experienced of the group, who yet had the sharpest eye. And it was he who caught the flash of moonlight, reflected through the leaves up by the ravine. He stopped dead and stared at the scrubby patch of brambles ahead of him. What had he seen? He was aware that Dunch, far away to one side, had also stopped and was looking his way. He risked a quick glance at his companion and gestured briefly towards the bushes. Dunch remained motionless, ready to cover any escape. Of Faro and Berin there was no sign, but Tuz was sure that they too would be watching and waiting for his lead.

There! Again, a brief sparkle of reflected light through the low tangle of brambles. Something, or someone, was standing at the edge of the ravine, hidden from view by the dark clump of foliage. Tuz peered closer, straining his eyes to see what it was.

Then, like a rising planet, a shiny orb appeared above the brambles, an eerie vision in the soft moon-glow – raised high by a slender arm, silhouetted black against a purple sky. Slowly the orb revolved, turned by the hand that grasped it, one way then the other, as though it were being held up to the light and examined.

It was the Touchstone. And the hand that bore it aloft was surely Una's. They had found her at last.

Tuz silently drew back his bow, waiting a few moments longer until he was certain. Through the brambles he could just make out the broken shadow of the figure beyond, the hunched shape of the wings, the slim torso. Then he heard a voice.

'Mine to hold, then. And now that my father is gone, the Orbis shall come to me also.'

The words were barely audible, but the voice was familiar enough. It was Una, the witchi child, mutter-ing to her mad self, gloating over her spoils. Tuz was sure, now. He aimed for the body, breathed slowly out and loosed the arrow.

There was a single cry, shrill in its agony, and a flurry of movement. The figure disappeared – a moment of silence – then a brief confusion of distant muffled sound . . . and no more.

Tuz calmly drew another arrow from his quiver and waited as Dunch scurried towards him. Together they stood, staring at the bramble patch, until Faro and Berin swept down from the nearby trees. Then the four of them advanced cautiously, their bows at the ready. They reached the clump of brambles and split into pairs, two to one side, two to the other, silently creeping around the tangle of leaves and thorns until they met on the opposite side. Nothing.

The bramble patch was at the very edge of the ravine, and now the hunters stepped warily forward and peered down into the darkness. They could see a hint of reflected moonlight on the black waters of the pools below, but no movement.

Dunch whispered, 'Faro, come wi' I. T'others bide here and keep a watch, till we whistle 'ee down.'

It was too steep and rocky to descend into the ravine at this point, and it took Dunch and Faro a little while to find an alternative route. At last they were able to slide and scrabble their way downwards until they stood among the rocks and shale beside the silent pools at the foot of the ravine. There was nothing to be seen. Nobody. Dunch lifted his head and whistled briefly, then began to cast about for some evidence of their prey.

Berin and Tuz soon joined them, and once again it was Tuz whose eyes proved the sharpest. He stooped and lifted something from the mud and rocks at the edge of the largest pool.

'Hsst!'

The others looked toward him. Tuz had found the Touchstone. He wiped it on the front of his rabbitskin jerkin and the hunters gathered round to examine it. As far as they could see it was undamaged by its fall.

'We s'll be King's Guard for exchange o' this,' said Berin. 'Good on 'ee, Tuz.'

A further discovery secured their promotion; a piece of material, just visible, floating a little way out upon the surface of the same pool. Faro found a long broken branch and waded a few steps into the waters. The ground shelved away steeply and he had some difficulty in keeping his balance, but he managed to hook the bough onto the material. The object sank beneath the weight of the branch as he pulled it toward him and he had to dip his bared arm into the dark water in order to retrieve it. As he bent forward he gave a sudden cry of alarm. In reaching for the material, his fingers had brushed against something else – the unmistakable touch of another hand, cold and lifeless beneath the murky swirl of the waters.

'Acchh!' Faro splashed backwards in horror, dragging the sodden lump of cloth with him. He couldn't get back to the shore quickly enough, and fairly ran through the shallows, lifting his knees high and dropping the object that he had retrieved at the water's edge. He clambered up onto the rocks, and hopped about with his fists tucked beneath his armpits. 'Ach! She'm down there! Ugh!'

'Did 'ee see her then?'

'Aye.' Faro shuddered. 'Touched her, anywise. Ugh!'

''Tis all to the good, then. For now we'm sure.'

Berin and Tuz wrung out the piece of material that Faro had brought ashore – and now they could be certain of their coming rise in fortune. They recognized the object plainly enough. It was Una's shoulder-wrap.

Once again there was sorrow and respect in Corben's voice as he addressed the Elders. 'This be a sad ending for one so young. 'Tis plain that my brother's child have drowned herself for shame, and it should never have been. But,' he sighed, ''Tis done. She lies beneath the very waters that took the life of her father, and now have taken hers. So be it, then. We must put our sorrows aside, and journey on. Our way ahead be clear, and the Stone safe. When once those that ail have recovered we shall set forth. 'Tis not far to go.'

'And now 'tis thee that we follow,' said Haima. 'Ye must take up the Touchstone, Corben, and lead us as King.'

'Aye.' Corben gave another sad sigh. 'That I must. Come sun-wane, then, I shall choose my Guard.'

He looked about at the gathered company, their faces solemn in the early morning sunshine. They would follow him, and do his bidding. He noticed the stooped and ivy-wreathed figure of Maven-the-Green lurking among the undergrowth at the fringes of the gathering. The mad hag. Something about her was different – a malevolence in her gaze, perhaps, that had not been there before. She had been friend to the witchi child, and might now be his enemy. No matter. He would deal with her as he chose.

Chapter Sixteen

All the little details of her surroundings were thrown
sharply into focus by the bright sunshine, yet to
Celandine this somehow had the effect of making the
world seem more dreamlike than ever.

She looked at the ragged shoulders of Fin's jerkin,
roughly hemmed now with the green fishing line that
she herself had supplied, and shook her head for the
thousandth time at the marvel of him. She saw
the rabbit that he stood on tiptoe to reach, a lifeless
body, surprisingly long, dangling from its snare at the
end of a springy bough. In the distance she could see
the grey-brown Naiad horses, ungainly creatures,
whisking at the summer flies with their tufted tails.
And there was Pato talking to one of the Wisp – a
young fisher they called Moz, who proudly showed off
the string of eels that he had caught. The skin of the
eels had already become dry and leathery in the sunshine. All the everyday sights and routines of the forest
Celandine watched, the ordered comings and goings
of the Various, as unremarkable as those of the farmworkers in the outside world, and yet she still

sometimes felt that she would suddenly wake up with a start, wide-eyed and wondering, in her bed at home.

Well, today she *would* have to wake up, if she was to accomplish all that she planned. It was time, Celandine had decided, to pay a visit to Mill Farm. She wanted books and clothes, and any number of other essentials, and she could delay no longer.

Many times she had rehearsed the late night foray in her mind, and always she hit the same stumbling block. Farm life was hard and sleep was precious, so there was little fear that any human head would be stirring in the dark hour when she intended to arrive. She believed that she could slip in and out easily enough – undiscovered by her family or their employees. No, it was not the weary inhabitants of the farm that worried her. It was the dogs.

Cribb and Jude were loosed every night, and were not fed until morning. The fearsome lurchers prowled the yard from midnight till dawn, their hunger keeping them sharp, free to deal with any intruder upon their territory. Cribb would not hurt her, she felt certain, although he might well raise an alarm, but Jude she was less sure of. Jude had never been known to bark, but his silence made him all the more terrifying. There was something mad in the eye of Jude, a cold splinter of iron in that look of his, so that it made you shiver just to walk past him, no matter how innocent your purpose. And if ever he attacked, nothing would stop him. Celandine remembered the foxhound, a stray from the local meet that had once made the mistake of trotting through the stableyard, following some scent of his own imagining. Jude had gone for him – no warning, no sound – and none of the stablehands could pull him off until the job was done.

Erstcourt had shrugged at the rueful expression of the huntsman who came to collect the torn and bloodied carcass of the hound.

'It's no more than his duty,' her father had said. 'They're all foxes to Jude, whether they've four legs or two.'

It was an exaggeration – Jude had yet to attack a human – but Celandine wanted to take as few chances as possible.

Hence the rabbits. Fin managed to unsnare the one that dangled from its sapling and handed it to her. Now she had two. She intended to use them as bait, or a bribe, if she should meet with the night-watchmen of the stableyard. 'Good lad! *Gooood* lad!' She whispered softly to herself, already picturing such an encounter. Fin grinned up at her, thinking that her words were for him.

She carried her empty canvas bag in one hand and the rabbits in the other as she made her way down the dark hillside. It would have been easier to transport the furry corpses in the bag, but she wanted them instantly available. She had decided that her first purpose must be to actively seek out the dogs and be friendly to them, reassure them that she meant no harm. Better that than try to avoid them and so risk a surprise attack. She hoped that they remembered who she was.

The noises of the night made her nervous and she glanced behind her once or twice, thinking that something was following her. No, nothing there. The scrubby hillside was bare in the moonlight.

It had been difficult to make Fin understand that she would soon return. He had been content enough to escort her through the dark wicker tunnel, but had become agitated once he grasped her intent of going further – without him.

'*Noooo!*' His earnest eyes flashed up at her in the darkness, and he tugged at her pinafore. 'Is *Gorji* there! Is *get* you!'

'Don't *worry*, Fin,' she had whispered in return. 'I'll be back soon. Yes, and I'll bring you some cake. Yes, I will. Some cake!'

'*Cake-cake-cake*. . .' The thought of it appeared to mollify him, and he remained by the brambles at the entrance of the tunnel, looking wonderingly up at the night sky and murmuring to himself, his attention already drifting elsewhere.

She didn't really suppose that there would be time to search for cake, but the ploy had served its purpose.

Now she crossed the thistly paddock and crept up to the big gate that led into the stable-yard. Her heart was beating fast, thudding in her chest, and she stood still for a few moments, trying to regain control of her breathing. So long it had been, since she was last here. Weeks. All was peaceful, no sign of movement among the cluster of dark buildings.

Celandine quietly removed her heavy shoes as she

362

had planned, placing them next to the gatepost. It would be impossible to walk soundlessly through the farmhouse with them on.

The grass was wet with night-dew and her stockinged feet were instantly soaked. No matter. She had suffered worse. A few more moments to gather her courage, then she leaned against the cool metal of the gate and half-whistled, very softly.

'*Whit-whit-whit.* Cribb! Come, boy. Jude! Come, boy. *Whit-whit.*' Her voice was barely a whisper in the still night air, but immediately she heard the scrabble of claws on cobbled stone, and the two great lurchers appeared beside the corner of the open barn to her left – first Cribb, then Jude. They stood close together, heads low, searching the shadows for the direction of the sound. Then they spotted her, and seemed to grow larger in response to the unknown threat. Huge they were, as big as wolves and easily as powerful, hackles raised, ready to defend their own against all comers. The air crackled with Cribb's deep growl.

'Good lad. *Goood* lad.' Celandine could feel her nerve going. Don't bark. *Please* don't bark.

Cribb lifted his head at her voice, seemed to recognize her. She saw his tail move briefly, just a quick swish back and forth. Jude still crouched low, teeth bared, unconvinced. Twin moons reflected in his eyes – pale yellow discs, blank and sinister.

'Good boys. Yes. Yes.' Celandine awkwardly thrust one of the rabbits through the bars of the gate, and both dogs stiffened at the sudden movement. Cribb took a step backwards, unsure, before stretching his head forward and sniffing curiously. Jude never flinched, never blinked. His muzzle remained fixed in a silent snarl.

Celandine swung the rabbit towards the dogs and let go. The limp carcass landed with a soft thump on the cobbles. Again Cribb stepped backwards – then another brief wag of the tail, and he approached the rabbit, sniffing at it, turning it over with his nose.

Still no reaction from Jude.

'There's a good boy. Good Jude. Good Jude.' Celandine threw the second rabbit. Jude didn't even glance at it. He was waiting for her, she felt, daring her to actually enter his territory.

So be it then. She hesitantly stood on the first bar of the gate, clutching her empty bag, never taking her eyes off Jude. Another step up, a huge effort of nerve, and she was able to get a leg over the top bar. This would be the moment, if it was going to happen. Celandine imagined the great beast launching himself at her throat, and the terror of it made her swallow. What was she *doing*? There was a horrible crunch of powerful teeth on bone. Cribb was gnawing at the rabbit. Jude turned his head momentarily to look at his brother. When he faced her once more, the moon had gone out of his eyes, and his fangs were no longer bared. The spell was broken. Now his gaze was simply cold. A grudging permission seemed to have been granted.

She climbed cautiously down from the gate. Again the muzzle of Jude wrinkled into a brief half-snarl, a warning that she had better keep well clear of him if she knew what was good for her. Celandine sidled past the two dogs and tiptoed across the yard. She glanced over her shoulder as she climbed the two steps that led up to the front path of the farmhouse. Cribb was lying down now, tackling his unexpected meal in grisly earnest. Jude was still looking at her, a motionless shadow in the pale night, his own rabbit lying untouched upon the cold cobbles.

The scullery door was unlocked, as she had guessed it would be. How strange it was to breathe once again that familiar atmosphere – of woodash, and washing soda, and piles of wet linen. It must be Monday, then, she supposed.

A little light filtered in through the unshuttered windows, but she could have found her way through the house blindfold. Everything would be as it had always been. She knew which door would squeak, which stair would creak, and where each member of the household would be at this hour. Celandine cautiously opened the door to the kitchen, feeling the immediate warmth of the big iron cooking range, banked up for the night. All quiet. Good. Before passing through the shadowy kitchen, she took a paring knife from the cutlery drawer, a half-used bar of carbolic soap from the draining board and a gardening trowel that had unaccountably been left on the window sill. Useful things. Celandine put them into her canvas bag.

In the hallway beyond she stopped for a few moments and listened. The dark staircase rose up steeply in front of her – a threatening obstacle, full of hidden creaks and groans, ready to give her away if she should put a foot wrong. There was a smell of oilskins and muddy boots. Celandine took a hairbrush from the hall dresser, put it in her bag, and gingerly began to climb. One step at a time. Gently . . . gently . . .

At the top of the stairs she let out her breath and listened once again. Thos's snoring was like the scrape of a barn door being pulled to and fro, rattling through the whole of the upper floor. So loud! Celandine blessed him for it, and crept along the corridor – keeping close to the wall, where the floorboards were less likely to creak.

Freddie's room. This would be the test, and she had tried to prepare herself for it. Here she had imagined that she might collapse in hopeless sobs, unable to bear the thought that Freddie would never open this door again. The books and the fishing tackle, the birds' eggs and the butterflies, the scuffed cricket ball – all his treasures – all would remain in here for evermore, unloved and untouched.

There turned out to be little time to dwell on such things. Standing in the open doorway and gazing into the moonlit room, Celandine became aware that the house was suddenly very quiet. Thos's snoring had ceased.

Had he woken up? Might he now be lighting his candle and pulling on his boots, some instinct telling him that there was an intruder present?

Hurry, then. She stepped into Freddie's room and quietly removed several of the books from the shelf. Put them in the bag. Hurry. Hurry. What else? A few items of fishing tackle. Don't stop to choose. Just put them in the bag. The cricket ball? No. Penknife? Yes. Put it in the bag.

Outside on the landing all was still quiet. There was a clothes chest next to Freddie's door, and from here she had intended to take a few articles. But what if Thos suddenly appeared? Or her father? Ignore the thought. She hadn't braved this journey to simply turn around and run straight back again.

The lid of the clothes chest was heavy, but it was soundless on its hinges. Difficult to see exactly what was in there. Freddie's old canvas fishing boots she found easily enough, and after that she just grabbed at whatever items of clothing came to hand. Her bag was filling up.

Celandine quickly lowered the lid, and then regretted her haste. The thing slipped from her nervous fingers at the last second, and banged shut with a noise like a cannon-shot. No! She hoisted her bag and hurried to the top of the stairs. The whole household must have heard it – they *must* have done.

Her hand was slippery with perspiration as she gripped the banister. Wait. Just *wait* for a second. She listened for the inevitable heavy footsteps, the opening of bedroom doors . . . There! What was that? A low grumble of sound from the end room . . .

It was only Thos, snoring again.

Celandine crept down the stairs, shaking with relief.

From the parlour she took a pair of nutcrackers – still lying on a bed of empty shells, in a bowl that might have been there since Christmas – and from the sitting room a big ball of wool and two knitting needles. What else? The schoolroom.

She found an unopened box of chalks, some pencils, and a couple of exercise books. There was very little space left in the bag now, but she hadn't quite finished yet. She opened the big cupboard in the corner of the schoolroom, and took out her old workbasket. The hated sampler that she had laboured over for so long was neatly folded on top, some of the spidery lettering just readable in the blue-grey light; *I Shall Not Want.* Celandine tossed the thing aside and delved further into the basket, drawing out the heavy dressmaking scissors that had played such a large part in all her troubles. She had another use for them now.

A packet of needles, a few skeins of thread, and her task was complete. There was nothing else she could think of that was both useful and easily portable.

Back through the ground floor of the house she tiptoed, lingering a little when she came once again to the sitting room – grateful for the warmth of the rug on the soles of her damp feet.

Before leaving the kitchen and making for the scullery, she decided to press her luck just a little further. It didn't take her long to find what she was looking for – a piece of Cook's lardy-cake, sitting on a plate in the pantry. Enough to fill the last corner of her bag. Good.

Once she had silently closed the outer door of the scullery, she felt her shoulders sag with relief. The night air calmed her, and she took a deep breath. She had succeeded. All she had to do now was cross the yard, clamber over the gate into the paddock, and she would be safe.

At the top of the steps by the balustrade wall, she took a quick look up and down the yard – and her heart gave such a jump that she almost choked. A tiny figure was wandering across the cobbles, clearly visible in the moonlight, wringing his hands as he looked uncertainly around him. *Fin?* No! This *couldn't* be. Her elbow bumped against one of the wall pillars as she momentarily lost her balance. What on earth was he doing here? He must have followed her after all – or somehow found his way. And now he was fooling about in the stable-yard, threatening to ruin everything, totally exposed to every danger . . .

The dogs! Where were the dogs? Celandine opened her mouth to hiss out a warning, but could make no sound – because now it was too late. She had spotted them. From the darkness of the open-sided barn they came, creeping low among the shadows, silently inching forward as Fin drew level with them. He was whispering to himself, completely oblivious to the peril he was in.

The twin lurchers crouched shoulder to bristling shoulder, teeth bared, quivering in the anticipation of their moment.

Celandine was unable to move, rigid with anguish. A terrible vision exploded in her head – of the foxhound slaughtered by Jude. The horror of it knotted up her tongue and her throat, and every bit of her. She could only stand and gape, helpless to prevent what would happen.

A great rumbling growl from Cribb, and Fin turned his head – saw them at last – such monsters as he could never have imagined. His pitiful little frame was dwarfed in their combined shadow. Cribb's final shattering snarl echoed around the cobblestoned yard as the two dogs stepped straight in for the kill, ferocious, unstoppable . . .

'*Hschhhhhhhhhhh!!*'

Fin put his finger to his lips and thrust his head towards the gaping jaws that were about to tear him apart. He hissed like an angry swan into the very faces of his attackers, sweeping his raised forefinger from one to the other. The noise was so piercing and un-expected that both dogs sprang backwards in alarm. They staggered clumsily against one another, a tangle of astonishment, unable to retreat quickly enough. Jude gave a loud yelp – a thing that he had never done in his life – and the shock of it dragged Celandine back to her senses.

She lugged her heavy bag down the steps, stumbled across the cobbles, and prayed that Fin's amazing reaction would hold the lurchers at bay a little longer. She made straight for the big gate, heaved her bag up as high as she could and somehow shoved it over the top. Then she ran back to grab Fin. The dogs had recov-ered a little, and now Cribb had begun to bark in earnest. But still the pair of them clung hesitantly together, skittering this way and that – and every time they came too close, Fin sent them into a whining retreat with his miraculous hissing finger trick.

A light flickered in an upstairs window of the farmhouse and there was the rattle and curse of someone struggling with the sash. Thos? The dogs looked up hopefully, distracted for a second, and Celandine grasped Fin by the collar. She yanked him over to the gate, and tumbled him through one of the lower bars. Then she squeezed between the narrow gap – it was quicker than climbing over – and picked up her bag.

'*I* all right! *I* all right! Ah-ah-ah . . .' Fin was jabbering away, but Celandine had no time for his nonsense. With one hand on his collar and the other gripping the handles of her bag, she hurried him as fast as she could into the safety of the beckoning shadows.

A loud voice shouted, 'Cribb! Come by! Jude! Come by!' Thos had apparently managed to get the window open, and was bringing the dogs to where he could see them. That probably meant that he had a gun. 'Cribb! Jude!' The barking ceased. Celandine struggled on through the darkness, panting with fear, desperately hoping that she could not be seen.

Ba-dooom! The shotgun blasted out, and even as she instinctively ducked, Celandine recognized the sound. It was the four-ten, not the twelve-bore. Good. She was already out of range.

'You keep out o' my yard – you hear me? Ruddy gyppos.' Thos's angry voice, fading into the distance.

Celandine kept going, furiously dragging Fin along by the greasy scruff of his jerkin until they reached the sheep-gate at the foot of Howard's Hill. Her feet were scratched and sore from trampling through the thistles, and it was only at this point that she realized that she had left her shoes behind. They were still beside the gatepost where she had taken them off. Well, she didn't really need them any more, and she was certainly not going to go back for them now. Would she ever go back again, she wondered?

Fin clambered up onto the stone wall beside the sheep-gate. He seemed happy enough, and already had either forgiven or forgotten her rough treatment of him. Together they looked back towards the distant huddle of farm buildings, silent now, and dark once more.

Celandine shivered, and was suddenly grateful that Fin was there. For all that he had caused her nothing but trouble, this would be a lonely moment without him.

'I'm sorry I was angry with you,' she said. 'I was frightened.'

Fin looked at her and solemnly nodded his head. Hadn't he warned her of such dangers before? 'Is *Gorji* there,' he said. He leaned towards her, and his eyes widened in the moonlight. 'Is *get* you.'

A penknife, a trowel and a kitchen knife. Half a block of soap. Some wool, and a pair of knitting needles. Nutcrackers. A couple of large shirts, minus their collars, and a Fair Isle jumper. Canvas boots. Pencils, chalks and exercise books. A hairbrush. Four woollen socks and a cotton one. A pair of cricket flannels, still grass-stained from when they were last worn. Bits of fishing tackle – line, hooks and lead weights. Sewing materials, and of course the dressmaking scissors. Celandine was pleased with her haul, and the cave-dwellers, gathered about her, were most impressed.

Best of all, though, were the books. Celandine laid them out in a row upon the warm stone floor of the cave entrance. *The Home Workshop, Campfire Songs, Old Moore's Almanac, Gamages Christmas Bazaar 1912,* and *Pears' Cyclopaedia.* Now she had something to work with.

She picked up the Cyclopaedia, and let it fall open. 'Look,' she said, 'It tells you how to make jam. Blackberry.' There was a murmur of polite interest and the dark heads moved in closer.

Chapter Seventeen

It was Rufus who first saw them as they appeared through the hanging mist at the edge of Great Clearing. Those to the forefront of the group were curiously attired in black and white, their weather-hardened faces made ghostly in the shroud of dawn. Spears they carried, and strange bowed implements, other weapons perhaps, all hung with magpie feathers. There were others, of plainer appearance, half-hidden among the background foliage: wives, childer – a very tribe – and all with that same gaunt look to them, dark glittering eyes, and deep brown skin. Who were these wild outlanders, and how had they found this place?

Two sinewy figures dropped down from the high branches of the trees and circled to the ground on outstretched wings.

Wings . . .

Rufus touched the ringlet of kingfisher feathers that hung about his neck. He had no great knowledge of the ancient lore and legend of the travelling tribes, but he was certain now of what he saw. He must go and find Pato, quickly, and tell him.

The Ickri had returned.

Celandine saw nothing, and the attack seemed to come from nowhere. She was looking for mushrooms – better to collect them at dawn than in the dull heat of midday – and the sudden clamour of pigeons' wings made her jump. Then something ripped into her hair, tearing it at the roots, and she ducked sideways, gasping with the pain and surprise of it. For a second it seemed to her that the birds were somehow the cause of this, and she glanced fearfully upwards, putting her hand to her head. Then again – *zhhhip* – a cutting blow across her fingers, another searing tug at her scalp, and this time she was away, every nerve of her body shocked into instant flight.

Around the high ridge of the main clearing she ran, gulping for breath, terrified that she was being pursued, yet not daring to look back. She dodged into the thick undergrowth, swerving this way and that among the dew-soaked bushes, down through the rocky maze of pathways, down, down, down, all her instincts driving her towards the safety of the caves. What was it? What had happened? Her fingers were sticky now, and she caught sight of the red smears on them, flashing in and out of view as she ran. But the pain in her chest was worse than the pain in her hand, or her head, and there was no time to stop and examine her wounds. She blundered into a group of Naiad horses, banged her shoulder against a tree-trunk as she tried to avoid them, regained her balance and carried on. Just keep going – don't stop for anything. Keep going. Run.

Nearly there. A scattering of white butterflies among the buddleia bushes, an awkward vault over the fallen beech, and then the mouth of the main cave was in sight. As Celandine crashed and slithered, whimpering with panic across the heap of loose shale, she heard the muffled sound of tuneful voices – a distant congregation, singing, '*Speed bonny boat, like a bird on the wing...*' The cave-dwellers. They were calmly practising one of the songs she had taught them, oblivious to all her panic. A last frantic scrabble and she was able to heave herself up into the mouth of the cave. The voices immediately ceased. Celandine stumbled forward into the welcoming darkness and then dropped to her knees, exhausted.

The stone floor of the cave was cool against her palms, a comfort. There was something caught in her hair, but she was unable to do anything about it until the pounding in her chest had subsided. She remained on all fours, her own loud breathing echoing all around her. And now she became aware of the murmurings of concern and of gentle hands, hesitant, upon her shoulders.

'What've happened to 'ee, child?'

'Mab – some water. And a cloth – she be hurt. Step back, Loren – Patty – and let her bide.'

'It's all right . . . I'm . . . all right.' Always her voice was so loud. The group around her fell silent. She eventually forced herself back onto her heels, calmer now, and raised her hands to her head. What *was* it that was tangled up in her hair? A stick? Celandine caught the look of alarm on the faces of the cave-dwellers, as she painfully unravelled the object, wincing as she drew it from the bloodied mass of knots. Then she saw, and knew, and the thing fell from her fingers, making a slight clatter as it tumbled end-over-end onto the stone floor. It was an arrow.

A faint *tink-tink* echoed from the distant tunnels, breaking the silence, and the spell that seemed to be cast upon them all. Micas stooped and picked up the arrow, holding it away from him and towards the light. He smoothed down the black and white feathered flights with his thumb, examined the scorched and fire-hardened tip of it.

'They'm come at last, then,' he said. 'As we knew some day they must.'

'Who has?' Celandine's voice was shaky. Even as she asked the question, she had begun to guess the answer.

'The Ickren.' Micas grasped the arrow with both hands and the sudden crack of splintering wood bounced about the walls of the cave. He held up the two halves of the broken arrow for all to see. 'And they come wi' trouble. As wappsies do come wi' a sting. Aye – as they left, so they return. Unchanged.' He looked around at the gathering of Tinklers and Troggles, his faded grey eyes moving from one to the other, as if measuring their strengths, their weaknesses.

'Bron, step with me – and thee, Garlan, and thee, Tammas. Bring each a staff. Let us see what we may learn. And all else here – biden close to the cave. Maid, thee must be seen no more. Stay in darkness. Heed what I say.'

Celandine, still kneeling, put her hand to her head, gingerly attempting to examine her scalp. Her matted hair was sticky with blood and it was difficult to get to the wound.

Elina said, 'Come, we s'll bathe it.' But Celandine had other plans.

Corben began to relax a little. It was plain that this lowly people would be of little threat to him. They carried no spears, no bows. The gathering of wingless simpletons that now stood before him bore only implements suited to digging the earth or cutting at plants – humble things such as he had seen the Gorji fieldworkers using.

Behind the few who chose to speak for their tribe, this *Naiad*, stood the main body of them, silent and respectful, timidly keeping to the background. As well they might.

Corben looked about the smaller clearing they had now entered, noted the woven shelters that were pitched beneath the overhanging trees, the scraps of clothing that were hung upon the bushes to dry, the baskets of roots and greenstuff that had been lately harvested in. A good place, and undoubtedly a safe one – as the Ickri had learned, in trying to gain entry through the surrounding briars. It had not been easy. Those who lived here would have little fear of being discovered by the Gorji. What was he to make, then, of the story he had been told earlier?

He turned to his Guard.

'Again, Tuz. Tell us what thee saw.'

'An ogre maid, Corben. Leastways I reckon 'twere a maid – she were a way off.'

'But here i' the woods – not beyond the briars?'

'She were here. As I reckon.' Tuz looked puzzled, as though perhaps he was beginning to have doubts of his own. 'I knows I shot her, thass certain. And I knows I hit true.'

'Yet now she is gone.'

Tuz hung his head. 'Aye.'

Corben looked at the Naiad forest-dwellers and spoke to the one that seemed to have the most sense about him.

'What say thee, friend – Pato? Be there Gorji here?'

A slow shrug of the shoulders, a pursing of the lips. 'None as I can tell of. We be safe enough from the giants. But I'd ha' thought to see their kind here long afore I'd see yourn, maister. Aye. 'Tis a long day since the Ickri were heard of in these parts. Bist truly they? Where have 'ee come from, and what can we do for 'ee?'

Corben considered. He had been prepared for immediate battle, but that would not be necessary, it seemed. This was not a fighting tribe, nor even a travelling tribe. A soft life they had made for themselves here, these field-grubbers, and his own people would be glad to rest easy for a while. The Orbis might be here, and it might not – and perhaps friendliness would prove quicker than force in retrieving it. Either way, it could wait a little longer.

'Long-seasons,' he said, 'we have sought for this place, and for our brothers, the Naiad. Now that our

journeying be over, we need but a little food and sleep.
Give us some ease, and we shall talk when we be rested.'

Celandine had imagined this moment so many times,
had anticipated it for so long. Standing in the bright
sunlight at the mouth of the cave, she grasped a fistful
of her thick hair and leaned forward slightly, head to
one side. She was ready. But as she brought the scissors
towards her, something made her pause for a second
– some movement among the scrubby hawthorn
bushes down below. She stared at the greenery, her
head still tilted, the scissors still poised in her hand.
The trailing strings of ivy puzzled her. She had never
noticed ivy there before. Another twitch of movement
– there! – and she realized that she was being watched.
Eyes, she could see, and then a face that grew around
those eyes. The face was green, everything was green –
the hair, the clothing . . . it was as if she were gazing at
some extraordinary picture puzzle . . .

The eyes regarded her for a few moments longer,
then slowly faded back into the deep shadows. Gone.
And the ivy was gone, and every trace of it was gone.

She hadn't been afraid, she realized. Whatever it
was that she had seen had brought no sense of danger
to her. Rather there had been an air of calm interest
about those eyes, calm and . . . what? Reassurance. Yes,
reassurance.

Her arm was beginning to ache from holding it in
one position for so long, and the cave-dwellers were
still looking up at her, waiting to see what she was
about to do.

The first cut was the best – the heavy scissors making a delicious grinding sound, like a knife upon an oilstone, shearing effortlessly through the mass of tangles. Again. And again. Celandine watched the twisted locks float gently to the ground, great snaking swirls of it about her feet. So many years of brushing and combing, and pinning up and tying back, all the burdensome rituals that she had endured, they now fell away from her – snip . . . by snip . . . by snip. It was that simple.

She shook her head, amazed at how light and free it felt. More. She wanted it all gone.

The Tinklers and Troggles gazed up at her, narrowing their eyes at each deliberate *schhhnickk* of the scissors, following the path of every tumbling hank with wonder and fascination. Some of them tentatively raised their hands to their own straggly heads, as if exploring an idea growing within.

Later, when she had bathed her wounds, Celandine stood once again at the entrance of the cave, dressed now in Freddie's old cricket trousers and a huge collarless shirt that must once have belonged to her father – or perhaps to Thos. The warm afternoon breeze whispered delightfully through her short crop of damp curls, and she thought that she had never felt so unrestricted in her life. For all the danger that might now be lurking out there – amongst those softly swaying branches, or within that tangled undergrowth – here was a moment to be joyful in. She stroked the back of her bare neck, pinched at the bits of hair that still remained, sable-short, behind her ears. She put her hands in her trouser pockets – such a luxury to have pockets! – leaned against the cool stone, and felt like whistling.

But no. That would be too dangerous, and Micas was right. It would be best to stay hidden.

She had half hoped that she might see that strange apparition once more, the little green creature that had appeared and disappeared like a woodland spirit. But there was nothing there.

'Yes, all right, then,' she said. Elina was tugging at her trouser leg. 'I'll come back inside now.'

The air grew heavier as evening began to descend, close and still, and as Little Clearing became filled with the coming together of the Various tribespeople, the skies were already dark with the looming of thunderclouds. The Wisp had arisen, ready to go to work, but their night-fishing expeditions had quickly been postponed upon learning of the Ickri arrival. Now they joined uneasily with the Naiad to watch and to listen as the leaders talked.

Two bindle-wraps had been laid out on the grass, close to the ancient beech tree that stood in the clearing, and upon these sat Corben, Pato, and Gwill of the Wisp. Pato and Gwill occupied one oilcloth between them. Corben sat alone on the other. A large wooden dish of baked meats – rook and squirrel – had been placed on the ground in the centre of the trio, so that each might lean forward and take a piece as they talked. Behind Corben sat the Ickri Elders, arranged in a half-circle, and behind them stood the Guard, then, at a respectful distance, the bulk of the Ickri tribe. The Naiad and Wisp tribespeople mingled together in a looser arrangement, jostling for position behind Pato and Gwill.

The children of the forest-dwellers sidled around the edge of the crowd, moving a little closer to where the strange outlanders were gathered, marvelling at their dress, and their manner. What fascinated them most of all were those astonishing wings, and especially the wings of the archers. They pointed out to each other the curious designs that decorated the flexing membranes, and they whispered amongst themselves, only to shrink back in silence should one of the archers glance, unsmiling, in their direction.

'How long it has been,' said Corben, 'since our tribes were met. And how long have we, the Ickri, sought our brothers. Now we have returned to our old lands, and we be right glad to see thee thrive so well. Once there were but tribe and tribe here – Ickri and Naiad. Now we see that there be another – the Wisp.' He looked at Gwill. 'How so?'

Gwill seemed puzzled. 'I casn't tell. But I can tell 'ee this – there be others here yet. Naiad and Wisp, aye, but then there's they Tinklers and Troggles, too. We be Various now.'

'Other tribes?' said Corben. He looked about him. 'Then should they not be here to meet with us?'

'I doubts they'd come,' said Pato. 'We sees little enough of 'em. They keeps away from we, and we from they.'

Corben reached forward and took a piece of meat

from the wooden trencher. 'But these others – they be not of the Naiad? Then my question is not for them. Tell me, Pato, what do 'ee know of the Touchstone – and of the Orbis?' Corben put the piece of meat in his mouth, and casually began to chew it.

'The Touchstone? And the . . . what did 'ee say 'twas? Orbis?' Pato looked at Gwill, and raised his eyebrows. 'Orbis? No, I never heard tell o' such a thing. Did thee, Gwill? No.' He turned back to Corben. 'We do sometimes say "By the *Stone*!" for a cuss. But I casn't tell what it do mean, 'xactly. We just says it – "By the Stone". See, if one o' our childer were mitherin' us wi' their plaguey nonsense . . .'

'Ye speak of it, yet never heard tell of it.' Corben's voice had grown harder. 'Ye never heard tell of the Touchstone. And ye never heard tell of the Orbis – that which was *stolen* from the Ickri . . .' He seemed to check himself, and paused to rub his eyes for a moment. One of the Elders leaned towards him and muttered a quiet word or two in his ear. Corben lowered his head and nodded.

' 'Tis an old tale,' he said, 'and 'twill wait till the morrow. We be weary yet from many long seasons journeying. But think on it awhile, if thee will. The Touchstone. There may be those among thee who remember tell of it.'

'*I* remember tell of it.'

Corben slowly raised his head.

Four pale-skinned figures, all dressed in grey, had made their way to the front of the crowd. They carried wooden staves, and though their manner was calm they looked somehow more purposeful than the hobble-de-hoys who had parted to give them passage. Corben glanced round at his Guard, then turned to face the newcomers once more.

'Then welcome,' he said, and his bearded mouth opened into a smile. He looked from one to the other, as if trying to decide which had spoken. Finally his attention remained upon the eldest. 'Aye, welcome. Come – sit with us.'

Pato and Gwill had turned to see who was now arrived. They muttered a brief acknowledgement to the cave-dwellers.

'Micas. Bron . . .' They shifted a little closer together, in order to make room on the oilcloth.

The newcomers nodded in return. 'Pato, Gwill. No – we s'll stand, thank 'ee.'

Corben was now forced to look up as he spoke, and this seemed to annoy him. His smile had disappeared.

'So, then, friends. The Touchstone. Ye know something of that tale? What be your tribe, then, and how came thee to this place?'

The eldest quietly spoke. 'I be Micas. A Tinkler. Tinklers and Troggles they do name us now, though once we were all Naiad. Aye, Naiad. We were here when the Ickren were here, and we stayed when they had gone. We stayed as could do naught else – for was the Stone not stolen from us?'

'*Stolen?*' Corben's voice was raised in astonishment.

'Aye. Stole by the Ickren – *your* kind, maister. And have 'ee now come to return it?'

'*Return it?*' Corben began to rise, his face reddening with anger. 'I am King of the *Ickri*! Aye, the Ickri! Ye think we would journey so far that we might put the Touchstone into the hands of a . . . a . . . what do you call theeself? A *Tinkler*?'

'Aye. Thee med put it in my hands, if 'tis true that thee have it to give, for 'tis our'n to hold.'

Micas spoke calmly, though Corben's angry face was now close to his own. The Elders were struggling to their feet, and they attempted to lay restraining hands upon their king – but Corben shrugged them off, cursing, as he rummaged within the folds of his cloak. He drew something forth and thrust it aggressively towards Micas. The crowd shrank back with a gasp – all eyes upon the shining jasper globe that Corben now held out.

'Take it, then, if 'ee dare! Take it, if 'ee believe 'tis thine!'

Micas paid no attention to the quivering hand that was stretched out before him, but looked steadily into Corben's narrowed eyes.

' 'Tis true then. The Touchstone be here at last.'

'Aye!' Corben snarled. 'The Stone be here! By its power we have come, and by mine, led to this place from lands so hard they would crack your old bones into dust. A king we have lost upon the way – my own brother, Avlon. And a king's daughter, also, be lost to us. My own kin have been taken from me, and now you think the Stone shall be taken from me also? No, friend, thee have it widdershins. I am come to take from *thee*. From thee. Show me the Orbis.'

'Orbis?' Micas shrugged his shoulders. 'Whenst did I speak of such? I but said that I knew of the Stone.'

Corben looked furious. He glared at Micas for a few moments, then spun round to face the Guard – raising the Touchstone high as if about to give an order. The archers immediately tensed, bows at the ready, waiting for the word . . .

But then Corben appeared to change his mind. He lowered his head and his deep breathing could be clearly heard in the surrounding silence. Slowly he brought the Touchstone closer to him, cradling it in both hands as he turned back towards Micas. He kept his eyes upon the surface of the orb as he spoke.

' 'Tis true,' he said, and his tone had become apologetic. 'Ye said nothing of the Orbis – and perhaps know nothing of it.' He sighed. 'We have been travelling for too long, and I am wearied and out of temper. I mean thee no harm . . . Micas . . . nor any here. By this Stone we be brought together, and by this Stone we shall travel on together – aye, to the very gates of Elysse – once the Orbis be found. So spoke my brother, the King that was, and I must believe him.' Corben threw back his head, and looked directly at Micas. 'But I forget – ye know nothing of such matters. I must explain then, perhaps tomorrow, when we be rested, and in better humour. Then all shall truly learn why we are come, and what it is we seek, and what great power we bring thee.'

Corben glanced upwards at the black thunder-clouds rolling in from the west, and then looked about the clearing. 'For this night we must ask use of your shelters. Not all – a half share of these will serve. Come the morrow we will begin upon shelters of our own. Aye, the morrow shall be a day of changes.'

It was very nearly dark by the time Micas and the others returned to the cave. None had ever heard Micas's voice sound so loud or so angry.

'Come! Come all! Leave off what 'ee be about, and gather to me!'

But as the hurrying figures of the cave-dwellers began to emerge from the tunnels, and the little oil-lamps threw dancing shadows about the walls of the entrance cavern, Micas's angry scowl disappeared. His bushy grey eyebrows shot up in astonishment. Fully half of those now before him had apparently lost their hair.

'Wha'ist this? What have 'ee done to theeselves?'

Celandine stepped from her side-chamber, and stood amongst the gathering.

'I've given them a haircut,' she said. 'They watched me do mine, and then they wanted the same.'

Micas seemed unable to speak. He ran his fingers through his own thick side locks, and looked about him in bewilderment.

'*Elina?*' The sight of his wife's head – now almost as bald as his own – freed his tongue once more. 'Thee also?'

'I were the first,' said Elina, with some pride. 'What say thee?' She turned once around, so that Micas could benefit from the full effect.

'Om,' said Micas. He was clearly shocked, but

managed to mumble, ' 'Tis . . . comely. 'Tis . . . om . . .
most pleasing.' He shot a desperate glance at
Celandine, but her own transformed appearance was
also too much for him. He rubbed his grey-stubbled
chin and stared at the ground for a few moments –
perhaps the safest option.

The muscular Bron, who stood beside Micas, was
less diplomatic. 'We'm fallen in wi' a gaggle o' coots!'
he said, and Garlan laughed. 'Aye. Or a clutch o'
goosey eggs.'

But Micas was looking serious again now, and
some of his anger had returned.

'Hold, Bron. And all of 'ee. We've more than this
to think on.'

He raised his head. ''Tis as we supposed,' he said.
'The Ickren be here, and here they means to stay.'

'Do they really have wings?' said Celandine.

Micas frowned.

'Maid, when I speken, thee do not. Thank 'ee.
Aye, they have wings, and each a pair o' faces to
match. A face that do smile, and a face that do snarl –
and neither would 'ee trust. They come bearing the
Touchstone with them. I have seen it, and Bron, and
Tammas here, and Garlan have seen it also. They
come bearing the Touchstone, but they seek the
Orbis. The Orbis, mark 'ee. And they s'll take it from
us if'n they can.'

There was silence at this.

Micas said, 'So here we be.' He looked at his
companions. 'Bron, what say thee?'

Bron folded his arms and threw back his broad

shoulders. 'If they'm to take the Orbis, then first they'm to find it. And how should 'em do that, when none but Micas knows where it be hid? Micas alone do carry the secret about him – to be passed to such of his choosing when his time be near. And this shall be our guard. Th' Ickren will never know where to seek for't.'

'I be wi' Bron,' said Tammas, though he hadn't been asked. 'They'll get naught from we. Let 'em huff and puff.'

'They may do more'n huff and puff,' said Micas. 'As we do already find.' He looked up at Celandine. 'They'd put a dart through any as crossed their way, be 'em childer or no. Aye, and we all have childer. Garlan, what from thee, as have also seen 'em?'

'They casn't kill us all,' said Garlan, 'for we be too many. Tribes and tribes we be. And mark 'ee; they've childer of their own. 'Twill come to parley, not to blood. We've naught to fear – and naught to tell.'

'Naught to fear?' said Micas. 'Then think on this; how did they find'n this place after so long, and from so far? The Touchstone did lead them here, or so say their *king*. And if the Stone have such a power as to bring 'em to these woods, then might it not bring 'em a little further yet – to the Orbis itself? Tonight the Ickren be weary and have already gone to their rest. Come the morrow, they would parley some more. We might then learn that the Stone have the power to find the Orbis, wherever it be hidden. We might learn that the Orbis cans't *not* be hidden from the Stone, and that if we do not willingly give it, then there will be blood. Aye, there will be blood – for hark 'ee; the

Ickren do reckon the Orbis to be their'n to hold, as sure as we do reckon the Stone to be our'n.'

There were murmurings of concern over this, and Micas had to raise his hands to still the crowd.

'We have this to choose,' said Micas. He waited for silence to descend once more. Then he lowered his hands, and turned them palm upwards. 'With this hand we med wait, and parley, and see if the Ickren shall find the Orbis and take it from us. Or with this hand, we med reach out and take the Stone from the Ickren. Aye. The Ickren must take from us, or we from they. Which hand shall it be – and which hand shall become the bloodier?'

The voices of the cave-dwellers rose once again, each with their own opinion, and this time Micas left them to their discussions. He beckoned to Celandine.

'Come, maid. Walk with me a step. We s'll see no more of the Ickren this eve, and 'tis safe to be abroad for a little. I must talk with 'ee.'

The night air was very humid, and by the time Celandine had followed Micas up the steep pathway to the high clearings, she felt sticky with perspiration. They stood beneath a hawthorn tree and looked out over the dark expanse before them. On the opposite side of the Great Clearing the far tree-line was just visible, a ragged horizon against a rumbling sky, and Celandine found herself thinking of the war. It was said that the terrible big guns could be heard clear across the English Channel. She wondered if this was how they sounded, a distant boom of thunder that threatened to roll ever closer – something that would surely happen, if it weren't for Freddie and those like him. Thousands like Freddie . . .

' 'Tis time thee were gone,' said Micas.

'What?' she said. Gone? Where?

'Thee c'nst bide here no longer, maid, though I be sorry to say it. A true friend to us thee have been, and have kept all your vow. But this be no place for a Gorji maid, now – if ever 'twere – for the Ickren bain't like we. They'll bring 'ee down like a throstle as soon as they sithee, and we casn't keep 'ee hid for ever. Thee must go back to where 'ee came from.'

'But I *can't* go back! You don't understand. You don't know what I've done . . . or . . . or what I've run away from. You don't know what they'd *do* to me . . .'

'Would your own put an arrow through thee? For tha'ist what'll happen if thee stay.'

'Well, no. But I'm sure that if I just *talked* to these others . . . like I did with you . . . if I showed them that I meant no harm. And perhaps they just shot at me because they were frightened . . .'

'No, child – 'twon't do. Not wi' the Ickren. They'm come for the Orbis – and there'll be blood. I s'll not have yourn on my hands, and my own also.'

'Well, but what *is* this thing that everybody wants? I don't understand it at all. I know that the Touchstone and the Orbis go together somehow, but what does it mean? And why can't you just . . . share . . . ?'

Micas's face was suddenly illuminated in a blind-ing explosion of light – like a photographer's flash –

and all the world around was momentarily as bright as day. A great crash shook the skies and Celandine ducked down with a shriek, thinking for a split second that the guns of war had indeed arrived and that Howard's Hill was being bombarded. Then she saw a crackle of flame below her, on the fringes of the woodland, and realized that one of the trees down there had been struck by lightning.

As she rose to her feet, the heavens lit up once more. A jagged snake's tongue of brilliant blue pierced the darkness, another tumbling roar of thunder, and this time she heard the nearby crack of splintered timber. Celandine turned to see more flames spitting upwards at the sky. The ancient beech – the one that stood alone in Little Clearing – had also been hit.

All her instinct was to draw back, to shrink beneath the cover of the hawthorns and hide herself from the lightning storm, but Micas stepped forward onto the verges of the Great Clearing, tensely looking toward the burning beech. A few more paces he took, then he turned to beckon her out into the clearing. In the light thrown by the distant flames, Celandine saw the look of panic in his eyes.

What did he think he was doing? It wasn't safe out there. And yet, after a few moments' hesitation, Celandine began to follow, keeping close behind Micas as he scurried between the vegetable plots and the wigwam rows of bean-sticks.

There was a gap in the line of low bushes that separated the two clearings, and here Micas paused, peering about him into the darkness. The flames from the stricken beech had dwindled now, but there was still enough light to see that the trunk had been split, where one of the massive limbs had been torn away. It was the limb itself that now lay burning upon the ground.

'What are we *doing*?' Celandine's voice was all but drowned out by the angry rumbles of thunder, but Micas immediately put his finger to his lips in order to silence her. 'Sh!'

For a long time they crouched upon the well-worn path between the bushes, and Micas continually looked about him, apparently waiting to see if any of the tribes would be roused by the storm. There was still no rain, but the thunder continued to grumble around the heavens and there were occasional lightning flashes, though these were now moving further away.

At last Micas whispered to her, 'The Ickren be all about here – sheltered b' the Naiad. We casn't let them sithee.'

'Then why are we here?' Celandine didn't understand. If it was so important not to be seen, then what on earth was Micas thinking of, to bring her so close to danger?

'Come.' Micas began to creep towards the beech tree, still looking from left to right, scanning the borders of the clearing for any sign of movement from the Naiad shelters.

Celandine put her trust in him, and followed. If any of the tribespeople had been awoken by the thunder, and had perhaps stirred themselves, then they had taken little further interest. Thunderstorms were common enough at this time of the year, and sleep was too precious to waste.

The resinous smell of scorched timber hung in the air and the fallen beech limb still smouldered upon the ground, though the flames had all but died out. It was dark once more, but Celandine could see where the trunk had been split – a huge gash of exposed wood, pale against the blackened bark.

Micas was moving around the bole of the tree, looking upwards.

'Hst!' He whispered for her to join him. Celandine crept towards him and followed the direction of his pointing finger. What? She could see nothing.

'Can 'ee reach it?'

Celandine peered closer. There was some sort of knotty protrusion from the trunk of the tree – perhaps the relic of an old branch, now long gone. Was that what he meant? She stood up on tiptoe, and found that she could just about touch what felt to be the lip or the rim of a hollow. Her fingers curved over the edge of it. There must obviously be a cavity, or a split in the trunk.

'Put thee hand in,' whispered Micas. 'See what be there.'

Put her hand in? Celandine wasn't sure that she was able to reach that far, nor was she sure that she wanted to try. Anything might be in there – an owl for instance, or even a buzzard. No, she didn't like that idea at all.

'I can't reach,' she whispered back at him. 'And anyway, what am I looking for?'

'A box'n.'

'A . . . box?'

'Aye – made o' tinsy.'

Micas dropped to his knees. He placed his hands flat upon one of the great tree roots and then braced his shoulder against the trunk.

'Climb upon me, child. Hurry!'

Celandine hesitated. Things were moving too fast for her. She looked doubtfully at the crouching figure of Micas, then up at the shattered trunk of the beech. What if . . .?

'Be *quick*, maid!'

She was panicked into action, and placed one foot on Micas's back. Then she put her hands upon the bark and pushed herself up – wobbled as Micas seemed about to collapse, clung against the broad trunk, and steadied herself. Now she could reach – just.

The hole was just above eye-level. Another wobble as she brought one arm upwards, and then she was able to grasp the edge of the opening. Again she hesitated.

'Are you all right?' She really didn't want to do this.

Micas grunted, and let out a sharp breath. 'Aye. Hurry.'

Celandine bit her lip and gingerly put her hand inside the cavity, slowly reaching forward, terrified that some unknown creature might suddenly grab at her fingers.

Ugh! She had touched something – it was spiky! Her hand jumped backwards. What was it? A hedgehog? No, it couldn't be. Again she reached into the hollow, and again her hand touched the spiky thing. It moved, but didn't seem alive. Once more, then . . .

Her fingers closed about the object, explored the shape of it, recognized it for what it was. Just an old pine-cone.

Micas shifted slightly beneath her. He wouldn't be able to bear her weight much longer. Celandine delved deeper into the hole. Leaves . . . bits of twig . . . moss. Feathers? She dug down through the pile of rubbish, her fingers growing bolder now that there seemed little danger of them being bitten off. How many birds and animals had made their home here? Squirrels, woodpeckers perhaps . . . There! What was that? Her fingertips had brushed against metal – the hard square edge of something. She tried to manoeuvre herself into a better position, and again there was a sharp hiss of breath from Micas.

The thing was just a little too big to grip with one hand, but it was definitely a box of some sort, and she was able to get her fingers beneath it and drag it up towards the opening. It was heavy. She tilted it over the edge, and it tumbled towards her, just as Micas's strength finally gave out. The box fell away somewhere, and Celandine slid awkwardly down the tree – scraping the side of her face on the bark and ripping her trouser knee on one of the protruding roots as she collapsed to the ground.

It took her a few seconds to recover herself, by

which time Micas was already back on his feet and retrieving the metal box from where it had bounced onto the grass. He took no notice of her, but instead looked furtively about him before concentrating upon opening the box lid.

Celandine struggled to stand up, angry that her own efforts and injuries should merit so little attention. Her knee hurt, and she was sure that her face must be bleeding. She put her fingers tentatively to her cheek. It felt grazed and raw, but no more than that, perhaps.

Micas had his back to her now, as though he didn't want her to see what he was doing. It was dark in any case. Why was he being so secretive?

'Well? Is it all right?' Celandine said, annoyed at being so obviously excluded. 'No *damage* done, I hope?'

Micas turned towards her, and the box appeared to be closed once more.

'Aye, all's well. I were feared that 'twere harmed by the rowdy-dow. But 'tis safe. And now we must put 'n back.'

Put it *back*? After all the trouble she had been to?

'Well, *you* must put it back then. Because I'm not going up there again.' Celandine folded her arms, intending to show that she had a will of her own in such matters, but Micas immediately agreed with her – and this annoyed her even more.

'Aye. If 'ee can bear me up, then I s'll do it.'

What? Was she now to take the part of a step-ladder in this ridiculous venture? She opened her mouth to protest, but then considered her situation once more. This was a dangerous place to be, and the sooner they were out of it the better.

She sighed.

'All right, then.'

Celandine crouched down onto the knee that didn't hurt, and Micas climbed onto her shoulders.

He was heavier than he looked, and she had to steady herself against the trunk of the tree – head forward, hands splayed on the rough bark – as Micas hid the box once more. What was he doing up there? It seemed to be taking a great deal longer than necessary.

At last he whispered, ''Tis well. Bringen me down, maid.' Celandine awkwardly moved her hands down the tree-trunk, one at a time, until he was able to slide from her shoulders.

They could still hear the distant rumbles of thunder – the 'rowdy-dow' as Micas called it – as they stole away into the humid warmth of the night.

Later, unable to sleep, Celandine lay upon her pallet-bed and stared up into the shadows. She was too hot, and the stone chamber felt airless and stuffy. Her thoughts raced round and round her head, everything jumbled up and confused. What was she supposed to do? Micas had said that she must leave, but that meant returning to the outside world again, and she didn't even want to think about the outside world. So long as she refused to think about it, then that other life did not exist. So long as she was not surrounded by reminders of the past, she could pretend that it wasn't there, that it had never happened. There was no other way of coping with it.

And it was the same with the future – she had simply avoided considering it. Today was all there was. Here. Now.

It was no good. She couldn't sleep, and thinking only made things worse. Perhaps a little fresh air would clear her head.

Celandine got up and pulled on her shirt. It was as big as a nightgown on her, and the stone floor felt cool against her bare feet as she walked silently out into the main cavern. An oil lamp burned steadily in an alcove, giving off its familiar scent of lavender, no breath of air to disturb the even flame.

As she glanced towards the cave entrance she saw a figure standing there and her heart gave a little jump – but then she realized that it was only Micas. He had his back to her. Perhaps he too was unable to sleep.

She watched him for a few moments. What was *he* thinking about, she wondered? The Ickren, most likely, and all the problems that their arrival had brought. And now she was a problem too – one more to add to his list. As if echoing her thoughts, she heard a rustling sound, and realized that Micas was folding a piece of paper. It must be a sheet from one of her old exercise books. Perhaps he really had been making a list, she thought, and smiled at the idea of it – although Micas was one of those who could write now, after a fashion.

How miraculous it all still seemed, that first chance meeting with Fin so long ago, and everything that it had led to. If she hadn't banged her head, then none of this would have come about.

Her eyes were drawn towards the yellow flame of the oil lamp, and she stared at it for a few moments, remembering. Where *had* this story begun? With Freddie, when they had played at rolling down the hillside? Or had it all been because of Miss Bell? Yes. If Miss Bell hadn't nagged at her so much, then perhaps she and Freddie would never have left the Coronation party. Then they would never have rolled down the hill, and she would never have hurt her head, and been put in a bassinet beneath the trees. She would never have seen Fin, or known any of this . . .

And now the cave-dwellers wanted to send her away. But they *couldn't*, not after all that had happened. Not now.

She opened her mouth to say something to Micas, and then realized that he had gone. He had slipped out into the night, without her even noticing. Celandine walked quickly to the cave entrance and looked about her, but could see nothing. It seemed odd that Micas should go out yet again.

Well, it was none of her business. She leaned against the wall of the entrance and ran her fingers through her short hair. What was she going to *do*? Her head felt a little clearer, but still she could find no answer.

As she turned to go, she thought she heard a voice – a low muttering from somewhere out there among the bushes. She paused, and listened. Nothing.

It occurred to her that perhaps she was being watched, that there might be unfriendly eyes trained upon her – or more arrows. She crept hurriedly back to the safety of her chamber and tried once more to go to sleep.

Chapter Eighteen

Celandine was awoken by the sound of angry words, echoing from the main cavern. Micas she recognized, and Bron. They were shouting at someone.

'This be no business o' yourn – and this be no place for thee!' – Micas.

Other voices, muffled, from outside the cave it seemed. Then Micas again;

'There be no giants here! Parley, do 'ee say? Then you med tell Corben us'll see 'un at sun-wane. Aye. All that be here – in Little Clearing. Now be gone with 'ee.'

A few moments of silence, and then Micas appeared at the entrance to her chamber. He looked tired – perhaps he had not slept at all – and his expression was serious.

'Bist awake, maid? Then maken theeself ready. We can hide 'ee no longer, for th' Ickren do now reckon 'ee to be here. Come sun-wane we meet, all tribes, and 'tis then thee must run to the tunnel. Aye, thee must go from here when all eyes be elsewhere.'

There was the urgent murmur of another voice, out in the main cavern, and Micas said, 'Aye, Bron. I

403

be with 'ee. Mark me now, maid – come sun-wane, when all tribes be met, get thee to the tunnel and away from here. Heed what I say.' Then he was gone.

Celandine sat on the corner of her pallet-bed, quite unable to get her bewildered thoughts into any sensible order. Was that it, then? Was it really all over? She looked at her canvas bag, tucked away in a corner of the chamber, and vaguely supposed that she ought to begin packing her things. But what did she need to take? Nothing. And where was she supposed to be going? She didn't know. She didn't know why she was leaving, or what she was running away from, or what she would do. She had never even seen the enemy – the Ickren – that were the cause of all this. What were they like, she wondered, these invaders? And what right had they to drive her out?

Corben was now certain that Tuz had not been mistaken after all. The tongues of the Naiad childer had wagged, and the rumours were too many to be ignored; there *was* a giant, a Gorji maid, living among the cave-dwellers – such common knowledge as could not be kept secret for long. The ogre had apparently been in the forest for some time and was considered harmless. Corben had despatched his archers to the caves, with orders to ask questions, but not to attack. They had returned empty handed, and with no further information, but certain that a giant was being harboured in there.

So be it, then. This Gorji was naught but a maid, and could do him no harm for the moment. Such a being could not be allowed to leave this place alive of course, but that could be dealt with later. He would have to discover how a giant had got in here in the first place, and ensure that any exit was blocked.

In the meantime he had other matters to consider. The Elders were grown impatient – and the Guard mistrustful. They wanted to know why he did not simply use the Touchstone to find the Orbis. Surely, when the Stone had led them so far, it would lead them to the Orbis itself? Did he not hear it speaking to him? He had claimed to have that power. Why then did he delay?

And there were others of the tribe who viewed him with dull suspicion, he knew it. The two scouts, Peck and Rafe, and the archers of the old Guard – they had followed his lead, but their reluctance had been plain enough. Their loyalty had been to Avlon, and to Una, not to him. Now they all waited to hear him speak.

'The Orbis be here,' he said. 'I know that these forest-dwellers have it. The Stone tells me so, and 'twould lead me to it if I asked. Aye, we could take it before sun-high, if we so wanted. But there would be blood.' He faced the archers of the old Guard. 'Would that have been Avlon's way, think 'ee – to take without parley? Have we not lost enough of our own already?' Corben paused here for a moment, and there was some cautious nodding of heads.

'I think of Avlon,' he said. ''Twas my brother's belief that the Touchstone and Orbis together shall lead us on – true travellers once more – and return us to Elysse. And I believe this also. But even when the

Orbis be ours to hold, we may be here a moon or more, as I and these wise Elders learn how such a thing be put to use. And how much harder shall our task be if all hands be against us? Would it not be better if the Orbis were freely given? If we can persuade these scare-a-crows by parley to give up that which be ours, then we might save ourselves an armful of trouble.'

Again there were some murmurs of agreement, but Dunch, now General of the Guard, said, 'They'll not give it up, not they *Tinklers*. I never saw their like. They that do live as moles and do give shelter to giants – aye, for I knows that there be such a one in there – they'll not be reasoned wi'. Us were there at sun-wax, as 'ee told us, Corben, and we did have some argle-bargle – but 'twere no good. They'll hold to whatsoever they have, till it be *took* from 'em, whether 'tis Orbis nor ogre.'

Corben gave a faint smile. 'Then Orbis and ogre *shall* be taken from them, Dunch. Yet I would try parley first. Let all tribes meet at sun-wane, then, and we shall see what a king's tongue may do to loosen their hold. If they will not then give, so we must take. In anywise we shall have the Orbis come moon-wax, I give my vow.'

It was a bold statement, and Corben saw that it had worked. The Ickri were still with him, and he had gained himself a little more time. But if the cave-dwellers could not be persuaded to reveal the whereabouts of the Orbis, then he was in trouble – for he had not the first idea of where it could be found, and the Stone told him nothing.

As the forest waited for sun-wane, when all the tribes would be awake and ready to attend the Ickri summons to parley, so Celandine made her miserable preparations for leaving. Micas's instructions had been clear enough. She was to wait until the Tinklers and the Troggles had vacated the cave, then, when all the forest-dwellers could be presumed to be gathered in Little Clearing, she was to quietly make her way to the wicker tunnel. She was not to linger, and she was not to let herself be seen. She was simply to return immediately to her own kind, and to not come back. This was for her own safety, but also for the safety of all forest-dwellers. The Ickri were savages, and would surely attack any that helped her or sheltered her.

Celandine looked around the dimly-lit stone chamber that had been her home since early spring. So warm and safe she had felt here. The thought of returning to that other world made her stomach hurt.

There was nothing that she wanted to take back with her – the books and the writing materials, and all the useful little odds and ends that she had smuggled in – everything might as well remain. She wished that she could magically turn herself into a pair of scissors, or a ball of wool. Then she could stay as well.

They had given her a present, a pecking bag, such as the woodlanders often wore when foraging for food. This was a large pouch made of some kind of soft leather with a flap that fastened over the top. It had two compartments inside, and in these had been placed some gifts for her – two tinsy pendants and a bracelet, a carved wooden comb, a toy boat made out of a walnut shell, and a folded piece of paper. The pendants and bracelet had each been decorated with a flower – celandines, she thought – very simply engraved, perhaps hastily. In the toy boat sat a little figurine, made out of beeswax. Two tiny feathers protruded from the figure, like oars, so that the boat appeared as though it might fly away.

When she unfolded the piece of paper, it made her want to cry.

' 'Tis we,' said Elina, and so it was – a crowd of names that covered the whole sheet, all higgledy-piggledy, and jumbled up together. The names had been written in pencil, some large and bold, some small and faint, but all were recorded there, down to the very youngest.

'I did wroten my own,' said Loren, very proud. 'And I did put Tadgemole's for 'un – see? There.'

Celandine looked to where the tiny finger pointed, but could only see a blur. She nodded, and brushed the back of her hand across her eyes. 'It's very good,' she said, and wondered how she could ever bear it. This wasn't right. She shouldn't be leaving like this.

At sun-wane the cave-dwellers were gathered in the main entrance, ready to go to the parley, and it was time for Celandine to part from them.

Micas helped her to adjust the pecking bag so that it would tie around her waist – the strap being too short to go over her shoulder. He shifted the bag around to the back of her, and spent some time making sure that the fastenings were secure. ' 'Twon't get 'ee all of a tangle, then,' he said. 'Best leave it so, till 'ee be safely whum.'

Home, she thought? Was that where she was going? She felt as though she were leaving home, not returning to it.

Micas looked out towards the evening sky. The light was beginning to fade, and a broad band of dark cloud had arisen, creeping threateningly over the high tree-line. Another storm seemed likely.

'We'm in for a soak,' he said, 'afore this night be done. Mark what I say then, maid, and don't 'ee tarry. Once 'tis dimpsy-dark, away thee go.'

Celandine nodded, but couldn't speak. She didn't know how she was going to say goodbye.

Micas raised his arm toward her, and she thought that he meant to shake her hand. She reached out uncertainly, but Micas merely brushed his fingertips against her palm and turned to go. He had said nothing. As her eyes followed him, she felt another brief touch, and then another – Elina . . . Bron . . . Mab . . .

One by one, the cave-dwellers filed past her, each reaching up and touching the palm of her hand, almost as though they were placing something there for safe keeping. None of them spoke. She looked down at the bobbing procession of heads and saw how badly she had cut their hair – the little tufts and wisps that she had missed, the bald patches where she had cropped too close. It seemed to her that she had spoiled them, had made them look ridiculous, and more vulnerable than ever. The other tribes would laugh at them, she thought. And that would be her fault. Everything was her fault.

The last of the tribe passed her by, and at the very end came Loren, carrying baby Tadgemole. Loren looked much healthier than he had done a few weeks previously. His cheeks had filled out and had a little more colour to them. The baby, too, looked well.

'Goodbye, Loren.' Celandine couldn't just let them go without saying a word.

Loren glanced back at her. He smiled, and then turned away once more – holding his little brother closer as he carefully picked his way down the bank of shale. He got to the bottom safely and hurried to catch the rest of the tribe as they disappeared down the winding path between the hawthorn bushes.

The final glimpse that Celandine had of them was of Tadgemole's tiny face peeping over Loren's shoulder, the dark eyes wondering, but calm, untroubled. The cave-dwellers had no way of saying goodbye, she realized – no word for it. And if none of them had ever parted from this place, or from each other, then why would they?

A terrible silence settled all around her. The cavern entrance felt cheerless now – no *tink-tink* of distant hammering, no snatches of song, no echo of laughter. There was nothing to be heard but the tiny sputter of a lavender lamp, somewhere back there in the darkness, the final *pitta-pit* of a spent wick, drowning in its dish of oil. Then nothing. Celandine was deserted.

Her shoulders gave an involuntary judder and she

stepped out onto the loose bank of shale at the cave entrance. The darkening woodland had also become depressingly quiet. No bird sang, and the air was growing damp and chilly. She had never liked this sad hour between evening and nightfall, when the light begins to fail and the day dwindles down almost to nothing – like a lamp wick. But tonight she felt completely desolate. There was such an ache of loneliness in her chest that it seemed as if the surrounding silence was pressing down upon her, squeezing the breath out of her.

The thought of Fin came into her head, and she realized that she hadn't seen him for days. Was she really to leave him without a word, and never speak to him again? Had she to keep this place a secret all her life, and to forget all that had ever happened?

No. This was unbearable. She would not be driven from here by an enemy she had never even glimpsed. She would not simply creep away to the tunnel. She had to know what was going on.

There were so many of them. Celandine had never seen the tribes all gathered together at one time, and now almost the entire area of Little Clearing was filled with the jostling murmuring crowd.

The laurel bushes that she crouched among were obscuring her view. By gently parting the foliage and craning her neck this way and that, she was able to get a fragmented idea of the proceedings, but little more.

Near the centre of the enclosed space stood the ancient beech tree that had been struck by lightning, deeply shadowed now against the summer evening sky.

Around the tree were grouped the Various tribes, spreading out towards the edges of the clearing. Immediately in front of her were the Wisp. Celandine recognized the back view of Gwill and Moz, and a few of the others. The Ickren were apparently on the far side, and she couldn't get a clear sight of them. Perhaps if she was able to get a bit higher . . .

She put her foot onto a low branch, and cautiously hauled herself upwards. The big laurel bush shook a little, but all attention seemed to be elsewhere, and she wondered if she dare risk another step. Again she found a branch that seemed capable of bearing her weight, and by clinging to the main trunk she was able to pull herself up. Now she was about three feet above the ground, and she had a much better view. And there they were. At last she saw them . . .

Yes, she saw them . . . but she had not been prepared for them. She had not been ready for this. The shock made her dizzy, and she had to lean against the trunk of the laurel, holding on tight, frightened that she would lose her balance and fall backwards. Because they were impossible creatures. The wings . . . those dark leathery wings . . . they were just as the cave-dwellers had portrayed them. And the bows and arrows . . . tall spears . . . the hard sinewy faces and the glittering gypsy eyes – she couldn't take it all in. Black hair, braided with feathers, black and white . . . and most of their clothing black and white . . . pied, so that they looked like condors, vultures, things that belonged upon some dusty plain. These were not the shy little fishers and cave-dwellers and crop-gatherers that she had become familiar with, miraculous though they were. These were not the little people she knew. They were creatures of another species altogether, bat-winged hunters from a different world.

Celandine saw their leader – unmistakably their leader – raise his arm into the air. There was something crow-like about him, dark-eyed, hook-nosed. His feather-braided black hair was swept back from his high forehead and his bearded cheek was gaunt and deeply lined. Around his neck, the one splash of colour amongst so much black and white, was a blue spotted neckerchief. What was he holding? It looked like a cricket ball.

His arm remained raised, and the crowded clearing fell completely silent.

'Here we be met, then – all in this place – and we be met to a purpose.'

Celandine was still trying to get over her initial shock. All she wanted to do was gaze in wonder. But she had to concentrate, had to listen.

'We be the Ickri – as were here of old. And this be the Touchstone as have been in our keeping since we left this place. The Stone be rightfully born by the kings of our tribe, and by none other. I am named Corben – King of the Ickri.'

The voice was clear upon the still evening air, clear and hard.

'The Stone holds great power, and have led us here through many seasons. Aye, but it would lead us further yet – far away from these Gorji lands – and we would take all here with us. We would journey to Elysse itself, my friends, the great home of all the travelling tribes. Too long have we been trapped among the giants. Too long have we lived in hiding, and crept in shadows for fear of being seen. We be not of this place, and nor be thee. Now, at last, we have a chance to return to our own, to rise above the stars, to cross the ages, and to find Elysse once more. Aye, it shall be so, mark me well. From Elysse we did once come, Ickri and Naiad, guided by this very Stone, and to Elysse we shall return, guided by the same. Who would not join with us, if so they could? Who would not lay aside their toil and travel free once more, to lands where there be no ogres, and where our childer would not be afeared?'

A murmur of approval arose at this and the crowd pressed closer, eager to hear more.

The leader of the Ickri raised his arms for peace and spoke again.

'This very night, my friends, may bring such changes. This very night. And yet we come seeking your aid – for the Touchstone be not complete. Aye, there be a brother piece to it. 'Tis named Orbis. Some here will know of the tale. Long-seasons since, the Stone and the Orbis were broke each from the other, parted as the Ickri and Naiad tribes did also part. The Stone travelled with the Ickri, but the Orbis stayed here with the Naiad – upon these wetlands . . .'

There was a sudden commotion from the high branches of the old beech tree – a squabbling band of rooks – and the Ickri leader broke off from his speech

414

to look upwards. He watched as the birds settled themselves again, and then turned to his archers.

'Tuz,' he said. 'Bring one down, for your king. Let us see some skill.'

The youngest of the archers stepped forward and fitted an arrow to his bow. He stood with it lowered for a few moments as he scanned the shadowy branches of the beech tree, choosing his target. Then in one smooth movement, he raised the bow, drew it back to its full extent and let the arrow fly.

There was an immediate scattering of birds from the treetop and a loud cawing as the rooks flapped away in all directions. But one did not escape. The crowd watched as the stricken bird dropped down through the foliage, a ragged bundle that twisted and tumbled amongst the lower branches to land in a feathery heap upon the rough turf. Awkward and misshapen it looked, one shiny black wing splayed out – the slim arrow, so neat and deadly, protruding from its back.

'Prettily done,' said Corben. He stooped, and gently placed the Touchstone upon the ground. 'Now bring me the arrow.'

The young archer strolled over to the dead bird, put his foot against it and calmly pulled out the arrow. He gripped the bloodied end and offered the other to his king.

'The bow also.'

Tuz handed the bow to Corben.

Corben raised the weapons high – bow in one hand, bloodstained arrow in the other.

'How shall the arrow find its mark, without it be

sped from the bow?' he said. 'It cannot. And how shall the bow bring me meat, without it be strung to the arrow? It cannot.'

Corben turned full circle, so that all tribes could see. Then he tossed the weapons towards Tuz and picked up the Touchstone once more.

'As with the arrow, so with the Stone. As with the bow, so with the Orbis. The one hath need of the other. Orbis and Stone belong as one. And we too – Ickri and Naiad, and all tribes – belong as one, to travel together, far from here.'

Corben looked about him, until his eye fell upon the cave-dwellers – partly hidden from his line of vision by the shattered trunk of the beech tree. He moved a little to one side.

'I know that the Orbis be in this place, for the Stone and mapskins have brought us here,' said Corben. His words now seemed directly aimed at Micas. 'And I know that it be close to where I stand, for the Stone tells me so. Aye, the Stone speaks to me, and would lead me to the Orbis if I so asked. But I do not ask. I ask instead that the keepers of the Orbis do willingly bring it forth, to be joined with the Touchstone. Let them be restored to each other, this day, brother to brother. And let all tribes be restored to each other this day also, brother to brother. For is this not to the good of all? Who shall keep us apart?'.

There was more muttering from the crowd, and all heads turned towards Micas.

After a few moments, Micas stepped away from the group of cave-dwellers and approached Corben. In his right hand he carried a staff. One or two of the archers raised their bows uncertainly – as though wondering whether this stout length of hickory should be regarded as a weapon, or merely as a means of support.

'And if the Orbis were here,' said Micas, 'and were joined wi' the Stone once more – then who wouldst carry it, maister? 'Twould need but one hand. Whose should it be?'

'Mine,' said Corben.

'Ha. Thine. As I supposed. And so we'm all to follow thee?'

'If not I, then who? Dost think it should be thee, Micas? We may quickly put it to a choice, if thee wish. Mark me now, all here . . .' Corben raised his voice and appealed to the crowd. 'When Stone and Orbis are joined – as they shall surely be – who wouldst the tribes have lead them forth; I, Corben, King of the Ickri, who have brought the Stone amongst ye, who have travelled through the lands and the very settlements of the Gorji, safely guided here by that which I already hold, and who know the ways of such matters? Or wouldst have Micas, a Tinkler, a cave-dweller, who hides in his mole-hole from the very kind he now seeks to lead – aye, and who would yet give shelter to the *Gorji*, the enemy of all travellers? Who should bear the Touchstone, he or I? Come, Micas, I give thee fair space. Make a claim in this. Let us hear thee speak.'

Celandine awkwardly shifted her position. Her ankle was twisted against the trunk of the laurel bush, and it was beginning to ache. Nevertheless, she had to try and bear it. She had to be able to see, and to hear. An

417

early moon had risen, but the sky was also streaked with heavy black rain-clouds. There might be a storm yet.

'It matters not what choice be made,' said Micas. His voice was bitter, resigned, as he in turn addressed the gathered tribes. 'The Ickren be come but to take from us. These be not our *brothers*, nor shall we be fogged by such talk. These be robbers. If'n we do not give, then shall they steal, as they did first stealen the Stone from us. Aye, the Stone be ourn – but we shall never hold it again, without we murder them all. And so our *choice* be no choice at all: to fight to keep the Orbis – aye, and lose it, as we should against such as these – or simply to give it. Which shall it be? Shall we see our childer struck down like this bird, or shall we give to them what they have come to steal? Very well, then. I wouldst see no blood over this. We shall give up the Orbis. But when 'tis given, *then* shall we see whether these be our brothers or no. Bron! Tammas!' Micas called across to the cave-dwellers. 'Your aid in this. Come.'

Why was Micas surrendering so easily? Celandine couldn't understand it. And why didn't he at least make Corben prove that the Touchstone had such magical powers as he had claimed? After all, if she had guessed rightly, the Orbis was only a few feet away from where the Ickri king stood.

She watched as Bron and Tammas approached, and saw that they too seemed puzzled and disappointed – angry perhaps that Micas had not put up more of an argument.

'The Orbis be here,' said Micas, 'hid in this very tree.'

418

Corben glanced upwards at the beech, but his face remained expressionless. Perhaps he had known it all along, perhaps not. He nodded, and said nothing.

Micas pointed out the hollow, high up on the lightning-scarred tree-trunk, and the crowd began to shuffle around as they tried to get a better view. Those who were in front of the laurel bushes where Celandine was hiding moved away from her, pushing themselves further forward. Micas directed Tammas and Bron to prop part of the fallen branch against the trunk of the beech. Bron then held the branch firm so that Tammas could scrabble up it.

Tammas steadied himself at the top of the branch. He reached deep into the hollow, his arm disappearing almost up to the shoulder. Eventually, after a couple of attempts, he managed to bring some object forth into the fading light. Those at the back of the crowd stood on tiptoe, trying to see. A metal thing, a box by the seem of it, dulled with age.

Micas laid his staff upon the ground and the box was passed down – from Tammas, to Bron, to him. There was a sombre and subdued air about the whole proceedings. The faces of the tribespeople looked apprehensive.

For a few moments Micas studied the box, cradling it in his two hands. Then he raised it up, and turned from one group to another. 'So be it then. And let what may betide, betide. This I now give to the Ickren, for the good of all. I put it in their keeping – and trust they will hold to their vow.' He extended the box towards Corben.

Corben was still bearing the Touchstone, and it was plain that in order to be able to receive the box and to open it, he would need both hands free.

Micas said, 'Let me help 'ee, maister.' He balanced the metal box on the palm of one hand, and offered the other hand to Corben – a cool invitation to place the Touchstone there.

The Ickri king looked into the impassive eyes of the cave-dweller. To relinquish the Stone would be to relinquish the very symbol of Ickri power, albeit temporarily. But to refuse a simple offer of help would only make him appear suspicious and foolish. It hardly seemed likely that Micas would try to make off with the Stone.

Finally he smiled. 'A kindness,' he said, and slowly placed the jasper globe in Micas's waiting hand.

He took the box and turned it around in order to study the clasp. ''Tis well-fashioned,' he said. 'By thee?'

'No,' said Micas. 'Not by me, nor any I knew.' He pointed to the clasp. 'See? A turn there, and 'twill open for 'ee.'

Corben unfastened the lid of the box and looked inside. He studied the contents for a moment and then cautiously put his hand in. With a brief questioning glance at Micas, he drew out a round bundle – something tightly wrapped in cloth. Protection, presumably, for the Orbis.

Once again Corben seemed to find himself in possession of more objects than he could comfortably cope with. He thrust the metal box upon Micas

420

and hurriedly began to unravel the cloth. Round and round his fingers flew, and the frayed strip of material grew ever longer. Not until the cloth hung in ribbons about Corben's feet did the precious cargo finally emerge. It was an old pine-cone. Corben stared at it.

For a few moments the silence held, the time it took for the stunned onlookers to believe what they were seeing, and then the tension began to crack. A stifled snigger, another, and suddenly the whole of Little Clearing was ahoot with mocking laughter. A piney-cone! Did 'ee ever see the like o'it?

But Corben's roar of rage quickly brought the crowd to silence again. He flung the pine-cone to the ground, reached forward, and yanked Micas towards him by the collar of his tunic. 'Dost think to make a gull o' me, thee old addle-pate?' The two faces – one dark with fury, the other pale and calm – were almost touching. 'Dost *dare*? I'll have 'ee so full of arrows, *Tinkler*, as to turn 'ee into a furze-pig! What be this nonsense? Give me the Orbis!'

'I thought 'twere wounden in the cloth,' said Micas. He stood unresisting, his arms slightly outstretched. He was still holding both the Touchstone and the empty metal box.

Corben dashed the Stone from Micas's open hand, then shoved him away. His breathing was heavy as he swayed before Micas, wings spread, eyes narrowed as though he would bore through that innocent expression on the old Tinkler's face to discover the truth beyond.

The Touchstone lay disregarded upon the turf.

Finally Corben nodded. He had apparently come to a decision.

Calmer now, his mouth set hard and vengeful, the Ickri king looked towards the gathering of Tinklers and Troggles. 'Very well. Let us see an end to this – and to all such *parley*. I'll no more of it. Guard! Bring me . . .' he raised his arm, '. . . bring me *her*. Aye, she with a head like a teasel.' Corben was pointing straight at Elina.

Dunch and Faro stepped over to the group of cave-dwellers and pulled Elina from their midst.

'Hold her against the beech,' said Corben, 'Archers – to your bows. And Tuz – give me yours.'

Dunch and Faro forced the helpless Elina back towards the beech tree, grasping an arm apiece and pinning her against the broad trunk. The rest of the archers raised their weapons, some trained upon Micas, some sweeping the crowd. All were ready to bring down any that might dare to interfere.

'I give thee no more chance but this.' Corben spoke to Micas. He drew back the bow that Tuz had given him and immediately fired at Elina – so quickly that the arrow was quivering in the bark beside Elina's cheek before any had realized what was happening. Elina gasped with shock and the two archers struggled to keep her upright.

Corben fitted another arrow to his bow. 'Now,' he said. 'Where be the Orbis?'

Micas looked towards Elina, horrified, and his voice was no longer steady. ''Twere in the box'n, but yesternight! I give 'ee my vow. And today 'tis gone – stolen, as I now see.'

'Stolen? Dost mock me again, old fool? Who knew that the Orbis were hidden there?'

'I and but one other,' said Micas. 'And on this too, I give 'ee my true vow, maister. Why'n would I think to give 'ee an old piney-cone, as would surely bring us all to this? What could be my gain from such a notion? The Orbis were in the box'n. I saw it yesternight, when I were stood here wi' . . . another. I were frit – for I thought the rowdy-dow might o' harmed the Orbis. Us . . . us did climb up to see.'

Corben slowly drew back his bow. 'Who were the other that were with thee? *Who?*'

Micas took a deep breath. ''Twere the giant. The Gorji maid – Celandine. 'Tis *she* who have taken this thing, I be sure of it, for there can be none other as were knowen where 'twere hid. Now I see her for what she be – a Gorji like all other Gorji.'

'A *Gorji*? Wast so foolish as to show this thing to a *Gorji*?' Corben was furious. He swung the bow around so that it pointed at Micas. 'Where be this ogre? In the caves?'

'She'm gone from here. Gone, and 'll come no more. We sent her back to her own, this very day, though 'twere against her liking. And now she have stolen the Orbis from us in her spite – and us'll see no more o' that neither. Aye, foolish we have been as to ever show friendship and trust to an ogre. We should have known her for what she were – a thief. Shelter we did give her . . . and food . . . and now see what she have brought us to.'

'Us did warn 'ee, Micas, that no good'd come of

it!' Rufus of the Naiad shouted up, and other voices quickly joined in.

'Aye – 'twere thee and thy kind as did put this upon us, Micas! Thee should ha' drownded her when thee could.'

'She were never wanted here – why did 'ee let her stay?'

But then some of the cave-dwellers began to retaliate.

'No! 'Twas the Naiad! 'Twas the Naiad as fust brung her here – not we!'

'Aye, that young zawney o' thine, Pato! His be the blame! That Fin . . .'

Corben's voice rose above all of them. '*Hold!*' he roared. '*Hold before I skewer the lot of 'ee!*'

He waited until the last of the muttering died away.

'If this be true,' he said, his voice now low, and dark with menace, 'then all our chance be over and done. We be trapped among the Gorji for ever, and I shall hold thee *all* for the blame of it. If the Orbis be gone from here . . . put into the hands of thieving giants by *fools* such as thee . . . then the Stone may lie there upon the ground, and stay there, for all the good it shall bring to us. But I tell ye this – there shall be some broken heads to lie there beside it this night, and keep it company . . .'

As Corben paused to take breath, the dull crack of a snapping branch echoed across the clearing – together with a cry of pain and alarm. Hundreds of startled eyes turned to look . . .

Celandine's right leg had gone quite numb. She hadn't known it, so horrified was she by the terrible blow that had been dealt her . . . the utter betrayal by those she had thought were her friends. As she leaned further forward, unable to believe what was being said – desperate to cry out her innocence – the branch that she was standing on cracked and gave way.

She tumbled down through the laurel bush and fell to her knees on the black earth below. Immediately she pulled herself upright, hanging on to the waving branches for support – and glimpsed the faces beyond, all looking her way. For the briefest moment it actually occurred to her to emerge from the bushes . . . to enter the clearing . . . to explain . . .

But then, through a gap in the crowd, she saw Corben – leaning forward, peering at the laurel bushes – and she knew that neither he nor anyone else had yet quite grasped what had happened. It was almost dark, and they hadn't yet seen her properly. She still had a chance to run. Run! And yet she hesitated . . .

'Guards!' Corben's voice. Celandine tried to peep out between the leaves. A pause, a few hastily muttered words, and then Corben again. 'Micas – be *that* her?'

'Aye, that be she. Let me to my staff, and I s'll crack her head wi' it!'

'No! Hold! Let none move!'

Corben raised his bow towards her in slow deliberation, and in that moment Celandine knew that there was no escape. He had seen her – and could see her now. She was fixed to the spot, mesmerized by the slight weaving motion of the arrow-tip . . . up, down . . . side to side . . . as though it were delivering the sign of the cross to her. But then Micas's head bobbed into her vision as he hurriedly rose from a stooping position, and the staff that he bore accidentally jostled against Corben's arm. The arrow zipped from the bow . . . and rattled harmlessly through the branches above her.

She heard Corben's loud curse, the rising hubbub of many angry voices – and at last she was jolted into action. Run!

Skidding and tumbling down through the tangled bushes, ducking beneath the treacherous branches of hawthorn and holly, her right leg in an agony of pins and needles, Celandine blindly fled the cries of her pursuers. Black waves of panic swamped over her, choking her breath, drowning all reason. She clutched wildly at whatever instinct bobbed to the surface.

The caves! No – not the caves. Not safe there any more. Where, then? *Think* . . .

The wicker tunnel. Yes.

Take the long way, the least obvious. And keep thinking . . . do the least obvious thing. Don't stop. Don't give up. Keep moving . . . quickly, quietly, through all the dark and difficult places . . . the briars and the nettles . . . not along the usual pathways . . .

'To the caves! Follow on to the caves!' Celandine heard the shout – quite distant. Was that Micas's voice?

They had guessed wrong, then. They were headed off in another direction – some of them. But surely not all? Surely some would think to make for the tunnel? Of course they would. The tunnel was the only way out of the forest. It would be guarded by now.

Celandine stopped for a few moments, holding her hand to her pounding throat, trying not to gulp so loudly, trying to think. Trying to think *properly* . . .

Where would they *not* be looking for her? Little Clearing? But when they failed to find her in the woods, then to Little Clearing they would eventually return.

Great Clearing, then . . . ?

Could she hide in Great Clearing? She had no better idea.

Her wrists and forearms were stinging from where she had brushed through the tall nettles, and her face and neck had been badly scratched on the holly bushes – but there was little time to think about it. She had to try and ignore the pain until she had found somewhere to hide.

Celandine began to climb once more, fearfully making her way through the dark and silent trees, doubling back towards Great Clearing . . .

She lay shivering upon the roughly broken earth, with her head upon her arm, and cried as quietly as she could. The wigwam construction of the bean-sticks rose about her, sheltering her from the night like a leafy tent, and at last she had time to nurse her injuries. Everything hurt – her arms, her legs, her head . . . and her heart. What had she ever done to deserve such treatment, and such unhappiness? All she had tried to bring to this place was good. And now they would hunt her down – kill her perhaps, if they found her. Why? She had stolen *nothing*. Why would Micas think that she had? And why would he turn everyone against her? What on earth did he suppose she would want with their stupid bits of magic? Stupid, that was what they were – all of them. Just as stupid as the people outside, with their lying and their bullying, and their silly prejudices, and their fighting over nothing. And if she ever got out of here she would show them just how stupid they were.

If she ever got out of here . . .

She knew that the Naiad would come to work in the clearing at first light. She would have to think of a plan before then, for once the dawn arrived she was sure to be discovered. No, she couldn't stay here for long . . .

Perhaps she had fallen asleep for a few minutes. There was a strange sound that hadn't been there before. Insects? No . . . it was something tapping. She sat up and listened. Yes, a faint tapping sound – coming from the far end of the clearing. Celandine cautiously pushed her head between the entwined leaves of the runner beans, and looked out into the night. The moon was very high now, appearing inter-mittently between the heavy clouds, and she stared and stared towards the source of the sound. Could she see some movement down there?

Tap-tap . . . *tap-tap-tap* . . . A creeping dread tightened the skin of her scalp as she realized what the tapping meant. They were beating for her with sticks –

spread out in a line across the clearing, moving towards her along the vegetable rows to drive her out of hiding . . . *tap-tap* . . . *tap-tap* . . .

'*Uhh!*' Celandine gulped in horror as something touched her shoulder. She fell forward, shielding her face with her arm – they'd got her! They'd got her!

'*No . . . don't!*' She could hear her own voice, a mouse-squeak of terror, barely there.

Then a familiar sound – *ah-ah-ah* – and the rushing flood of relief. *Fin*. It was only Fin. He had found her, somehow. The breath hissed out through her teeth.

Celandine grabbed him by the tunic, dizzy with shock, and put her finger to her lips. Shh. Fin kept quite still, and she could see his wide fearful eyes in the patchy moonlight as together they listened. *Tap . . . tap . . . tap . . .* a steady rattle of sound, closer now.

'Is . . . is . . . *get* you,' he whispered.

The tunnel. Whether it was guarded or not, it was the only way out. She *had* to try and get through the wicker tunnel. Celandine moved forward, and as she did so the little pecking bag that the cave-dwellers had given her got caught among the ivy-like creepers. She yanked it free. If there had been time to untie the straps she would have left it behind. Stupid thing.

'Come on.'

Together they scuttled between the bean-rows, keeping low, and at every pounding heartbeat Celandine expected to hear the shout of triumph that meant they had been seen. She was horribly aware that her white shirt and trousers were the worst things that she could be wearing for trying to stay hidden at night.

But they reached the end of Great Clearing with no alarm being raised and began to creep down among the grove of spreading cedars towards the tunnel stream. There were bramble patches dotted along the banks of the stream and they dodged between these, from one to the other, until at last they could see the tunnel entrance.

There was no one in sight. The dark mouth of the tunnel was just a few yards away, sideways on, and from behind the covering of a blackberry bush they crouched, and looked, and listened.

Fin was being so good. *So* good. He was as silent and watchful as she – aware, it seemed, of the danger she was in, and the need to be quiet.

How easy it would be for her to slip forward from her hiding place, to jump across those rocks and enter the tunnel. Celandine tried to pluck up the courage to do it, but the fear of what might be lurking in there held her back.

What if Fin went first and had a look? He was in no real danger. It wasn't him that they were after. Perhaps he could tell her if the tunnel was clear.

She looked down at him – saw the way that his straight dark hair fell across his wondering eyes, the way that he sucked in his top lip, how his thin shoulders just begged to have an arm about them. How lovely, and perfect and wonderful he was.

Could she make him understand what it was that she wanted him to do?

'Fin . . .' She bent closer, and whispered to him as quietly as she could.

His big solemn eyes turned towards her, and he put his finger to his pursed lips. For a terrifying moment she thought that he was going to perform his loud hissing trick – but instead he gave a tiny whisper – 'I. . . is look. I is see. I.'

She clutched him to her, couldn't help it, though she squeezed the very breath out of him. The tears sprang to her eyes at the sudden conviction that this was it – that if she once let him part from her, she would never see him again. She felt the tiny pat of his hand on her shoulder, a brief touch of understanding, and then he was writhing in her embrace, trying to break free. He pushed himself back from her, and she could see the whiteness of his broad grin. 'I all right. *I* all right . . .'

Then he was turning away from her empty arms and creeping out into the open, silently making his way towards the stream.

He didn't get more than a dozen paces. Celandine saw his shadowy little figure hop onto the big flat rock near the tunnel entrance and, even as he steadied himself, he was caught.

'Bide there!'

It was Corben, suddenly appeared from the darkness, and standing on the opposite bank of the stream. He had a bow and arrow.

From the wicker tunnel, three more archers hurriedly emerged.

Corben turned, and growled at the guards. 'Were

thee *asleep*? What be this capering nary-wit doing here?'

'We didn't see 'un.' One of the guards spoke.

'Did ye not? Then ye see him now. Bring him to me.'

Don't hurt him, don't hurt him, don't hurt him. Celandine was on the verge of showing herself, of giving herself up.

Two of the guards collared Fin and dragged him onto the opposite bank, to stand him before Corben.

'Speak then – if thee can. What business do thee have here?'

'Ah – ah – ah . . .' Fin was trying to wriggle free, beginning to panic.

'Hold still, thee mad little coney! Have 'ee seen the giant – the Gorji?'

'Gorji is *get* you! Is *get* you! Ah – ah.'

'Have 'ee *seen* her?'

'*I* all right . . . ah – ah – ah . . . Shhh!'

'Ach! There's not scrap o' sense to him. Get the mazy young fool away from me.'

Celandine watched as the guards hauled Fin a short distance along the bank of the stream and sent him on his way with a parting kick. She saw him scamper off, apparently unhurt. He turned once, a last sly little grin in her direction, *ah – ah – ah*, and then he faded into the night and out of her life.

'Thee've seen nothing, then?' Corben sounded angry, frustrated.

'Nary a twitch. She've not come this way.'

'She will, though – for there *be* no other way. And

the beaters shall drive her here soon enough.' Corben was looking directly towards the bush where Celandine was hiding, his bow at the ready. Celandine held her breath and tried to crouch a little lower. Had he seen her? Corben moved sideways a little, as though trying to get a better view – but then a loud splash came from the stream behind him. *Ba-loosh!* Corben spun round, pointing his bow at the water, moved a couple of paces towards the source of the noise. Nothing there.

'But what if she got here afore we? She might a'ready be gone.' The low voice of one of the archers.

Corben looked about him once more, before replying.

'No. She'd not be quick enough. We were straight here. But if she *were* gone, Dunch, then I should send 'ee after her.'

'Would 'ee? Well I shouldn't go, then.'

Corben turned on Dunch – amazed at this sudden show of disobedience.

'What's this? Thee'll do as I say, *General.*'

'I'll not, though, and I'll tell 'ee straight. We'm safe here – for the fust time I've ever knowed. Aye, as safe from the Gorji as we s'll ever be. I'll not set my foot among ogres again – and nor will any here, I reckons. Thee may keep the *Orbis*, if 'ee find it. Much good may it do 'ee. But I be a sight too seasoned for any more o' travelling. I be done wi' it, and shall bide my days here, thank 'ee. I'll help 'ee find this giant, if she be here – aye, and put an arrow through her, gladly. But if she be gone from here, then she be gone.

I ain't a-going back out there among the Gorji to look for her.'

'Do thee say so? And what if she comes back with a tribe of her own kind – a tribe of giants to hunt us down? What do thee say then?' Corben was losing his temper.

'That we s'll be no wuss off than ever we were . . .' Another of the guards spoke, now. 'And anywise, we reckon her to still be in here. We s'll bring her down yet. All we say is, *if* . . .'

'We? *We?* Be all of thee in this, then . . . ?

Celandine began to quietly back away. Whilst Corben and the guards were arguing, she at least had a chance of avoiding immediate discovery. Gently, she inched herself further from the scene at the wicker tunnel, keeping as close to the border of the forest as the tangle of brambles and briars would allow. Finally she was hidden from view, and was able to turn and weave her way through the undergrowth beneath the trees until she had put a safer distance between herself and the Ickri.

But now what should she do? She was at the very edge of the forest, so close to the outside world, and yet without a chance of breaking through that impossible barrier. The tall sycamores, some of which overhung the wall of brambles, mocked her. She could never climb up to those high spreading branches. It was hopeless.

And what was that? Celandine stood still and listened. *Tap-tap . . . tap-tap . . .*

The sound came from the clearing above, but now . . . yes . . . *now* she could hear it to the side of her also.

They were coming through the woods, along the inner edge of the wall of briars. Corben and his archers were to the right of her, and from above and to the left of her the beaters were closing in. There was nowhere else for her to hide. She might crouch among the undergrowth for a while longer, but soon they would arrive, beating with their sticks, to drive her like a pheasant towards Corben and the Ickri archers.

It was over. All over. They were sure to find her in the end.

Celandine sank to her knees, defeated at last, and closed her eyes. *Our Father, which art . . . which art . . .*

No. Too many other thoughts were crowding her brain to be able to pray properly – pictures and visions that sprang into her head, unbidden. Tobyjug . . . why did she suddenly see him, trotting happily through the paddock on his leading rein? And Young Wilfrid, driving the dung cart. Fin – dear Fin – staring down at her from the trees. Miss Bell . . . and Nina . . . Mary Swann. Why on earth would she think of Mary Swann? *Tap . . . tap-tap . . .*

Her heart lurched with fear and her throat grew tighter. Beamer, the great shire horse, she saw, leading the team back into the stable-yard . . . William, the school porter . . . and Freddie . . . poor, poor Freddie . . . there he was, in his Christian outfit. Around her and around her they all paraded, an endless circus of faces, as the hot tears rolled down her cheeks and splashed upon her shaking hands. *Tap-tap . . . tap-tap . . .*

'Come.'

Celandine opened her eyes at the unfamiliar voice and gazed upon the moonlit figure that stood before her. Through starry tears she saw a wavering vision, a tree-spirit, a fantastic thing of leaves and vines, with wild hair that shone blue-green beneath the moon. Cascades of ivy fell about the hunched shoulders and the skinny fingers that extended themselves towards her were as green as willow twigs. The eyes she had seen before – yes, once before – peering at her from the hawthorn bushes below the caves. Reassurance they had given her then, and reassurance she took from them now. She was not afraid.

'Celandine. Come.' The voice was cracked, with age, it seemed, but there was a beauty in it, a quiet confidence that held the approaching danger at bay.

No, she was not afraid. This creature meant her no harm, would never hurt her. Celandine raised her hand automatically, with no second thought, to touch the fingers that reached out to her – and a tiny spark of electricity sprang between the closing gap. It made her jump, but still it did not frighten her. Again Celandine stretched forth her hand, and this time she gently took the offered fingers between her own, so cool they felt and so healing. She rose to her feet.

'Ye have the Touch, maid – as I did know when I saw thee first. Come, then. Follow.'

Celandine allowed herself to be led, even though she was being led towards the terrible sound of the oncoming beaters. *Tap-tap . . . tap-tap.* Towards her own death-rattle she walked, guided by this spirit of the woods, and found herself willing to go. Closer came the insistent tapping, and closer yet, but the hand in hers was calm and Celandine drew calm from it.

'Here thee may climb.'

They had stopped at the foot of a spreading oak, one of the great trees that bordered the woodland. Climb? How? Moving around it, Celandine saw that the back of the trunk was damaged. There was a smell of scorched bark and moss. Then she remembered. This was the tree to have been first struck during the lightning storm – before the beech. She had seen it from above, when she had stood with Micas at the edge of Great Clearing.

Now she saw that the trunk had been partially split – a huge strip of splintered bark torn down almost to the undergrowth – and that she would be able to get a foothold here. She would be able to climb up and crawl along the stricken branch that dipped across the wall of brambles. She could escape. She really could . . .

The brambles tugged at her clothing as she pushed herself around to the back of the tree. She could just lift her foot high enough to wedge it into the split of the thick bark. Gripping onto a shard of splintered wood, Celandine hauled herself upwards, then again, until she was able to squeeze in to the vee where part of the massive branch had twisted away from the main trunk. She peered down at the ground. Her strange little saviour looked vulnerable now, hump-backed and frail, although there was a quickness of movement about that tiny frame that was unusual in one who appeared to be so old.

'Who *are* you?' Celandine said.

The ghostly face, so solemn and wise, studied her for a moment.

'I be Maven-the-Green. Or so 'tis reckoned. Now go well, maid – and harken to me. Thee'm one wi' a gift.'

The beating sticks were drawing horribly close. *Tap-tap . . . tap-tap . . .*

'A gift?'

'Aye, the Touch. And 'tis a gift to be given – mark it well. But thee've another gift, and this must be hid, 'till better times than these. Thee shall know the day, when it comes. Help me, maid, as I help thee. Now away with 'ee.'

Celandine clambered up the angled split in the trunk until she reached the horizontal branch that extended out over the brambles. Down through the black woods came the sinister rattle of the sticks, and she was suddenly terrified that her white shirt and trousers would give her away at the last. She must be so visible up here. She risked a quick glance below. Maven-the-Green had gone.

Along the thick tree limb she crawled, trying to push aside the heavy foliage as quietly as she could. Finally she had reached a point where she could go no further – the leaves and branches were just too awkward for her to be able to get past. She lay on her tummy and fearfully looked down once more, to see how far she would have to drop. She could see a pale patch of moonlit earth below. An overwhelming certainty came over her – a feeling that blotted out all else for a moment. This was the tree where it had

438

all begun, on Coronation Day. And down there, in that patch of moonlight, was where the bassinet had stood – where she had lain and looked up at Fin in such wonder. This was the very branch . . .

The patch of bare earth dissolved into pitch darkness as the moon disappeared. Celandine was aware once again of the danger she was in, and she clung to the overhanging limb in renewed dread – because now the tapping was all around her. The sticks were beating at the coppices in the darkness below, and she could hear the sound of many small bodies swishing through the undergrowth at the foot of the tree – but worse . . . oh *worse* . . . now it seemed that they were coming *up* the tree . . . tap-tap-tapping all around her . . . battering at the leaves and branches . . . hundreds of them . . . thousands . . .

Celandine swung herself over the tree limb, gulping in terror, hung there for a moment, then dropped down into the darkness. A horrible thump as she hit the ground and the breath was knocked right out of her. But immediately she forced herself to get back on her feet, though she was doubled over with pain and fear as the terrible rattling above her grew to a roar. Celandine staggered from beneath the tree and felt the first of a thousand stinging blows – on her face, her arms, her bare neck . . . hailing down upon her defenceless being. Hailing down . . .

It *was* hail. A summer storm . . .

The freak downpour whipped across her shoulders as she stumbled away from the forest and began to run down Howard's Hill. Away, away, away –

from the terror that snapped at her heels, the panic that clawed at her back, and down towards the distant lights below. Faster she ran, careening through the stinging bullets of hail as though through enemy fire, and faster still, until suddenly her legs were out of her control, her steps grown too long – impossibly long – and she was springing into the darkness seven leagues at a time, a leaping, bounding, pounding, tumbling giant. She was utterly helpless – launching out into deep black space, with arms outstretched. Over went the world, and over and over, the wheeling world that turned its circle, so that everything that ever had been came round again... and again she was rolling down Howard's Hill in the sunshine with Freddie beneath a spinning summer sky. The peewits sang, and the party people roared with laughter, and the sun went *bang* and shattered into a million red planets, just as it had before.

Chapter Nineteen

She was a pine marten in a glass case – a weasel, a stoat, an otter – and even though the world might peer in at her, and poke and pry, she was protected by an invisible wall and they could not reach her. If she stayed quite still, and said nothing – *nothing* – then eventually they would have to go away and leave her alone.

Her mother, her father, her Uncle Josef – they were all at her bedside, just as they had been the first time. But now there was a fourth figure also. Another doctor.

Their mouths were moving. Celandine could see them out of the corner of her eye. She could see the shapes of the words that came out of those mouths, and the colours of them. And she could hear all the questions – Where had she been? What had she done? What had happened to her hair? – but the questions were just shapes and colours and sounds. If she stared for long enough, and didn't blink, then she could see right through them and through her bedroom wallpaper, the ceiling, and the roof. She could just drift upwards into the blue stillness of the sky and continue to say nothing.

'Some concussion, certainly, but perhaps shock also. It's difficult to say how severe. What do you think, Wesser?'

'Um. I am not yet sure. She seems comfortable at the moment, but I am afraid that the leg will be quite painful. Try to move her as little as possible, Lizzie.'

'Of course. But Josef, it frightens me that she will not speak. I must know what is *happened* here. Where she has been so long . . .'

'Give her a little more time. This is a very bad fall, and she needs rest. Doctor Lewis and I have both examined her, and . . . well . . . we can find no damage apart from the leg, and bruising on her head. The leg will be in splints for some weeks. But this is an accident, we think, rather than any attack, or . . . assault upon her. As for not speaking, she is perhaps in some shock, as Doctor Lewis has said, and it might take a while for her to recover. Erstcourt – this boy who found her – William, did you say his name was . . . ?'

'Young Wilfrid, the carter's boy. What the devil he was doing up on the hill at that time of night, I can only guess at. Says he was out with his dog, and got caught in the hailstorm. After a rabbit, if I know anything about it. Anyway, it was the dog that found her, for which we must be grateful, I suppose, and so I didn't press the matter further. I've already spoken to the local constable and got the search called off, but I daresay the police will have some questions that need answering – and so shall I, for that matter. When do you think she'll be in a fit state to tell us what she's been playing at, Josef? Lizzie and I have been worried to death.'

'Try not to be too impatient with her, Erstcourt. She will tell us in her own time, and I'm sure there will be an explanation for all this. Lizzie, you must stop crying. She is safe. That is the only important thing.'

'But her beautiful hair . . . and what are these *clothes* that she was wearing? Trousers for cricketing? Yes, and a man's shirt! What *can* be the explanation for this? And she is so thin! For *weeks* she has been gone. Where? *Where?* I must know. Celandine, do you hear me? Were you taken by the gypsies? You must *tell* Mama what has been happening to you . . .'

'Now, Lizzie . . .'

The shapes of the words bounced about the room, and it was curious to see the different colours of them – her mother's a kind of orangey-pink, her father's blue-grey, like the smoke from his pipe. She had never noticed that words had colours before.

And it was so simple to hide from them. The shapes and the sounds could not reach her. Nothing could touch her, because at last she had found the perfect place to hide – the best hiding place of all; inside herself. The invisible wall was all around her, and she was hidden inside herself. Nobody could find her here, and nobody could make her come out if she didn't want to.

They fed her, and they bathed her and they brought her books to look at. Celandine opened the books, one or two of them, and looked at the black and white patterns that the words made. If she made a circle with her finger and thumb, and looked through it, like a telescope, then she could move the telescope over the page and watch the patterns. The black shapes looked like fuzzy caterpillars, but the white spaces in between were more interesting – like a maze. Sometimes she could see white wavy lines, running from the top of the page to the bottom, that reminded her of twisted vines or brambles.

Pencils and paper they brought her also, and the pencils were useful to poke down the inside of the heavy bandage on her leg in order to reach an itch that she couldn't otherwise get to. She tried to find a way of folding the pieces of paper in half eight times, because she knew that it couldn't be done.

It got dark, and then it got light, and then dark, and light again. Sometimes she slept when it was light, and sometimes she lay awake when it was dark, listening to the mouse in the attic. Once she heard a squeal, and Cribb's savage snarl, in the dead of night. An awful, gurgling rattle of a sound. The dogs had caught something . . .

'Lizzie, I think perhaps it would be good if Celandine came to stay with Sarah and me, for a week or two. A holiday, yes?'

'A holiday? Do you mean at the clinic? Oh Josef! Do you mean as a . . . a patient? I don't know. I am so *worried* about her. She says *nothing*. But really, she has not been so many days at home – and now for her to

go away again . . . and to a hospital . . . with all those
. . . and now that Freddie is gone, she is all that I . . .
she is . . .'

'Yes, I know this is very hard for you, Lizzie. But I
think it might be for the best. And the children – they
might cheer her up a little. Perhaps it is not good for
her to be so much on her own. No, she would not be
a patient as such . . . not really . . . but she does not
progress as I had hoped, and I should like to keep a
closer eye on her.'

'Is she so bad? Perhaps just a little more time.'

'Yes, I am sure that a little more time is all she will
need. But Lizzie, I am seeing this with many of the
injured soldiers who are my patients. They suffer a
very deep shock, from the constant bombardment.
Whatever it is that has happened to Celandine seems
to have had an effect very similar. She has become
entirely withdrawn, and I need to be able to watch her
more carefully.'

'But you won't put her with those poor
men . . .'

'No, of course not, Lizzie. This is just a little
holiday with us – a change of scenery, and some
younger company. Peter and Samuel would love to see
her again, and of course her Aunt Sarah will enjoy
having a girl to make a fuss over . . .'

Later they lifted her into Uncle Josef's smart gig,
with a rug over her knees, her walking sticks propped
up beside her and a basket for the journey. She felt
nervous. It was not so easy to keep the world away
from her now that she was out in the open air, and

there was so much of the world that she did not wish to see . . .

But as they pulled out of the gate Uncle Josef turned to her and said, 'Celandine, let me make you a promise. I shall never try to make you tell me where you have been or what has happened to you. When you feel like talking again, you will do so – and I shall be happy to listen. Until then I am equally happy with silence.'

She turned her head away from him, partly so that he should not see the sudden tears in her eyes, and partly so that she could avoid looking at Howard's Hill. As they passed through the farmyard gate, Celandine saw a scrap of dark-stained material lying beside the grass verge. It was blue and white spotted, or it had been once. She thought that she had seen it before, but she couldn't remember where.

Her cousins had wandered away from the dining table, bored with their jigsaw, and bewildered at her lack of communication.

'But *why* won't she speak?' Celandine heard Peter whispering to Aunt Sarah.

'Because she prefers not to,' said Aunt Sarah. 'And please don't whisper. It's not polite.'

The jigsaw pieces were spread out over the table, a great sea of them surrounding the pitiful little island that Peter and Samuel had managed to assemble. Celandine looked at the picture on the lid of the box. It was quite a famous one – of a horse and wagon, standing in the middle of a stream, with trees and sky,

446

and an old farm building in the background. A mill. She began to push some of the pieces around, but then realized, out of the corner of her eye, that Aunt Sarah was watching her. Celandine took her hands off the table and put them back into her lap.

Later she sat with the family at the same table for supper.

'The whole business is quite pointless.' Uncle Josef was talking. He sounded unusually cross and gloomy. 'They send them to me, I help to patch them up, and then what do they do? Why, they post them straight back to the battlefront, of course. As long as a man is able to stand and see, then as far as they are concerned he is fit for fighting. A week later that same man is either missing a trigger finger, or deserted. Or dead. And in the meantime they send me more of them to "cure". How ignorant they are.'

'Perhaps *not* whilst we're at supper, Josef,' said Aunt Sarah. 'And particularly . . .' Her voice trailed off.

'You can't cure Olive, though, can you, Papa?' Samuel's voice was sad and faintly accusing.

'No, darling. I can't cure Olive.'

'Olive is Samuel's kitten.' Aunt Sarah turned to Celandine. 'He dropped her in the bath-tub, and now we think she has influenza, or pneumonia, poor thing. But speaking of bath-tubs, you two boys, it's time you were both in yours. Yes, you may get down. Say good-night to Celandine.'

'You will try, though, Papa, won't you? To make Olive better?'

'I'll try, sweetheart. But really, we can only wait and see.'

'Can I take her upstairs with me?'

'No, leave her in her box by the fire. She'll be warmer there.'

Aunt Sarah shooed the boys off for their bath. Uncle Josef rose from his chair and went over to the bureau. He took out some papers and said that he had some work to do before he began his rounds. Then he left the room also, gently closing the door behind him.

Celandine remained at the uncleared table, aware now of her solitude. The clock ticked on the mantelshelf. From upstairs came vague bumps and thumps, muffled voices and footsteps, but then she picked out another sound, quite close by. There was something else in the room after all. Of course – the kitten, in its little box near the hearth. She could hear its snuffly breathing.

By using the furniture as props, she was able to lurch over to the fireplace without the aid of her walking sticks. She awkwardly lowered herself to the floor and peeped into the box. A small bundle of tabby fur lay curled up on an old woollen scarf. Beside the box was a baby's bottle with a little milk in it. Celandine looked at the kitten for a while and then leaned closer, listening to the feeble rattle and wheeze of its breath. How helpless and fragile it was. Another casualty. Another sufferer, in an unsafe world. Like Uncle Josef's poor soldiers. Like her . . .

The fur moved beneath her hovering hand as if

blown by a breeze, or as though a magnetic current was passing over it. Yes, as though her palm was magnetic. Celandine slowly moved her hand back and forth, stroking, but not stroking, watching the fur rise and fall. She bent her head as close as she could, to watch how the tiny hairs shimmered gold in the firelight, drawn towards her palm. A waving field of corn that reached up for the sun.

Come out, then, she whispered. *Come out of there, and be gone* . . .

The chink of crockery made her jump. Aunt Sarah had come back into the room and was beginning to clear away the supper dishes. How long had she been there?

Celandine sat up, and took her hand away from the box. Aunt Sarah smiled at her, but there was puzzlement in her eyes.

The next morning, Samuel was ecstatic. He hugged his father's leg and said, 'See? You *did* make her better!'

Olive was out of her box and making shaky progress around the hearthrug. She mewed and mewed – or rather she croaked and croaked – and Uncle Josef remarked that any kitten that could make as much noise as that was probably capable of tackling a dish of milk.

'You're so *clever*!' said Samuel. 'I knew you could do it, really.'

Uncle Josef shrugged modestly.

Celandine smiled as she watched the kitten. She avoided looking at her Aunt Sarah.

'Your aunt has to take the boys to school tomorrow morning,' said Uncle Josef. 'It's the first day of their new term, and she may stay there to help for an hour or two. I thought that perhaps you might like to walk over to the clinic with me, if the weather stays fine. The grounds are very pleasing, and there's a small private garden that I think you would enjoy. There would be nobody there who would see you. And you could take a book, or do some sewing, or make a drawing . . . or none of those things. Whatever you prefer. Then I should bring you home at midday, and Aunt Sarah would be back by that time.'

Celandine said nothing.

Just before bedtime, she heard her aunt and uncle talking.

'Will it be all right, Josef, do you think – to take her to the clinic? She won't see anything that might . . . upset her?'

'No. There is nothing there *to* upset her, my dear. There are only a few of my patients who are able to get about by themselves. She will not be seen by anybody in the Hart Garden at that time of day, I promise. She can come to no harm, and I should prefer it to leaving her here alone. And besides, it will do her good to be in the fresh air. It's only for an hour or two, don't worry.'

The Wessers' house turned out to be quite close to the clinic where Uncle Josef worked – just a short walk through the walled grounds – but Celandine was once

450

again feeling nervous about being outside. She didn't like the winding pathways with their high rhododendron bushes and tall overhanging trees . . .

And there was something grim and imposing about the clinic itself, a square white building with black-painted window frames and big double doors, also black. The doors and the windows were all closed – to keep people out, or to keep people in?

'Ugly place, isn't it?' said Uncle Josef. His voice was quite cheerful. 'The gardens are pretty, though. Come along – this way. I am a little late, I'm afraid.'

He led her past the clinic and down a smaller pathway that wound between tall neatly clipped hedges of golden yew. They stopped at a place where two paths crossed.

'And now, if you follow this way down, you'll come to a little garden. We call it the Hart Garden. It's named after a benefactor, Amelia Hart. You'll find a bench there, and a summerhouse and a fountain – it's really rather lovely. You can sit there and read, or play, and at midday I will come and take you home again. But, Celandine, if you want to walk around and explore, then of course you must do so. There is no danger, and there is nobody here who would harm you or frighten you. And if you should want to see me, then just come and ring at the bell. It's in the main entrance to the clinic, and it has my name on it. I shall come down personally. You won't have to speak to any-one, I promise. Is that all right? Off you go, then.'

Celandine had become quite adept at using her walking sticks, but the journey from the house had tired her and now her wrists were beginning to ache. Her splinted leg was also throbbing quite painfully and the narrow pathway was turning out to be longer than she had expected. The high walls of yew on either side made her feel that she was becoming trapped, confined, as though in a maze.

The entrance to the garden appeared quite suddenly, a hedged archway after a tight bend in the gravelled path. The top of the arch had been clipped into the shape of a heart.

Celandine stood beneath the arch and looked in. A tingle of shock ran through her scalp and she immediately lurched backwards. In the centre of the enclosed garden was a white stone fountain, and on top of the fountain was a dark figure, a bronze statue. The figure was winged, armed with a bow and arrow – and the arrow was pointing straight at her. One of her sticks fell from her fingers, and bounced onto the gravel.

It was a cupid, of course – or perhaps it was Eros – but the sudden image of it had been so like . . . so like . . .

The breath whistled out of her and she had to hold onto the metal gate in order to steady herself. Her head reeled. After a few moments, she stooped to pick up her fallen stick. The effort made her dizzier than ever, so that she felt as though she would collapse. She really needed to sit down.

There was a long white bench, just to the right of the gateway.

'*Donated by Amelia Hart. 1879.*' Celandine read the

little brass plaque on the bench as she gratefully sat herself at the furthest end, and stretched out her injured leg.

The garden was a circular enclosure of tall clipped yew with a cheerful border of flowers and shrubs and a gravel path running around the central fountain. Set back amongst the shrubs was a green wooden summerhouse with wooden steps leading up to it and a weathervane on the roof. Old Father Time. It looked cool and peaceful in the summerhouse, but Celandine stayed where she was, too exhausted for the moment to move.

Gradually the fluttery feeling in her chest subsided and she became aware of the sounds and scents around her – the blackbird singing in the holly bush, the warm smell of the roses, the hypnotic trickle of the fountain. A lone bee buzzed lazily among the hyacinths. Uncle Josef was right. It was very beautiful here.

Calmer now, she allowed the peace of the summer morning to settle upon her. Yes, she would be very glad to just sit here, protected from the world, and feel the warmth seeping into her skin. Perhaps she might go and explore in a little while. But not yet.

She squinted up at the bronze cupid, shading her eyes against the sun, and decided that it was silly to have mistaken it for . . . anything else. It was just a chubby little cupid – a childlike figure with feathery wings. But it had reminded her of everything that she was trying so hard to forget. It started her thinking, and she didn't want that.

No. She would not look at it. Instead she made herself be interested in the weathervane on top of the wooden summerhouse – the silhouetted figure of Father Time, burdened down by old age and the heavy scythe upon his shoulder, leaning wearily upon his stick.

Tap-tap . . . tap-tap . . .

Celandine's fingers instantly gripped the hard edge of the wooden bench seat – and her head swivelled round so fast that she felt her neck click. *What was that?* Every muscle and bone in her body was locked solid as she strained to listen. She could hear nothing but the blackbird whistling in the holly bush, and the bee that still bumbled among the hyacinths.

Where had the sound come from? Was it . . .

Tap . . . tap-tap . . . tap . . .

There! To the left of her – somewhere beyond the gateway! Coming along the path? But it *couldn't* be . . . not here. It just *couldn't* be. And yet it was that same sound – that of a stick, tapping at branches, swishing at the undergrowth . . .

But also tapping on gravel.

Tapping on the gravel? In broad daylight? Celandine kept her head turned, eyes fixed, unblinking, on the gateway. The shadowy opening was no more than a few feet from the other end of the bench, and there was no other way out of the enclosed garden. *Tap-tap . . . tap-tap . . .* Closer it came, and now she could also hear the slow and deliberate crunch of footsteps upon the loose surface of the gravel path.

A flicker of movement – the end of a waving stick

– and then a figure emerged from the shadow of the arch, just a few yards from where she sat. A man. A young man in pale summer trousers, his army battle-dress jacket slung loosely about his shoulders, collarless shirt unbuttoned at the neck.

He stood just inside the garden, lifted his head up to the sunlight, and breathed in the scented air. A flash of green reflected from his dark glasses as he turned in her direction and began to move towards the bench. The stick probed low, sweeping from side to side, feeling its way ahead. It was a white stick. The man was blind.

Tap . . . tap-tap . . . The stick gently struck the end of the bench. The man leaned forward, fingers out-stretched, reaching out for something to hold on to. He found the curved arm of the bench and gripped it tight, resting his weight for a moment, head lowered. Then he manoeuvred himself round and cautiously sat down. He finally leaned back with a long sigh of relief.

Celandine was pressed hard against the bench, wedged into the furthest corner from him, motionless, unable to breathe. She stared at his boyish face, saw the scrap of peeling skin on his nose, the tiny shaving cuts on his neck, and was amazed. This must be how he spent his days now, sitting in this garden, listening to the blackbird sing – so far away from the war and the awful things that he was once able to see. And did he see those things still, surrounding him in the dark-ness? Were they the things he would see for ever?

She wanted to know. And she wanted to help.

The man's body suddenly stiffened, a little jolt of the shoulders, and his face slowly turned towards her. The centre of his brow was creased into a frown above the blank stare of the sunglasses. He had realized that he was not alone on the bench – knew that someone was there. And yet he said nothing.

She could get up, she thought, and she could walk away from him in her own secret silence. He would never be any the wiser. But that would be very rude. It would be rude, and cruel and unnecessary. Celandine made a decision. There was no point in trying to hide any more – not from him, and not from herself. There was no point in trying to hide from anything in this world. It was time to step out into the open again.

'Hallo, Tommy,' she said.

She saw the lines on his forehead deepen. Was he puzzled or annoyed? She couldn't tell. For a long moment he faced her, but remained silent. Then he suddenly threw his head back and gave a quiet laugh. He had remembered.

'Good God,' he said. 'It's . . . Celandine, isn't it? What on earth are *you* doing here?'

Josef appeared at around midday, strolling through the archway with his hands in his pockets, and Celandine felt guilty, as she watched him approach. He must surely have overheard the two of them talking. The game was up.

Yet her uncle seemed as cheerful as ever.

'How pleasing it is here,' he said. He looked around the garden with approval. Then he added, 'And how glad I am to hear your voice again.'

'Yes,' said Tommy – and he sounded shy and hesitant, as though he too had been caught out. 'We've been telling each other of . . . our adventures. Some of them.'

Celandine looked up at her uncle. *How glad I am to hear your voice again.* He had been addressing Tommy, not her. She began to understand something. This meeting had not happened entirely by chance, nor had it been for her benefit alone.

'Did you *know* that was going to happen?' she said as she and Josef walked back to the house.

'I did not know. But perhaps I hoped. Yes, I hoped. Tommy has been . . . quiet . . . for a very long time. I did wonder, if the two of you were put together, whether possibly one of you . . .'

'We've met before – did you know that? On a train.'

'No. I did not know that either.'

They walked on in silence until they reached the wicket gate of the doctor's house.

'I heard you talking to Aunt Sarah,' said Celandine. 'And I heard you promise her that nobody would see me in the Little Garden. But you knew that Tommy would be there.'

'Hm. And *did* he see you?'

The penny dropped. How careful she had to be with this man.

'Uncle Josef?'

'Yes?'

'I still don't want to talk about it. What . . . happened.'

'That is perfectly all right.'

'Thank you for . . . not asking.'

'You're welcome.'

There were things that she couldn't speak to Tommy about – things that she didn't even want to think about – but she told him what she could, as they passed their mornings together in the Hart Garden. She told him about Tobyjug, and Miss Bell, and about Mount Pleasant and how she had run away. She even told him about the strange ghost-girl that she had seen, the way that she could sometimes feel the hurt in people, the way that words had appeared to her as coloured shapes after her accident.

And he in turn told her about the war in France, and all the things he had seen there, some of them funny, some of them terrible. But when he learned about Freddie, he wondered why she had not been to see his grave. She should go and visit Freddie, he said. She must.

Tommy was right, of course. She had run away from this, hidden herself from this as she had from everything else. Freddie's memorial was almost within walking distance of here, and yet she had pretended to forget that it was so. She had pretended that one day he would just roll past the parlour window once more, face screwed up against the rain, on the back of a rattling motorcycle. But he never would . . .

He never ever would . . . and she cried and cried at last as she stood in front of the newly carved stone angel in Staplegrove churchyard with her mother and her Aunt Sarah. There were too many new angels here, too many bright stone crosses, too many polished headstones and fresh wreaths. There were too many Freddies.

Her bitter tears raged against the stupid war and her own helplessness in the face of it. Knitting balaclavas – was that all she could do? Dig potatoes? Throw away her German dictionary? Would that bring Freddie back, or be of help to one more like him? What could she do that was of any *use*?

Celandine was glad of her mother's arm to rest her aching head against, and of her Aunt Sarah's handkerchief to bury her face into. And when at last she could cry no more, she was glad to walk between them as they began to make their way back along the church path towards the cemetery gate. They were not alone, she realized. Beside another grave, in a further corner of the cemetery she saw a similar group – three bowed figures in dark clothing – a mother and two daughters perhaps. Others like themselves. Other Women of Britain, who had lost their fathers, sons, husbands, brothers, and who now felt as she did.

Celandine put her arms between her mother's and her Aunt Sarah's, and held on tight. No, she was not alone in this.

Her mother took her walking sticks from her, and carried them in her free hand. 'Freddie wanted to go, Celandine. We could not have stopped him, I think.'

'I know,' said Celandine. She looked down at the three sets of feet that marched slowly along the mossy path, and adjusted her stride so that they were all in step.

Her mother said that she could stay with the Wessers for a few more days, and then she must come home – for the weekend at least – in order to decide upon what was best for her future. There was still the possibility of a new governess, although Celandine was perhaps too grown-up for governesses, now. Certainly she would not be going back to Mount Pleasant – it being doubtful that they would even have her. She was of a legal age to leave school, of course, but that would mean working. And what work could she do? They would talk about it at the weekend.

'I have brought for you the clothes that you asked for. And the leather bag, and the shoes. Oh, and Celandine – do you remember the photograph? When Mr Tilzey came, yes? So *long* ago, it was, and yours was become lost. Yes? He found it again and posted to us. Here – I have it.' Her mother rummaged in the little overnight suitcase she had brought with her and found an envelope. 'See? How *pretty* you are. But oh! Most serious!'

Celandine took the envelope from her mother and drew the photograph out. Her hands shook a little as she quickly glanced at the picture. The child that stared out at her might have been a complete stranger.

'So lovely your hair was – see? We shall have made a bigger one. Yes. To hang on the wall, next to Thos . . . and Freddie.'

Celandine remembered how uncomfortable she had felt that day, and how, when the photographer's flash went off, she seemed to become somebody else for a few moments – that other girl. It was the day before she started her first term at Mount Pleasant. And it was the day that she had first encountered the cave-dwellers . . .

It was too much to remember. She didn't want to look back to that place, and yet found that she had to – didn't want to think about it, and yet found that she must.

'I like my hair better now, though, Mama. I know that it doesn't look very nice yet, but I like the feel of it, shorter.'

'Well, we shall see. And is easier for brushing, I know. But Celandine . . .' Her mother reached out and grasped her hands between her own. 'I am so glad to see you better, that I don't care if you have no hair at all. I want only to see you well, and happy. That is all I ever want.'

'I know, Mama. And I am better. Really, much better.'

'Good. And one more other thing. Josef says that when you come to the farm, I must not ask you questions, so many. I must be happy that you are safe, and not wish more. Josef is my brother, *liebling*, and so I trust him – as Freddie was your brother and you would trust him. I am only frightened for you, that is all. But I make him my promise. So you will tell me when you can, and I say no more, yes?'

'Yes, Mama. I'll tell you when I can – whatever I can. I promise.' Celandine put her arms about her mother's neck and gave her a long hug.

'That is good, *liebling*. And all will be well. And now I must go to the station. Sarah! It is the time!'

'Where did you put my clothes – and the bag?' Celandine brushed her hands across her eyes.

'All is upstairs on your bed. But you must throw that bag *away*, *liebling*. Piuu! Where did you find it – in the barn? I get for you a new one, when you come home. Sarah!'

Celandine sat on her bed, and held the pecking bag in her lap. She didn't want to see it, and she certainly didn't want to look inside it. But it had been a day for seeing those things that she did not want to see, a day for looking inside those places where she did not want to look, and she would face whatever she needed to face.

Not here, though, and not now. She would go to the Hart Garden – nobody would be there at this time of day.

The low rounded wall of the fountain was a comfortable place to sit, and a peaceful one. Celandine dabbled her fingers amongst the lily pads. The garden was silent, apart from the gentle trickle of the water. It was still warm – a lovely summer's evening – but it was that hour of the day that always seemed to make her sad. She looked up at the bronze cupid, forever about to fire his arrow at the archway. And yes, now she could see why. He was aiming straight for the heart – the neatly clipped topiary heart that topped the arch. The heart garden. Of course.

She sighed, and looked down at the pecking bag

that lay at her feet. One of the corners had been repaired with red wool – wool that she herself had brought to the forest . . .

The forest. Did it really all happen? Had the person who had seen such things truly been her?

This was hard. She had managed to push that other world away from her, tuck it so far into the back of her mind that it was almost forgotten, and now it was horribly painful to drag it out again. She had been so frightened, and so hurt by them – hunted down and driven from the woods like a wild animal. Why? What had she ever done but keep her promises and try to help?

She should throw this smelly little bag away, as her mother had advised, and then go back to the business of forgetting once more. To open it up and take out all the presents they had given her would only bring more pain and confusion.

But no. Just one last look, she decided, and then she would put it all behind her for ever. Celandine picked up the bag. It had been very securely fastened, the leather straps bound together with a length of string. She had no memory of doing that. It took her a while to get the thing undone.

The tinsy pendants lay heavy in the palm of her hand. Now that she had taken them out, they did not seem particularly meaningful. She felt no greater sensation of fear or loss for seeing them. This was a good thing to be doing – easier than she had imagined it would be. Celandine held the pendants up by the thin cords that were threaded through them, and dangled them over the water. They twisted and turned for a moment in the evening sun – the flower engravings flashing against the light. Then she let go. The heavy discs hit the water with a satisfying little *gloop-gloop*, and somersaulted away into the darkness.

Celandine delved into the bag and brought out the bracelet. This also was made of metal – a circular band with a gap in it where it was supposed to slip over the wrist. It was far too small for her. She tossed it into the fountain and it felt like another release, another satisfying act of revenge.

The little walnut-shell boat was less easy to discard. It puzzled her. Why would the tiny wax figure be using feathers for oars? She held it up, and moved it across the light of the dying sun, sailing it through the sky. A boat in the sky . . . a sky boat. The sudden understanding of it tugged at her heart. The Skye Boat Song.

Speed, bonny boat, like a bird on the wing . . . over the sea to Skye . . .

She had taught them the song, and this was how they had imagined it – a boat with wings . . . carrying the lad who was born to be king . . . over the sea to sky . . .

Her nose began to tingle, and she felt her eyes water. Why, after giving her such a gift as this, had they been so cruel to her? She gently placed the little boat in the fountain and watched as it bobbed away amongst the lilies. It sailed perfectly.

The piece of exercise paper she knew she would have to keep. No matter what they had done to her, she would not be able to just screw it up and throw it away. She had taught them how to write. That crowded pattern of scribbled names was as much her achievement as theirs. She hesitantly unfolded the sheet.

thee orbis be not saf and so it must leev this . . .

What was this? Celandine glanced at the dense paragraph of pencilled text, quickly turned the exercise sheet over, and then back once more. This was a different piece of paper. This was not what they had originally given her.

She started again:

thee orbis be not saf and so it must leev this plas with thee this da i sl tel thee icren that twer stoln and can not bee fownd ffor thay wood but tac it from us if twer cept heer ther bee wone as nos mor and i do this with thee ayd of shee non other nos of this ceep thee orbis hid for wee till better tyms be comn and wee med meet with thee agen thee sl no thee da thee bee owr tru frend as wee bee yorn and wee sl not fforget from micas

Celandine shook her head in amazement and spoke to herself out loud. 'What *is* this? I don't understand . . .'

Again she tried to puzzle her way through the scrawl of pencil marks, but was hardly able to make any more sense of it than on the first hasty reading. Micas's name was written at the end. Was this from him? She picked out the word 'orbis' once or twice . . . *ceep thee orbis hid . . .*

Keep the Orbis hid? Was *she* being asked to hide it? Did Micas still think that she had taken something? It made no sense.

Celandine looked down at the pecking bag. Could there be something she had missed? She picked the bag up and gave it a cautious little shake. There *was* something else in there. She put her hand inside, and reached down to the bottom of the left compartment. Her fingers closed around a bundle of cloth, and she felt her shoulders tingle.

Wary now, and with half averted eyes, Celandine drew the object from the bag. A round thing, wrapped in oilcloth. She held the bundle in the palm of her hand for a moment and caught a faint whiff of linseed from the stiff dry cloth. Another few moments of hesitation and then she cautiously began to peel back the material, keeping her head turned as though she were unwrapping a grenade.

Part of a metal frame appeared, a kind of circular cage. It didn't look dangerous. She felt more confident now, and she steadily unwound the rest of the cloth until the object was revealed.

Such a strange thing. A curving piece of metal, shaped like the letter 'C' – the kind of frame that might support a miniature globe of the world. At the top and bottom of the 'C' were knurled knobs that could be turned, adjusted to grip something between them. Were these what held the Touchstone in place? There were other parts to it – sliders that moved up and down the curve of the 'C', and two more circular supports for the main frame. The whole thing looked as though it belonged in an observatory or in the navigation room of a ship.

And so this was it. This was their Orbis – the thing that the Ickri would do murder for, and which the cave-dwellers considered so precious that they would risk smuggling it out of the forest in the pockets of a giant, rather than see it in the hands of their enemy.

Celandine studied the piece of paper once more. It was no good. The words were barely legible. This needed working out a bit at a time, with pencil and paper of her own. She put the Orbis back into her bag, along with the letter, picked up her walking sticks, and then hobbled around the fountain to look for the Skye boat.

It was as much a matter of punctuation as anything. With a fresh sheet of notepaper, and the letter beside her, she began to peg away at the meaning of it, word by word.

thee orbis be not saf and so it must leev this plas with thee this da i sl tel thee icren that twer stoln and can not bee fownd ffor thay wood but tac it from us if

467

twer cept heer ther bee wone as nos mor and i do this with thee ayd of shee non other nos of this ceep thee orbis hid for wee till better tyms be comn and wee med meet with thee agen thee sl no thee da thee bee owr tru frend as wee bee yorn and wee sl not fforget from micas

The Orbis be not safe, and so it must leave this place with thee this day. I shall tell the Ickren that 'twere stolen and cannot be found, for they would but take it from us if 'twere kept here.

So far so good – and Celandine could hear Micas's dry voice speaking the words as she wrote them out. She turned up the gas mantle above her bedroom table, in order to give herself more light.

There be one as knows more, and I do this with the aid of she. None other knows of this. Keep the Orbis hid for we, till better times be come and we may meet with thee again. Thee shall know the day. Thee be our true friend, as we be yours, and we shall not forget.

From Micas.

Slowly it began to make sense – not just the letter, but some of what had happened to her in those last few hours among the Various. Celandine tried to think back. Micas had been frightened for her safety, frightened that the Ickri would kill her, and so he had told her to go. That much she remembered clearly. But then he must have decided that the Orbis was also too vulnerable to stay in the forest, and that it too would have to go, smuggled away to safety before the Ickri either found it or forced him to reveal where it was. And she would have to be the one who carried it out of there for him.

So had Micas only been *pretending* to believe that she had stolen the Orbis? Had he laid the blame for its disappearance upon her so that blame would not fall upon the cave-dwellers? Yes, that would make sense. He was trying to save his people from violence and destruction. And he must have thought that she would be safe by then. He must have assumed that she was out of the forest and far away, long before he revealed where the Orbis was supposed to be hidden. How horrified he must secretly have been to find her still there, amongst them. Celandine thought of the terrible moment when Corben had raised his bow to shoot her – and how Micas had jogged against him so that the arrow had missed her. Had he done that on purpose in order to try and save her?

Other details were still hazy though. What was all that business with the pine-cone, and when had the Orbis been hidden in her bag? She couldn't see how that had happened. And how could Micas have been sure that she would even open the bag once she had brought it to safety? She might easily have put it away without looking inside. Nor could she see why the Orbis would be so very much safer outside the forest than in. Wasn't the Touchstone supposed to be able to seek it out wherever it was? And who was this other person – this 'she who knew more' – who Micas spoke of?

But it was late, and her head was aching from all that had happened today. It was too much for her to cope with. Celandine looked at the little Skye boat, now sitting on the dressing table in front of her.

. . . carry the lad that was born to be king . . .

Smuggling a precious cargo away to safety, just as she had . . .

Celandine yawned. She couldn't think about it any more. It was time to go and say goodnight to Uncle Josef and Aunt Sarah.

Later, before she closed her eyes, she thought of the last words in Micas's letter.

Thee be our true friend, as we be yours, and we shall not forget.

That was the only important part, really. Micas knew all along that she had taken nothing from them. And now she knew that Micas had not really betrayed her. She hugged that thought to her as she turned down the gas mantle above her bed.

Chapter Twenty

'*Onward Christian soldiers, marching as to war . . .*'

Celandine barely needed to glance at her hymn book, so many times had she sung 'Onward Christian Soldiers' since the war had begun. Now the words and the prayers came automatically, so that by the time the Sunday morning church service was drawing to a close she found that most of it had passed her by unnoticed.

Vague pictures came into her head: Micas on her shoulders, replacing the box that contained the Orbis . . . the pine-cone . . . Micas adjusting the straps on her pecking bag . . . Had there been something surreptitious about that?

She saw herself standing at the mouth of the cave on the night before she left, and remembered that she had heard voices whispering in the hawthorn bushes . . .

Who might that have been?

'*In the name of the Father, the Son, and the Holy Ghost . . .*'

Celandine closed her eyes for the blessing.

'*Amen.*'

It was time to leave the church.

More glimpses of the forest: Micas, knocking his staff against Corben's bow . . . Fin, magically there, just when she needed him most . . . and Corben again, down by the wicker tunnel, suddenly distracted by the splash in the stream, just as he seemed about to discover her . . .

But how much of it had been planned, she wondered, and by whom? Was it all Micas's doing? No. He said that there was another, one who knew more.

Then she thought of Maven – that wild and mysterious figure who had helped her to escape and so saved her life. Maven-the-Green. An ancient spirit of the woodlands, humpbacked and apparently wizened, yet as graceful as a cat. Perhaps she was younger than she looked . . .

Was Maven the one who knew more? Was it Maven who had planned the spiriting away of the Orbis? Why? Who was she, and where had she come from?

Celandine put her penny in the collection dish, and lifted Samuel up so that he could do the same.

'Will you help me with the jigsaw when we get home?' he said.

'Yes, all right.'

She was still confused, but she was feeling so much better. She liked her cousins, she realized, and it was fun to sit together with them, and slowly watch the jigsaw grow. They had managed between them to assemble most of the hay-wain and the mill, and now they were working on the trees and the sky.

Aunt Sarah put her head around the parlour door.

'A visitor for you,' she said.

Celandine looked around. It took her a moment to recognize the figure in the doorway – now out of uniform and with shorter hair – but then she jumped up so quickly that her chair rocked backwards and tipped against the wall.

'Oh – I can't believe it! Nina! But you look so . . .'

'And *I* can't believe you didn't tell me you were here! Idiot!' Nina ran across the room and gave her a big hug – an action so out of character that Celandine stumbled backwards against the tilted chair, and sat down on it with a bump.

'I didn't think! I didn't think!' said Celandine. 'I don't know why. I just forgot that you were living in Taunton now. And so much has been happening . . . but it's so lovely to see you! Peter, Samuel – this is Nina. My *best* friend.'

The boys looked a bit embarrassed, but politely said their hellos.

'Well, I don't know about "best" friend,' said Nina. 'I do think you might have written, or come to call, or something. I'm only just a few streets away, after all. But what have you done to your leg? You've been in the wars, I gather.'

'Yes. I have. I'm getting better, though.'

Aunt Sarah said, 'Come into the sitting room, both of you, and I'll put out some tea for you. I know you'll want to talk in peace – and these poor boys won't have to be on their best behaviour then.'

'She's nice, your aunt,' said Nina, when they were alone.

'Yes, she is. She's lovely. But Nina, tell me . . . well . . . just tell me *everything*. You look so different!'

And she was different. As Nina talked about her new school, and her friends, and all that she had done since they had last met, Celandine wondered what had happened to the frail and stuttering girl that she remembered. There had always been an underlying strength to Nina, a refusal to give in even to the worst of all the bullying, but now she just seemed so confident and cheerful. And normal. Nina had grown up.

'But talk about me being different,' said Nina. 'What about you? You're so thin! What happened to your hair? And tell me about your accident.'

'Oh, my hair. I just cut it off, that's all.' It sounded very lame, and Celandine was conscious of what a fright she must look to anyone who hadn't seen her for a while.

'You did it yourself? Well . . .' Nina sought for something nice to say about it.

'Oh, I know it looks awful. I just got so fed up with it. As for my ankle, I broke it falling down Howard's Hill.'

'What, again? Didn't you hurt yourself there once before? You should stay away from that hill, dear, it'll be the death of you.'

'Yes.'

Celandine tried to smile, but the tears weren't far away. Nina suddenly seemed so strong and full of life, whilst she felt so weak. Once it had been the other way round.

'And I hit my head. I . . . I haven't been very well.'

'I know,' said Nina. 'Your mother told me. I wrote you a postcard, you see. To Mill Farm. And then your mother sent a card back, to say that you were staying here for a while. She said that you were ill. Anyway . . . now I can come and visit you – every day, if you like.'

'Yes, I would like that. Although I'm supposed to be going home next weekend.'

They fell back onto the common ground of the past, talking about Mount Pleasant and all the awful people there – Miss Craven, and the Bulldog, Mary Swann and the ridiculous Pigtail Twins. They could laugh about it now.

'It wasn't very funny at the time, though.'

'No,' said Celandine. 'It wasn't. I thought they'd . . . killed you.'

Nina was silent for a few moments. Then she said, 'That time – when I was in the san, and you came down to visit me. What did you do?'

'Do? I don't know what you mean. I just sat by the bed.'

'I think you do know what I mean, though. You . . . took the pain away somehow. It was like . . . like it was being drawn out of me. By you. I could feel it happening.'

'Oh. Well . . .' Why shouldn't she just tell the truth? Nina was her friend. Weren't friends supposed to confide in one another? And she had already told Tommy about it. She couldn't help the way she was, and it was nothing to be ashamed of.

'If I tell you, will you tell me the truth about something in exchange?'

'Yes, of course – if I can. You first, though.'

'All right, then. It's . . .' Celandine sought for the words. 'It's as though, sometimes, I can feel what's inside other people, when they're sick . . . and animals too . . . but only sometimes. Not always. I mean, if I put my hands over where it hurts, I can somehow feel it too, and help to take it away . . . oh, I'm not explaining this very well.' But she tried, and when she had said all that she could say about it, she stopped and waited.

'Gracious,' said Nina. 'It's a good job it's 1915 and not 1515. They really *would* have burned you for a witch.'

But that made Celandine feel cross, and she said, 'I'm *not* a witch. And I can't help it – it's just what happens.'

'Sorry,' said Nina. 'I'm only teasing. And just a little bit jealous. I wish *I* could do something like that.'

'Well, it's not a conjuring trick . . .' Celandine began, but then decided that she shouldn't be angry with Nina. It wasn't easy to explain, and it probably wasn't easy for anyone else to understand. 'And anyway,' she said, 'now it's your turn.'

'All right. What do you want to know?'

'I want to know the truth about the lockers – that first night at school, when all my things got moved around and put back in their right place. And the sweets and everything – how they got into those other lockers.' Celandine's voice was shaking. She had the strangest feeling that this had also been due to some weird capability of her own – some wishing-power that she was unaware of. It was just too frightening to contemplate, and she didn't like it. 'Tell me the *truth*, Nina. Was it you?'

Nina looked at her with wide innocent eyes.

'Me?' Then she laughed. 'You nincompoop. Of course it was me.'

'Ohhh . . . *Nina!*' Celandine felt the relief rushing through her, but then looked round as she heard her Uncle Josef's polite cough from the doorway.

'Nina – your mother's here. She's come to collect you.'

Nina came to visit every day after school, as she had promised, and by the time Thursday evening came around Celandine was very sad to part from her. Even sadder, in some ways, was the fact that they had begun to run out of things to say to each other – because it was almost impossible to make any future plans together. Celandine had no idea what would be happening to her next, and could only promise that she would make a better job of staying in touch this time. It wasn't a very satisfactory way of saying goodbye, and both girls were subdued.

'Oh, I *wish* you could just move the whole of Mill Farm to the middle of Taunton,' said Nina.

'Yes. Or perhaps you could learn to drive a tractor and come and be our new ploughman.'

Neither of which flights of fancy raised much of a smile.

The next morning, a half-hour or so before she was due to catch her train, Josef said to Celandine, 'Come into the sitting room for a few minutes,

Celandine, please. I wanted to talk with you a little.'

Uncle Josef's Austrian accent could sometimes make his speech sound rather formal and severe, and Celandine felt uneasy. Was he now going to break his promise and start asking awkward questions? She sat down at the little table by the window and waited.

Her uncle sat opposite her and rested his bearded chin on his hands. He thought for a moment and then said, 'There will soon be some choices to make, Celandine, over your future – over what will happen to you now. And perhaps when you speak with your mother and father, it might help them if you had some ideas of your own to offer. I wondered whether you had been giving this any thought.'

Celandine shook her head.

'No. I don't know what will happen. Perhaps another governess . . .'

'Hm. It is important to be with friends, Celandine. I do not think that being so much alone is what is best for you. Nina is a good friend, yes? A good friend. So I have two suggestions for you to think about. Here is the first: if you were to return to your schooling, then perhaps you should go to school with Nina, here in Taunton. What would you say to that?'

Celandine could say nothing for a few moments. Here was a possibility that had never occurred to her. It hung before her, shimmering, and yet she hardly dared reach out for it. 'But . . . I can't,' she said at last. 'Nina's at a day school now, and it's too far away from home to travel to.'

'Well, you could lodge here. By that, I mean that

you could stay with us during the week, and go home to your mother and father at the weekends. This would be quite practical, I think. Yes?'

Yes, it would be very practical – and suddenly the world was changing. Within the space of a few sentences, a different and more hopeful future had begun to appear.

Celandine blinked, and struggled for something more to say. Uncle Josef had not finished, however.

'I have also another suggestion for you – but first a question. Do you believe in magic?'

This caught Celandine off-guard, and she shrank back inside herself again, instantly wary. What was he getting at?

'Magic? No. Not really. Or at least, I don't think I do.'

'Good. Nor do I. I believe that there is an explanation for everything – although we shall never *know* the explanation for everything. Not everything in this world can be understood by us, nor should it be. It is not necessary.'

Uncle Josef looked out of the window, watching the market day traffic pass by – the farmers' traps, and the horse-drawn wagons loaded with produce.

'Some people have special abilities, Celandine. Why this should be, or how this should be, I do not know. I only see that it is so. I prefer to think of such abilities as gifts, rather than powers. A gift – something given. Rather than a power – something to be wielded.'

He turned to look at her again.

'I think that perhaps you are such a one. One with

479

a gift. I overheard part of your conversation with Nina the other day, and must apologize for that. It is not my habit to listen at doorways. But I have had some thoughts on the matter before. Doctor Lewis, my colleague, has also spoken to me on the subject. You may not have made the connection, but he has a daughter at Mount Pleasant – Margaret Lewis. A talkative young lady, apparently, and quite close to her father.'

Margaret Lewis? Ah yes. Tiny. Tiny Lewis, who had been watching her, that night in the sanatorium with Nina. So Tiny had told her father what she had seen. A talkative young lady indeed.

'And there have been other instances, of course, Tommy Palmer being the most notable.'

'Tommy? But all I've ever done is sit with Tommy, and talk to him. And he talks to me.'

'Quite so. He talks to you, who would talk to nobody else. I had begun to wonder – for all my magnificent skill as a doctor – whether Tommy Palmer would ever talk again. You have a very nice way about you, Celandine. That is a gift in itself – and it is all that the clinic would require of an assistant. This, then, is my second suggestion: that you should come and help at Hart House. There would be a place there, I think, for a girl like you – a girl who has sympathy for those who have suffered ... damage. We could pay you, a little, and once again you could lodge here during the week, and go home at weekends. You would also be able to see Nina, of course, which would be good for both of you, I am sure.'

'You mean – come and *work* there? But . . . aren't I too young?'

'Yes, you are.' Josef gave a grim little smile. 'You are far too young for all this – but then many of my patients are also far too young for all this. We are living through times where the young must carry burdens that they should never be asked to carry. Ridiculous times. But what can we do? When an Austrian doctor is asked to treat soldiers who are at war with his own countrymen – so that those soldiers may then return to fight with his countrymen some more – then we live in ridiculous times indeed. Nevertheless, that is my job. I cannot stop the war, and nor can you. We can only help where we may, with whatever small skills we possess. None of this is your responsibility, Celandine, but perhaps there is a role for you to play – if you wish it.'

'I . . . don't know. This is such a . . . a . . .'

'A shock. Yes. And too much to decide all in a moment. You don't have to decide anything – but think about what I have said, and talk to your mother and father about it. They want only what is best for you. They love you, and they will help you. Listen to them. But listen to yourself also. You could go to school with Nina, or you could leave your schooling and work at Hart House. You are of a legal age to do so. Either choice would be good, yes?'

'Yes. Oh *yes* – it would. Thank you. I'm just . . .' Overwhelmed was what she was. And utterly confused.

'Try not to worry. There is plenty of time. But . . .' Uncle Josef glanced at the clock on the mantelpiece

481

'. . . not much time before your train leaves. Come, we should go to the station. Sarah! Are you ready?' Uncle Josef rose from his seat. 'A railway carriage compartment is a good place for thinking,' he said as he walked towards the door. 'There is something about a railway carriage compartment that clears the mind. Marvellous! Quite magical. Of course, there will be a proper psychological explanation for this, but I cannot think what it is – possibly because I am not in a railway carriage compartment.'

Celandine sat in the corner seat and looked out of the window. There was nobody else in the compartment, and nobody but Uncle Josef and Aunt Sarah on the platform, waiting for the train to leave. Aunt Sarah was saying something to Uncle Josef, and he was looking down at his feet, nodding and smiling.

How kind they had been to her, and how understanding. They had never questioned her about her mysterious absence, or her sudden reappearance. One day she might try and explain it all . . . but not yet. It was still too muddled and confusing. Here she was, in her railway compartment, and yet her thoughts seemed as cloudy as ever.

The whistle blew and her aunt and uncle looked up from their conversation. They smiled at her, and as the carriage shuddered into life, they raised their arms to wave. *Thud-thud-thud* . . . the couplings took the strain and the platform began to slowly roll by. Aunt Sarah and Uncle Josef walked beside the train for a few paces and then stood together beneath the station clock, still waving. Goodbye, goodbye . . .

And this time, Celandine knew that it would happen, a split-second before it did. She looked beyond the figures of her aunt and uncle, beyond the flash of Roman numerals on the overhanging clock, and saw the girl standing at the back of the platform. That extraordinary girl. Their eyes met and she saw the look of sudden puzzlement on the girl's face, the fleeting half-smile of recognition and the bare arm beginning to rise, hesitantly returning her own wave. Goodbye . . .

Then the girl was gone, and her aunt and uncle were gone, and the station clock was gone. The rolling platform disappeared abruptly, to be replaced by white fence posts which ticked past the compartment window, lazily at first, and then faster, as the train picked up speed. Tick tick tick went the white posts, and the 10.25 was on its way.

Celandine leaned back against her seat and thought about the girl. Who *was* she, this person who seemed somehow connected to her? And why did she keep appearing?

'. . . *there is an explanation for everything – although we shall never* know *the explanation for everything, or understand. Not everything in this world can be understood by us, nor should it be. It is not necessary.*'

Her uncle's words. It was a comforting idea – that it was not necessary to understand everything – but she did want to understand more about the ghost-girl. She couldn't just ignore something like that, or help but wonder about it. Although she should try not to worry about it, perhaps.

And what about the Various? Should she worry about them? Their troubles were not her fault, any more than the troubles of the outside world were her fault. She would keep their secret, as she had promised – and perhaps someday their lives would cross again – but she would not go looking for them.

Would they come looking for her, though? She didn't think so. Corben's archers had made it very clear that they were unwilling to leave the forest again.

But then an image came to her, of the scrap of material that lay in the mud near the farmyard gate. Blue-spotted it had been, torn and stained. Now she remembered where she had seen it before. It had been tied about Corben's neck . . .

Another flash of memory – the sound of Cribb's rasping snarl, and the cry of terror in the dead of night.

Were those two things connected? Had Corben come searching for her after all, perhaps alone, as she lay ill in her room? Celandine pictured herself waking in the darkness to find such a nightmare perched at the foot of her bed, leathery wings outstretched, bow and arrow pointing at her. Ugh. She shuddered at her own imagination. It could have happened, though . . .

No. Put that thought away. Perhaps Corben had escaped from the dogs, and perhaps he had not – but either way, she didn't think that he would ever trouble her again.

She looked up at her canvas bag, perched on the netted rack overhead. The Orbis was in there, and Micas's letter, and the Skye boat, and the little wooden comb. If it weren't for those things, she would struggle to believe that any of it had ever happened. Whenever she had been away from the forest for any length of time, she had begun to doubt what she had seen.

Then she understood something. Nobody really believed in the little people, and that was how they managed to survive. They were there, right under everyone's noses, and sometimes they were glimpsed, by accident. But those who had seen them would soon forget that they had done so, because they would not believe it. The Various were protected by disbelief. It made them invisible. That was their magic.

Even she, who had seen so much of them, might cease to believe and so forget. Already it was becoming difficult to picture the faces of those extraordinary beings. They were slipping away from her, disappearing. And everything that had happened to her was beginning to feel as though it had happened to someone else, in a story that she had read, or heard somewhere.

She would put the Orbis and the letter and the Skye boat in her jewellery casket at home, and she would turn the key. And some day she would perhaps open the casket again and look inside, and wonder how she had ever come by such things.

Micas, Elina, Pato, and Loren, and even Fin seemed hazy beings to her now, characters that she had imagined. It was the strange and wonderful Maven-the-Green, the one she had seen the least of, who still appeared to her most clearly. And Maven's was the voice that she could still hear.

You have the Touch, maid . . . Aye – the Touch. And 'tis a gift to be given – mark it well.

The Touch. A gift to be given.

And her Uncle Josef had said the same thing. A gift. Perhaps it was so, and perhaps that should be the choice that she made – to help at the clinic, in any way that she could, and with whatever ability she had. Or perhaps she should wait a little, until she was older, and in the meantime go back to school, with Nina. A happier school than Mount Pleasant.

Either prospect seemed equally exciting, equally wonderful, and she felt a sudden shiver of anticipation, a little burst of gladness inside her – something that had been absent for so long.

She thought about the Orbis, that unfathomable device, and Maven's voice came back to her again.

. . . thee've another gift, and this must be hid – 'till better times than these. Thee shall know the day, when it comes.

Thee shall know the day . . .

Would she? And would that day come? It might, and it might not. But of one thing she was certain – she would never climb Howard's Hill again, not if she lived to be a hundred.

The late summer countryside came back into focus as the train began to slow down on its approach to Withney Halt. Here were the familiar fields of home, with their ancient orchards and their withy beds, their rhynes and ditches – poppy-bright – and their curtseying lines of willow trees. And there stood the forest on the distant hill, unchanged, as innocent looking as ever against the bright horizon. She could gaze upon it now. She could take it out of its box and look at it, and then put it away for another day. The day that might or might not come.

Celandine pressed her cheek against the window – looking for Robert. Yes, there he was, calm reliable Robert, patiently waiting for her with the pony and trap, ready to take her back to Mill Farm – and to the beginning of all that lay ahead.

All that lay ahead . . .

A picture appeared before her, of herself in that future place. She thought that she could see, now, where she would be, and what she must do.

She picked up her walking sticks and heaved her canvas bag down from the luggage rack. Uncle Josef was right. There *was* something marvellous about a railway compartment. It had worked its magic upon her and her thoughts were suddenly as clear and as cloudless as the blue September sky.

Celandine glanced around the empty compartment one last time, and then swung her bag out into the narrow corridor. She drew the sliding door across, so that it closed behind her with a firm and satisfying click. Her mind was made up.

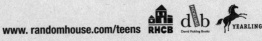